# For The Crown & The Dragon

## BY STEPHEN HUNT

### First Book In The

### *Triple-Realm*

### Fantasy Adventure Series

**Cover Art By Philip Rowlands**

*For The Crown & Dragon is dedicated to my family. Also with many thanks to all of my test readers, including Jeremy, Andrew, Mark, Jessica, Lesley and Karl ... business thanks to Graham Edmonds & the WH Smith crew, Jonathan Barnicoat & his merry band, plus Titan's Jenny Boyce – with last mentions for CN Gilmore, who started off as an Interzone critic of fierce renown, but kindly ended up as my copy editor.*

First Published in the UK 1994 by
Green Nebula Publishing
PO Box 491
Coulsdon
Surrey CR5-2UJ

Typeset & designed by Green Nebula Publishing, London.

Printed by Guernsey Press, The Channel Islands

ISBN 0 9522885 0 8

Cover Illustration by the ever-talented Philip Rowlands (available for freelance commissions c/o of the publishers).

# CROWN PRINCEDOMS OF THE REALM

## – SHOWN WITH THE LARGER NATIONS OF THE MAINLAND –

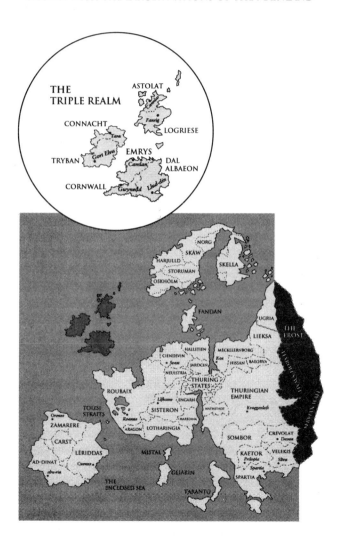

# Prologue

S creams poured into the evening air as the crucifixions continued, a long line of wooden crosses stretching across the city parades and into the gentle hills beyond. Creon's gaze shifted upwards towards Rome's sky, a flight of geese silhouetted against the blood-stained sun. Blood red, an appropriate augury.

Creon was joined on the palace balcony by the Emperor's Visigoth General. Another mercenary of course, most of the legion's officer class having fled months ago to swell the ranks of the Emperor's rival. A truly vicious scar ran down the General's face, as if his head had been split in half, then somehow joined back together again by force of will alone.

"Does the sight remind you of your god perhaps, Greek?" Kahr asked.

"They had run out of crosses by the time they got to him," Creon said. "And he isn't our god."

Kahr touched his wolf pelt cloak, a superstitious gesture. "Child of, then. Perhaps in another three hundred years, one of those men will also be proclaimed holy by some priest. You like thinking don't you, do you think that is likely?"

Creon knew his religion held a strange fascination for the tree-worshipping tribes. That vision of a man dying nailed to a Lebanese oak had proved a powerful image for Kahr's people.

"Another three-hundred years. You are an optimist, what makes you think we have that long left now?"

Reinforcing the Greek's words, a set of manic cries echoed from within the palace behind them – a tortured high-pitched sound, and unlike the columns of crucified turncoat legionnaires outside, a pain that was completely self-inflicted.

"The Emperor has at last heard, I think, that our rebellious friend Licinius is advancing on the capital," Creon noted.

"You see beyond the river?" Kahr pointed to the hills. "The smoke? His troops are burning the estates. Your *good* man is no longer in control of his army. Licinius called my people savages, but we never fired our own tribe's villages. My scouts tell me over half his army is composed of the ex-legion's demisapi. Beasts. How can you expect to control beasts? They should have banished every last one of them into the wilderness after the slaves' uprising."

"There's still time," Creon pleaded. "You have control of the garrison here, take Maximinus Daias's head and offer it to Licinius. Give Licinius Rome. You can stop the civil war, finish it before the Emperors destroy everything."

The Visigoth General shook his head. "You are a fool, Creon. The Caesar is paranoid, he's always surrounded by his guard of demisapi; those monsters would rip anything apart that tried to touch a hair of their precious master. Besides, your rebel friend Licinius will try to slaughter my people whether we run or stay, surrender or fight. Let him bring the Empire down, *Donner,* what do you care?

"They used daemonry to crush Athens and enslave your people. How can you care for Rome? They have twisted the world into an abomination with their enchantments and sorceries, weirded animals and the forests into horrors. Let Rome fight to a standstill and rip herself apart like a wounded animal, then my tribes will come as free men. We will come to remind them there are some things silver still cannot purchase!"

"You have not joined with a tutor," Creon said. "You can not understand what the Emperor is going to do, the raw power he has under his control. Even Maximinus Daias does not understand the toys he's been left to play with. We should never have let another Emperor into Rome without undergoing the rites."

Kahr laughed at this, but it was not a happy sound. "Caesar may be as crazy as a leper, but there are some things even he won't sleep with. Your daemon's three years gone now, and its prohibitions with it. If you still adhere to its teachings, you get your savants to stop Caesar, let them try and say no to the Emperor – we'll be hammering up your body in the Citizen's Way before nightfall."

"You think I fear him?" Creon said, a trace of anger infecting his normally calm voice. "If I could bring him down, I would do it in a second. But you know it would mean nothing. The brotherhood has been shattered into pieces by Vulcanus's departure: the Emperor's found no shortage of lapdogs from within our ranks to help him. I have already told my party not to assist Maximinus, but over half of them are partisans of one of the Emperors. I can't even control my people anymore, let alone the other parties."

"Not so loudly, Greek," Kahr said. "Caesar's mood will not be visibly improved if he overhears your view of his reign. He thinks he is a god now, and very shortly I expect he will discover he is all too mortal. That is not an easy thing for a god to do, and it won't be easy on those around him either."

"We are all dead men today, General," Creon answered.

"Come with me then," Kahr said. "I do not intend to be caught here when Licinius's rebel legions fall upon the city. My men control the east gate, you can slip out with us tomorrow, leave Rome to her insanity. By the time we escape, Caesar's demisapi will be far too busy to chase a cohort of foreign deserters."

Creon shook his head. "No. We should have stopped this

a long time ago. I will call the Senate together and hope enough savants answer the call to council to put a stop to this madness."

"Tread carefully, Greek," Kahr growled. "As you said, your people have splintered into many factions."

Pinched and tired eyes looked at Kahr as he stood in the shadow of a temple on the city outskirts. His centurions had gathered slowly around him, many wearing common armour so the unscheduled concentration of officers would not be noticed.

"You know what to do," he explained. "Fall back towards Natiaum in unit and avoid contact with any other legion. If you run into loyalist forces this side of Atiati, tell them Maximinus Daias has heard the rebels have split their forces to flank Rome, and you've been sent to harass his rear. The Emperor's crazy enough to waste his troops like that."

That drew a bitter laugh from the General's ragtag legion, hired killers who'd had their fill of Rome's inhumanities, of household pets being appointed to the Senate, beasts being raised into races of slavering half-men, sorceries and bewitchments that could shock a normal person insane with their world speeding through change after change.

Far to the south, a series of hollow concussions cracked the air, dust from the baked ground which surrounded the city filtering up into the wind.

"Damn, but they're close," said a soldier.

"When you have travelled far enough north of the central provinces, we'll meet up in the border forests, then back to our villages before autumn settles," Kahr went on. "Let whoever wins here choke on his victory."

"But the forests have been weirded," a legionnaire protested. "There is no living to be had there now. If our villages are even standing where they were it will be a miracle."

The General's scar seemed to draw his upper lip into a sneer, making the man's face appear even crueler. "You have spent too long living soft in Rome, boy. We are still part of the order, the World-Tree will draw us under the cover of her branches. Froh and Wotan will not forget our people, not in this moment."

Abashed, the legionnaire dropped his gaze. There was no challenge to the General and his party as they left through Rome's east gate.

Kahr stood under the massive arch a moment, looking to the sky. A thin vapour trail marked the passage of a solitary flight of the Emperor's Aviatis; Kahr had heard that it was difficult getting them to work now. First another tutor would start to decompose and grind to a stop, then one more savant would disappear in the war, or be lost as prefects jostled for the ever-dwindling supply of luxuries.

Everything was breaking down. Rome had built her glory out of a house of cards, and now their Daemon Prince had fled, what little was left of the natural order was reverting. Vulcanus's passage had provided the gust of wind that would bring it all down.

That fact gave the Hunnic warlord some small grain of satisfaction. The Caesars had partied with dark forces and had obviously become twisted in the process, extending their corruption across the globe, ruling through a potent mixture of fear, force and the supernatural.

Natural vengeance, retribution in the form of Wotan's will was destined to strike back in the end, and he would tell his grandchildren he had been there at the end to see it.

Pushing their way through swarms of broken retreating maniples and confused refugees, the Visigoth mercenaries headed away from the Imperial capital. As if reminding them of the Emperor's reach, demisapi soldiers hammered away under the burning morning sun – the line of crosses reaching, it was rumoured, as far north as Dianis.

Kahr stopped under the irritating clouds of dust, unslinging his waterbag and walking quickly towards the orchard of crosses off the road.

One of the demisapi standing at the grass's edge moved to intercept Kahr, the origins of its breeding obviously canine. The Visigoth officer was reminded of the wolves that had terrified him as a boy, grey shadows darting through the shadow of the trees at dusk under his rough wool blanket while he shivered and the pack scratched around his mother's fence, four-legged killers made bold by the winter desolation.

"No water," it growled. "Traitors."

"Get out of my way," Kahr snarled back. "Move, or I'll break your filthy back."

Sweeping up its pilum the creature stepped back, menacing Kahr with its barrel. "No water. Orders."

Kahr slapped the gold eagle holding his short crimson cloak to his breastplate. "Orders, is it now! Can't you recognise an officer when you have one in front of you? Step out my bastard way or I'll see your brothers have your rotting carcass nailed up along with these."

"Orders," the beastman sulked, moving aside to let the General reach the field of crosses.

Kahr grabbed hold of one of the wooden cross-pieces and pulled it at an angle so he could reach its occupier.

Greedily the crucified prisoner lapped at the water dribbling from Kahr's drinking skin.

"No crown – of – thorns for – me?" husked Creon.

"Where would I get those from at this time of year?" the General said. "You should have listened to me, Greek. I take it your people didn't live up to your expectations?"

Creon coughed up blood as the liquid hit his stomach. "So – stupid. It's over – for – civilisation. Why? So much – pain."

"Rome was a sickness." Kahr looked at Creon's sweating face, convulsed in agony. "Do you want to hold a sword?"

Creon gasped, almost laughed. "No – no – sword. Never lived by – that."

Kahr nodded then hugged Creon and slid his blade into the man's heart, the bearded Greek arching once on the cross then falling slack.

"He's killed, killed," the beastman whined accusingly behind its officer.

Kahr brutally pushed the creature out of his way. "Haven't you heard, legionnaire? We are all dead men today."

Six days later, the world shattered.

# Chapter 1

Death was in the valley. An evil fate for a region which was used to being one of the few isolated islands of safety among the wild, terrible beauty of the tumble.

Pwyll raised the heavy metal spyglass to his eyes, the device capturing the carnage of the valley floor, bringing it leaping into sharp clarity.

Below, thin spirals of smoke stretched high into a drizzling lacklustre sky; Pwyll's gaze following the smoke trail down towards Drum Draiocht castle. Here and there angry gouts of smoke erupted from an already pockmarked curtain wall, stark testament to the accuracy of the besieging army's culverins.

A blackened strip of ground circled the moat where Duke Matholwch had fired the town's slum tumble-downs, depriving his enemy of any cover the buildings would have afforded. The question of whether the nobleman would have razed the entire town was made academic when Drum Draiocht's own starving militia had mutinied.

"The farmhouse is this way," coughed a voice behind Pwyll. Pwyll's escort was a fencible from the Princedom of Emrys, a short brute armed only with a sergeant's spontoon, but one who looked like he could wield the pike to wicked effect.

As a member of the Queen's Household Cavalry, Pwyll shared the cavalryman's disdain for the ball-fodder which formed the greater part of the Realm's muster; men fit only to clear the field for the glorious charges which he and his comrades were addicted to. And among all the unwashed rabble, the fencibles were the worst of the lot, auxiliary militia who only enlisted to escape their counties' press –

scum who took part in more disturbances than they ever put down.

"You're taking a message to the farm then?" asked the fencible.

Pwyll did not see fit to answer the impertinent soldier and merely grunted.

The fencible grimaced, accustomed to the beatings and brutality that most officers used to keep their fighters under discipline, as well as the cold disregard they held for those that were not 'quality.'

"Them at the farm don't normally get much attention," continued the levyman. "Except when there's some cess that needs cleaning. Then they're called quick enough, I hear."

"There's always a use for scum," Pwyll said, making it clear in his tone that he counted his escort as one of them.

With a grin the levyman kept walking. He knew the best way to annoy someone like Pwyll was to keep rattling away as if he was an old servant who had served a lifetime on the man's estate, ignoring the officer's aloof manners, tipping just enough deference towards the cavalryman to escape a flogging.

Pwyll had been lumbered with the talkative fencible by his squadron's Colonel. With the confusion of the siege, there had been a near total collapse of the efforts Drum Draiocht's muster put into guarding the town from the encroachment of the forest. Wild hidden things had sensed the absence of order and grown bold, sometimes striking in daylight.

As if an extra man would make a difference to the sly faerie creatures that lurked in the tumble.

"Yes, Captain, always a use for scum. I hear the muleteers brought up a train of fresh powder yesterday, fine stuff too, carries roundshot nearly as third as far as that mulch they were using before.

"I suppose they'll thunder on all of tonight now too,

make it fair impossible for us to sleep they will."

Pwyll hawked a gob of spit into a thornbush. Curse the luck that had brought him here. The rest of his squadron were coursing hares with the local squire, riding hedges and hunting, and he had to listen to this lowborn fool. "Drum Draiocht will lose her walls faster than you'll lose your rest, you blasted idiot."

"Well, here we are then sir," the soldier indicated a farm building resting on the crest of the valley. "There's your farm, and now I'll be reporting back to the light company for fresh duty."

Pwyll thought of ordering the fencible to stay, but was reluctant to endure the soldier's prattle for any longer than was absolutely necessary.

The fencible saw the officer hesitate, then dismiss him with a contemptuous wave. He smiled to himself as he picked his way back to the main camp: they were certainly not quality at the farmhouse, and he had no desire to play the part of witness to what might follow.

In the farm's main yard a canvas canopy had been drawn over two of its walls, and a collection of dragon-browns lay sprawled underneath, throwing dice, shaving, or sharpening their sabres. Keeping the flintlocks serviceable from the damp, their puffers' locks were wrapped with rags while the barrels had been corked.

Dragon-browns: *brown* for the tattered dirt-coloured uniforms they wore, *dragon* for the rearing serpent which fluttered on the Queen's green flag. Foot soldiers. Pressed horse-thieves and highwaymen. Gutter scum.

"Where's the senior officer?" Pwyll demanded, angered that nobody stepped out into the sleeting rain to challenge him.

Underneath the canopy, the dragon-browns ignored him, the only sign he had spoken at all being a slight fall in the level of conversation.

"I asked where's your senior Captain?" Pwyll repeated

furiously. Seeing not one man was paying attention to him, he moved under the canvas and singled out a dark-haired soldier sitting on a chest.

Pwyll was tall among his cavalry fighters, so it was unusual for him to come across someone as big as himself. Not only was the seated man tall, but he had the muscles of a bull, looking as if he could assault the castle down in the valley singlehanded, just by ripping her stones out.

The soldier was cleaning the barrel of his holster-puffer, the handle metal rather than carved from wood, a sure sign the dragon-brown originally hailed from the barren highlands of Astolat. A strange sight to see an Astolatier in the Realm's army, given hardly a year passed without some mountain village having to be massacred in an uprising.

"Damn your eyes, sir, you will tell me where your senior Captain is, or I shall have you strung up and flayed until I can see the colour of your miserable spine?"

Pwyll was fixed with an icy gaze, the soldier's cold blue eyes gazing carelessly into the cavalryman's own. It was a curiously young face to have such a look of brutality etched in its lines.

Above Pwyll, a pool of water had formed in a sag in the canvas, freezing drips splashing down onto his head. The soldier looked lazily up at the sag, as if suggesting it was of more import than the officer's threats. He tossed his head in the direction of one of the farm buildings.

Pwyll started to stay something, then, burning with anger, marched out towards the building.

When he located their officer, Pwyll swore to himself, he would make sure every last one of those low-born lackwits pay for their insolence.

Pwyll practically kicked in the farm door, surprising a cluster of men sat gambling around a table. He searched for their Captain. Only one of the dogs was out of the dirty brown uniform, and he was dressed like a city dandy ready to trawl the street for brothels. The man divided his attention between the cards and a plate of cheese and chutney. The dandy's features were almost too delicate for Pwyll to believe the man was a soldier, perhaps a card-sharp who had wandered in to play for his supper.

Pwyll was about to ask the dandy if he was the senior officer when it occurred to him that the gambler was not that much older than the blue-eyed highlander who had insulted him with dumb silence outside. Many young noblemen purchased commissions, but what quality would be so desperate as to buy one with this pressed company of thieves and rufflers?

"After the Captain?" the dandy asked, seeing Pwyll looking at him. "Upstairs in the loft, you won't miss it, it's the only room there is."

"Upstairs, *sir*," Pwyll spat, angry at the friendly familiarity in the fair-haired soldier's voice.

"Yes sir," said the dandy. "Look you, shall I show you up?"

He made it sound like Pwyll might not be competent to walk it by himself, and fuming, the officer pushed past the table.

Pwyll rapped on the only door and went straight in. "I have – "

Amazed, he stopped. By a small window, the only inhabitant of the room lay stretched out on a mahogany drum-table hastily converted into a bed. Unshaven, the man had a pair of worn trousers with the blue stripe of a Captain down them. The thirty-year-old officer also wore the faded brown jacket of a Cornwall Pioneer.

Underneath an unkempt tangle of brown hair, a dilated half-drunk pupil focused on Pwyll, a black eye-patch covering the officer's other eye.

Pwyll regained his composure. "You are neede – "

"Sod off, cavalry," the Captain interrupted, rubbing his ill-shaven chin and sitting up blinking in the stream of sunlight though the lead glass windows. "What day is it?"

"Captain Pwyll, Royal Emrys Cavalry," Pwyll growled saluting.

"Taliesin, Old Shadow's own favourites, and you can still sod off, cavalry."

Pwyll looked with utter distaste at his brother officer. "You presence is required by General Teyron, Taliesin."

Taliesin scratched his eye-patch as if his eye was still there. "What are the charges?"

Pwyll looked aghast at Taliesin. "I don't – "

"What have I been charged with, cavalry?"

"There are no...," Pwyll began, distracted. "You have been ordered to attend the General's staff meal this evening, along with your company officers."

Taliesin started to laugh, a loud booming sound which filled the small bedroom like culverin fire. "Dinner is it? Dinner with the Butcher. That's a rich one."

Pwyll started at Taliesin's casual use of the General's nickname. The Butcher. The name fit Teyron like a well-sewn lace glove, a noble every bit as brutal as the killers he commanded with measured and ruthless efficiency. Queen Annan's favoured executioner, whenever a need arose for the Princedom of Emrys to show it still clung to the nominal over-kingship of the Triple Realm, Teyron would be dispatched to build a pile of corpses. Ironically, Teyron considered himself a cultured man and loathed the ugly name his troops had thrown on him.

Taliesin reached out and extracted a bottle from the mess on the floor. He took a greedy swig and rolled back over again, his face buried in a paisley-patterned pillow. "Tell the butcher I'll be glad to *attend* him this evening, cavalry."

"There is also the matter of your company," Pwyll added. "You will see the ones in the courtyard are lashed. They are in need of discipline, they have not even mounted a sentry on your position here."

"There's a whip in the stable behind the barn," Taliesin said. "You try to flog them, if you feel the urge."

"I demand you punish them," Pwyll shouted, moving towards Taliesin's bed. "They are insolent bordering on mutiny, if you fail in your responsibility I'll come back with an army provost and see them striped raw myself."

Taliesin twisted over, moving his feet to hang off the table's edge. "There's dying to be done, cavalry, and I'll wager you a sack of silver angels that it's going to be my boys that'll be doing it. You just remember the battlefield's a big place. There's plenty of room for a horse-riding fool to be rolled into a ditch somewhere. Your colonel wouldn't even notice you were dead until the campaign was finished."

"It's not going to end here," Pwyll threatened, swivelling to stalk out the room.

When the Household officer had disappeared, Taliesin followed in the soldier's tracks and joined the dragon-browns in the kitchen downstairs.

"There was a swine none too full of the joys of existence, man," laughed the giant who had ignored Pwyll in the courtyard.

"Was there a sentry outside, Connaire Mor?"

"Aye, of course," the highlander answered. "We saw him coming almost as soon as he was on the road."

"I meant a buggering guard looking down towards the castle, not into the forest."

Connaire Mor shrugged his shoulders. "If there's trouble for us, it lies in the tumble, no with that pack of hired blades trapped down in Drum Draiocht."

"Mount a bloody guard looking to the castle."

"Something came out of the forest last night, sniffing around," Connaire Mor insisted. "The men in the cottage barn heard it."

Taliesin shook his head. He knew the superstitious mountain-man had been leaving plates of milk out for the faerie folk for the last few nights, trying to placate the creatures of the witchwoods.

"Probably no more than wolves prowling around. The siege may be as good as over, but there's been night sorties this late into a fight. The rebels are desperate down there, they have to know they are finished. Matholwch's hired regiments may try to break out, and I don't want the first I know about it to be them stealing in here and slitting my throat. So mount a damn sentry!"

Still at the table, the dandy looked up from his game. "What did the horse buggerer want?"

"What did he want, Gunnar?" Taliesin laughed. "The good fellow has invited us to the Butcher's table tonight. It seems the General wants to give us a good meal to steel us to the hell he'll inflict upon us tomorrow."

"Aye, and the man's got a big heart."

Outside the local squire's manor house, a set of guards stood posted in silver dress-cuirass, their armour feathering the moon's ghostly wash with the mansion's candlelight.

Saluting, the guards moved their flintlocks aside for the officers to enter. Taliesin and his two escorts were led across quarry-tiled floors to a banqueting room filled with staff officers. A line of colourful army standards marched down the wall – Emrys, Dal Albaeon, Logriese, Connacht, Astolat and Tryban – as if the act of grouping them would create a unity among the Realm's feuding Princedoms.

"So the Butcher has not arrived yet," Gunnar noted, gazing across the room.

Connaire Mor smelled the lemons stuck with cloves which the local landowner had used to scent the air. The squire was probably only too willing to accommodate the Realm's officers, to distance himself from the losing rebellion. "Keeping a man waiting is one of the laird's ways of demonstrating his superiority."

Taliesin glanced around. By and large, the chamber's occupants were junior staff ranks, although the officer recognised the Adjutant-General and a handful of the corrupt commissaries. In the captain's mind, the commissaries' main contribution to the Princedoms appeared to be delivering rations late or siphoning them off to merchanteers. Either way, the dragon-browns lived on weevil-filled bread and whatever poultry they could steal from cottage yards.

Stewards dressed in green uniforms were serving the officers veal and hare from metal platters, a traditional serving of game brought down in the day's hunt. Conversations buzzed around the room: culverin officers arguing about the grade of powder that should be used in damp weather; Dal Albaeon loyalists complaining about the poor quality of their fencibles' flintlocks; dragoons debating the appropriate weight of a gentleman's sabre and the sudden fashion for the lance which had been imported from the mainland.

Standing at the opposite end of the table, Taliesin noticed a priest of the Tree Martyr arguing with a weirdsman, brooding eyes bulging out like a stunned frog's from underneath the enchanter's thick white eyebrows.

The ageing weirdsman, Gwion Bach, was attached to the Butcher's own staff and stood as one of the more imposing figures in the chamber. Whether at the Butcher's own urging or as a spy for the Queen was a moot point.

The monk at the old man's side belittled Empedocles, which meant little to Taliesin, and poured scorn on his cycles of eternal recurrence for fire, which meant even less to the dragon-brown. Gwion Bach endured the Martyr man's self-important lecture with the look of one who was born to suffer fools.

Suddenly a startled half-strangled voice sounded across the room. "Those men!"

Pushing his way past a throng of officers, the cavalryman Pwyll shoved his way through to face Taliesin and his soldiers. He stared in open-mouthed disbelief at the dandy and highlander who had ignored him in the courtyard. "Are

22

you trying to mock me? These men should have been tied to a post and whipped by now. You dare to bring them here?"

"Your orders called for me to bring along my company's officers, cavalry," Taliesin said. "Here they are. Gunnar of the merchanteer House of the same name, and Connaire Mor, late of the Astolat forces of Congal Cáech."

"Congal Cáech?" Pwyll erupted. "A Martyr-damned mountain rebel! There are rebels by the hundred in this valley, and you expect me to fight alongside a dirty Astolat secessionist?"

Pwyll fought his way forward. In a single fluid motion Connaire Mor had drawn a heavy boot dagger. There was a sudden flurry of fists as Pwyll's cavalry brothers restrained their colleague, Taliesin and the dandy lunging to stop Connaire Mor from gutting the riding officer.

Still struggling, a space was cleared between the two antagonists.

"You know the punishment for officers duelling on campaign," a booming voice sounded.

General Teyron stood by a pair of open ironwork windows. The Butcher. Chill rain and leaves blew in from behind him, the wind-driven halo of some warlock out of the tumble. "If either of you fools cause so much as a nick to the other, I'll have you both strapped to a culverin barrel for tomorrow's bombardment."

Warily the two men were released, staring poison at each other over the wood-grained floor.

The Butcher moved forward "They'll be blood enough for everyone by the morning, if that is what you have a taste for. One of our spies inside the castle has just passed word that the Ruri of Dal Albaeon was garroted three nights ago in his dungeon. Duke Matholwch has got rid of his hostage. Our hands are free."

There were gasps from the Dal Albaeon loyalists around the room. Their Ruri-Prince was dead, with only the pretender left in Drum Draiocht's granite fastness. Some began to weep at the news.

Teyron continued. "If it was Matholwch's intention to strengthen his claim to Dal Albaeon's throne, then he has failed.

"The Peers of the Dail Oireachtas have met across the border in Emrys, the Prince of Cornwall is supporting the claim of the Ruri's nephew, as is the Queen. If Matholwch still lives we will take him to Camlan for judgement by the Doomsmen's star chamber."

Overwhelmed by the news, the officers drifted apart to talk over what the murder would mean for their campaign, eager to discuss the regicide's implications on the politics of their own Princedoms.

Teyron was in fine form, with his high-collared coat, spurred leather boots reaching almost to his knee and turned back to display the decorative lace of the boot hose. The knowledge of the Ruri's death had left little impression on the beak-nosed man – regicide just one among the prerogatives of nobility.

The Butcher drew Taliesin aside from Connaire Mor and Gunnar. "How much longer do you think the Prince of Gwynedd's favour can protect you and your misfits, Captain?"

Taliesin was taken back to a mountain pass outside Cannlar, the thunder of hooves and screams of men dying in an ambush. Taliesin pulling a dazed lady out from a coach and the falling dirks of Astolatier raiders. It was only after he had stumbled and clawed his way back to Fanrig with the half-delirious noblewoman that Taliesin discovered he had rescued the youngest daughter of the ruler of Cornwall. She had been picnicking with her friends on the edge of a battlefield, courted by officers who would gallop over with trophies, bloodstained dirks and Astolat shields, watching while the scrapings of the Realm died for her pleasure. When he found out, Taliesin had cursed his foolishness and sworn to the dragon-browns that he should have left her there to die with her spoilt friends. But she had offered her reward later, and Taliesin had taken it, her manicured fingernails raking his back as she moaned and buried her face in a pillow.

Then he had found out the real reach of milady's favour.

How the Butcher's face had burned with anger when the commission of Taliesin's Captaincy arrived out of the blue, the royal seal of Gwynedd still soft on the envelope. A low born-killer from the crumbling slums of Llud-din commanding men in Teyron's army, and forced upon the General by the machinations of the painted pasty-faced courtiers he so despised. But even in accepting an appointment which had been forced upon him, the General found a use for Taliesin. Every rogue, thief, drunkard, deserter and murderer Teyron's army threw up was guaranteed a place in Taliesin's company sooner or later.

Given Taliesin's successes on the battlefield, another General might have grown used to the situation. But the Butcher was paranoid. Teyron recognised the power of the mob, and feared in his black heart all that separated his soldiers from a riot was the discipline and fear imposed by the army. One small step across that thin line, and his killers would be off the leash, savaging their masters like ill-trained hounds.

Taliesin was the incarnation of those nightmares.

The Captain ignored the Butcher's implied threat. "I'll rely on a sabre for my protection, sir, if it is all the same to you."

Teyron glowered at Taliesin. "Your men will be the Forlorn Hope – heading the attack on the breach at the south wall tomorrow. Now the Ruri is dead, I no longer need to play soft games with Matholwch. You just make sure your devils take that wall."

Connaire Mor and Gunnar came over as the Butcher moved off towards his staff officers. "Dancing on the point again, man," Connaire Mor said, more of a statement than a question.

Taliesin nodded. "Every cess-hole job that comes along, Connaire Mor, every cess-hole job."

Inside the shadow-draped hall of Drum Draiocht's keep, the other target of the Butcher's enmity, Duke Matholwch, sat sprawled in his luxurious leather wing chair. Having reached late middle age, the rebel Duke's receding hair hung as downy as a babe's, spread damply across a beetroot-red forehead. Matholwch's face was ashen, a sensuous expression touched with melancholy. It was a face few of those who still dared count themselves among his friends would have recognised.

Outside, the Realm's bombardment continued.

Matholwch had to raise his tremulous voice to be heard. "Those soldiers begin to tire me with their constant thundering. The noise. The clatter. It is so jiggered churlish. And who are they, eh? Eh, Dordias? You said we could not lose, and yet these are not our allies, oh no. If they were, they would not disturb my sleep so, Dordias."

With robes cut in the style of a Martyr monk, the target of the Duke's complaints was hunched over a brazier, the thin man burning pieces of paper with an incense, blackened curls floating upwards, scratching trails of smoke as they drifted.

Seeing the servant was ignoring him, Matholwch continued. "Your powder, Dordias. I need some more of it. It makes everything so clear and clean. I must have it, I must."

Seeming to hear him at last, the man turned, fixing the Duke with an indecipherable look. "Soon, my friend, soon. You will have more soon."

With a peaceful, sigh the Duke rested his head and listened to the echoing crack of roundshot striking the keep.

# Chapter 2

Dawn found Taliesin in one the narrow cobblestoned streets of the town. Few townspeople remained in Drum Draiocht, most had fled when news of the advancing regiments reached them. Candle-lighters and brewers, rat-catchers and blacksmiths, nobody wanted to risk the insanity known to grip troops when a stronghold fell, the orgies of burning and looting.

Occasionally a curtain fluttered as one of the holdouts peered down into the road, quickly drawn back when they saw the line of dragon-browns outside.

Eerily deserted, the thoroughfare was empty of everything except the distant clamour of battle; the sinister whir of roundshot passing overhead, the fireplace crackle of flintlocks.

Behind Taliesin, Connaire Mor checked their company was ready for the fury of the assault. On the other side of the road Gunnar was joking with the men, his garish clothes out of place in the wet drizzle which was the only weather Drum Draiocht received; death's own joker come to leap and jape while soldiers fell and writhed on the battlefield.

Taliesin nervously fingered his sabre, wishing the blaring music of the trumpets would call the assault. Not that they needed the bandsmen's signal, the sudden silence of culverin fire would announce men were preparing to charge, and Matholwch's mercenaries would rush out from their rubbled fortress to man the defenses.

Some among his company were hungrily eyeing a posthouse tavern back down the street. Deserted, its sign cracked and flapped in the wind, a temptation goading weary men to risk the army's prohibition on looting.

As an infantryman in the ranks of the headcount, Taliesin had succumbed to that temptation before, but he prayed his dragon-browns would resist the lure of plunder today. The Butcher knew as well as anyone the trouble partisan regions created, when the nearest civilisation was a perilous journey through the dark corridors of the witchwood. Provosts prowled Drum Draiocht with nooses ready for the fools found provoking local people.

Taliesin stared down the ranks of his men. There were few who would be hailed as saviours by the Princedoms if they survived this day: highwaymen and rufflers escaping the doomsman's gibbet by joining the regiments; poverty-stricken farm boys who had accepted recruiting company silver after some sly sergeant got them blind drunk; rag-pickers bludgeoned senseless in the city rookeries, waking to find themselves pressed and in the ranks.

By the wall was Laetha, a hunchback forester turned murderer, Pikva, the coachman turned horse-thief, Helig the ex-dragoon cashiered from the cavalry in disgrace, the two fisherman brothers, twins who, ironically, had killed a sailor while resisting the naval press – having to join the dragon-browns just to escape execution.

They were scum. But they were the best scum in the Realm. They were Taliesin's killers, and he would have it no other way.

Gunnar walked over to Taliesin. "They'll be expecting their words now."

Taliesin grunted, but acknowledged the dandy officer's comment. He was not one for speeches, but the men expected it. Fine words came easy to the aristocratic gentlemen that commanded the Realm's headcount, but Taliesin was of a different breed. He found it difficult to fill the desperate silences which preceded a slaughter.

He stood up and looked down the mass of dragon-browns. "There's those that say leading a Forlorn Hope is a great honour, being the first to break through a breach in the wall."

Sarcastic muttering came from the ranks. Taliesin recognised the woodsman Laetha's voice – ever the troublemaker.

"There are officers that say it is the greatest honour a company can ask for, to haul their colours across that hell out there, that it is a sign they are trusted for a bloody and noble task."

Laughs lifted from the company.

"Well I say toadshit to that!" Taliesin pointed to the valley crest with his sabre. "We all know the Butcher is trying to do for us again. He is sending us in because we are sewer-hunters, rat-catchers and rufflers, and there is not going to be one household in the Realm that will shed a tear if we don't come back. I say bugger him, we'll take the wall and return alive to give the bastard some more sleepless nights."

The men cheered and made obscene signs at the valley's crest. Taliesin hoped the butcher had one of his aide's telescopes trained on them.

"We'll take the wall because there is not another company in the army worth a copper angel. We'll take it because we are the only ones who can and still spit in the quality's face."

Stamping and jeering, the dragon-browns waved their puffers in the air, the octagonal barrels of the weapons rising in the rain, wicked muzzle-swords fixed to the flintlocks.

Around the corner lay a hundred feet of scorched ruins, the wasteland created by the Duke's act of arson. No cover there. Just a killing ground before the Realmsmen reached the breach in Drum Draiocht's wall.

A still quiet fell over the valley as for the first time in

weeks the culverin drank silence.

"Move!" screamed Taliesin.

Rounding the corner to the distant call of trumpets, the troops streamed towards the fortress wall. Taliesin prayed they would reach the steep counterscarp of the drained moat before defenders appeared to rain fire down on them.

Charcoaled wood splintered under Taliesin's boots as the one-eyed Captain willed his legs to pump faster. The curtain wall was still obscured behind a thinning mist of destruction, but from the battlements the first cracks of the enemy's puffers sounded, the whistle of balls passing through the charging ranks, dragon-browns dropping to the dirt clutching their wounds. Howling like devils, the soldiers smashed through the debris of burnt buildings and closed on the defenders.

Suddenly they were overtaken by rolling thunder, clash and crash followed by gouting masonry flowering from the wall ahead. Taliesin threw himself to the ground, Connaire Mor landing nearby. Granite chips and hot iron splinters showered down across them.

"Swining bastards," shouted Connaire Mor. "You swining bastards!"

Taliesin looked back. He could see the struggling figures mopping out the Realm's culverin on the hillside, ramming down fresh balls and canvas bags of powder. Their assault had been dangled as bait! Drawing out the reluctant defenders so the rebels could be pummelled by the Butcher's battery on the slopes.

The rebels had not been expecting that. And why should they? The Butcher's own men were being cut to bits by the battery fire, roundshot falling short and lifting dragon-browns into the air, masonry from the walls shredding the company where they lay huddled.

"On your feet," Taliesin shouted over the violence of the salvo, waving his sabre towards Drum Draiocht. "If we stay here they'll be scraping us from the bloody walls. On to the breach."

Taking up the cry, the sergeants urged the soldiers up. "For the walls, for the walls!"

Charging through geysers of flame and earth, the company cleared the rubble in the breach. A figure appeared from behind a makeshift barricade blocking the collapsed rampart, and Taliesin flung up his puffer. Smoke billowed from the pan at the side of the Captain's weapon, the single ball slinging the mercenary back. Taliesin drew his sabre, the Realm crown-and-dragon stamped on the cheap workshop steel.

The officer took in the scene of the outer ward. Defenders' corpses lay scattered unburied across the yard, the few remaining rebels turning from the protection of the battlement's teeth, not believing that their attackers had dared the devastating hail outside. A hound had escaped from the hunting kennels, running in maddened circles while the Butcher's culverin shook the earth.

About to seek cover and ram another ball down his puffer, Taliesin noticed a flicker of movement at the corner of his eye. As he sidestepped to the left, a blade cut across the space he had just vacated; swinging around with his sword-arm, Taliesin continued his turn and slashed his opponent across the spine. The dead soldier fell away from his sabre, an incredulous expression on his face, as if he had been shocked by the fact of his own mortality.

Along Taliesin's side, the dragon-browns poured through the breach, breaking left and right for the steps to the curtain wall. Paltry resistance remained on the battlements, but flames still leapt out from arrow slits in the inner keep, balls slapping down men and fleeting past the Captain.

With his own battery case still raining down around him, Taliesin took cover from the murderous crossfire and cursed the Butcher's name.

Blocking the portal in the central keep, an arched door grinned like a black mouth. The Realm's soldiers grouped outside, crouching behind a pigsty's wall as Duke Matholwch's men kept their heads down with the occasional fusillade.

Gunnar stooped by the shelter, huddled alongside Connaire Mor. "Look you, there's a small matter of a keg of blackstrap owed."

"Manawydin got here ways before your lot," one of the dragon-browns argued.

"Manawydin was taking a leak behind the stables," another of Gunnar's troops retorted. "We were the ones who made it through the gap first. You owe us a keg, friend."

Taliesin was about to settle the matter when a precise voice sounded behind him. Slan Daoine, one of the Butcher's Colonels, a bloodied sabre clutched in his left hand, a flintlock in his right. "You think perhaps the General has lifted the barrage so you can settle your wagers in comfort?"

"No sir," Gunnar said, flashing a grin and mocking Slan Daoine with his surprised tone.

"Then perhaps, sir, you'll be so good as to gather your men, sir, pick up that fallen support, and smash in this door which seems to be blocking the passage of my soldiers."

Taliesin prepared for the charge, pulling out his sabre. He winced; the fractured crash of the makeshift ram too similar to the floggings handed out in the Martyr poorhouse – no good place for any child to grow up in. Damaged by the salvo and having stood six passes of the ram, the keep's door collapsed inward.

Before the door echoed off the marble floor of the entrance, Taliesin and his dragon-browns were lurching inside, flattening to the sides of the portal. The boom of the door hitting the floor was followed by a series of retorts, return fire from inside, while Slan Daoine led his company through the gap.

Ringed by balconies, the hall was surrounded by an ancient minstrel-gallery accessed by a barricaded staircase. Eight columns supported the hall's stone and timber ceiling, Taliesin and his men taking cover behind the pillars, firing up into the balcony then ramming fresh powder and ball back down the barrels of their puffers. They charged their weapons with a professional's smooth rhythm. Bite off the paper-wrapped cartridge, prime their pan, out with the maul, down with the remainder of the powder then spit in a ball and slap it down.

Along the balcony, Matholwch's hired killers laid a desperate cover of fire from behind their chipped banisters; they knew foreign mercenaries could expect little quarter from the Butcher and his troops.

Gunnar's puffer jerked in his hand, the dandy's ball catching one of the mercenaries in his head. Spouting blood, the soldier hit the wall behind, then crashed through the guard rail, twisting towards the floor.

A heavy throwing-knife spun lazily through the air, past Taliesin's position, embedding itself in the chest of a rebel on the staircase. Taliesin did not have to hear Connaire Mor's battle cry to recognise the highlander's handiwork.

"See there, you're losing your civilised accent," Gunnar called across to the giant mountain-man.

"Och away, this is the only civilised accent in the regiment."

Waving the company forward, Taliesin took the stairs. "Dragon-browns, for the stairs, for the stairs!"

On the balcony above, a sudden rush of Realm soldiers pushed their way across the landing – another entrance obviously having fallen to the Butcher. With a murderous flurry of muzzle-swords the melee was finished, the rebels in the hall routed. More dragon-browns poured through the broken portal, dispersing across the keep.

"Search every room, you dogs," cried Slan Daoine. "Take Matholwch unharmed, the Queen desires the pleasure of the Duke's company back in Camlan."

Pushing their way through the barricaded staircase, Taliesin sped up the surviving steps. First up the stairs, he glimpsed the back of Slan Daoine's escort disappearing down a corridor.

"Does Slan Daoine know these halls?" Gunnar asked.

"We'll find out," Taliesin said.

Standing there among the panelled wood, a bloody blade in Taliesin's hand and an eye-patch draped across his face, many of his dragon-browns wondered if they were being led by a killer who had careered out of some coaching-inn tale of pirates and corsairs.

Passing a buttery blocked by a number of collapsed beams, the soldiers slowed. Behind one of the walls came shrieking; not the death throes of a defender, but a wholly female cry.

Kicking their way into the room, Taliesin's men confronted the source of the mewling. Five soldiers surrounded a woman hugging the floor, her clothes ripped and torn. She lay there dazed and still, a blue swelling rising from her cheek Among the troopers circling her was Pwyll, the tall cavalryman's belt already loose around his waist.

Seeing they were no longer alone, the girl's tormentors turned, Pwyll's face glazing when he saw who had come up behind him.

"She's one of their dollymops," Pwyll brayed, as if it explained everything.

Taliesin's mind flashed back to a damp room, the shadow of a Martyr churchman heavy on him with the lash.

"Too good for you, whoreson," Taliesin struck out with his sabre, the metal weight of the guard catching Pwyll on the nose. Pwyll twisted to the floor, his face smashed and bloody.

There was a long second where the cavalry officer's men stared dumbly at the fallen Captain, then burning with rage they reached for their weapons. Behind Taliesin, his men jarred their puffers level and Pwyll's bullies pulled short, realising if they finished drawing arms Taliesin's criminals would think nothing of loosing a volley first and explaining it later.

Connaire Mor waved his flintlock. "Not so much fun is it, man, when you're on the receiving end?"

"You low-born one-eyed shit," Pwyll spat, feeling his bleeding face. "I'll call you out after this is over, Taliesin, I'll have satisfaction from you."

"Whenever you feel up to it," Taliesin said.

Behind him, the dragon-browns had lifted up the limp body of the woman, and Taliesin backed out of the room, keeping the Household soldiers under his barrel as he retreated.

Gunnar laughed. "You stick to your horses in future, cavalry, if it's satisfaction you are after."

In the safety of the corridor, Taliesin detached a group of men to convey the woman back into the town.

"Aye, and you can be sure he meant what he said."

Taliesin shrugged at the highlander. "That toadshit is only used to flogging estate hands. The idea that someone might actually turn around and fillet him will not have entered his mind."

"Come on then, sir," Gunnar said. "Let's be finding the fellow who deprived me of a comfortable season in garrison."

Gunnar gasped, short of breath as they continued their pursuit up a granite staircase. "Some of these paintings would pay off a good number of my debts."

Taliesin shot Gunnar a foul warning look. The Butcher would as like hang him with the dandy if he found the company had looted the castle.

The Captain thanked his fate they encountered no opposition on the spiral stairs. Turning to the left, no right-handed fighter was able to bring a sabre around effectively, while defenders would have space enough to hack a full swing at their foe. At the top of the stairs, a long wooden hallway led onto a set of doors inlaid with Matholwch's falcon crest.

Taliesin nodded. "Quality's chambers."

Ahead of them, Slan Daoine's escort had just broken through the doors. Taliesin followed.

Matholwch's shadowed great-hall lay chill in a candleless gloom, the Duke still sitting in his easy chair, chuckling idiotically to himself.

Behind the Duke, his bald retainer Dordias was on his knees, turning through the contents of a faded deer-skin chest.

Seeing none of the Duke's soldiers in attendance, Slan Daoine moved forward, his sabre balanced in a duellist's poise.

"Matholwch! Your rule ends here."

The Duke gazed vacantly into space, ignoring the Colonel.

Finding and pocketing what he was hunting for, the robed man stood up and turned around, running his sly eyes over Slan Daoine and the Colonel's escort.

"Really," the monk-like man spat. "The Queen's lapdogs should work at being less predictable."

As Taliesin and his soldiers flew into the chamber, Dordias made a contemptuous wave of his right hand, as if dismissing the intruders from his presence.

*"Quid vides volvitur in rota."*

Suddenly a shocked Taliesin found himself falling to the

floor, paralysed and unable to even croak a protest. Around him, the dragon-browns collapsed as if they had been hamstrung by a master butcher.

Only Slan Daoine remained on his feet.

"There now," said the man. "I value intimacy."

Sensing the sorcery of a weirdsman, Slan Daoine swung his flintlock up to fire.

Lunging with a strength and speed that should have been impossible to the spindle-shanked man, Dordias seized the Colonel's arm in a vice-like grip, the other hand locking onto the soldier's throat. "Rude. Rude. Such indecent haste. What would the quality back at Camlan say, eh?"

Taliesin could only look on. The ludicrous sight of the slight man lifting Slan Daoine from the floor like a pillow. Slan Daoine was gagging and spluttering, his face becoming a continent of red blotches.

Ignoring the violent thrashing of the Colonel's legs, Dordias continued. "No more clichés fighting man? No more 'it is all over for you', or 'in the name of her gracious majesty'? Well then, if you are not going to add to the conversation, you will just have to leave."

His arm became a blurred arc, and Slan Daoine was flung through an oriel window. His windpipe savagely crushed, unable to scream, the soldier spiralled to the ground in a shower of stained glass.

The gargoyle-like man clutched his hand to his brow in a show of mock tragedy. "What, you mean we are not on the ground floor?"

Taliesin stared in silent horror, unable to close out the terrible leering face.

The weirdsman addressed the felled dragon-browns. He knew them for what they were. Gutter scum and rufflers. Hardly worth his attention. "Tell me you feel it's like a dream. When you are being chased by something and your legs will not move; rooted to the spot. Well, that is the effect I always try for."

"Let me have the powder now," Matholwch called out, oblivious to the murder committed by his servant. "There is such an emptiness inside me. Please."

"Busy, busy, busy. So many distractions," Dordias complained. "If there is emptiness there, I shall just have to let it out."

The weirdsman was out of sight again from Taliesin's position on the floor, but the Captain saw the eldritch spark leap across the room to strike Matholwch in the stomach.

*"Est idoneum bello."*

Collapsing backwards with the impact of the lightning bolt, Matholwch spilled out of his chair, a gaping smoking hole burned through the furniture.

Matholwch's mutilated remains were hidden from Taliesin's view, but he could not ignore the sickening roasting smell which began to waft across the stone-flagged floor.

"Painless, really. Now, I must bid you farewell. I have tarried here for too long, and there is a full day in front of me."

So saying, the long-legged man took three striding steps, leaping out of the shattered window Slan Daoine's body had passed through moments earlier.

# Chapter 3

Watery sunlight glowed behind iron-sheet cloud. In front of Drum Draiocht's walls, the regiments stood arrayed in the parade order of the Realm's Princedoms.

Squares of Connacht fencibles, Tryban light foot, Cornwall pioneers, columns of Emrys dragoons and hussars, and at the rear, a line of the dragon-browns, killers drawn from every tumble-down and rookery on the island.

In victory, their petty politics had been thrown aside. The regiments which had fought under the command of the Butcher stood momentarily united, bound together by fear of the fate of failed rebellion; a lesson which the soldiers would be expected to carry back to their homes.

Gallows stood where the town once hugged the fortress's curtain wall. Above the grubby ashes which had been Drum Draiocht's slum quarter, trapdoors clacked and men thudded down, their necks snapped instantly, or if they were unlucky, dangled kicking for a minute, long seconds spent thrashing themselves into burbling silence.

Representing the victors were three dragon-browns from Fanrig; unlucky looters caught rifling the dead Ruri's bedroom. They were allowed the noose first, followed by the grim-faced ranks of the captured mercenaries. These were hard men, mercenaries from the kingdoms of the mainland and Dal Albaeon secessionists. There would be no quarter for them. The Queen had troubles enough in the land, without encouraging the hordes of free companies swarming the mainland states to seek employment in her islands.

Taliesin stood with the line, rubbing circulation back into

his arms. After a party of Realmsmen had discovered the Duke's smoking corpse – the carcass surrounded by bodies sprawled across the floor – Gwion Bach's imposing presence had been summoned by the staff officers.

Following a few perfunctory prods, the weirdsman had raised one of his massive white eyebrows, then, for reasons known only to him, scattered a peppery ash across Matholwch's body.

"They will live," he had announced indifferently. "Which is more than I can say for this one."

Gwion Bach waited with the Butcher, apart from the ranks and behind the scaffold. General Teyron watched the line of condemned snaking to their left with a quiet satisfaction. "You have been in contact with your fellowship in Camlan?"

Gwion Bach nodded. "You will hardly be surprised to learn the manner of the Duke's passing has become a matter of concern in the highest councils."

"Your senders have been discreet?" Teyron asked.

Gwion Bach narrowed his eyebrows at the Butcher. The question was an unnecessary one. "Only a handful know of it. Officially, Matholwch will have been killed during the weeks of bombardment – an important fiction to maintain. Those present at the Duke's murder must go to Camlan, to stop the truth spreading. And to make themselves available for inquisition by the mummers.

"Ensure you bring the Duke's clothes and a scattering of objects from the hall, the mummers will want to try for a scrying from them also."

"There is nothing you can do from what is here?"

Gwion Bach shook his head, a barely perceptible movement. "That is not my path. Besides, the Queen will not trust results given to her secondhand, and would certainly not wish them produced outside of the capital."

"Does the Queen think I would fake the death of Matholwch?"

"More curious things have happened," Gwion Bach said. "And more trusted servants betrayed a mistress for the right price."

The Butcher glanced across the black mess of the town, towards Taliesin's troops. Even stiff on parade, the devils managed to look as if they were lounging outside a coaching-inn. "Of all the people who had to be present at Matholwch's end. Of all the scum we have in the ranks, it had to be Taliesin's rabble."

"Impress upon them the need of silence, General. If the other Princedoms learn too much of this, it will weaken Emry's position. They will start wondering about the nature of our enemies. They will start plotting more schemes to lever at our weaknesses."

Teyron sneered. "A city has just fallen to an army mustered from every territory in the Realm. Whatever we do here, the blasted rumours will get back to the Princes soon enough."

Gwion Bach's lips curled up, what passed for a smile from the frog-eyed weirdsman. "You might find the Queen's own factors spreading another story. About how the Realm reached into Drum Draiocht. Putting a quick end to Matholwch to stop the friction that would have been created by a trial in the islands."

The General eyed Gwion Bach suspiciously, a sudden unpleasant thought crossing his mind.

"No," Gwion Bach said simply.

Across the wreckage of the town, Taliesin noted the Butcher's cold stares in their direction.

Losing the Butcher's aide had not improved Teyron's

disposition towards the dragon-browns; whatever lay in their future, Taliesin knew it would not be the easy return to garrison life he and his men were after.

The best his company could hope for was a posting to a Martello tower in the highlands. Out of sight out of mind, and the only tales they would be telling would be to mountain eagles and cotters. The worst he could expect to receive would be the flicker of an assassin's knife, a blade flashing out of the shadows one sentry-night.

Connaire Mor had also seen the Butcher's calculating gaze. He knew the perfidy of the Realm only too well, and despite his massive muscled bulk, the young mountain-man shivered under the watery light.

It had been four years ago, in the same sunlight which washed Astolat's sparse granite slopes like a corpse's spittle. Dead men. Shallow graves full of them after Congal Cáech's final show of bravery, the last act of a desperate Prince who had pushed Astolat's claims to independence too far, too fast.

Their clan's blacksmith and his assistants had to hold Connaire Mor down while his two brothers and a dozen more rebels trod air, legs fluttering like pinned moths. The jeers of the Logriese soldiers, laughing and joking about the finest mountain dance they had ever seen.

His father's voice had been harsh in his ears. "You remember, Connaire Mor, how the buckler and knife struck their squares and shattered against their heathen ways of fighting. Never forget the weakness and stupidity that led to this day."

Connaire Mor choked with shock and shame when his father told him how they planned to become strong again, that the clans were paying for him and others like him to be commissioned in the army of the Realm, to learn the ways of the heathen. He had screamed and railed, but his family had cursed him back and then threatened to disinherit him.

Twelve days after his brothers had jerked their last breath away in the city square at Cannlar, misting the air in the shadow of the great heights, Connaire Mor had walked into the garrison of the hated lowland army.

Escaping the cruel procession of executions in front of Drum Draiocht, Connaire Mor recalled his first meeting with the one-eyed rogue who had become his Captain and the events which had led him to this strange situation.

Staked out in a garrison yard, the highlander had been freezing to death for assaulting two of the Realm's gentleman officers. Dead he most certainly would have been, if Taliesin had not held off a Logriese Major with his sabre, the companymen sawing through Connaire Mor's cords, bribing the gate sergeant to draw up papers of transfer to Taliesin's band of dragon-browns.

It was not a debt the mountain-man would forget.

# Chapter 4

Morning had arrived and a chill wind was whipping across the valley, tossing up clouds of leaves and making the trees shiver.

Standing outside Drum Draiocht, Taliesin watched the regiments bent around the main road, heading back for Llud-din and her coffin-cover pall of workshop smoke. Flintlocks shouldered, the men's marching songs were gladdened by the fact they were heading home, off to garrison – or in the case of the fencibles, back to their farms and estates and town trades.

Towering alongside Taliesin, one of the Butcher's kettle-blacks waited as sullenly as an iron menhir. Even on horseback, the ugly felloe of her wheels reached high over the Captain's shoulder, black-iron plates damp from the drizzling showers. Steam from the automaton's aeolipiles hissed across the road's floor, curling around his horse's hooves, making the beast skitter and prance.

Uneasy on the piebald mare, Taliesin cursed the creature and tried to rein her in. A childhood in a rookery slum had proved little qualification to become a rider, but Teyron seemed determined to turn him into a gentleman. Good horses cost as much as sixty angels – more than Taliesin could afford on a Captain's coin – so on the Butcher's instructions, the beast had been lent to him by an unhappy lancer with a drooping moustache.

Teyron needed speed from his party. Not for the dragon-browns the relative safety of the busy southern road; the General had other plans for the company. The eldritch forest. Close to three days' journey, the majority of it along a dangerous slim path which threaded and twisted its way through the heart of the tumble like a muddy, mutilated serpent.

Late the night before, Taliesin's soldiers had discovered they were to be detached to the capital in Queen Annan's own Princedom, royal Emrys. What luck would Taliesin's unhappy stars bring when they reached the richest city in the Realm?

Nothing good, the officer was willing to wager. No good fortune to be found in Camlan, where courtiers poured vitriol on each other like siege oil, daggers were kept close at hand, and every day saw some new way to circumvent the laws on duelling inside the royal estate.

Climbing down the steps of the kettle-black, two artificers in garter-blue uniforms and silver shako hats jumped off the ladder and onto the ground. Trudging through the thick mud, one of them nodded at Taliesin and rolled his eyes in theatrical despair. Behind them, a limber of eight horses struggled along with its great cannon, the long brass culverin moulded into a four-wheeled wooden bed. Rolling the fieldpiece to the back of the kettle-black, her gunnery officers and the artificers laboured around the trail, lifting and locking it to the heavy war machine. But no kettle-blacks would be travelling their route, the ravaged western road traders had cut through the enchanted forest; the clumsy automaton would have had her iron wheels trapped by a pothole before an hour had passed.

Down the valley, Taliesin saw a turnpike-keeper coming out of his cottage to open the gate to the Llud-din road, light dragoons cantering past long columns of dragon-browns, the plumes on their tarleton helmets sagging in the rain. The Llud-din road had been one of Blind Tierney's undertakings, the Realm's notoriously eccentric road builder. Layered with small stones and staged with coaching-inns every sixty leagues, the army would reach Llud-din with only four days of hard march on the road.

Separated by the marching regiments, Gunnar and Connaire Mor waited on the other side of the thoroughfare on their own mounts. Taliesin knew the dandy had more reason than most to regret their journey to Emrys. Gunnar had killed a powerful nobleman's son in a Camlan duel, and had only escaped the Baron's toppers by hastily accepting the Queen's coin. Taliesin grimaced. He had problems enough, without adding the ranks of the capital's assassins to his list.

Spilling across the baggage on two stage-wagons, the remainder of Taliesin's company laughed and joked at the novelty of being carried somewhere for a change. Their horseplay was watched with studied indifference by the squadron of hussars that was the Butcher's escort. It had not escaped the one-eyed officer's notice that only the soldiers present at Matholwch's murder were being ordered to the capital; the half of his force which had remained scattered fighting in the carnage of Drum Draiocht were now on their way back to garrison. A soldier lived by two things, his instinct, and his superstition, and Taliesin's told him his company might be just as well off deserting into the forest, joining one of the ruffler bands that scratched a living in the faerie forestland.

Taliesin had no idea who the Duke's gargoyle-like killer had been, and as far as the officer was concerned, he would not even break a wind for the Peers' intrigues; the complex, delicately deadly labyrinth of Camlan politics – Emrys trying to tie the land into an ever closer unity while the Princedoms chaffed at the bit to assert their independence like badly broken horses.

Putting his gloom-ridden thoughts behind him, Taliesin looked over to the Butcher, General Teyron sitting on a slate-grey mare which looked ill at ease next to Gwion Bach and his mount. The eyes of the weirdsmen's horse burned with an intelligence no animal should possess.

"Our way lies to the west," said the Butcher, watching the slow passage of his army in the opposite direction.

Gwion Bach nodded. "Let us make haste then."

Riding rapidly along narrow roads, the party passed rows of landowners' hedges, the fields around Drum Draiocht thick with turnips which would become winter fodder for the region's cattle. Labourers worked the land, figures in the distance tilling soil and burning the stubble of the crops – a second glance needed to check they were not scarecrows.

As the Butcher's group clattered across the lanes leading up to the enchanted forest, the farmhouse walls grew thicker and the holly-hedges taller, the villagers' protection against their proximity to the wild border.

Then at last, opening up in front of them like the mouth of a mineshaft, the entrance into the tumble reared up over the road. Taliesin remembered the name foresters and poachers had given to this region of the tumble. The Céannans Mor. A scrubby desolation of dense oak and elm, haunted by nameless creatures and those that the kingdom had banished, tobymen, thieves and other brutal undesirables.

No-one in the group made conversation, echoing the silence of the ancient place hemming them in. Even Gunnar, with his impetuous humour, seemed intimidated by the presence of the boundless place.

For two days the company cut through the deep mantle of the forest, stopping overnight at well-fortified posthouses, the only outposts of civilisation in the thorny, impenetrable faerie-land. By night they drank hot grog in common-rooms filled with men lathed hard by the witchwoods, trappers, royal coachmen, merchanteers and travelling monks of the Martyr. And by day they pressed on for Emrys, their hussars acting as escort for any travellers that dared the road.

Happening across nothing more sinister than a family of forest hobs, their hairy hemlock-coloured bodies fleeing up the trees as they heard the Realmsmen, Taliesin counted himself lucky. Forest imps were known to throw stones at farmers' windows and tease squires' hunting beagles, but they were infinitely preferable to the other dark beasts which slunk through the heartwood.

As with the previous two days, the third found Taliesin

passing along the cool gloom of the Céannans Mor road, although the officer was reluctant to dignify their passage with the title road; more a passage which saw enough traffic to wear away undergrowth from the rut-deep track.

It was hard for him to place the trees; the forests had been weirded so long, the verderers who penetrated the wooded caverns told tales of new joinings every year. Only Laetha, the hunchback forester in their company, could have put names to the princely green monarchs of the Céannans Mor.

Taliesin passed a cluster of trees that had once been holly, but were now stretched as tall as living sentinels, needle-like leaves waxy and the size of an Astolat warrior's shield.

As they moved on, a stand of Logriese pine forced its way to the road's edge, clawing at the sky as if trying to scratch a way into the firmament. There was little foliage on the pines' lower branches, but near the crown, a beard of pine cones and leaves spread out to dissipate the falling sunlight into a hundred thin shreds, making a chequerboard out of the forest floor. It was impossible to see far into the witchwood, but the Captain and his dragon-browns could smell the carpet of decaying leaves.

Of all those in Taliesin's party, only Gwion Bach appeared truly to belong in the shady tracks of the forest, a pale rider on a paler mount. His steed moved from shadow to shadow, snorting contemptuous clouds of mist from its nostrils like a dragon preparing to gob flame. Giving it a clear berth, a hussar fiddled nervously with his fur busby, letting the horse move forward surrounded by its own island of space.

Drawing up beside Taliesin, Gunnar's breath misted in the clean air. "Camlan. I never thought I would be returning there."

"Perhaps they've let the price on your head drop with the toppers."

Laughing, the dandy shook his head. "Damn unlikely, sir.

Gold angels do not much matter to the family that's after me. If it did, my father's House could have bought the bastards off."

"You never did tell me," said Taliesin, "what the duel was over."

"It was a stupid thing. There was a player with a capering idiot on a leash. The one I killed thought he could beat the cripple for the amusement of a tavern. He was trying to impress his lady."

"You fought a duel over an entertainer's fool?"

"No. When I stopped the beating, I tried to buy the fool from his owner. The gentleman didn't care for that and so we played cards for the boy. If I won, the cripple was to go free ... I won."

Taliesin knew what would have happened next. "And the quality didn't like it?"

"He accused me of cheating."

"Were you?"

"Of course," Gunnar sounded pained. "But he was too stupid to know that. We settled for grass before breakfast, on the lawn of a Cornish Baron. Damn large crowd. I won that too. The dolt! Look you, it was only to go to first blood. I spared his life, then he tried to fillet me as I was walking away. He left me with no choice."

"Ah," said Taliesin, understanding. "Embarrassing. As long as you stay alive, you are a reminder of his dishonour to his family."

"As crazy a reason to end up here as any. I could almost have stood what the buck was doing to the cripple, but for his woman. She was fair as a goddess and she was laughing. It did not seem right that such beauty could be so cruel. It sounds stupid now... I had to stop the fool being beaten."

Shaking his head, Taliesin barked a laugh and rode on. He had escaped a life of poverty and worthlessness by taking the Queen's coin, while the dandy had fled a life of wealth and comfort. Landing them together, life had completed her hardhearted symmetry with a perverse flourish.

With the chill of morning passing into evening, layering the forest tunnel with a crust of frost, the party crested a shallow rise and came across a welcome sight. In front of them, a half-timbered posthouse rose in a clearing, a run of buildings scattered alongside a glacial river, her waters foaming rapidly towards the emerald faerie-world. Behind the hold's coach-house lay a pier with merchanteer riverboats moored in its shadow.

Part of the waters had been diverted to fork around the building's walls, a miniature moat crossed by an arched granite bridge. Stout oak beam-pieces girdled the red stone, giving the posthouse a feeling of permanence its guests surely valued as much as the opportunity for a warm bed for the night. This far into the isolation of the tumble, any sign of humanity was a welcome sight.

Opening the posthouse door, a figure stepped out, the fragrance of scented lavender bags drifting across on the breeze. He wore a green uniform with red facings, one of the Queen's Foot Guards.

Pulling off his shako and holding the hat under his arm, the man hailed them. "Good evening to you, General. Major Fangel, sent to bring you fellows to Camlan. Damnable cold night, eh?"

Whining growls came from behind the Major, and Taliesin saw a cage had been set up in the shadow of the stables. Behind wooden bars, a dark shape clung miserably to the cage and trembled in the damp weather. It was a beastman – demisapi in the old tongue – a weasel-faced creature with silver whiskers, staring unhappily at the soldiers in the last rays of the forest's lemon-yellow light.

"What is that foul animal doing here?" demanded the Butcher, dismounting.

"That?" their escort said. "Ran into some fuss and bother last night, sir. Damned pack of his kind attacked the mailcoach from Neronnotar. Luckily for the coachman, we had arrived by river an hour or two beforehand. With the rebellion, the dragoons haven't been seen on the road for months; these brutes have been taking advantage."

Teyron slapped angrily at his boots with his rider's crop. "I meant, what is it doing in that cage?"

"The tavern-owner's idea. Wants to sell it to the Duke of Llud-din for his menagerie. Said the demisapi have given him enough bother while the campaign's been going, the least he is going to do is make an angel or two out of the thing."

One of the dragon-browns laughed. There were ballads about the mad Duke's collection of animals, theatre-pieces based on the adventures trappers got into trying to satisfy his grotesque tastes.

Dismissing the notion as the worse sort of foolery, the beak-nosed General left the hussars to rub down their mounts and walked into the posthouse.

Looking over the low barges in the river, Taliesin gave his horse to a young groom along with a copper angel, Connaire Mor and the dandy following suit. The hussars might not trust the care of their beasts to the stablehands, but the Captain's plans for the rest of the night did not include ending up smelling of horse dung and saddle polish.

So. If they were to travel the rest of the way to the capital by boat, then they might be in Camlan before the next night. Not a prospect that appealed to Taliesin.

Leaving the warm stone-vaulted drinking room, Connaire Mor saw Taliesin standing outside the coaching-inn. Waiting alone, the officer watched the shadows of the clouds crawling across the stars.

"You're not for a turn of the ale then?"

In answer, Taliesin raised a wood-carved mug filled with the local cider, nearly as potent as the army grog the soldiers called blackstrap.

The Captain preferred the company of solitude. Inside, the rooms spilled over with dragon-browns, hussars and the Foot Guards, adding their ranks to a crowd of riverboat merchanteers and tinkers, royal coachmen in striped waistcoats, thronging the tavern with their carriages' passengers.

From behind the cage's bars, the beastman looked at them with ancient eyes, its fur-lined muscles tensing and relaxing as it tried to ward off the cold wind.

"Ugly beast," said the highlander.

Leaning against the posthouse wall, Taliesin downed his sweet-tasting drink. "I remember the Duke of Llud-din; he was a bastard as well as crazy."

Settling on Taliesin, the monster's unblinking gaze moved across to the mountain-man. "Aye, poor bugger. I wonder if the Duke will feed the thing well."

"Better than he ever fed his people," Taliesin spat.

"There were demisapi in my mountain forests that could speak, man. As true as I stand here."

"But of course they did," Taliesin grunted. "And no doubt they played cards with your hermits and danced jigs for your lords."

"Ah, you're a heathen, man."

Drawing his sabre, Taliesin walked up to the cage and wedged the blade between the lock. "Sod the Duke, and sod every dragoon that ever served under him."

He heaved the sword under the lock until its mount groaned and snapped, the cage door swinging open. Like a lightning bolt, the beastman was out of the stall, climbing the wall and fleeing towards the dark spiny bushes.

"Martyrs," Connaire Mor swore at the Captain. "Are you daft? What are you about?"

"We may die in the capital. But he'll be free."

Shrugging, Connaire Mor opened the door into the posthouse. "I'm no corpse yet, and you, you've got the luck of Old Shadow about you."

They would need it for Camlan. Every last bit of it.

Travelling on the river, the dragon-browns ate up the leagues towards Camlan, morning mist closing in on itself as their barges followed the current. Each boat had two triangular sails, a hump in the planking beneath which a small paddle laboured, the craft's aeolipiles pumping steam through the roof of the forest canopy.

Made green by the filter of the ferns, watery sunlight bathed the landscape of serrated witchwood, otters gliding by the boat's flat-deck. Taliesin realised they had entered the Princedom of Emrys when the ranks of weirded trees receded, the tapestry of wildflowers and mountainous evergreens replaced by tamed meadows and the sight of grazing sheep.

Villages and the chimney smoke of towns drifted alongside them, the river widening by the afternoon and growing busy with barges and boats. At one point, a canal's aqueduct bridged the river, the sails of the boats above billowing as Taliesin's craft cut underneath.

Gunnar pointed out the great houses on the estates, elegant and collonaded, the dandy naming the noble families that lived in the white mansions, amusing the company with tales of their indiscretions. Taliesin knew one of the river's tributaries reached as far as the sea when he noticed a small navy cutter trailing behind them, a brutal cauldron-shaped culverin on her prow.

With the Realm's taxes on wine and lace, there was a healthy trade in moonraking, smugglers making a fortune by dispersing illegal cargoes across the islands; 'free trade' was so widespread, few of the Princedoms' people viewed it as a crime; just another profitable sideline for those that worked the seas and rivers.

The soldiers' lighters finally anchored at a custom-house, the smell of backyard industries from the town strong after days in the pristine forest; the scent of dyers, soap-boilers and brewers rank in the air. Artful custom officers lounged around the mooring, cleaning flintlocks, warm in their heavy coats and trademark red bicorn hats. Most of them would be receiving coin from the smugglers to turn a blind eye, as would the local lords – that was if the region's squire and doomsman magistrates were not already the ringleaders.

Waiting down in the town was a column of kettle-blacks, the wind buffeting their wrought-iron sides as drizzle flailed the cobbled streets. Emrys' pennant flapped in the squall, the dragon rearing on a field of green proud over the cabins. Crowding into the decks to the rear of the automata, the dragon-browns watched the local lamplighters climb the town's metal rails with their candles and flintboxes. They were having a job firing the wicks in the icy weather.

Coughing greasy smoke, the war-machines pulled off, following the Camlan road and trundling away into the rain.

Emry's roads were lively with gigs and post-chaises, lone riders and foot travellers, farm wagons bumping along beside the Queen's kettle-blacks. Numerous turnpikes funded her well-kept roads, as good as any the Captain had travelled in the other princedoms. When they neared Camlan, sedan chairs began to dot the road, borne down the flagstones by rugged chair-men, nobility being carried from outlying mansions towards the capital's fashionable balls. The carriers had to be hale men, to lift the sedans as well as to fight off Camlan's cutthroats and street beggars.

Behind Taliesin, two stage-coaches cracked along the road, racing to overtake the Crown automata. Eyes intent below low-brimmed hats, both coachmen switched their whips down around their team's ears. Each coach was decked in laurel.

"Martyr's teeth," said the Foot Guard Major. "But their horses are not going to last long at that pace."

Taliesin looked over the rail, the carriages passing them neck and neck. "Why the race?"

"Accession Day, Taliesin. First mail-coach from the coast to reach the palace wins a prize of silver coins. Why do you think Teyron is in such an all-damned hurry to reach the capital? It will mean double the prestige if the fellow can claim a campaign victory during the Queen's celebrations."

So the Butcher was out to curry favour with the Royal House. Taliesin should have guessed. The dragon-browns were being dropped into the great spider's web, and all Teyron was considering was how best to please the woman at the centre of it.

A jolt followed by a rasping sigh of steam announced the kettle-black's arrival at their destination. Taliesin climbed down the iron steps to find himself standing in a large stone courtyard, the heavy automaton having pulled to a stop under a stretch of canvas. Beyond the courtyard, the mouth of an arch swallowed the other kettle-blacks.

Silhouetted against the leaden night sky, a line of megalithic towers crept high into the darkness, the scale of the Crown's citadel overwhelming. Built on four hills, Camlan lay across the land like the belly of a ruddy-faced squire; corpulent and swelling across the slopes, filling every fold of land. Beyond the royal estates they could see the lights of the city, pale constellations of oil lamps twinkling below.

"Every new ruler adds another tower, an extra wing," said their guide. "Parts of it date back to the old kingdom. Damnable cold of course."

"The builders should have asked to have been paid by the brick," said Taliesin, gazing along the bloated length of the battlements.

Climbing down from their kettle-black, Connaire Mor and the dandy joined the other officers.

"Keep close to the main corridors," advised the guardsman. "Entire wings are falling into collapse."

Following his weirdsman, Teyron walked up to the Guards officer and encompassed the party with a perfunctory wave. "Garrison these rogues, and Captain, if I hear of anything of value going missing around your devils, I shall personally see every one of your rufflers and thieves flogged."

"Sir," Taliesin saluted the Butcher carelessly.

Across the tower beside Taliesin, warm lights smudged the sheeting water, shadows shifting behind one of the rain-slipped windows. Two figures stared down into the courtyard, watching the brown motes below. One was a Prince-Regent by marriage, the other a Prince of the Church by cunning.

"Is it they?" asked the Prince-Regent, peering through the drumming rain.

"They are hardly aristocracy from the Foot Guards," sneered the Arch-Truron. Why had the Martyr saddled him with this asinine ally? Had he risen so far and fast among the ranks of the blessed that he needed such a painful lesson in humility?

Behind the churchman, a pair of the Prince-Regent's spaniels worried at his cope, chewing on the fine silver cloth. Angrily, he brushed them back and looked at their foreign fool of a owner. "The Martyr save your majesty, but the Martyr damn your dogs."

"Gracious, stop that you two fellows. Over there with your cousins, or no pork lumps for you tonight."

Abashed, the golden spaniels scampered away across the polished boards, barking and yapping at the other puppies.

Looking back into the courtyard, the Prince Regent shook his head. "Why, they are rogues, sir. Hardly gentleman at all. Would she use such scum as these?"

"She will use anyone and everyone. As you should well know."

"That I do, sir. It is insufferable, insufferable. I show my hounds more respect than the Queen returns to me. It stands against the natural order, sir. I will not stand to be one of her poodles, no, not at all. I am a man!"

You are a dullard, thought the churchman, but he nodded sagely. "But of course you are, your majesty. And we must show her. Strike out, demonstrate that you understand her schemes and can be a worthy partner... or a worthy enemy."

"Yes, I can see that. But I must be circumspect, holy

father. The bitch's informers are everywhere, and she knows who in the capital is taking my coin."

"You are wise indeed," said the churchman. "But I already have a man in mind. One I understand will be only too glad to help us in this matter. The Queen might wish to make those gutter-scum her tools, but we might blunt them a little first, eh?"

With the Prince-Regent's eyes flashing, the nobleman turned away from the filthy weather outside. "Those damn low fellows, we will give them something to remember. And the bitch too."

The Arch-Truron smiled. And on ground where the state floundered, the servants of the Martyr would be all too ready to step in, to swell the church's coffers with tithes. Glory be.

Major Fangel led the soldiers to a two-story structure falling off the curtain wall, part of the barracks. Inside, the Royal Guards wore green uniforms similar to Fangel's, their cuffs and collars piped with red facings. Patent leather crossbelts cut across their breasts, and Fangel noticed the mountain-man glancing towards the Guards' flintlocks. "Outside the Foot Guards, no jack in the estate is allowed a weapon with a reach longer than the length of his arm. Sabres only. Less trouble for us that way, eh?"

"A mug-hunter can murder you as well with a sabre," said Taliesin. "Is this where we are to be billeted?"

Fangel shook his head. "No, Someone must have taken a liking for you fellows, I was told to put you near the chapel. Damn warm there. Too good for those monks and holy crows anyway."

"I expected to see more folks about," said Connaire Mor.

Fangel levered open an oak door leading to a spiral staircase. "Most of them will be getting ready for the Accession Day, either that or getting Accession Day ready. Fuss and bother, Taliesin, fuss and damned bother."

At the top of the staircase they came to a long passage

tilting down into the distance. The plain-spoken Major ran a finger along a trace of water dribbling down the bricks. "The west wall was Macsyn's. Outlasted the King, anyway! His aunt poisoned the fellow a year later."

Halfway down the corridor, a side-entrance breached the wall. There was no door, but rusty red hinges showed where one had rotted away.

Curious, Gunnar poked his head through the gap. Inside, the dandy found a slab-like porch overlooking a semicircular chamber. The sides of the chamber plunged the height of two men, the brackish green surface of a pool lapping against stone. The walls of the chamber were green with slime and mould – an unhealthy odour lingering in the dank hollow.

"No water pool?" Gunnar said. "It's stagnant."

Fangel looked into the well room. "It is connected to a flow in the caverns underneath the estate. Macsyn liked to fish, so on a whim the fellow had this place constructed with the wall. Should have stuck to fishing, eh? Politics will kill you every damned time. Anyway, there were other fish down in the caverns, blind and hungry, ate every salmon the fool had it stocked with. Had to abandon the idea in the end. Confounded ass! The Aled runs through the capital, he could have fished there."

With the wet corridor leading to a balcony, the party stared down towards a marble floor. The hall looked as cold and miserable as any of the others Taliesin had seen since they had arrived.

Fangel sneezed. "Dust, the damn lazy fools never clean the place. You'll soon realise, Taliesin, this place is full of fools. More fools to the league here than any other princedom in the Realm."

The Guards officer continued to lead Taliesin and his company through the citadel's labyrinth, its construction a bizarre lesson of architecture from a dozen ages. By the time they reached their quarters, only the Major was able to retrace their steps. Alone among the dragon-browns,

Taliesin felt strangely at home. Suddenly he realised what Camlan reminded him of: Llud-din, the brutal smoke-filled streets; cobbled pavements choked with age and the debris of abandonment. He was half expecting to come across a gin-house in the narrow passages, drunken artisans spilling out across puddles of urine and dodging hissing alley cats.

Fangel led them into a gatehouse, where Taliesin discovered their rooms had once been monks' cells, a view into a quadrangle enclosed by the chapel. Originally intended as a priest's herbal garden, the garden had become littered with debris and mud. Outside, the rain still whipped angrily across the walls, rubbish below smeared across pools of water and bobbing in the overflow.

"Rather sparse, Taliesin. Rather sparse. But warm, eh? The ghosts like it, the staff have seen enough Kings and Dukes along these corridors to stock someone's parlour of oddities."

"We'll live with spirits," said Taliesin. "At least they are nobody we have killed."

"Good fellow. Now, let me have your sizes. I shall see what I can do about finding you dress uniforms."

"Dress uniforms?" Taliesin said disbelievingly. "Are we expected to join the Guards, on parade?"

"The Accession Day, Taliesin. You know how the fools in this place enjoy their trophies. Most the Court will want to hear how you chased off the damn insurrection."

"This is a pressed company, sir, not a troupe of dancing bears. That is all that Camlan's Court want. A trained bear they can pet, preferably after it has savaged the hand of someone they dislike. You may make our excuses, Major, and tell Camlan's quality we will be stowing our gear tonight."

Fangel looked sternly at Taliesin. "No excuses, Taliesin. You know how the courtiers pout and sulk when they don't get their way. If you are not there this evening the Queen will only send someone to drag you out!"

Taliesin gave the Major a look indicating this would suit

him fine. "You can tell her most serene majesty to – "

"Taliesin," Connaire Mor laid one of his massive fists on Taliesin's shoulder. "You'd not be turning down the chance for the best feed we have had since Dal Albaeon?"

With relief, the highlander saw a glint of sense begin to return to his officer's remaining eye. Connaire Mor hated the Royal House with a passion – he knew what they were capable of if slighted.

"No buggering good will come of this though," said Taliesin.

Taking this as a tacit acceptance on the foul-mannered Captain's part, Fangel departed to make the arrangements.

Half an hour later, three Whitestaves returned – part of the Court's army of orderlies and runners. They came with an ill-matched pile of clothes, the only common feature a luxurious cut in the cloth, material that could have paid for an entire company of dragon-browns to be fitted out. Their uniforms dripped with hussar-style braid, shining buttons stamped with the Realm crown-and-dragon, the jackets dyed in an explosion of wild colours: purples and golds, whites and silvers, fiery magentas and garter-blues.

"What in the Martyr's name is this?" Taliesin demanded, examining the bundle. "My men have been in the field for over five months, drinking pond water and eating maggot-infested beef courtesy of the army. And now you want me to dress them up like Roubaixian whores, then take them to a royal banquet. Like poxed Roubaixian dollymops! Do any of you also wish to tell me how I am to get them to fight again when we leave Camlan?"

"This is appropriate wear for the Court, sir," said one of the Whitestaves, his voice dripping with disdain.

Taliesin shook his head. "If the devil must, I shall play like a good puppet for all the fine people, but I shall be dammed if I will dress like one for them too! If they want to see the army that fought for them in Dal Albaeon, they can see the real thing, not some perfumed troop of tin soldiers."

"Mark you, it is Accession Day," Gunnar laughed, trying

onc of the jackets. "If they want to dress us up like the Butcher's staff, then damn, but I say let us take salutes from the Guards."

"Martyr's teeth, give these to the others. They fight like a bunch of pirates, they may as well look the part too."

Connaire Mor looked at the uniforms. "When the man was telling us we'd be expected in their hall, I do no think he was extending the invitation to the entire company."

"I didn't hear any specific orders," Taliesin said. "I told the Major we would need to stow our gear, and he ordered us to attend."

"Aye and you're crazy. We're not back in Cornwall with the Prince to look after our hides now. This is the capital. You start playing with any of your games here, and the swining Queen will stick our heads in a gibbet."

"Just give out those uniforms," Taliesin said.


With a hare lip and overweight belly, the Whitestave who had remained with the dragon-browns had always been held in low esteem by the other servants. Nervous and stuttering, he crept around Camlan trying to find jobs that kept him out of the way of anyone with authority; sweeping the roof walkways had always been a favourite of his.

Now the sweating youth was faced with a company of strutting brigands; a gang of rufflers, murderers and drunks. And he, he, was expected to lead them to a banquet being attended by every notable he had spent a lifetime studiously avoiding.

The one-eyed devil who was their leader had not even bothered to change, he was still wearing his faded brown jacket – complete with bloodstains and powder burns. The Master of Revels would flog his hide raw for bringing these devils in front of the Court.

"Come on lad," one of the soldiers shouted behind him. "We want to get to the blackstrap and celebrate our promotion." This raised a round of raucous laughter from the others.

"Just don't be expecting me to salute you," said the highlander.

Envious of Connaire Mor, the young Whitestave wished he had the giant's bull-like frame – no more days scraping at the bottom of the pile – under the thumb of every other toadshit in the Royal Estate. His revenge fantasies were interrupted by the capering devils behind him.

"Come on boy. Damn but these boots are tight."

Leading them across Camlan's honeycombed corridors, their hare-lipped guide opened a door into a dusty barrel-vault.

Set four stories above them, a series of crystal panes circled the vault. Candlelight spilled out, catching motes of dust swimming up through the illumination, moving slowly towards the ceiling's black ribs. Like a child's shadow-play, figures moved in silhouette behind the glass.

"The lib, library," coughed the Whitestave, seeing the direction of Taliesin's gaze.

"Oh paper and paper, and more paper still."

Turning, Taliesin found the source of the voice, for a moment confusing the man with Gwion Bach. But another figure emerged from the shadows, hobbling on a cane. Taliesin saw the old man was dressed like a tinker, shabby and gaudy, his eyes crafty with a mischievous sheen.

"No librarian, you," Connaire Mor said.

"Do I look like one?" he replied, falling into step alongside the soldiers. Then to the Whitestave, "You are going to the Accession Day hall? Hey-ho, I am passing that way myself. Save your hands for something else, I shall guide these ones."

Relief vied with gratitude on the boy's face. He had been spared the beating he had coming to him.

With a nod to Taliesin, the Whitestave made himself scarce, but not before the old man lent over in passing and whispered: "Use the south passage, there's nobody by the roof stairs."

Never having seen the old man before, the boy skittered

off. Swearing under his breath, that tales of his quirks had spread so far he was now being assailed by complete strangers in the corridors.

"Dressed for the festivities?" Gunnar said, looking at the patchwork cloak and frayed trousers.

"Would the Foot Guards refuse a lonely traveller warmth and company on this foul night?"

"Aye and we'll find out together," Connaire Mor said. "Have you travelled far?"

"Far enough to recognise a mountain accent," he replied. "You men have the look of a tale about you. Perhaps you've been travelling too of late?"

"You're a right canny one, you," Connaire Mor said. "But then a little slyness never hurts on the road. It's a tricky tinker that travels the forests, as my cousin used to say."

The old man seemed amused by this. "Yes, a very tricky tinker indeed."

Following the spry old man through the passages, Taliesin began to notice a gradual change, the faccade of the corridors better cared for, increasingly ornate, plank floors replacing cold stone passages, burnished panelling taking the place of shabby tapestries.

"And are you having a name then?" Connaire Mor said.

"Oh yes," he said. "The tinker, sir, the tinker. Or, *you fool*. Or, *you dirty ruffler*. Answer to many but heed to none, that is my motto."

Climbing a staircase, they came upon another hall, an arch of golden metal leading into a garden. It was one of the crystal gardens that were fast becoming a rage in many of the big cities, the greenery enclosed by iron arches and covered in a magnificent sweep of glass. Pipes lined the wall behind them, hot water steamed by the furnaces of an aeolipile somewhere inside the palace.

Walking along a pebbled path, the party wound its way through a trail of tall shrubs; orange, red and pink blooms marking the way. Herbs of every description lay behind the ferns, gathered from the enchanted forests at no small risk to the collectors. Tamed here, they provided a wealth of medicines and remedies for the palace leeches, as well as flavourings for the court's Master of the Bakehouse – and no doubt a store of poisons for the noble's toppers, the retained assassins that were whispered to serve the Queen.

Butterflies fluttered past, bright and brilliant, small cousins to the eagle-moths which sometimes swooped out of the enchanted forest, scattering sheep and impaling unlucky farmer's hounds on their wicked serrated tails.

One of the men saw a dwarf-tree heavy with apples and stretched out to pluck one, but the tinker's cane flitted out with toad-tongue speed to stripe the soldier's hand.

"One to make you sick. Has the word of the Martyr not reached your village yet?" said the tinker. "There are some apples that are far better left on the tree."

"No bleeding harm in a little scrumping," the soldier complained, his face flushing with anger. But the tinker had already moved on.

Coming out of the passage of evergreens, the dragon-browns walked along the edge of a landscaped pond, walled in red stone and its surface thick with floating bronze leaves. The sound of laughter drifted across the water. On the other side of the bank, a group of courtiers were cooing over a young deer – feeding it snuff, which the tame creature clearly enjoyed, nibbling away quickly.

"Now there's a sight," said Gunnar.

The dandy referring not to the deer but the woman; one of the quality, fey-like in a satin black gown. Flowing freely, the tresses of the girl's long red hair curled seductively across her shoulders, orange freckles scattered across a beautiful, child-like face.

"A beauty for your arm, and a blade for your hand," quoted the tinker.

"You know her?" Gunnar asked.

"Of her, of her. You would be better off naming the men that have been called out over her. Bodies more than have your eyes seen."

"I would not count on that," said Taliesin.

With a curious glance, the tinker looked at Taliesin. "Never a rule crafted to cover all, Captain. Your lady opposite is Elaine, ah, beautiful and perfidious Elaine. Bucks who can not claim a friend for their second, they usually make the mistake of trying to fly away with the lady."

"She is well placed?" Gunnar asked.

"Is there anyone here not well placed?" said the tinker. "Elaine is the prize daughter of a great and prized family; a family noted for fine bladework and the employment of toppers with a taste for dipping suitors in the Aled – as many a buck has discovered to his cost. Eyes to drown in, if you will!"

Twisting around the water, the company passed the revellers resting on the bank.

"By the Martyr, sir, our Colonels are getting younger all the time," one of the men called, seeing the ill-fitting uniforms. His blades laughed with drunken good humour."

"Ah, ladies and goodmen, do not mock the gentleman fighters back from Dal Albaeon. These are heroes all, if you please."

With a start Taliesin looked at the tinker; before he could voice the unspoken question, the tinker leant in close. "You had the smell of that place about you, Dal Albaeon is all turf and tumble."

Gunnar looked poised to capitalise on the tinker's introduction, embellishing the campaign into an epic of near classical proportions, but his dragon-browns pushed the dandy along with friendly abuse.

"She would eat you alive, man," Connaire Mor said, looking back at the red-haired beauty.

Gunnar shook his head. "No. She was looking at me, definitely."

"You're daft, you. What would a Court beauty see in a ruffler like you?"

Leaving the crystal garden, the group came onto a section of the estate congested with staff and functionaries. Busy to the point of distraction, none of the clerks paid any attention to Taliesin's men. Kitchen workers and Whitestaves, guests and courtiers, they scurried back and forth, as if any slower and the business of state might congeal right there in the palace corridors.

"Ah the smell, the smell ..." said the tinker.

"Dal Albaeon again?" said Taliesin sarcastically. "Or has it the smell of a tale about it?"

The tinker just smiled. "Better than that, young Captain. Or worse perhaps, depending on your point of view. The fragrance of power."

"I haven't been young for longer than I care to remember," said Taliesin.

"You won't have smelt power like this for quite a while either." The old tinker sniffed the air theatrically. "Pure. Refined. Nothing quite like it, if you've the nose for a heady brew."

"Aye, or the stomach for it," said Connaire Mor, remembering the mounds of Astolatier corpses Emrys had piled up to keep the seat of power within their Princedom.

Green-uniformed Provosts with burnished flintlocks and neutral stares saluted as the party passed into the Accession Day chambers; slack in admitting such an obvious pack of thugs and thieves masquerading as officers. Or better informed of their attendance than Taliesin had been.

"Hey," Connaire Mor called out, "where's the tink about?"

"He was by us just outside the hall," said one of the soldiers, staring around.

Taliesin shrugged. "Dressed like that, the bugger probably decided not to risk being turned away by the Guards."

"Daft man, we could have got him in," Connaire Mor said. "No problem. Travelling man like that, aye, he would have been full of tales too."

A vaulted dome crowned the space above the party, painted with a panoramic scene of the Martyr's crucifixion on the tree. Pastel angels and clouds on an impressive scale, beautifully rendered but hardly original. Unpleasant memories for the Captain. There had been similar scenes on the lead windows of his poorhouse too.

His childhood custody in the 'gentle' church's care – it made the Captain shiver to think of it. Three years eking out an existence in Llud-din had seemed a kindness after he had run away from the cold cells and colder hearts of the poorhouse.

Luckily for the boy-Taliesin, peace was always short-lived among the Realm's feuding Princedoms, and the crumbling slums on the outskirts of Llud-din an ideal recruiting ground for the Queen's press. For a single silver angel he had exchanged the listless life of a street waif for the brutality and discipline of the Cornwall Pioneers. And had been surprised to discover he had found a family at last.

Taliesin had beat a tune while the army's old hands burnt villages in Tryban; hanged rebels in Dal Albaeon and Astolat by the time he was twenty; had watched helpless while the quality and Crown spent the ranks' lives like water. Nobles called the Realm's army the scourings and refuse of the Three Isles, but every soldier in the companies looked out for his brothers; if a married man died, the chances were one of his friends would marry the widow; if a soldier lost a leg and was thrown out, his comrades would hold a collection to see him back to his village. For Taliesin, starved of human affection and dying the slow death of worthlessness, it had been like coming home for the first time.

"Take your pleasure then," Taliesin said, turning to address the company. "And mind your manners. If one of the quality wants to hear how brave you were, you just spin them a good tale full of courage and clever sodding leadership."

"A fairy tale then," shouted one of the soldiers as they all scattered.

Connaire Mor shook his head. "You're crazy… cutting them loose in here, man."

Taliesin laughed, a rare sound, booming across the chamber like culverin fire. "There's not one of them with a uniform ranking lower than Captain. Officers are expected to act badly, especially when they've come from good families."

"Have a care man, if a real General catches one of them pissing in some Doomsman's pudding while his back is turned, we are all going to be strung out like the time you first happened across me."

Gunnar came over holding a tray of crystal, blood-red wine spilling over the glass's sides. "That could happen yet. The Butcher didn't drag us the distance to the capital just so his favourite soldiers could get drunk in the company of the great and good."

"That's been on my mind too," Taliesin said. "The quality are going to want answers about what happened over in Dal Albaeon, and they might be none too fussy about how they go about obtaining them."

"What have we got to be telling them anyway?" Connaire Mor asked. "A tale of some weirdsman pulling limbs from officers and Dukes, like legs off a spider, before jumping out of a window."

Taliesin sipped back on the wine, his good eye thoughtful under the chandelier light. "Somebody put the Duke up to his mischief in Dal Albaeon. But who had most to gain?"

"It could have been any one of the Realm's Princedoms," Gunnar said. "Dal Albaeon, Astolat, Tryban, Logriese, Cornwall. Martyrs, even Emrys maybe. The Queen might have decided the Ruri of Dal Albaeon was up to be replaced by somebody more tractable and engineered the entire scheme herself."

"Whoever was responsible, the bastards aren't going to cough for it," Taliesin said. "So watch your back for their blades. Somebody out there doesn't want us to give evidence. Even if the Crown had nothing to do with Dal

Albaeon, it may just suit a purpose to have us killed and the blame lain at the feet of one of Annan's rivals."

Gunnar laughed. "You should have been a courtier."

Taliesin looked around the chamber, hoping for distraction from the worries playing across his mind. Three arched entrances led to other chambers, the distant strains of music drifting in from one. It was a sprightly tune, leaping and springing like a field of cavorting horses. There had been little time for music in the officer's life, and he valued the chance to hear the merry rhythms. For the quality here, such extravagances were so commonplace they hardly noticed anymore, just a backdrop to their struggles for power and position.

The chamber they stood in had a chequered marble floor, tiled as if for a massive board game. Groups of well-to-do moved and chattered across the chamber, hundreds of small cliques shifting and politicking, mixing scandal with their wine. Crescent-shaped tables filled with food and drink followed the curve of the far wall, etiquette precluding the guests helping themselves, waiting instead for Whitestaves passing among the crowd, hands heavy with trays.

"See if you can find the men. Make sure they have not offended some Baron's mistress," said Taliesin.

"If they haven't," said Gunnar, "then we will know our devils have swopped duty with someone else's regiment."

Gunnar was leaning against a column, his back supported by cool marble speckled as green as the shell of a duck egg.

Camlan had not become more interesting during his long absence from the capital

In front of him a group of peers argued about the latest ministry appointed by Queen Annan, one of the lords waving a cheaply printed scandal sheet in the air. Denouncing the rogues that had printed it, the obese nobleman complained that the Crown's patronage of common trading men was corrupting public life and lowering the standards of government.

"Seditious libel, you see," roared the peer, devouring a whole ham. "A laxity of morals. Only last month they caught a group of levellers pamphleting a town near my estates in Cornwall. Scoundrels – they want one chamber do they? Away with tyranny of Queen, peers and army, by the Martyr! If I catch them I'll have their tongues bored through with a hot iron for their troubles."

"Ruffians and rebels," agreed one of the peer's colleagues. "Why, the doomsmen in Logriese tried to pass a restriction act on their dram-shops last week, and they got two days of looting from the mob. Couldn't even send in Fada Óiche's Foot because the garrison warned their men might mutiny."

His arm swaying back to illustrate his point, the ham in the peer's hand slapped back against someone behind him. There was a squeal of annoyance, and Gunnar saw it was the young crimson-haired woman from the crystal gardens, Elaine. She looked at the smear of grease on her black gown and the peer turned around.

"Watch where you're walking, girl, I nearly lost my food to the floor."

"Food is it?" she howled. "You jiggering fat pig!"

Turning around in astonishment, the peer was in time to see Elaine picking up one of the meats from a Whitestave's tray. She smashed the man's jowls with the joint, kicking him as he slipped over. When he was on the floor Elaine tossed a glass of wine over his balding pate then gave him another kick for good measure. "Consider where *you're* walking in future, you ill-mannered cove."

One of the peer's friends looked like he might intervene, but another guest stopped him. "Do you want to have us all called out, you damn idiot? That's the daughter of the Duke of Fastain."

Gunnar laughed and walked after the woman.

Camlan was surprising him after all.

"That was uncommonly fast of you, milady."

"My dress is ruined," Elaine complained. "I can't stay

here – every woman at the ball will be laughing at me behind their fan." She seemed to notice Gunnar for the first time. "Who are you?"

"Your servant, if you will," Gunnar bowed.

"Yes, yes, of course." Elaine looked bored. "Ruined! And all because of that fat imbecile. It's perfectly intolerable. Well, are you going to walk with me? I can't stay here."

Surprised, Gunnar took the proffered arm. "It seems I have discovered a rose in a garden of briars."

"Oh please. You can stop that nonsense – it may go down fine with your farmgirls out in the counties, but I have been put on by balladry from the poet laureate, and he does it with far greater proficiency than you. Tell me of our recent victory. Tell me of that."

Victory. Gunnar remembered the siege's aftermath, the army surgeons holding down wounded men as they sawed through smashed limbs, closing wounds with hot iron and stitching skin to the sound of agonised drunken screams.

"There was ... much glory."

Pointing to a door hidden by the side of a stone recess, Elaine led him across the chamber. "I feel like seeing the sky, can you climb stairs as well as you win battles?"

Opening the door, Gunnar realised the stairs coiled up though an old winter hunting tower, where the quality could go to release their hawks and falcons, watching them glide over the deep mantle of the forests below and hunt while their masters and mistresses sipped warm wine.

They ascended the stairs, granite laid over with a line of herringbone carpet, and Gunnar listened to the wind scraping the tower. Lifting a brass candle-guard off the wall, Elaine let Gunnar light it with his flintbox. "It will be dark at the top, hardly anyone comes up here now."

Gunnar nodded and continued climbing.

From the vantage point of the turret-top Camlan fell away before the couple, frosted crystal windows opening out and revealing first the citadel walls, then the city lanterns reflected through the rain. Hearing the regular creak of iron above them, Gunnar wondered in what direction the weather vane would be facing.

"I come here more often in the summer; when you can feel like you're sitting on top of the islands, alone with the sun."

"It's a good view," Gunnar agreed. Above him the clouds peeled back from the moon and Gunnar was jolted. There was something silhouetted against the moon.

Elaine saw the officer gazing up towards the clouds. "What is it?"

Screened by clouds again, Gunnar blinked at the dark horizon. "There was something up there, in front of the sky. It was a parcel shaped like a cigar and it had the face of an eagle... but there were lights along it, lights in the name of the Martyr."

Elaine laughed. "I hope you haven't drunk *too* much."

He continued looking, but when the moon was stripped bare again there was nothing in the sky but a sliver disk. Staring intently he thought he saw a twist of smoke, but the rain crept across the landscape and smudged the night. No. If it had been aeolipile smoke, it was from one of the workshops down in the city... that was the only explanation. "Curse my eyes, the ghosts of Camlan are playing tricks on me. Either that or your wine is spoiled."

"I wish I had your eyes, you lucky fool. You've seen the whole world while I have been stuck away in these corridors."

"Stuck here, that's not quite the words I would choose."

"What do you know?" Elaine replied. "You're a man – when did you have a choice forced on you? You're in the regiments now, but you could have become a priest, or a peer, or joined the navy. What choices do I have?"

"What choices do any of us have?"

"A typical answer," Elaine said. "A typical useless answer from a man who has everything. I'll tell you the choice I have – the *only* choice – to marry a dried-up bag of

72

bones with all the vigour of a starved billygoat, just to please my cursed family."

"And would this aging billygoat be pastured in an ancient pile and sitting on a throne of silver coins?"

"Of course he would," Elaine shouted. "You don't think my father would put me off on anybody less than a Baron, do you? Don't be insulting."

"Well it's a waste," Gunnar laughed. "And damned unhandsome of your father. A woman like you deserves better air than dust to fill her lungs."

"Have you heard of my family?"

"There were certain tales mentioned, I seem to remember. The respect is still there in people's voices when they talk of your father, in coaching inns and the like. He was one of the best fencers in the Realm. In his day."

"He still is. And that doesn't put you off?"

Gunnar shrugged. "I've met people for grass before breakfast before – I can hold a sabre."

"The fashion these days is for a brace of pistols, although my father still prefers the old ways. He says any fool can bag a ruffian with a puffer. You're an unsteady rogue," Elaine said, moving closer to Gunnar. "You've all the charms of a streethawker selling silk and the smile of a highwayman. But how reckless do you feel tonight?"

"How reckless am I allowed to be?"

She stood on her toes and kissed Gunnar. "You could start like that. Do you still think I'm uncommonly fast?"

He felt for the tiny ivory buttons along her back. "I think you're trouble."

Elaine bit Gunnar's upper lip and hooking his belt tugged the officer to the floor. "I think you're right."

Moving towards the tables at the far side of the chamber, Taliesin manoeuvred through the press of guests. Camlan was packed out with visiting notables who had made the dangerous journey through the forests, country gentry and wealthy merchanteers from all the Princedom's counties and many of the cities, arriving just to have their presence counted during the Accession Day season.

Taliesin found their desire to enter the fashionable season of balls, dances and sights incomprehensible. Even travelling on Crown-patrolled roads, few sensible people voluntarily ventured through the badly maintained paths which penetrated the wilderness. Each village and farm where the tumble had been cleared was an island of safety; outside lay only unknown green depths. In the uncharted tumble, nature had grown wild and fey, turning in on itself like a snake swallowing its own tail. Haunted by an intermingling of sly feral things, joinings the old Goddess never intended to exist, enchantments given life by the ancient Demon Prince Vulcanus.

Cavalrymen patrolled the tumbles' paths, hussars and dragoons paid by the quality to do their dying for them. Merchanteers too, driven by the smell of quick profit; even pedlars, travelling monks, players, and the fierce Royal coachmen. But ordinary folk were quite content to stay in filthy cities filled with the smoke of aeolipiles, or tenant farmers sheltering behind landowners' hedges and the manor's ditches.

At no table was there any sign of Taliesin's dragon-browns, although by the mess of spilled drink, the officer saw they had been there recently. He was about to continue his search when he saw a patchwork harlequin cloak among the scrum of Whitestaves. It was the tinker, and in an outrageous display of cheek, the old man was openly filling his pockets with silver sauceboats. Turning, he waved happily to Taliesin.

"There's not too much left now," the tinker explained as Taliesin drew closer. "Your people took more than their fair share before I showed my hair."

"My soldiers – " Taliesin began, surprised.

"Yes, they are not amateurs, are they? Know what they are about, they do. One lot distracted the pages, the others swept the table. You should be proud of your rufflers, they are disciplined, they work together like a unit."

"How did you buggering get in here?" Taliesin said.

"I walked through the door, of course. Nobody around here has got much time to notice me, so on balance they don't usually bother. Hey-ho, that is the curse of being old, you know? Few have time for you unless you're on your last legs and there is a large legacy involved."

"You talk too much, old man," Taliesin said.

"It has been noted before. Come, I shall reunite you with your soldiers, before they deprive me entirely of my meagre pickings."

With the tinker leading the way again, Taliesin was led into the chamber with the band, musicians set against a window balcony.

"A merry tune," said the tinker. "But there is nothing so useless as a dance."

Taliesin cocked his head. "Useless, how?"

"Useless to me. You can not sell a dance, or eat it, or wear it, so what use is it? None of course, which is why the nobles here enjoy it so much."

"Martyrs. And I thought all honest travelling folk loved a merry fling."

Continuing as if he had not noticed the sarcasm in the officer's voice, the tinker assailed those too slow to move out of his way with his cane. Interrupting the tinker's progress, the two men came across the dragon-browns.

"So you got in after all, man? You must have some luck about you." Connaire Mor was with the company, the mountain-man weaving a little more uncertainly now he had punished a few bottles.

"Why, it is my friend from Cannlar," said the tinker.

Taliesin gladly surrendered the rakish old man and his taste for conversation to the highlander.

When a silence descended across the rowdy behaviour of his company, it was enough to make Taliesin spin around. Connaire Mor was staring at an officer on the dance floor. At first Taliesin assumed the man must be one of their company – a whore's uniform loaded down with braid and buttons. Then he looked at the face, hawkish and sombre, not one Taliesin recognised; but the Colonel had stopped his dance and was matching Connaire Mor gaze for gaze.

"I thought we had hanged the last of your filthy damnable clan years ago," the officer spat.

Connaire Mor moved out of the crowd of dragon-browns. "Man, you missed one. But then you were too busy raping the bairns at the time, you piece of Emrys shit."

Taliesin swore.

One of the army killers responsible for putting down Congal Cáech's rebellion of secession. For all Taliesin knew, the same man that had hanged Connaire Mor's brothers. Now the huge Astolatier looked set to repay the debt in kind. Drunk as they were, a couple of the soldiers grabbed Connaire Mor, but he shook them off his powerful frame with a careless ease, then barrelled into the officer with the force of a dragoon warhorse. There was no skill involved in the exchange, the two men rolled across the floor, savaging each other like street dogs while a massive hush fell over the chamber. This was not one of the duels Annan Pendrag had banned from her citadel, this was a mutual murder in progress, and few of the guests could believe that anyone would violate the spirit of Accession Day with this brutality.

Before the two could get any farther, Taliesin's men were upon them, more than six dragon-browns needed to wrest the blood-crazed Astolatier off his foe.

Too late to do anything, a party of the palace's Foot Guards skidded to a stop on the slippery marble, Connaire Mor's victim pummelled and bloody in the arms of the two soldiers restraining him, incoherent with rage.

One of the green-coats spoke harshly to Connaire Mor. "Striking a superior officer inside the Court! Who in the name of the Martyr do you think you are? This man will be placed under arrest for mutiny."

"I do not think so," said Taliesin.

This took back the Guards, unused to receiving anything but unquestioning obedience inside the capital. "There is no question of innocence. Half the confounded hall saw him strike this officer; he is nothing but an animal. We are going to take this bastard away, and if you, Captain, have any sense, you had better go back to your garrison and measure a hitch of rope for him."

The Foot Guards moved to seize Connaire Mor, but Taliesin's troops stood the soldiers off, a sudden rush of concealed weapons coming out into the chandelier light. With horror, the Guard's officer realised the devils he was facing not only had knives, but flintlocks, ranged weapons forbidden to everyone save the Queen's own men.

With the nobles' constant paranoia of assassination, the officer knew he would would suffer a severe penalty for letting these brigands come armed to an Accession Day ball. Accession Day no less! His career was over as surely as these gutter-brawler's lives were forfeit.

"You had better be a bastard lot faster than you look," Taliesin told the Guards officer, seeing the man's eyes glancing down towards his sabre.

Cutting through the crowd of nervous on-lookers, an imperious voice sounded above the embarrassed quiet. "Let them go, and take him with you."

It was the tense and clipped tones of a man used to being obeyed, and turning around, Taliesin saw a noble clad in black, an austere jacket balancing a serious expression and savage eyes.

The Foot Guards bowed, dragging the victim of Connaire Mor's violence along with them, the beaten Colonel stunned and incredulous by the pace of events.

With a wintry gaze which perfectly complemented his voice, the man looked over the dragon-browns. Many men as powerful as this one might have looked across the collection of rogues in front of him with distaste, but this one gazed appraisingly, calculating, as if he thought each soldier had an exact worth that could be set on his head. It put Taliesin in mind of a man he had met in Llud-din as a street ruffler; a dead-faced man who had made a living killing criminals for the Doomsman's bounties, silver angels in exchange for outlaw's heads.

He looked at Taliesin – his dirty uniform and faded trousers – and appeared to take it for granted that this was the company commander. "Keep them on a leash. They will live longer."

With that, the grim-faced man turned and walked off, the crowd parting for him.

Behind him, the tinker again answered Taliesin's unspoken question. "Domnal Mac Aedo, one of the Queen's favourites."

"Her lover?" Taliesin asked.

At this the tinker laughed, finding the question genuinely funny. "No, at least nobody speaks about it if he is. An advisor, and rumoured to be the head of her network of eyes and knives. Not exactly noted for letting people out of the noose, so I would guess your men must be of great use."

"Yes, but useful to whom?" said Taliesin.

Except the tinker was no longer there.

# Chapter 5

Morning light slipped down the wet quadrangle walls, bringing Taliesin out of a fitful sleep and back into his miserable cell.

Then he remembered Accession Day and groaned.

Today the festivities were well and truly over; every bone in the soldier's body told him this day was the culmination of events his company had been witness to in Dal Albaeon. It was a battlefield feeling, the dread that knots every soldier's stomach before a slaughter.

But this was a battlefield he had no map for, reduced to a weapon in someone else's hands. Taliesin grunted and got up. Even a sabre could be dangerous to its master, especially if the swordsman did not understand the nature of his weapon.

Gunnar was in uniform, up, and in the corridor, the sand-haired dandy having missed the previous evening's entertainment.

"I heard about Connaire Mor's run-in with the old friend of the family."

Taliesin was irritated that whatever the company's circumstances, the young hell-rake found humour in the situation. "So where in the Martyr's name were you, when we were running off the Guards?"

"I had my own run-in, with the woman you saw in the crystal garden. Elaine."

Shaking his head in despair, Taliesin clipped on his sabre. "The Foot Guards will be looking to settle the score after slighting them in front of half the palace, and that is only if the Butcher doesn't hear of last night first. And what do you do? You start chasing some dollymop who has already had half the Court slitting each other's throats for the chance to tumble her! I don't need to be watching out for her family's hired knives too."

"She's not like that," Gunnar protested. "She is being forced into marriage with some noble pig old enough to be her grandfather. She needed comforting and she is – "

"Trouble, sir," Taliesin said. "If her damn family hears of any of this, they'll disappear you, truss you like a pig and dump your body in the nearest forest. Your father might not be short of a few angels, but do you think you are going to be seen as a prize for one of the Great Families? You think it'll matter to her if one more fancy gets drowned when she's done flirting? Martyrs, start thinking with your brain."

Gunnar shrugged and looked unrepentant. "One of the Court's peacocks has been here. They have given all the company times to report to the mummers, myself and Connaire Mor first."

"Truthseekers." Taliesin looked unhappy. "Never seen a mummer, but I heard stories they leave your mind a sodding cess-pit by the time they've finished – drive you crazy."

Gunnar laughed. "Fishwives' tales. My family hired a mummer once, when they were in dispute over the terms of an agreement. Our people and the other merchanteers both submitted to the touch and they were perfectly fine afterwards. Besides, you don't have to worry. Your name was not on the list, they have cut different orders for you."

"Different?"

"Somebody high wants to see you," Gunnar said. "The Whitestave did not say who, but I think you are expected to be properly grateful to the quality."

"That will be my promotion for last night then," said Taliesin. "Make sure you tell your mummer story to the company. I don't want any of them deserting when they hear where they're going today."

Guiding Connaire Mor and Gunnar to the mummers, a retainer led them across the estate, a Logriese burr in his accent.

As confusing as ever, their journey through Camlan's labyrinth eventually led them to a cage, the stall looking as if it had been buried inside a wall. Estimating their weight, the retainer scribbled the figures down and passed the paper to another man standing by the cage.

"What was that for, man?" Connaire Mor asked.

"Counterbalance," said the retainer, tapping a twisted nose and knowing this would make no sense to his massive countryman.

Having seen the pulley-workers lifting bales out of merchantmen in Cornwall's harbours, Gunnar was better informed. "Hey you, is this safe?"

"Is life?"

Entering the confined space with the retainer, twisted-nose pulled down a gate, blocking the opening, then tugged on a chain in the ceiling. With a jolt the cage started to descend, the corridor rising upwards to be replaced by gray rock-face.

As minutes passed and the cage failed to plunge downwards, Connaire Mor relaxed his grip on the cage's railing. The Logriese Whitestave seemed disappointed. He took malicious delight in frightening his charges with the cage's descent.

Growing cold, the descending rock face dropped away to be replaced by a deep well, illumination from a phosphorous moss staining the shaft. Light bleached the three passengers – washed and pallid – shades visiting the underworld.

"This pit, is it natural?" Connaire Mor asked.

"Aye, maybe natural, maybe not," the retainer declared. "There are beasties that like digging down here. They leave walls rough, not brick and slab, so it's hard to tell."

Leaning out of the cage, there was no visible end to the drop, just an inky pool of darkness beneath. As Gunnar looked down, a single eye of light began to lift out of the night. The young dandy saw the rising light was a loft window, lead panes in the roof of a twisted house. Piled haphazardly on a natural outcropping of rock, the cranky building looked seconds from sliding off and into the void below. Apart from the loft lantern, there was no sign of life in the strange cottage.

"Somebody lives there?" Gunnar was astonished.

"Could say that laddie," the retainer replied. "Hermit. Daft of course."

"He would have to be."

Reaching the well floor, their cage put down on a wooden platform.

"Out with you, now."

Stairs had been hewn out of the rock. As was often the case with ancient fortifications the dragon-browns had been billeted in, the treads were too small to use comfortably.

Letting the retainer descend the stairs ahead of them, Connaire Mor drew back to whisper to Gunnar. "I'm not liking this one little bit, man. This swining place is too much like a dungeon."

"There has got to be more than one way back to the estate. These caverns must stretch for leagues. If it comes to it, we could make a break and hide out, I haven't seen anyone up to stopping us yet."

"It would no be this lowland devil," Connaire Mor agreed.

"Full kit?" Gunnar asked.

Connaire Mor opened the jacket to reveal his powder horn, a pouch for paper flintlock cartridges – the Crown stamp silver-leafed on its leather – and his iron pistol, the little flintlock Realm workshops called dumplings. "If it is treachery they are about, I'll trade them hard, you can be be sure of that."

Gradually their passage levelled out and ended in a low-roofed cave, Connaire Mor having to stoop his massive bulk to avoid cracking into stalactites. Smelling of chalk, a lime-coloured underground lake lay in the cave's far corner. Fascinated, the highlander saw a group of figures trawling nets across the pool – demisapi, small beastmen with woolly white hides. Clicking like tree rats, they paid no attention to the visitors from the world above.

"Not for you, laddie," said the retainer, his voice ringing in the cave.

"What are they?" Gunnar asked, peering through the half-light.

"You ask too many questions. Things are different down here, aye, different that is all."

Led along an oak-panelled corridor hung with oil paintings, Taliesin ignored the proud faces staring down from the canvas. Clothes and manners dated them, necks haughty above ruffs, legs ballooned in breeches. A few figures were shown rearing on horses, or leaning on thin blades, ridiculously impractical for any real butchery.

Pacing ahead of him, his Whitestave guide raced to their destination. Muttering to himself, the demented servant mouthed nonsense words of which the officer caught only half.

*"Quick as a fox. Haggard. Too much to clean."*

The retainer failed to notice the tinker coming out of a side-compartment, attaching himself to the back of their sprightly procession. Taliesin realised he had been half-expecting to see the garishly dressed old man. "You travel a distance, sir."

"That is certainly the traveller's way," said the tinker.

Taliesin noticed the tinker was holding his left arm as if it was supported in an invisible sling, a leather hood balanced on his arm.

"Have you been *earning* your living in the citadel again, old fellow?"

"There are some things you can not steal, Captain, yes there are."

"And do your traveller's wiles stretch to knowing who this wizened tree-monkey is taking me to see?" Taliesin asked.

"Fi and fo," said the tinker. "They have not let you know?"

"Obviously not."

The tinker winked. "This leads to the Queen's apartments, and what do you think of that?"

Taliesin was caught off guard by the revelation. "You are playing a joke on me, old man! What in the Martyr's name would they want with me? The Queen doesn't grant audiences to the headcount. Nobody has even ordered me to put on one of their whore's uniforms."

"What does a Queen ever want? She wants to see you as you are."

Dumfounded, Taliesin continued down the passage. People of his low station had a monarch, they did not visit them. Annan Pendrag was just a name, an abstraction – Old Shadow, the Martyr, the Crown – not something to reach out and touch.

The tinker hobbled along, keeping pace with the mumbling Whitestave. "Not what she used to be, our Annan Pendrag. Old and tired before her time, but she still likes to be flirted with. Remember that. She likes a rogue, so you should do. There's many the man been marked her favourite through flattery, but she is not stupid, far from it. She understands the game, and when it comes to keeping the Realm together, she will sacrifice anything she needs to."

"Well informed," said Taliesin. "For a tinker."

Mischievous eyes glinting, the tinker scratched his nose. "Never met her. But you get to hear all sorts in these corridors."

"Pity the audience isn't with her husband. It's the Prince-Regent they gossip about in the streets. Talon and his damn fool foreign antics."

The tinker nodded at the truth of the words. While the distant, reclusive Queen remained in favour with the town mobs, the foreign Prince she had married was reviled. A Ruri from one of the Roubaixian territories, Talon was popularly regarded as a treacherous milksop of little account. Neither of them, it was frequently whispered over farmer's hedges, liked the marriage, but it had guaranteed peace between the Realm and one of the most powerful empires on the mainland. Their union had also swelled the bags of the Realm's mail-coaches, gossips exchanging news of every infidelity, tales growing wilder with each telling.

The tinker lifted the bag off his arm, revealing a kestrel resting on his sleeve, claws digging into the frayed cloth. Suddenly Taliesin noticed its eyes, pure gold sown with purple flecks.

The colour!

Eyes described in a thousand child-time tales. *Chimeras*. Cousins to the beastmen, though enchanted in subtler ways.

"It can talk?" Taliesin said, half a question.

"In a manner," said the tinker.

"They are wild, their kind can not live in captivity."

"Can you ever tame something truly wild? Cage it and it dies. That is why they are worth so much. Did you never hear the tale of Blodevedd and her horse? The mare stayed with her because it liked her company – no other reason."

"How did you come by it?" Taliesin was suspicious.

The tinker laughed. "How? How and the King's cow. Am I not likeable enough on my own account, Captain? But no, like our own Queen she is getting old, her wings will not carry her to food like they used to. Being nimble is something that is prized out in the oceans of the forest, for my friend here, you could say this is her dotage. Here…"

Pressing his arm against Taliesin's, the creature hopped across, clutching the Captain's arm with a sharp grip he could feel through his uniform.

Coming to the end of the panelled corridor, a series of feelings showered through the air like rain – part melody and part communication – an impression both aristocratic and high-souled.

*Room. Queen. Food. Safety.*

Taliesin knew it had to be the golden-eyed creature. Turning around, the nimble-footed retainer looked warily at Taliesin. "What's that, eh?"

Unsure if he meant the voice or the appearance of the

strange bird, the officer looked to the tinker for an explanation. The ossified old man was nowhere to be seen.

"Martyrs, the old sod moves as if he were an assassin."

"What was that, eh, eh?" muttered the retainer, barely loud enough to be heard.

"Are you deaf, sir?" Taliesin said. "The man I have just been talking to for half the estate."

The retainer tapped his head. "You're touched, plain daft. There's been nobody along here save us two, and that's the way her Majesty likes it, you mark me. This corner of Camlan is a closed wing."

Ushered into the Queen's presence, Taliesin was expecting a chamber on the same scale as the rest of Camlan: spacious, empty with shadows and the delicately filtered light, built to overween onlookers with a swell of stone and pillar. Instead he found himself in a boardroom full of warm panelling, pier-glass mirrors and oakwood bureaus.

Sitting on a chair built into the wall, simple and stately, was the woman in whose name Taliesin had butchered and killed for most of his adult life. In her middle years now, she affected a stiff dignity, as natural as a swan and without any trace of the vainglorious.

He kept the presence of mind to bow.

She laughed. "You see Mac Aedo, we are courted like a peasant girl."

Domnal Mac Aedo stood by the side of the chair, still clad in the simple black tunic he had worn on the Accession Day. He had since added a black velvet cloak to the ensemble, and there was an absence of guards in the room. Taliesin let himself relax slightly, reading this as a sign he would survive the audience. Domnal Mac Aedo was unemotional and dangerous, no fool to think he could run Taliesin through without making a fight of it.

With an unexpected flutter of wings, the kestrel left Taliesin's arm, landing on a vacant four-poster bed by the window. Again, the liquid musical feeling.

*Queen. Queen. Air. Flight. Queen. Queen. Land.*

Annan Pendrag gasped, a gentle intake of air. "A rare gift, indeed."

Taliesin recalled the tinker's advice for dealing with the Realm's most titled noblewoman. "My most difficult task – to find a gift as rare as your highness's majesty."

Annan Pendrag inclined her head, a polite look of doubt on her chalk-white face. "One of the houses of Skäw received a vixen cub with the eyes of gold last year. If my memory serves me, it cost the bearer four times his own weight in silver angels... this is, you will agree, an unusual gift from one of our own Captains."

Still following the tinker's guidance, Taliesin took up another of the old devil's traits. Outrageous invention. "Your soldiers seized the creature as a prize after a battle in the tumble, your highness. She was caged by forest beastmen, but we freed her. Once she was a leader among her flight, an Empress of the air, but now her best days are past and she wishes nothing more than to grow old under the patronage of a noble lineage."

"So this is the man." The Queen laughed. "The man who bearded our own Guards. They have been in here you know, begging me to allow them to hang you. Something I understand your own General would also take great pleasure from. It still chafes on Teyron that he should have been forced to promote you; you not even a new man, without a merchant charter to your name. Who was it again Mac Aedo?"

"A daughter of Cornwall, your majesty," said the grim-faced advisor. "The campaign in Astolat."

"There are so many of them too, they breed like hares down there," the Queen said, playing with her neck frill. "Still, I suppose it *was* your duty to save her. But look at where your Captaincy has got you now. Your soldiers are the scrapings of the headcount. Thieves, highwaymen, rufflers and palmers. Your men are, to put it quite simply Captain, a gang of pirates."

"Your pirates, milady," Taliesin bowed his head.

An appropriate response, the Queen's pale face lighting up with pleasure. "Yes. And never forget that, sir. For much of my life I have found myself surrounded by unwatered pedigree, but it is not always the animal with the shiny pelt that gets the job done." She indicated Domnal Mac Aedo, and a slight flush rose to the man's cheeks. A sight few saw, and one fewer still lived to boast about.

"Take my dear hand Mac Aedo here. He has titles and honours enough, estate and land, coins by the chest-full. But this was not always so, was it?"

The man replied with his measured voice, flat and toneless. "We have all prospered under your reign, your majesty."

"My poor Mac Aedo, I really shouldn't tease him. But sometimes his stony demeanour is too much to resist. Mac Aedo started his career as a knifeman, when my father was still on the throne. You see, Captain, I tell you this so you may know I value proficiency more than lofty blood; it is why Emrys is still the glue which binds this land together. If you act like a ruler for long enough, it is the act that becomes the truth, the act which shows out, not your origins."

Taliesin stood waiting and listening, biding his time, curious to see when her real hand would be revealed. She exchanged banalities for a while more, but the Queen did not make him wait long.

"You will have heard something of my younger sister, Ariane?"

Taliesin had. "I have never seen her in the flesh, your majesty, but the people speak of her as a great beauty. It is said Ruris travel from as far away as Roubaix and Fandan just for the chance to court her."

Annan Pendrag laughed that her officer could talk of the Realm's neighbours with such an awe of distance in his voice. "You see Mac Aedo, it is far past time we started a war outside the Princedoms. My people are starting to think their village pastures are all there is to the world. Yes Captain, Ariane is certainly a beauty. Unfortunately, she has no more good sense than an unsteady butterfly. We can all offer prayers to the Martyr that it was I who was born first, not Ariane. The course of our land's fortunes would have been very different had that circumstance been reversed."

Taliesin said nothing.

"At the moment the Court thinks she has caught a chill and is taking the sea air at Fawr, our family's coastal estate."

"They *think* that?" Taliesin said.

"A necessary deception: a little time ago she left Camlan – departed the very Realm itself. And in answer to the question in your eye, I did not give official approval to her departure."

Domnal Mac Aedo took up the story. "Some years ago, Ariane had a fancy with a Prince from Sombor who was visiting our land."

Taliesin shrugged, the name meant little to him.

"It is a minor land far to the east, at the end of the world for all the dealings we have with them," Domnal Mac Aedo continued. "Theirs was a most careless affair. When Ariane marries it must be as one of the cords the Realm requires to tie the Princedoms closer together. Sombor's King was hardly pleased either, his kin had also been brought up knowing their lives would be needed as bridges to secure prosperity for their own state, not married off in a meaningless union half-way across the world. The Prince was rightly ordered back to his land in disgrace."

"In their parts they actually regard us as barbarians," the Queen added. "Can you imagine that. Us! It is very tiresome. I am constantly thankful our land is separated from the rest of the world's sordid affairs by such a convenient distance of water."

"It did not end there, though?" Taliesin probed.

"Would that it had," replied the Queen. "The Prince's father died recently in an intrigue, along with the son next in line for the throne. Our Somborian friend now sits in Sombor as King, and on his accession he sent word to Ariane that their way was clear."

"She has run off to him," Mac Aedo said. "Not only that, but before she fled, Ariane had been promised to a son of Logriese."

Shaking her head in anger the Queen shook her finger at Taliesin. "Logriese has always supported Emrys. Without them the suppression of the Astolat insurrection would have been impossible. But our problems do not stop with the potential insult to one of our own Princedoms. Word from the east suggests war is burning across the nations of the mainland, not that those devils ever stop fighting long enough for anyone to notice.

"Sombor could fall, Captain, and should Ariane be discovered in the ruins, it would be the most complete disaster I could imagine. I had to marry that pig from the Empire of Roubaix. Do you understand? I gave myself to Talon just so the other Princedoms would have to figure support from the mainland into their future scheming. If an Emrys Princess is found bawling over the corpse of a foreign monarch, every nation from Roubaix to the Wall at the end of the world is going to believe Emry's ambitions have inflated way beyond our means. Roubaix could easily be forced to disassociate itself with us just to survive in the games on the mainland."

Domnal Mac Aedo looked sternly at the Captain. "The Realm cannot afford to lose more support. As it already stands now, my people are treading on assassination plots and secessionist schemes with every turn of the calender. Your campaign in Dal Albaeon was but a very small turn of recent events."

"Martyrs, you want me to bring your royal waif back before word gets out she has run away," said Taliesin, his part in the Queen's affairs suddenly becoming clear.

"I do not require a royal poodle to go to Sombor and argue niceties and protocol with their Court," said the

Queen icily. "I need a devil, no I need a pack of devils to go over there and slit the throat of anyone who gets in the Realm's way. Drag Ariane out of her wedding trough if you have to, but bring her pretty royal face back to me untouched."

Domnal Mac Aedo flourished his dagger at a framed parchment on the wall, a faded leathery map. "My merchanteers say this part of the world is a madness now. Reports from this distance are vague, but alliances seem to be shifting with each telling, territory changing hands with equal rapidity. Given the unrest, you should have little trouble in finding Sombor's Court without too many questions on the way; mercenary companies swarm over the continent like fleas."

"Do this for Emrys, Captain," the Queen said, "and I shall buy every one of your bandits in Realm uniform out of the army and into their own coaching-inn, or whatever else your men might desire that is within my means."

"Your majesty knows how to capture a common soldier's heart."

Fluttering a peacock fan, the Queen leaned back in her seat. "My heart is our peoples', kindly spare it from further burdens. You will be in sole charge when you make land, you will acknowledge no higher authority on the journey. Yes ... I thought that might appeal to you. Just do the job Captain, and *do* try to be circumspect about it."

"Your majesty, getting the task done is all I have ever asked," said Taliesin.

"Apart from ourselves," Domnal Mac Aedo explained, "the only person to know all the details of where you are going is one of my ship masters, Bron. He has a private vessel waiting for your company, private, but as well armed as any ship of the line. Bron will furnish you with a miniature of the Princess so that you may recognise her."

Annan Pendrag looked tired, as if all the talk of her younger sister had proved exhausting. "Bron is also my pirate, Captain. As are you, now. But expect no letters of marque on this mission. Wait until you are at sea before telling your men of Ariane, and as you value your life, talk to not one other soul of what has been said inside this room."

With a cursory wave the interview was over, Taliesin bowing before leaving.

"May your majesty's choice prove to be a wise one," said Domnal Mac Aedo, after the Captain had left. "He is no gentleman, not a gentleman at all."

Sighing, the Queen lay back in her chair. "We have no choice, all the other candidates have too many suspect loyalties, any one of which could wreck the Realm given the chance. Besides, he is a total scoundrel, who else would you send to do this? Did you see the way his eyes lit up when he heard this would be only his command. Yes, he is hungry, he is my hungry-man now, Mac Aedo."


Back in the painting-lined corridor, Taliesin discovered a man draped in a silver cope waiting outside. By the tracery on his cloak-like vestment, Taliesin realised that this was someone who had climbed high in the hierarchy of the Martyr, one of the Princes of the Church.

"Ah, the Realmsman's campaigning hero," the Arch-Truron's voice was as unctuous as oil. Taliesin took a quick dislike to the man. "You are most fortunate to have been granted an audience so quickly. I have been waiting since yesterday."

So, the church knew who he was. A bad premonition gnawed at the Captain's gut. Why should the servants of the Martyr be concerning themselves over a company of pressed cutthroats?

Taliesin stepped around the churchman. "Keeping the Queen's many possessions united, sir, the army doesn't get to sit on its arse in Camlan every day."

"The Realm have always been united under the Martyr, my son," the Arch-Truron hissed. "One church, one land, one God. If the Princedoms put their differences to the church's mediation as civilised nations do, your army would be troubled far less."

Which was of course the unspoken ambition of the church. Taliesin had never travelled outside the Realm, but he had spoken to enough seamen to know the Church of the Martyr played more significant roles in state matters across the sea. Mediation equated to filled coffers, treasure chests full of tokens of 'faith'.

"Those *civilised* nations are plagued by heathen beliefs. Why not give faith for the Realm's faithful?" Taliesin recalled the doctrinaire tones of his poorhouse jailors.

He had struck a sore point with the Arch-Truron. Religious wars were as regular as sermons across the sea. If the foreigners were not burning pagans, they were suppressing heresies, or killing each other over the ever-elusive crown of spiritual leadership.

"Oh but I do," the Arch-Truron lisped insincerely. "But these are weighty issues, of little interest to the military mind." This was said dismissively enough to be taken as the end of the conversation.

Taliesin snorted and walked off.


Sniffing the cool air with his twisted nose, the Logriese retainer stopped by an opening in the stone passage. "Aye and you'll remember the way up again?"

Gunnar nodded.

"Then I shall be making my way back. My work does not stop for showing the likes of you swine around."

"Hey, wait a minute man, what are you about?" Connaire Mor reached out to stop the retainer. "Where are these mummers we are to see?"

Wagging his finger, the retainer pointed towards the opening. "They're down there. Do no worry, they'll come out and get you when they're good and ready, not before. And you can be sure they'll know you're here."

"After all," he laughed, walking back down the passage. "They're mummers, aren't they?"

Departing, the Whitestave left the two officers waiting in the brazier light, pools of slow-burning oil smoking across their brown uniforms, their nerves growing frayed.

The dandy regretted his earlier bravado. Gunnar's kin had hired one of the truth-seekers, but that had happened while the dandy was young enough to still be sleeping in a cot; since then the story had been passed around like a spice bowl at every supper the family attended: an old merchanteer's bravado, communing with Old Shadow himself if it meant not being cheated out of a profit. Supporting common sense over superstition might be the merchanteer's way in the warmth of a coaching-inn's common room, but waiting for the unknown in the near darkness of an underground maze was quite another matter.

Blocking the corridor with his bulk, Connaire Mor put a finger to his lips, Gunnar starting to say something.

"Do you hear that, man?"

"Nothing," Gunnar said. "Martyrs, how can anybody see anything down here?"

From beyond the opening a tapping sounded, slight at first then louder, soft echoes ghosting every knock back into the distant silence.

Nearest the passage's opening, Gunnar started as a cowled figure emerged from the darkness, shades of grey shrouding whatever colour it might have possessed. Gunnar saw the figure was a woman. Skin had grown over the flesh where her eyes should have been, a horror worse than any blind beggar to be seen in the streets of the cities; even if the poor devils eyes were not functioning, the beggars at least had them. But here there was nothing, not a void or a scar, just an absence. *Blind to see*, the ancient saying came back to him now – the code the mummers were reputed to live by.

In the woman's hand she held a globe, milky and metallic, Gunnar not recognising the material even as the dandy saw how the noise was being produced. The old hag tapped the globe with a miniature hammer gripped in her claw-like hand.

"Dragon-soldier," she said, a throaty voice and an indifferent tone. "Killer in silk."

Gunnar realised she was staring at him, or would have been if she'd had the eyes to see him with.

"Follow me. You wait, big man. You wait until it is your time."

Dragging his feet through the darkness, Gunnar left his fellow officer and followed the old women, moving by tracking the hollow tapping sound. How far they travelled or how many turns they took, Gunnar found it impossible to say, his world reduced to a darkness and the monotony of rapping.

Why she never stumbled the dandy could not understand; on every step of the darkened corridor Gunnar stubbed his boots against loose rock chippings and uneven paving. When light did come again it was harsh on his eyes, tripod candleholders flinging orange shards into the night. Gunnar blinked. Together they had emerged into a room, walls smooth, bare apart for rusting torch holders.

"Sit," she indicated a heavy chair carved above a stone dais. Doing as he was bid, Gunnar sat and looked around the room. In front of him, four rock steps led to an opening, the door arched and traced with intricate patterns – meaningless to the eye, although imagination might have made them snakes curled around coronets, or faces leering from the stone.

Appearing from nowhere, another woman moved to flank him. She was identical to the first, as if the original hag had grown a sister, multiplied like frog-spawn in the darkness outside while he had been groping through the rubble.

A third women emerged from the door ahead. Dressed in the same unflattering cowl, and sharing their blindness, if not their age. Despite the unnerving absence of eyes and her knife-cropped hair – as golden as Gunnar's own – the woman was possessed of a perfectly formed face, all the chiselled symmetry of one of the Sunken Empire's long-forgotten goddesses.

"Dragon in silk," the youngest woman announced. "Lift your arms. Place your hands on the globes."

Moving close enough for Gunnar to touch, the two hags lifted their milky spheres, orange torchlight reflected in the burnished highlights.

Dropping his fingers onto the globe was like experiencing the cold kiss of brass. Against expectation his arms did not feel heavy, his entire body was fever-light, as if he would float away in a dream or a faint.

"Just as there is a time for what is not true, there is also a time for truth," the youngest women continued. "Sharing this knowledge, you will see beyond yourself."

Her words carried across to Gunnar as if from a great distance, heavy with ritual – boredom almost – as if she had worn this speech out like the frayed ends of a well-trodden carpet. "There is a battle in the islands, what do you see?"

His voice answered her. But it was not his mouth moving, both the hags were speaking in unison – speaking with his voice. "I see a fortress, a hill, a farm on its crest. I see an officer insulted."

Gunnar was frozen, a dream where his legs would not move. It was not mimicry – that was his own voice, his own thoughts spilling from the hags' mouths. Part of Gunnar was horrified, but that part was buried deep, the rest of his consciousness was smothered by an unseen weight, lost, directionless.

Torture would have almost been preferable. What was any torture compared to this? The scrape of metal across a skin, the impact of a fist in a stomach, molten iron dribbling across the sole of a foot. Just one object being pressed to another.

More precise, more measured and intimate than any beating, the dandy's inquisition continued.

Looking with suspicion at the elegant script on the note, Taliesin saw the highlander had noticed the frown creasing his features. The Whitestave who'd handed him the scrap of paper had vanished as suddenly as he had appeared.

"What is it, man?"

"Orders from the Butcher. He wants to see me. A private meeting."

The mountain-man shook his head. He and Gunnar still looked white from their ordeal at the hands of the mummers – this news was not helping improve their mood. After their preternatural inquisition, the soldiers had returned to their rooms tired and hungry, drained of energy yet uneasy and restless at the same time. Now this. On the battlefield, every order from the Butcher normally meant deaths and maimings among the company. Connaire Mor tried to shake off his headache. "He is no going to be too happy about our company being detached away from his merry band."

"I thought the bastard would be glad to get us off his hands. Still, what can he do to us that he hasn't already?"

Gunnar laughed. "He'll find something. It was bad enough when Teyron had the Prince of Cornwall interfering with his command. And now the Queen too?"

Placing the note in the small fireplace of the monk's cell, the Captain watched it writhe and twist in the flames. "Yes. The Queen. The Queen."


An army of gardeners toiled in the lawns and woods below the Citadel; the Crown estates raked for the wild progeny of the witchwoods, weeding for faerie growth creeping back into the lands tamed by man.

Wind groaned across Taliesin's position on the roof, a flat plain of granite among an orchard of chimneys and slate gray slopes. Below was the courtyard where the dragon-browns had arrived two days earlier.

Appearing by the battlement tower, a staff officer turned his face into the moaning gusts. What was his name? He could not place it, but Taliesin had seen him at General Teyron's side before. Accompanying the officer were three

Foot Guards with stove-pipe hats. As many as he expected.

"Is the Butcher not fit today?"

The stone floor was still slick from the rain, and the staff soldier had to hold onto the crenellations to stop himself sliding over. "Fit enough, Captain."

"He must be absent-minded, then. He does not seem to have turned up."

Smiling, the staff officer pointed back to the tower. "But he did send a message for you."

Stepping onto the roof, Pwyll pulled out his sabre, the cavalryman disguised in a green Guards uniform. He must have ridden hard to have caught up with them in the capital. But then Taliesin suspected his vicious enemy had help; an army pass and authority for a relay of posthouse horses. "I told you back in Drum Draiocht we would meet again, one-eye."

"So you did, horse buggerer."

All four men had their swords drawn and stalked towards Taliesin.

"I'll carve out your heart for daring to humiliate me in front of my men, Taliesin. We'll see how unkillable you are now, you piece of gutter shit."

"That you will."

As the soldiers advanced on Taliesin, a wave of dragon-browns surged from behind the roof towers, charging the Foot Guards with daggers and metal garottes – the wicked wires rookery stranglers knew as velvet coughers.

They took the four killers like an avalanche, slipping the coils over the Guards's necks, pulling the loops taut and watching as the royal soldiers struggled and thrashed under the garottes' touch. While the soldiers were pinned, shuddering and grappling with the company, other dragon-browns slipped up and plunged daggers into the Guards' stomachs, thrusting back and forth as they spilled their entrails across the battlements.

"This one is mine."

"Get back with you, that's my blade in his sodding

throat." Dragons-browns bickered and pushed each other in their eagerness to strip the wealthy corpses of their coin and finery.

Walking over to where the tall cavalryman lay, chest fluttering as his blood warmed the rain-soaked stone, Taliesin looked down at Pwyll's pained face.

"How – how?"

"Your note. When was the last time the Butcher began an order to us with 'I request'? Every company in his army had that courtesy. Never mine."

Pwyll's eyes slipped skyward in understanding, then grew wide with death.

Four corpses lay slumped across the roof, and Taliesin watched as Gunnar kicked one of the Foot Guards. The Guard was gone. "What now?"

"Now, sir?" Taliesin said to the dandy. "That anglers' pool below us... Macsyn's was it? Weight the bodies and the fish can have them. Martyrs, I wonder which bugger sent these blades after us?"

Gunnar laughed. "Take your pick."

Cleaning his dirk on the corpse's emerald uniform, Connaire Mor looked up. "Aye, he's right. The bastard bairn-killer I tried to do for on Accession Day, the Foot Guards we showed up there, the Queen, one of the Princes, the Butcher, toppers from the House Gunnar's red-haired dollymop hails from. We can take our swining pick from our enemies."

# Chapter 6

Unlike Llud-din's river port, Taliesin could see Ellsemar was no commercial centre. The craft lying off the docks were dominated by the Realm's small navy.

Dipping in the frothy spray, lines sharp and haughty, these were vessels that could only be men-of-war. Their worth measured in culverin, judged solely on the fact they were strong enough to join the line of battle. The warships were carvel-built, a skin of planks fitted edge to edge over a weighty internal frame – the heavy slopes of their sides curving inward to prevent the weight of the upper gun decks making the killers top heavy.

Casting his eyes about, Gunnar was the first to spot the white-wolf pennant of Bron, the Queen's shipmaster. Bron was no pig-tailed stiff-shirt of the navy, but he served the Queen every bit as faithfully for love of gold. Free with her letters of marque, Annan Pendrag had attracted a cadre of unpleasant talent to the Realm's shores, supplementing her small force of ships-of-the-line with hell-rakes and braggarts, men accustomed to routine violence and quick lives of sea-borne butchery.

During an attack of irony, Bron had named his ship the Gogmagog, *giant* in the native language of Cornwall. But riding the spray alongside the warships of Emrys, the Gogmagog appeared little more than a minnow. A three-decker carrying thirty-five culverin and sporting three masts, the Gogmagog might have been dwarfed by the more formidable looking line-ships, but Taliesin was sure that if Annan Pendrag had entrusted the success of their mission to this man, her master's crew would be the equal of every other craft afloat.

Gunnar ran his knowledgeable gaze over the Gogmagog,

then he laughed, his seal of approval. Like the wolf totem on her banner, the ship was sleek and narrow, low in the waves, her masts arrogantly prodding the milky sky.

They were on their way to the Gogmagog's gangway when trouble distracted them. A woman, fallen over on the dock's slippery cobbles and wrapped in heavy shawls against the wind. She was being abused by a man in a seaman's woollen hat, the words drifting in and out of the wind. "Clumsy slut – can't – walk straight?"

As the bedraggled woman tried to rise up, the seaman shouted something drowned in the wind, then lashed out with his boot, catching her in the chest and turning her over with the shock of the blow.

"I'll not be standing for that," Connaire Mor said, the huge Astolatier halting the group.

Moving closer, Taliesin saw a vicious mob had come from under the shelter of one of the rotting dock buildings, but far from stopping the beating the on-lookers urged the seaman to greater violence.

From behind the dockers appeared a figure dressed in the common brown habit of a Tree Martyr monk. "Ah lad, there is work here for my precious healing hands." Bleary-eyed and ragged, the priest emphasised his words with sausage-like fingers.

"She's a useless bleeding dollymop, this one," said the seamen. "No cracking good to anyone."

"A little mercy might be in order, lad," said the priest.

Angrily the other seamen turned, looking at the priest for the first time. Broken and bulbous nosed, the monk had the hang-dog face of a carouser, hard-bitten and over-used in the excesses of life – a face more suitable to the unkempt dockers ringing them, than a representative of the holy source.

"And what do you know about women?" spat the seamen. This raised jeers of agreement from the crowd. "Women should submit to their men, she has heard that one in church enough. This is the only thing she understands."

He kicked the woman again to cheers from the rough mob.

"The beloved of the Martyr shall dwell in safety by him; and the Martyr shall cover them all the day long, and they shall dwell between his shoulders," quoted the monk. "There's a mortal wickedness in you. But a laying on of my poor shaking hands may heal your soul."

So saying the priest drove an oversized fist into the seaman's stomach, doubling the squalid man up, a look of astonishment frozen on his face. Leaning forward with the casual ease of a priest applying benediction, the Tree Martyr brought his knee up, connecting with the seaman's chin and hammering the man backwards.

While the seamen groaned on the floor, his friends in the mob rushed the priest. Until that point Connaire Mor had been content to look on, but now the mountain-man piled forward, tossing dockers aside and cudgelling attackers with his ham-sized fists. Taking the Astolatier's lead, Taliesin led the rest of the dragon-browns into the mob, the soldiers matching the hardbitten dockers viciousness for viciousness.

One man came at Taliesin with a baling hook, but the Captain used the longer reach of his leg to bludgeon the docker's knee, a sweeping kick which shattered the man's bone. To Taliesin's left a townsman flailed down to the cobbles with a nose spouting blood, one of his soldiers still mauling the man's face.

With a detached professionalism, Taliesin noted it was in melees like this the pressed company really stood out, his soldiers bringing to the table a lifetime of previous experience from lock-ups, street brawls and the city's rookeries. They might be a disorderly drunken disaster in garrison, but if they ever closed close enough with an enemy for muzzle-swords, he knew the battle was as good as won.

At last the dockers decided they had got the worst of it and disengaged from the clash, running bruised and bleeding back down the warren of warehouses and sailor's flop-houses.

"Liked that, I did," said a soldier, summing up most his comrades' feelings and hawking a gob of blood across the dock.

The priest helped the seaman's wife to her feet and said a few words of comfort to the sobbing woman, then turned to the soldiers, rubbing his hands together. "Take the shield of the faith, where you shall be able to quench all the fiery darts of the wicked. Ah but mercy, but that was a blessed good spot of work you boys did back there."

Even with the priest's broad Tryban accent, Taliesin could hear the slur in the man's voice – not that he needed to look any farther than the ruddy bulbous nose for signs of his fondness for drink. Scratching a tonsure that was little more than a concession to a bold-spot, the monk wheezed. "There's a mortal lot of wickedness loose in the Realm today, but I think I have earnt the sleep of the just tonight, after chastising so many mortal sinners."

Taliesin nodded. "Blest be the father of all mercies."

"Ah, there's a mortal tone of disrespect in your voice," said the priest. "But the Martyr will forgive you; though if you hadn't been about his work today, I might have been a little more harsh in my judgement."

Taliesin spread his hands in supplication. "We have just spent the last six months fighting the rebels of Dal Albaeon, I have no desire to add Tryban to the list."

"I was baptised with a good name, Finbar to you," said the monk. "You've got the look of privateers about you, so it's wicked odds you will be bound for the Gogmagog."

"Well met," Gunnar laughed.

"Ah, well. You are not marines or the navy press, not dressed like that. Besides, if anybody in port has use of a pack of devils like yourselves, it would be Bron."

Taliesin nodded towards the ship. "What sort of man is he?"

"Well that is the question to be asking me, for sure, me

being the ship's churchman. Bron is partial to his religion, so he is. In his line of work it makes sense to have someone standing by to grant him indulgences."

Taliesin was surprised. "And the Arch-Truron is happy to let you dispense mercies to a man like that?"

"Well now," said Finbar, "there was a slight falling out between myself and some of the good fellows back in Tryban. A mortal disagreement over interpretation of the true book you might say. Ah, never has a man had my luck before. Pity my poor old head, driven out of my own home and forced to take up with a pack of vicious killers. Though there's grog on Bron's ship, a blessed small comfort for an honest servant of the Martyr."

As if in answer to the priest, a penetrating voice rang out from the ship's deck, lucid and loud. "Finbar, when you've finished making trouble with the townsmen, you'll do me the courtesy of hauling your damn hide aboard."

A short man leant over the upperdeck's rail, a beard sharply pointed at the front, putting Taliesin in mind of a satyr.

He did not look much like the man Taliesin had imagined. In his mind, the officer had depicted the Gogmagog's master in the same mould as the Queen's favourite, Domnal Mac Aedo. A ruthless killer clad in black. The only notable thing about the short man above them was his lack of remarkability. If it had not been for the nautical cut of his clothes, this could have been any one of the nondescript tallymen and clerks working for Camlan's trading houses.

Eschewing trousers in favour of cloak-bag breeches tucked into leather boots, Bron wore a brown jerkin not far in colour from Taliesin's jacket, the seaman's arms emerging from shoulder wings, sham hanging sleeves draped behind him like a twin cape.

"You are late, sir," said Bron as the company climbed the gangway and made their way up to the poop-deck. "But then I wouldn't expect a bunch of lubbers to know about tides and such."

"Taliesin," said Taliesin, louder than he intended to be heard above the wind. "Annan's special cargo."

"So you're the Queen's new pet. You might as well say it," said Bron. "*Captain* Taliesin. Just as long as you remember, there's only ever room for one master aboard a ship. That's doubly true on *this* ship."

Taliesin indicated the Gogmagog. "Your command, then."

Bron nodded. "Well, at least you've got some sense about you. The last cattle job we had from Annan expected me to run around after him as if we were a damn pleasure barge. Finbar, you take them down to the steerage, show them where to stow their gear and introduce them to the pleasure of the hammock. We'll be casting off as soon as the last of your people arrive."

"The last?" Taliesin said. "This is all there is."

Bron shook his head. "Not by my orders, Taliesin. There's still one Gwion Bach, who I was told will be arriving separately."

"That'll be the Butcher's weirdsman," said Connaire Mor. "Aye, here's me thinking we were shot of him."

Taliesin looked thoughtfully up at the sailors climbing over the rigging, clutching on tightly in the face of the bracing gusts. "Well, he could earn his keep yet."

Climbing down a narrow set of stairs, the priest led them past individual cabins and along a roofed deck where culverin snouts pouted out of neat square gun-hatches. Taliesin saw that ropes had been run through rings in the weapons' stubby rears, preventing carriages sliding back across the deck in rough seas. To balance the ship the heaviest culverin were carried on the lower decks, the lightest above them.

Another ladder led still farther into the Gogmagog's depths, the orlop-deck below the waterline. They passed a cattle pen strewn with straw where geese and chickens clucked, picking their way across a deck littered with bales and barrels.

"Well now, here's your new home," said Finbar. "Bron won't mind if you move about on deck once we get going, taking some precious air. But don't be getting in the way of his men."

Taliesin was standing near the Gogmagog's forecastle, one hand resting near the fierce wolf-head carving which reared up at the ship's prow. Eager to catch the best of the tide, Bron was getting impatient for the weirdsman's arrival, tapping his fingers on the ship's wheel and staring up towards the cloud-obscured sun.

Just as Bron was about to give the order to cast off and to hell with the weirdsman, a peculiar figure on a donkey cantered from behind the sea-front buildings, clattering rapidly across the cobbled dock, sea-spray and crosswind making his cape flap noisily in the squall.

"Stand to, damn it," shouted Bron with resignation.

"Man, that is no Gwion Bach," said Connaire Mor. "Don't tell me they've gone and found the bodies back in that pool in Camlan?"

Gunnar laughed and pulled at the holster-puffer tucked under his belt. "If there's any trouble we'll settle it quick and be sailing out of Emrys before anyone's the wiser."

Taliesin pushed the flintlock back in Gunnar's belt. "Use your head. Even if the Queen has found out, she wouldn't jeopardise our journey, not for the sake of that slug Pwyll."

Hobbling up the gangwalk, the figure hopped across onto the quarterdeck, almost knocking over a sailor lugging two buckets of water.

Rapping his cane onto the deck as if it was a staff of office and he a page announcing the arrival of a monarch, the figure turned towards Bron, flipping back the cowl of his tattered cloak. Taliesin saw the mischievous face of Camlan's tinker revealed. Beneath the cloak, his patched and frayed jacket was a splash of colour against the drab ship and slate-gray sea.

"Gwion Bach?" said Bron, suspicion and surprise in his voice.

"Is he back?" said the tinker, looking around. "No, no I don't think so."

Bron put his hands on his hips and stared at the tinker. "Don't play me for a damn fool, matey. What are you doing here?"

"Why, I'm here to help," said the tinker. "Them, in fact. I thought that was obvious."

"Camlan sent you?"

"Does it look as if Camlan sent me?"

Bron tugged angrily at his sharp little beard. "Malan and Sepptis, listen old man, what has buggering happened to Gwion Bach?"

"Him? Sick. Too ill to take to the sea."

Bron shook his head in disbelief. It was on the same scale as the Gogmagog's overweight priest refusing to lead prayer because it just so happened the Martyr was feeling a little under the weather and had taken to bed for the day. If a weirdsman ever suffered something as mundane as a common illness, word of it had never reached the Realm's coaching-inns.

"Well I hope you can buggering stomach boiled salt-meat and hard biscuits, old man," said Bron. "Because, matey, you have just signed yourself up for a tidy little voyage."

Slipping into a mild breeze, the squall had died away by evening, clouds stripped away to reveal a sky as black as the sea, dark pitching waves lit clearly enough by the half-moon and a sprinkling of stars.

Lanterns swung with the play of the sea, Taliesin laying with his back against the wall of the gundeck, warmer and dryer than their sleeping quarters down in steerage.

Feeling sleepy, the officer climbed up the steps to the open quarter-deck, the freezing night slipping between the seams of his jacket and rubbing the weariness away. There was a coop on the upper deck for poultry, and beside it

Bron stared out across the waves, clutching a tricorn hat behind his back.

"Do you know these waters well?" Taliesin asked.

"Well enough," said Bron. "We'll be entering the mouth of the Tolisi straits before long. It narrows for nearly a day and that's where it's worst. There are Martyr-damned reefs all around those waters, shallow draft, currents pulling in every direction. Yes, many a good ship's been splintered up the Tolisi."

"One of my officers – he is from a merchanteer family. Reckons the Enclosed Sea is none too safe."

"Traders," Bron said it dismissively. "They prefer to hug the coastal routes like scared pigs, Nor-east to Fandan and Cindsoven, Roubaix. But there is trouble enough in the Enclosed Sea, matey. You don't even have to go looking for it. Slavers from the sand-kingdoms, pirates from Aragon and Gliarin, and every piss-handed noble with a scrap of land to call a harbour handing out their letters of marque to privateers and no-goods."

"People like you," said Taliesin.

"Ha, yes, damn right. People like me. But don't go saying that too loud in front of my crew. We have got official marque from the best Queen of them all, so they are a might touchy about their status. It's gentlemen of a private company to you."

Taliesin breathed in the sea air. It was clear, cold, and he could almost taste the salt. Bron continued, as if the sea spume and night wind had made his tongue restless. "You're a soldier, used to land, towns and the forest, so I'll tell you: there's things out here you wouldn't believe. It's always been wild and hard.

"Now, I have been in enough damn port taverns to know fifty of every hundred tales you will hear are all piss and wind, and the other half so tall they have to be true. But since last year there's been talk, things been happening on the sea. Ships come out and just don't sail back again. And that's not even the half of it."

"There are times in the forest," said Taliesin. "When you travel with dragoons or not at all. When the wood's darkness is close to your door."

Bron shook his head. "It's not that. I've seen some damn bizarre sights swimming out in the deep ocean, but this is something new, recent."

Taliesin shrugged his shoulders. Poachers and farmers were the same, there was always something unexplained, deadly, lurking in the Realm's green cathedrals. The wilderness wrote her own rules.

Using his vantage point on the poop-deck, Taliesin stared down the length of the Gogmagog. At the far end, near the snarling wolf-head, the soldier saw another figure looking out across the moonlit waves. Bulbous-nosed and wearing a brown habit, it was Finbar.

Bron saw where the soldier's gaze was resting. "He's a strangeun, that one," said Bron. "Every night he comes out and stares out into the damn darkness. Myself, I love the sea, this is all the life I ever asked for. But that priest doesn't, a shipman develops a nose for the ones that have been pressed. Martyrs, half my crew's deserted from a navy at one time or another. But the sea has a way; they like the life enough not to return to their farms or their city workshops. Him though, he just stands and stares, and dammed if any of us know what he's looking for."

Finbar stared out into the darkness, but it was not the swell of the sea the monk saw, it was the placid calm of a Tryban stream, bubbling and carrying away a bounty of autumn leaves.

Finbar had been sitting by the stream, contemplating the tumble's bounty. Then his meditations had been interrupted by one of the village girls running from behind the church's shadow.

"Brother," her voice breathless, choking back the horror. "The Militant Order have arrived in the town, they're gathering people from all the villages."

"Blessed life, take yourself a breath," Finbar said.

His voice was calm, but behind the composure he had known this time would come.

The wolves were running at last.

Centuries past, in one of the cruel quirks of fate which composed history, Tryban's south-western shores had been the landing point for Martyr missionaries, not the orthodox orders of the central mainland, but Palispitian's from the north, Fandan.

Was it only five years ago that the Arch-Truron had sent Finbar and his minorite brothers out? Gently weaning the people from the distortions of belief which were perverting the true faith in the Realm's eyes. Weighing his heart heavy, Finbar remembered the Militant Order: blades and racks, trials and confessions, an artist's creative touch with blunt instruments. Passing away like his autumn leaves, now the time for gentleness was being swept down the stream.

"You get your mortal family together, girl," said Finbar. "If you see the Order coming, have your village's foresters take you all into the edge of the tumble. Sure and none of the soldiers will be following you in there"

Lines of villagers were being led past the walled gate of the town. They looked like refugees, pitiful, dragging children along in clusters. Most obeyed the command to come to town without coercion, but some of the men were being escorted by soldiers of the Martyr.

Looking around, Finbar could see few foresters. He nodded to himself, they would slip into the boundless woods, taking the ones they could. Few of the priests that followed would ever be found again.

Finbar walked to the gate and addressed one of the Order. "And where would I be finding the fine person in charge of all this now?"

The soldier saluted. "He directs from the keep, merciful father."

"Merciful is it?" said Finbar. "There's precious little of that here, lad."

Five stories tall, the town's keep was unimpressive. The priest stopped to look at the moat, it had been allowed to lapse into disuse, too shallow to stand off any decent assault. Just deep enough for the Order's ducking boards.

Finbar recognised some of the faces from his church: the stubborn ones, the ones who clung to the old ways, refusing to recant. Up they came, blue faces spluttering and gasping for air, too exhausted now to even respond to the Order's Inquisitors. The questioners looked as if they were angels. Such young faces above their white surcoats, the humourless features of fanatics, sure of purpose and pure in the violence of their methods.

Huffing from the exertion of climbing the stairs, Finbar paused at the top of the keep. He could see out to the west of the cleared estates, in the far corner of Finbar's parish, a scrap of land that men had clawed back from the forest, paid for with generations of hard effort and toil. Black smoke billowed into a clear sky.

It was not farmers burning their stubble.

"Mercy me," Finbar said to the back of the only other observer. "But you are quick with your blessed bonfires."

Turning, Finbar noticed his fellow spectator's translucent pupils, as if those eyes had been diluted by all the blood and pain he had visited on the Realm during his long life. He wore the white surcoat with the red outline of a fish in its centre: the multiplication of miracles, a bitter joke.

"Ah, yes," said the Master of the Militant Order. "I remember you from the meeting in Gort Elva. You and your minorite brothers' ways have proved ... insufficient, haven't they? How many years have you been here, four, five? We've been on the coast for five days and the Order's already brought more back to the true salvation than you and your friars managed in all your years here."

"The Arch-Truron ..." Finbar began.

The Master of the Order barked a hollow laugh. "You really are out in the tumble, aren't you? He passed away four weeks ago. The Covenant elected a new head two days after."

"So that's the way of it, is it?" said Finbar. "And now we're to be putting our wicked house in order."

"He was weak," said the holy General. "If but one soul falls to Old Shadow through our weakness, then we have failed in our trust. If we are to lead the people on the true path then we must be pure in our methods, as strong as the Martyr on the tree."

Screams hovered over the moat below. The men's corpses were being cut off the ducking boards, a line of struggling women being held to take their place.

"Well, I see blessed little method out there," said Finbar. "But I do see you are a mortal modern-thinking fellow. Didn't you burn the women in the old days?"

"So many saved," said the man, oblivious to Finbar's sarcasm. "Can you see it? We have the chance to do such work across the land. By the end of our lives the plains of Old Shadow will be barren and empty – the fields of paradise as thronged as a market day. There will be a cushion there for each of us, by the very Martyr himself."

"And how will you be doing all that now?" Finbar asked. "When you'll be getting there so blessed early yourself."

It took little exertion for someone of Finbar's weighty bulk, seizing the man's legs, flipping his body over the battlements.

Flapping onto a stone lion on the keep's bridge, the Master of the Militant Order jounced across into the moat, then settled, bobbing face down in the mud-clotted water. On the bank, the soldiers of the Order looked up in dumbfoundment, as if their God was dropping priests from the very heavens that day.

Slapping against the wooden planking of the Gogmagog, the sea brought the priest back to the present.

"Ah," Finbar muttered to himself. "There's another one fallen from grace."

Though it was still dark, the first thing Taliesin's nostrils detected was the approach of dawn's first gleaming, the second was the foul-smelling seaman shaking him awake.

"Up and out, eh," the sailor said. "Bron wants you and your man on the deck." He pointed at Gunnar.

Taliesin pulled off the dewy canvas sheeting he had been using as a blanket. Asleep, the dragon-browns were still stretched out across bales and packets in the damp steerage hold. Reaching out with his boot, Taliesin pushed the dandy off his perch.

"Come on," Taliesin said, then to the sailor: "What is this all about?"

"The Cap'n. You see, he is wanting to ask your opinion on a little matter."

Taking Taliesin and Gunnar up onto the quarterdeck, the seaman led the soldiers to one of the ship's longboats. Lashed atop a pair of the Gogmagog's spare spars, the longboat was being used as a sheep pen by the crew.

A group of seamen bunched around the boat, Bron standing there thoughtfully, stroking his satyr-like beard.

"This one says she's yours," said Bron, turning one of the group around.

Struggling with her arms pinned, Gunnar was shaken to see Elaine being held by the sailors. She looked a distant relation of the creature he had last seen in Camlan, adorned in loose sheep-soiled cotton trousers now, her scarlet tresses hidden beneath a woollen cap.

"You're jiggering pigshit," she spat. "I'm of the House Fastain, you'll know who I am alright when we get back to land."

"And I suppose you *don't* smell like week-old sheep shit? I know who you are," said Bron. "I always make a point of knowing any damn clan that's got more pirates in it than my crew, even if your family is landlocked."

"You putrid little bastard," she erupted. "I'll have your head on a pole for speaking about my family like that."

Bron turned to the soldiers. "Do you really want her,

matey? It'll make for a lot smoother voyage if we just feed her to the damn fish now."

"You wouldn't," Elaine fumed.

Bron leered at her, a dolphin-like expanse of white teeth revealed. "You remember how your father treats the buggering servants back on your land? Well now, you just put it into your head the idea that this ship is my Dukedom, and think how your family might treat a traveller who's been found kipping in one of your outhouses."

Gunnar ran a hand through his blonde hair. "What are you doing *here*?"

"I'm coming with you," said Elaine. "They moved forward my marriage to that bastard in Llud-din, so I slipped out of Camlan last night."

"You're crazy, girl," said Taliesin. "We're not skipping through the Realm on some royal progress. There's seven sorts of hell waiting for us at the other end of this voyage, I have made enough enemies in the Realm without bringing your corpse back to your family."

Elaine was jarred by the ferocity of Taliesin's curses. She turned plaintively to Gunnar. "You don't want me to end up married to him, do you?"

"Martyrs," Taliesin shoved Elaine around to face him again. "There's worse fates then waiting around in a manorhouse for some senile old quality to die of gout and leave you a widow. Have you ever seen a soldier lying out in a field, screaming because his stomach's been opened up by a sabre? Or cut in half by culverin fire? Stumbling around in powder-smoke that's so thick you'd think you were fighting in a chimney, balls splitting your friends, waiting for some gallant on a horse to ride you down with a lance. That's what we are about, we are not on some fairy-tale pursuit to recover the King's sceptre."

Elaine jerked her head away, avoiding Taliesin's gaze, her freckled face sour and hostile.

"You still don't understand, do you, it's – " Taliesin begun. He was interrupted by a bare-chested sailor, shouting down from the rigging. "It's out there, It's out there."

Looking up, Taliesin saw the seamen was pointing into the darkness. A trail of cloud uncovered the moon, revealing a shadowed hulk off their starboard.

"That is the one, the thing they've been talking about," cried one of the sailors holding Elaine. "The ship with wheels."

"Hold your damn tongue bosun," said Bron. "I don't want any panic here."

It was a distance into the night, but squinting with his good eye, Taliesin could see the hull of the ship was raised off the water, eight solid spokeless wheels burrowed through the hull – four each side of the vessel.

It was turning towards them.

Between each pair of wheels a fort-like superstructure rose into the air, lights sparkling there and losing definition as the first tinges of morning infected the horizon. Black dot's peppered the hull, row upon row of culverin hatches.

"Who the hell are they?" Taliesin asked.

Moaning, a sailor gripped his head. "It's a devil ship. They'll do for us."

"I told you to shut that up," Bron railed. "I don't know what that bastard thing is out there, but two months ago when one of Ellsemar's fisherboats pulled a man from the sea, all the wretch could rant about was the ship with wheels. It is that thing that has been doing for our ships."

"There's no sails," Gunnar said, surprised. "And at this distance, it must be massive. Why, if we had our spars down we would sail right underneath her."

Bron nodded, shoving his men away from the rail. "That's right, army. Just like a bloody great Zamarorian galleon, too high for her own damn good. Run her on the port gybe!"

Scattering, the sailors dispersed across the deck, shouts from below decks raising the crew still sleeping.

One of the seamen – scarcely a boy – flew over the

planking to hand Bron a flared speaking trumpet. Taking the brass trumpet, Bron barked orders across the Gogmagog. "Damn your eyes there, clear for battle, clear for battle. Are you manning that damn culverin or brushing it clean?"

Bron turned to Taliesin. "Your free ride's over, matey. Get your men up here. I'm taking the ship underneath that thing's culverin and see how well she sails with a broadside across those buggering wheels. When your people get near enough to see their crew on deck, start sniping them off."

Taliesin moved to go.

"And take her damn hide with you," Bron said, pointing at Elaine.

Like rolling thunder, the strange ship let loose a volley, a hammerfall starting from the forecastle and echoing back to her stern, spouts of black smoke leaking out into the night.

The first five shots lashed the sea, spouts of purple-black water climbing towards the night sky, another discharge dynamiting over their heads. With an incredible explosion the last part of the volley slammed into the Gogmagog' poop-deck, heaving the ship up and slicing down the mizzen-mast.

Collapsing over the deck like a falling tree, the broken mizzen-mast crushed one team of sailors while three seamen pitched away from the rigging and fell into the sea, others slapping the deck with the wet sound of fruit shaken from an orchard. Billowing in the slight wind, the collapsed sail was on fire, flames leaping across the rear of the ship.

His feet hooked from under him, Bron climbed to his feet. "Bucketmen, bucketmen to the poop. Martyrs, what the hell size are their damn culverin? We're not even close to range yet, their balls should be falling short, not cutting above us."

"You tell that to them then, you jiggering milksop," Elaine shouted at Bron, Gunnar dragging her towards the stairs.

Taliesin did not have to make his way down into

steerage. Before the eight-wheeled ship had hurled her third ball, the company was packed and racing up the stairs, survival heavy on their minds.

"You did no have to arrange a practical demonstration of seamanship for us, man," Connaire Mor shouted up to Gunnar. Then he saw the woman. "Martyrs! Gunnar, it is not her swining father chasing us out there is it?"

Taliesin waved the company up the stairs. "On deck, keep your heads low, and when we get near enough to the other ship, you take down anyone you can."

"Same routine as the field," Connaire Mor ordered the dragon-browns. "Go for the silver-buttons first."

Barefoot in their striped cotton trousers, a snarl of gunners struggled around the culverin below decks. Loading ship cannon involved a longer, more intricate process than that of the company's flintlocks. Wheeled back from the hatch, a bag of powder was rammed down the culverin's barrel, followed by a felt wad to hold it in place, then the ball was pushed in – an extra wad of felt to secure the ball. A sailor with a spike thrust it through the touch-hole, piercing the powder bag inside the barrel, a fuse hastily jammed after the charge. Another sailor jumped forward to fire it with his blazing torch.

Sweating crews manhandled shot down the poorly lit length of the under-deck, hauling the heavy culverin carriages, powder monkeys toiling with leather bags full of the deadly black grain. Near the stairs, a sailor sliced the air with his cutlass.

"Fire."

Standing above-deck the enemy's volley sounded as if it were thunder, but here the explosions were deafening, like some pagan storm god breaking the back of the world on his anvil.

Culverin after culverin recoiled back on their wheeled carriages, smoke curling across the enclosed deck, the familiar smell of sulphur overwhelming in the enclosed space. Already the crews were attending their metal charges again, moving in with damp fleeces fixed to their mauls. Sponging with precision and urgency, they swept the barrels clear of any remaining powder, smouldering remnants which would ignite the next powder bag; erupting iron and flame across the deck and slaughtering the crew before the battle had begun.

Another shuddering impact threw Taliesin sideways, flinging him into a sailor's small card table.

Yawing at an angle now, a culverin broke its ropes and rolled across the tilted deck, missing the Captain by inches and hammering into the back of a battery behind him. Taliesin slid over and helped the sailor's mates pull the weapon off the bloody bodies mangled by the collision.

Screaming with tears in their eyes, the injured were carried below to the orlop-deck, where the ship's sawbones was treating the wounded. Having already seen the drunken fool's instruments, Taliesin knew they were screaming as much from the thought of what the surgeon would have to do to them to save their twisted bodies, as from the terrible injuries.

With no hatches for Taliesin to see out of, marking the accuracy of the Gogmagog's culverin, the soldier climbed out onto the quarterdeck clutching his flintlock rifle. Listing in the water, the top-deck of the Gogmagog was a scene from hell. Along with the mizzen mast, the main mast had been punched to the deck, even the remaining foremast's canvas was shredded, her topsail blazing in the night and lighting the ship with capering orange flames. Unable to tack, at the mercy of the Tolisi strait's currents, the wheeled warship was standing comfortably off the Gogmagog. Abandoning the discipline of volley fire, the enemy ship's culverin whipped random balls into their vessel, cracking the hull apart and flailing the remaining canvas into ribbons.

It was no wonder Bron had not been able to close with their bizarre foe as he had intended; even in the twilight Taliesin could see the wheels churning the pitch-black waves in reverse, matching the Gogmagog's helpless course by powering backwards. However skilled Bron's crew were, no sailing ship could hope to match that manoeuvrability.

Standing under the burning sail with his satyr-like beard, Bron looked even more like a devil. Wheeling his cutlass above his head he cursed the wheeled ship, threatening his crew into continuing the action, flaming canvas raining down around him.

Across their ruined topdeck the culverin had fallen silent, covered by tangles of sail, rigging and broken spars. Hiding in this wreckage, the company were using the cover to shoot at the wheeled ship, useless unless the wind caught the balls. But Taliesin understood the feelings of impotence which underlined their fusillade. His men were trained to get in close, spear and hack the enemy, then wheel away to inflict havoc on another part of the foe's line. Here, there might as well have been the fleas on two dogs, snarling it out in one of Llud-din's twisting alleys.

"It is a sight, isn't it?"

Taliesin turned around. It was the old tinker, the hellish flames reflected dancing across his mischievous eyes. "You wanted in on this trip instead of Gwion Bach, old man," Taliesin said. "How about you get us out of this fix?"

"Weirdsmanship?" the tinker said. "Call up a beast from the deep to wrap its horned length around that ship, for instance?"

"Something like that," Taliesin growled.

The scruffy tinker shook his head. "Ah, the mixture of superstition and worldliness, it all adds to the fascination of our age doesn't it?"

"That is what I thought," Taliesin said, hunkering down as an explosion scythed a shower of wood across the quarter deck. "As much buggering good as a bloody fart in the wind."

Splintered apart in the attack, the longboats had broken open. Adding to the insanity, penned sheep were escaping, jumping about the wreckage, bleating in terror while the

Gogmagog burned and bleeding sailors cried into the darkness.

"Come on in, you great damn monstrosity," Bron shouted. "Come on in like men and try to finish us off, you bastards! I'll see I slide this through one of your ribs before I go."

Beneath them, one of the decks finally shattered, spilling flaming debris onto the storage holds below the waterline. Holds where, for safety's sake, the powder barrels were stored. An echoing concussion slammed into Taliesin, a sheet of darkness sliding across him.

He was rising blind, rising far into the sky, impaled on the stars and the night, rising so high he would never have to fall again.

Rising and falling. Rising and falling, Taliesin wondered if he was running. Who was he running from? His face felt different, did he have a beard? He scratched his face, grit. No, not grit – sand.

"Precious life," a voice scraped in. "He is awake again."

Blinking, Taliesin saw Finbar's ruddy features floating above him. "You are sure enough a strange sight to see, priest."

"Many are the afflictions of the righteous, but the Martyr delivereth him out of them all," said Finbar. "Ah, lad, but we didn't think to be seeing you up so soon."

Groggily Taliesin sat up. They were on a sandy beach, golden and warm, his legs still in the water, bobbing with the rise of the gentle surf. Behind them the flat stretch of sands turned into dunes, then the cool deep turquoise of the forest.

Taliesin was no poacher, but he could tell it was not the watery-green forests of the Realm. Lush and verdant, the trees were redder and richer, far warmer in hue – but for all of that, Taliesin was sure the goddess of the green darkness would prove no less capricious here than she had been in the Princedoms.

Scattered across the beach were bodies. Some living, others corpses. Seeing Taliesin awake, the huge highlander picked his way through knots of men.

"Man, it's good to see you are all there."

"Who else made it?" Taliesin asked.

Connaire Mor shrugged. "Not many. The ship ripped itself in two and the ones that weren't blown into the water jumped soon after."

"Gunnar, Bron, the company?"

"I've found three-hands of our men along here, twenty of them alive. No sign of Gunnar, five sailors alive, and Finbar here of course."

"It was a mortal miracle," said Finbar.

Taliesin coughed up a gob of salt water. "You'll forgive me if I don't share in your enthusiasm."

"No man, listen, it was last night," Connaire Mor said. "We were clinging onto what was left of the ship – we had already found you floating on your back by then – then we were rescued by these ... fish."

If they had not been lying washed up and broken on a hostile shore, Taliesin would have laughed himself fit to choking. "You've had too much bloody sun."

"It was a merciful miracle," Finbar said. "Dolphins. Hundreds of them swimming out of the night with their kind smiling faces. They whistled like blessed angels and helped push us to the shore."

"Our seamen said they have never been hearing of anything like it before, not in all their years. There would have been more of us here, too," added Connaire Mor. "But when the ship went down the wheeled thing came over. Man, the sailors treading water with us thought they were coming to pick us up, they all started yelling."

"It was a wicked bad thing them shouting like that," Finbar said.

"Aye," Connaire Mor agreed. "The thing came over us and ran us down, the wheels churning the sea and our people being sucked underneath, the poor wee buggers coming up drowned or not at all."

"We'll find that ship again," Taliesin promised, a demonic expression on his face. "Get on board her and rope her bastard Captain up by his bastard balls, pay them back for Gunnar and all the rest."

"Well man, we better be getting out of here first," the giant said. "I found some footprints back of the dunes. They were barefoot, so it looks as if some of the sailors might have reached here first and tried to get through the forest."

"Damn idiots," Taliesin said. "They won't last long in a small group. What have we got?"

Connaire Mor looked down the beach. "I still got my knives man, five sabres as well as yours, sailor's cudgels, there are a handful of puffers, but the powder's only fit for porridge after the water."

"Better than nothing."

"Laetha made it along with the dragon-brown's survivors," Connaire Mor added.

In the face of all their misfortune this was a small consolation for the Captain. "What does he say?"

"Aye, well you know Laetha. He's a miserable bugger. It's not the same as the tumble back in the Realm, but he says he's still got enough woodsman in him to give us half a chance."

Taliesin called the soldier over, Laetha walking with a pronounced stoop. If his infirmity had been a degree worse when he was an infant, his village would have marked him as a hunchback and left him to the forest. They had reason to have wished they had abandoned Laetha anyway, and not only because the grim man burned the air with constant profanity. The Realm's landowners valued the estates they cleared from the dangerous wilderness, and Laetha had not only been found poaching on one, but, it was also rumoured, had lured a pursuing party of wardens to their deaths in the tumble. Laetha's village had been razed to the ground in retribution by a troop of the county's dragoons.

"Laetha," Taliesin called. "You reckon you can survive out there?"

"I can," Laetha spat, eyeing his officer with suspicion. "But I don't know about the rest of you. You've done a piss awful job of getting us anywhere alive to date, haven't you, one-eye?"

Like all his company, Taliesin understood the taciturn man's quirks and how best to deal with him. "Listen to me, you bent-back piece of toadshit, you'll get us out of here and through that green hell over there, and you will get us there alive. And you are going to do it because we are your very good friends."

"Well that's a different matter," Laetha said caustically. "I'll do any bastard thing for me mates."

Preparing to enter the forest, the exhausted survivors were preempted by the appearance of a figure rounding the dunes; swinging his cane as if he were walking one of the capital's crystal gardens. The old tinker hummed a tune. While everyone else's hair was matted with sand and saltwater, their clothes crumpled and soiled with powder, smoke and brine, the garishly coloured jacket still hung about the tinker under his cloak. Frayed, but no worse for wear than before.

"Sun and sea," the tinker called ahead. "If I was the settling sort of man, I might put down some roots in a place like this."

"Old man, you can bloody put them down," said Taliesin. "We are out to cut our way back to whatever passes for civilisation around here."

The tinker shook his head in puzzlement. "If that's the idea, you will lose a lot less men if you walk back to the harbour here."

"What?"

"You thought I was breaking bread with the Sea Goddess this morning?" said the tinker. "There's a harbour down there."

"Martyrs, tink, where are we down, then?" Connaire Mor asked.

"Now what did I have?" said the tinker to himself. "Endive and guinea fowl. That was it. Well I suppose it must be Roubaix. Morning food in Lérridas is a lot simpler, and Aragon has more fruit with their – "

"That's fine then," Taliesin cut in. "Roubaix! Annan married into the Empire. We'll get to the tinker's port and see whether we can ship out back to the Realm or keep on going."

"Man, we can no go on like this," Connaire Mor protested. "We've lost the ship, three-quarters of our men... most the weapons."

Taliesin felt the stubble on his chin and grunted. "You didn't get to meet that ruthless bitch back on the throne, highlander. I'm not going to scuttle back to Camlan to discover if she has a sense of compassion. Martyrs, I would sooner sign up with the first free company we happen across in this poxed land."

Finbar stood up, brushing sand off his robe. "Pedlar, this blessed harbour of yours, would it be possessing one of those fine little places where they might offer a poor fellow a mortal sip of the barely bloody drinkable?"

# Chapter 7

S omewhere far into the distance Gunnar heard the eery muffled thump of the six-wheeled ship. It throbbed as if it were the heartbeat of the sea-serpents his father used to scare him with. Monstrous black humped things, surfacing from the deep to crack open ships as easily as his family smashed open crab shells at the dinner table, scooping out the salty-pink meat inside.

He had come round from the shock of the explosion as if he was in a dream, no visible boundaries between the visions of sleep and the cold nightmare he had been plunged into. No sign of the Gogmagog, it had gone, that much was sure. There was so much wreckage about it had to have sunk. Gunnar's voice had become sore from screaming, but if there was anyone out there they were not answering him.

Caught in the same current as the Realmsman, a body floated past Gunnar on its back. Still holding onto his cracked spar-piece, Gunnar thrashed his numb, soaked legs, pushing himself painfully towards the bundle. Reaching his target Gunnar grabbed hold of the body's jacket and pulled it closer, fighting the slap of the waves.

Bron.

Half the Captain's face had been burned black but Gunnar still placed his hand over the curled mouth. Nothing. No breath, not even a hint of warmth. Gunnar coughed up some of the ocean of briny water he had swallowed.

"Well Captain, I hope you wanted a burial at sea. My family would envy you."

He fought back the panic. The pulse of the devil-boat

growing fainter still. "Damn you, damn your rotten eyes, I didn't want to go to sea. Why would anyone want to go to sea?"

Bron's body floated off, unmindful of his ex-passenger's fears. Gunnar wondered if he should let it go. Even a dead body seemed company of sorts, in these freezing black swells.

In truth he was terrified of the ocean. Dark, empty, bottomless. Curse his family for all those stories at his bedside. Somewhere far beneath him was the seabed. Filled with the wrecks of ancient galleys, merchanteer cogs wrecked by storms, men-of-war from every nation and age smashed by conflict and squids the size of ships. Dead seamen scattered across the black sands, their marrow sucked out by the filthy scuttling things that swam unseen below. United in death.

Gunnar screwed his eyes shut. Where in the name of the Martyr was the ancient land? The Sunken Empire. Had Rome not wrecked the world with its black necromancy and daemon pacts, the Martyr returning from his tree to flood away their evil with a tidal wave taller than mountains? Gunnar saw the corrupt hands of a thousand skeletons clawing up through the watery green light, children, men, women, clawing towards the life above.

Fighting off another coughing fit he held onto the memory of his tutor's globe, that worn wooden ball wrapped by strips of painted parchment. The Sunken Empire's cursed lands must lie submerged farther to the east, they had to. What were the nations on either side of the straits? The first was Roubaix – that was too easy, most of the islands trade came from that sprawling, powerful Empire. A mere day's journey by sea. And on the other side of the straits? Strain as he might all he recalled were vague impressions. His family's agents brought back a pale gold wine from the nations there. They called it Xeres, but his father had great difficulty selling it, the Realm's villages and towns preferring the cheaper, sweeter Roubaixian grapes. How he had railed against losing so many gold angels on that venture. And then there were those piquant little black vegetables with stones in them. And there was constant warfare across there too. Over worship of the Martyr, something his atheist tutor had shown a philosopher's practised disdain for.

Think. Sunshine and trading ships, anything but the barren watery wilderness waiting to suck him down as his numbness spread. How much easier to let go, just cease struggling. A strip of cloud peeled away from the moon and Gunnar saw something in the distance. By the Martyrs, it was another survivor! His eyes itched from the salt, but without a doubt there it was. A shadow laying on top of something flat. Flailing his boots the exhausted Realmsman moved slowly towards the shape, creeping closer and closer as the weight of the dark sea toiled against him. His muscles scorched with agony, he closed on the makeshift skiff. They were barrels – barrels lashed together with a web of rope. It had to be from the Gogmagog's cargo hold, part of the privateer's supplies. Gunnar might have even been lying on it before the attack began.

"Look you to your side," Gunnar gagged, reaching out a deadened hand to haul himself up onto the barrels. "Martyrs but I'm freezing."

"Bastard."

A wet fist broke against Gunnar's nose and he nearly flipped back over the side of the raft.

Instinctively Gunnar lashed out and caught his cursing assailant squarely in the face. Whoever he was, he must have been every bit as weary as the dandy because the attacker collapsed on to his chest – a near-spent force.

Crawling across, Gunnar turned the body over, moving his shadow out of the way of the shallow radiance of the moonlight. His eyes felt as if they were burning. Elaine! The consummate survivor had survived even their sinking. Gunnar felt his bleeding nose.

"Something vexes you?"

She squirmed away to the corner of the raft. "You bastard. Look at this, I'm soaking, I own more bruises than an autumn peach, and it is – all – your – fault! Now you've even gone and hit me, you *utter* scum-bastard."

"My fault! You, you stowed away on the ship! Your family are going to be sending every mug-hunter and topper on the island after me when they realise where it is you've disappeared to. Just how is this *my* fault?"

Elaine waved her fist at the soldier. "Don't you understand? You made me, you made me by the words you said that night."

"Words are just words."

"Oh that's right," she shouted. "You're not even real quality, but you can just say words you don't mean then walk off again. Leave on some great mystery while I have to stay behind and marry some unctuous fat squealing pig even older than my father. I *do* think not."

Gunnar glared at her. "Well you, it might not take half an evening to introduce all of my titles when I go to a Camlan ball, but I still piss in the same water your family does."

Sniffing her turned-up nose at the Realmsman's opinions, Elaine huddled down and frowned at the dark swelling sea. Gunnar ground his teeth in frustration. Bron's corpse had been better company.

With the thud of the strange attacking ship disappearing into the slap of waves, the two survivors let fatigue turn their sleep into dull, infertile dreams.

# Chapter 8

The tinker's harbour was a half-hour walk from where the Realm survivors had been washed up, a tired slog along sea-licked dunes marking the forest's limits.

Red-beaked cormorants shrieked and dived over the town's anchorage, worrying netted fish piled across the boards of two fishing craft. The anchorage was almost empty, whatever fishing fleet the port possessed out on the waters. Narrow in her length, the largest craft docked was a three-masted packet, her stern graceful with carvings of seahorses and starfish. No fisherboat this, her gilded carvings pointed to a rich purse with a taste for decoration and luxury.

"What is the harbour's name?" said Taliesin.

The tinker shrugged. "Hey-ho, they all sound alike to me."

"Martyrs! So much for traveller's lore."

"Do you know any more about a place for the labelling of it?"

Coming onto narrow streets, the survivors of the Gogmagog drew suspicious and sometimes hostile stares. It was not that men had turned up dirty, desperate and unheralded. Their foreign uniforms played on the onlooker's fears. Never having travelled beyond the Princedoms, the Captain recognised the fear well enough. Tobymen, raiders and occupying armies were no less common on this side of the sea.

The harbourmen's apparel was also noted by the dragon-browns: fishermen going about their business armed, less wealthy citizens wearing knives, deadly thin scabbards dangling from swordbelts – duellists' weapons.

"These laddies are not too pleased to see us, if I'm any judge of character," said Connaire Mor.

"Do not be too insulted highlander," said Taliesin. "You can clean the seaweed off your sabre before you start making trouble here."

Passing a cluster of drinkers resting under the shade of a building, Finbar spotted a fellow brother in the robes of the Martyr. Finbar raised his arm to wave but the monk disappeared in the press of bodies.

"Mortal rude."

Taliesin moved the company on. "Even your own people don't want to get involved, priest."

Ahead of them a man stepped out to block their passage, bowing and sweeping off his hat, a dandy-like cavalier's coptain with a black feather stuck behind the brim.

"You make for a most queer sight, if I may say so."

Marking the two men behind the spokesmen, Taliesin saw they faced a party of sailors with flintlocks and cutlass.

"My tailor, he had an accident last year," Taliesin said, still walking forward.

"Hold there fellow."

Taliesin stopped as the sailors moved the flintlocks from their chests, dropping them level. Curled hair framed the speaker's pocked face, and he lowered one hand to the pig-sticker hanging from his ornamental shoulder belt.

"It's not good manners to walk off when someone's speaking to you."

"It was my tailor that tried to teach me manners. Some say that is why he had his accident."

"I believe your tailor may have died, fellow. You look as if you haven't changed clothes for a year."

Taliesin waved towards the sea. "That happens when your ship sinks. Why don't you recommend somewhere I can get a new coat, one with as many ribbon loops as yours. Is that a fashion over here?"

The speaker twitched his nose, ignoring the officer's impertinence. "Yes, I know about the sinking. There was a cornicle out last night, the fishermen heard the battle."

"Perhaps then, sir," Taliesin said, "you would be so good as to get out of our way. That is unless you have any more musings you would care to share with us."

Pock-face moved apologetically out of the group's way and gestured for them to continue, then at the last minute he twisted out his walking cane and blocked the path. "One thought does spring to mind now I come to think about it. Small matters of coincidence."

Taliesin stopped again.

"A deuced queer thing washed up last night."

His hat in hand, the speaker pointed towards the harbour front. Alongside one of the nets lay the Gogmagog's lupine figure-head, cracked, splintered, and almost charred beyond recognition.

"You see, it was only a short while ago that a ship with a figurehead just like that one was raiding my country's ships. But then, and this is the deuced coincidence, the Moon Queen's cousin married the Queen across the waters, and the attacks stopped."

"A lucky marriage," said Taliesin.

"Lucky for some, fellow, less lucky for others. But now, and here's another one of those dashed coincidences: there's a battle in the straits last night, and then this figurehead comes a-floating by here in the night. Followed this morning by your good self."

"Now those," he pointed to the five surviving sailors. "They look like the sort of scum that Bron used to crew his ship with. But you, you and your friends are cut in just the sort of gib noted on soldiers of the very same Queen across the waters we were just talking about."

"I knew if we travelled far enough we'd find a wise man," Taliesin said.

"Better travelled than you, one-eye."

Finbar pushed his way past the soldiers. "You're a man with a precious kind face, so I know you'll be eager to help a pitiful poor party of shipwrecked souls like ourselves. Just point us to the nearest coaching-inn, lad, and we'll be having no more talk of sinking ships and brigands and wickedness."

Behind pock-face, the two seamen began to pull back their puffer's flint heads. With experienced ease Taliesin read the signs in the speaker's eyes: the momentary glance backwards; the tightening pupil.

"If you can describe my face as kind, priest, you have drunk too much already. But I think we can manage to extend some of Roubaix's hospitality to you."

Before the last word had left his lips, Taliesin was moving. With the leader still in front of his men, Taliesin jerked one of Connaire Mor's knives out from his belt and lunged forward, crossing the distance like a whip. Pock-face's sailors were drawing their flintlocks around for a clear shot. Taliesin had the blade pressed close to their leader's throat.

Taliesin wrestled Pock-face around. "Neatly down, navy. Unless you've been paid in advance and don't mind me improving his face."

"The roof, fellow."

Taliesin looked up. From the harbour building roof, a row of light-cavalrymen in blue uniforms met his gaze, the octagonal barrels of their puffers pointing down at a sharp angle.

Pock-face broke free and adjusted his dandy-like hat. "You are deuced churlish, aren't you? We can't have you leaving Roubaix in such a poor state. I really think you should accompany me on my little trip to Roanne. You can explain your interesting choice of company to the authorities there."

Connaire Mor lent over to whisper. "You know, this devil is meaning to embarrass us."

Taliesin shook his head. "The Queen will not cough for the truth. Bugger this bastard. When word gets to Annan and she disowns us, they'll stretch all our necks for privateers."

Looking up at the blue uniforms and white facings, the tinker smiled. "Ceroliné."

"What's that old man?" asked Taliesin.

"They're the Queen's men, The Empire's Moon Queen that is."

"Does it matter?"

"But of course, everything matters. Do try and pay more attention."

Pock-face swaggered along the dock front, extra soldiers appearing behind Taliesin's men to shove the dragon-browns forward. "Being islanders, I expect you fellows won't appreciate the magnitude of your situation, or know the quality of the man you're facing. Suffice it to say that I am a person of some station in the Empire's matters of state. You are more than fortunate to have fallen into my hands, rather than those of the prefecture's militia."

"You're the courtier, Six dam Saldair," the tinker replied.

"Deuced if I haven't had a pedlar make a lie of my words. And who would you be, sir?"

The tinker pointed to the luxurious vessel bobbing in the harbour waters. "Just a humble fool. A pedlar travelled enough to recognise the crest of one of the Twelve Houses."

"Ah yes, of course, the ship. I need some solace sailing to the northern marches, the people there are nearly as low as you coves. Except being in the Empire they haven't the excuse for it."

"I have been meeting some peacocks in my time," Connaire Mor whispered to the tinker, "but this one has it practised."

"Don't let that donkey voice lead you into underestimating him. He is competent – one of the Moon Queen's stilettos, if you please."

Taliesin agreed. "Those men on the roof, he's no buggering fop. If he had put them on the ground we could have made a decent fight of it. He knows what he is doing, sure enough."

Rounding a corner, dam Saldair vaulted onto a slate-gray stallion, the soldiers following his lead, mounting alabaster piebalds which matched the colour of their uniforms' facings.

Disarmed, Taliesin's company were forced into a pair of empty haywain carts. Sitting on the boards, they were flanked by cavalry, watched by a brawny pair of turnkeys on the rider's mount. Each guard had a puffer with flared lips, brutal charges of nails, glass and stone packed down on top of the powder. At close quarters, it would be a cloud of flesh-ripping death if any of the dragon-browns made trouble.

Finbar wiped the beads of sweat from his forehead. "Ah, this is a grand old scrape. First my ship is smashed out from underneath my feet, then I'm pushed around the ocean like a spinning-jenny by a school of monstrous grinning fish, and now I'm marked for a pirate by that pock-faced devil, and a terrible step away from being walked down their wicked Execution Dock."

"You don't suppose these swining devils were the ones who sent us to the bottom?" Connaire Mor asked.

Taliesin scratched his face, still raw from the salt water. "No. They might have liked to have done it, but I'm dammed if I can see them having a craft like that bastard thing on wheels that did for us. Tinker, have you ever heard of a ship like that?"

"It is a bore, but I have never seen a ship like that before."

"I did not ask if you had seen a ship like it, I asked if you had heard of one."

The tinker looked up into the sky and Taliesin let the matter drop.

Crossing a small street market on the edge of the port, none of the Realmsmen noticed the priest who had fled from the company earlier. He was on a roof, carefully viewing the departing carts from the cover of drying washing. Satisfied they were leaving by the main road, the monk released a pigeon, morning light glinting from its bronze leg clip. A flutter of wings and it had disappeared into the firmament.

Passing the fishing port's gates, the two haywain carts clattered onto a cobbled road, diving into the dense press of the enchanted forests. Unlike the Realm, high stone ramparts enclosed the road at either side, small keeps and turnpikes – some manned, others crumbling into disrepair – the buildings marking the steady progress of their journey. As high as the walls were, the greenery always towered over, at times looking as if it was set to push the stone down and reclaim the toll-road.

"This is new," said the tinker, pointing at the ramparts. "They must be getting fancies of civilisation from someone."

Connaire Mor looked at the walls with interest. "Aye, it must be a piece of work to keep the forest from growing back again."

From beyond the battlements the scent of the wilderness filtered through, a constant reminder of the baleful forest's proximity. As if the act of closing her out had spurred her to haunt travellers with nature's presence, lush combinations of fern bouquets played across the wind.

Taliesin found the fragrance evocative, the play of scents teasing out half-forgotten memories from his childhood. An old blanket, the stroking warmth of a hand washed in rosewater, the lemon-flavoured drink cupped in the hands of a distant relative. He shook it off. His real childhood had been in the rookeries and violent twisting alleys of Lluddin, and though no estate gamekeeper, Taliesin knew the forest's scent could serve a crueller purpose.

There had been the war in Astolat, fighting Connaire Mor's mountain villages. A Logriese pioneer, picking his way through the impenetrable trees in his coat of velvet-soft deerskin. He had led Taliesin and a handful of dragon-browns to a clearing, pointing out the Butcher's company of missing soldiers.

They had been lying face down in a clearing of purple flowers, petals the size of small shields. Quite dead. But that smell, like apple blossom, the perfume of paradise itself.

"You've been in their capital before?" Taliesin addressed the tinker.

"Roanne? In passing."

"Well, are they likely to bloody string us up or not?"

The tinker sighed. "Better for us if they don't."

"Damn your eyes, tinker, you recognised pock-face from the crest on his ship. Who in the Martyr's name is he?"

"One of the twelve great families. Between them they have carved up the Empire. From his uniform, your admirer looks as if he is in the service of the Moon Queen, a station quite distinct from the King."

"Mortal me, but you're not saying that with much blessed faith," noted Finbar.

"Annan's husband, Talon, he's a cousin of the Moon Queen. The Queen here and Talon were *very* close, if you please. After Roubaix's new King married Céroline, he made a point of removing Talon by packing him off to the Realm for a loveless marriage of state. The King claimed he needed to secure his coast from the Realm, but knowing how much Talon hated us, he probably would have packed

Talon off to the islands anyway."

"Pock-face is bringing us in to gain favour with this bitch, then," said Taliesin. "And if she is still sulking about the fact her lover's married to our Queen, she's not going to be overworried about sparing Annan or ourselves face."

"Hey-ho, she does not sulk. She is like your pedigreed poodle over there. The Moon Queen might act the ingenuous girl on the outside, but inside there lies a heart of refined crystal."

Finbar moaned. "Dear life, this is a wicked situation. Caught like flies in their wicked web of ambition. The Realm will forget all that Bron and his men of courage did for the Crown when these devils drag us in front of their terrible naval court. Annan Pendrag will be all for letting these miserable sinners send my poor head back home in a sack."

The tinker shrugged again. "Maybe yes, and maybe no. But the Realm and Roubaix stand close on one matter – if a faction tries to stretch us, there will be a dozen others plotting to get us out, to spite the Moon Queen's people just on principle."

"This is the Empire, man, not the Princedoms."

The tinker looked at Connaire Mor. "No Ruri-Princes, but a fair few families have taken turns at being *Laird* of the manor, if you understand me. And there are a good few more waiting in the wings for the next act."

When the wagons and their escort broke out onto tableland, the sun had drifted up towards its afternoon zenith. Her light was harsh and sharp, making angular shadows of the fences and ditches, barb-edged shadows quite different to the diffuse filtered shade of the Realm.

Burnt stubble around the wood's beard hinted at the expansion of man's domain in Roubaix, well-irrigated fields running right up to the forest's edge, although there was little sign of anyone tilling the land.

Thatched cottages began to dot a landscape of low rolling hills, shabbier than the farms of the Realm, houses obviously poor despite the profusion of good agricultural land. In the distance, walls enclosed what looked like substantial estates, and the Captain did not have to guess to see where the kingdom's affluence was concentrated. Landowners and rich nobles, safeguarding their rights with gamekeepers, iron traps, and floggings for those that trespassed.

Connaire Mor noted the wealth. "Man, you could feed the highlands with a half of the crops they're raising here."

"Lad, you head for where the sun rises and they say the land treats her people like precious Kings," said Finbar.

The tinker snorted. "Travel there to get lost, if you have a soul to be stolen away in the Frost."

"Let's not be making ditties of the darkness and the shadow now, sure and no good will come out of it." Finbar made the sign of the Martyr on the tree.

"Old soak's tales," said the Captain. "The other lands are no better or worse than ours. Just farther away. I'll wager there are mothers in far lands that scare their children with stories of how bloody awful it is to live on islands surrounded by the Cold Sea."

In answer to this, the old tinker began to croon a pedlar's ballad.

*"In the land of the shadow*
*Pepin the short lost his bow*
*Laid low after the darkfall*
*Then came Lexrolf and said make me a wall*
*Oh veni, vidi, vici."*

Some of the sailors picked up on the song, the brawny pair of oversized thugs on the front boards scowling at the tinker. Prisoners in his situation were not expected to be as carefree as the garishly dressed old man.

Rounding the curve of one of the hills, their road slipped downslope in a long lazy curve. The city of Roanne in the distance.

Spotting the capital, Connaire Mor looked up in surprise. "We're only coming back to the swining sea again."

Six dam Saldair rode by, his elaborately curled hair jouncing as the slate-gray stallion reigned in. "Sea! You dashed fool. This is the lake country, have you never heard of the majesty of the Watered City? The City of Isles?"

"Don't be daft. Before I fell in with this pack of thieves, Logriese was as far foreign as I had a care to visit."

Six dam Saldair shook his head. "If your barbaric country ever united, you would be quite a threat, sir."

Given its scale, confusing the lake for the ocean was a common mistake for visitors to make. There may have been no tang of brine or circling stain of gulls on their approach, but pristine waters lifted out to the horizon in a clear, fan-like sweep, an immense weight of water.

Roanne was set along a series of islands dusted across the lake like stepping stones; many isles not big enough to support a single street of houses, others miniature peninsulas; overflowing with warehouses, tanneries, taverns, merchant houses and royal government buildings. With nothing to compare it to save cramped Realm streets in the mould of Llud-din and Camlan, the foreign architecture appeared generously noble and spacious. Only on narrow bridges – crisscrossing the islands in a plait as complex as their captor's wig – did the buildings begin to knot into each other in the familiar way.

Sitting up in the cart, the tinker nodded to himself. "Take a boat out on a cloudless day and you can sometimes mark the ruins at the bottom of the lake. Unhappy luck, if it's fish you want to take."

"The Sunken Empire," whispered one of the soldiers.

"I haven't a map in my possession, but I believe you will

still find that that lies at the bottom of the sea, not a lake," said the tinker.

Heading towards the nearest of the crowded bridges, they heard a cry from the houses lining the causeway. Six dam Saldair stood up in his saddle and stared at the red-coated figures pouring out onto the bridge's span.

"Damn the fellow, Buonapar, Buonapar!"

Hearing the nobleman's warning, his squadron of light cavalry wheeled their mounts away from the bridge. The turnkeys on Taliesin's cart lashed the whips down on their straining shire horses. Twisting about on two wheels, the draught horses nearly pulled the haywain cart over in their desperation to turn, the prisoners sliding across the boards as they took a turn of speed which would have done a charge of dragoons proud.

Taliesin grabbed onto a handhold. "Martyr's teeth. What was that he was screaming?"

"Buonapar's the King," shouted the old tinker. "And given the sudden departure, I would say our self-serving noble had not counted on the royal army holding that bridge."

"I thought these dogs were the royal army!"

Billowing in the rush of flight, the tinker's patchwork cloak made him look like a rainbow-coloured crow struggling for a perch. "They are the Moon Queen's royal guard, and in this Empire, that is something else again. It is not illegal to keep private forces, in fact they are positively encouraged."

"Martyrs," Connaire Mor looked back at the pursuit. "Aye and Emrys only took the clans to the slaughter for the same."

The tinker jolted into the air as the haywain took a furrow. "If it is any consolation, you will find this sort of incident is usually the result. Most of Roanne's prefects are one step removed from brigands, although your noble friend would as like have it as a mark of their political sophistication."

"This Buonapar, pedlar," said Taliesin. "I trust our turn of speed indicates the King does not see eye to eye with his wife."

"Hardly. The circumstances of his marriage to the Moon Queen were less than cordial – somewhat strained you might say. But judging by the improved state of the tollroads, not to mention our current bout of exercise, my guess is that Buonapar's star is definitely on the rise."

Finbar clutched on to his plain habit for dear life. "So now we are being run out by a pack of hounds fighting among themselves. It is a precious sad state of affairs we have fallen to, so it is."

Without horses, their pursuers quickly lost ground. Forced with the choice of continuing a fruitless chase or abandoning their post, the royal redcoats slowed to a stop by the lake's bank, then began walking back to the bridge.

Six Dam Saldair slewed his slate-gray mount around in fury, slicing the air with his gentleman's pig-sticker. "I'll have a head for this. Damn it to hell, that deuced bridge has always been the province of the royal guard."

One of Saldair's mounted soldiers cantered alongside. "All-hallow bridge sir, that'll still be ours."

"It had better be. Damn it all, Buonapar will know we have arrived back now. All those extra days at sea so we could use a discreet port, I could as well have used the main road and ridden a gold-plated carriage for the same effect."

Cursing fate's cruel nature, Six dam Saldair's two cavalry-flanked haywains sheered around the lakes, detouring the waters in favour of a more peaceful entry to the City of Isles. Taliesin and his fellow prisoners sat out the remainder of their journey in silence.

The hangman victim's deathly hush.

# Chapter 9

Blinding sun stung Gunnar awake. But he was not facing
the sky, it was the sea, dawn transforming the black
wastes of the previous night into an undulating plain of
glints and glitters. Light-headed, Gunnar inclined his neck
to look at his fellow passenger of fortune.

She was awake before him. "Why didn't you come and
hold me last night, I was cold?"

"Would I still have the use of both my eyes if I had
tried?"

She smiled. "Does that mean you aren't going to hit me
again?"

"I wouldn't have hit you if I had known it was you in the
first place; even after you tried to put a dent in my nose."

Elaine dragged herself to the other side of the raft with as
much allure as she could muster. In the circumstances
Gunnar had to bite his tongue to stop himself laughing.

"Do you find that funny?"

"I have just never seen a lesson in deportment carried out
on a handful of barrels lashed together in the middle of a
sea before."

She felt his face. "Such a nice nose too. I hope I didn't
hurt it too much."

"I have to say you did. Where in the Realm did you learn
to punch that hard?"

Elaine laughed. "The Countess of Aneiddylad taught me.
I think she had a less satisfactory childhood than I."

"Elaine, everyone had a less satisfactory childhood than
you."

She shrugged her shoulders. "I'm so hungry, I don't
think I have ever been this hungry before. And thirsty.
Martyrs, I promise I shall never complain about what I eat

again, not as long as I live."

"Don't drink the seawater," Gunnar told her. "It will only make your thirst worse, much worse." He did not disturb her with the source of his information. All those tales. Shipwrecked survivors lunching on each other during their last fevered days. Surely they would have killed themselves before it had come to that?

Rummaging through one of his uniform's worn leather pouches, the soldier withdrew a hook. "The Butcher's idea of living off the land usually consists of stealing some old cotter's poultry, but this works for the river fish. I doubt if the ones out here are that different."

"Fish, I loathe fish. There's not even any sauce to make it bearable."

"Well, there's one thing that I can guarantee you, I won't be ruffling any chickens out here."

Before his mouth had closed, the obvious struck the Realmsman like a roll of thunder.

He had unclipped his sabre the night before, its weight adding to the terrible exhaustion of staying afloat, but he still had his muzzle-sword. Elaine looked at him as if he might have sunstroke as he brandished the dagger-sized weapon.

"What?"

Gunnar rapped the blade on one of the barrels – already splitting apart with damp. Cracking the weakened staves, splinters and oak fragments stabbed at his sun-raw skin as the wood broke apart. He reached in, drawing out a fist of salted jerky wrapped in waxy-brown paper. For the first time since they sailed, Gunnar was glad that their secret passage had been arranged on a privateer's vessel, not a Realm ship-of-the-line. This was one of the reasons why all sane sailors sailed with merchanteers like his father, having to be press-ganged into royal service. By the time the Victualling Board, a ship's Purser and the Port Master had all creamed off their illegal profits from short-measures and fouled meat, the navy crews would be lucky for a ration of slimy butter, maggoty cheese and loaves so hard sailors carved them like wood.

"Sweet rapture." Elaine took the bundle as Gunnar broke holes in the remaining barrels, limiting the size so no sudden waves would send them the way of their last vessel. They found cured sides of beef, powder for the Gogmagog's culverin, and oatmeal, but no drinking water. How long could they last without water? Their throats were as dry as parchment already. Damn the salt air.

Gunnar carved himself strips of leathery beef to chew while he pondered their situation. They had passed through the worst of the straits – if the Gogmagog had sunk before the passage narrowed into its steaming, foamy cauldron, then they would have been feeding the fishes for the last day or two. These currents must be pulling them towards one side or the other – if they could only last out until they spied some coast. His years spent carousing and gambling were looking as wasted as his dear father had always reminded him they would be. Gladly he would now swap at least *one* of those happy years for the skills of navigation by kamal and astrolabe, or to know if this part of the sea had a storm season.

Elaine seemed unperturbed at their situation and Gunnar wondered what had become of the light-hearted dandy who had stepped onto the ship at Emrys. He had faced death dozens of times before – on the battlefield, the duelling grass, even in the occasional bedroom – and always with an arrogance that made friends speculate Milady Chance must surely owe him some sizeable card debt. But then the triumph of cheating life out of her ultimate victory, with a grin on his face and sabre in his hand, it all seemed such a long way removed from this distanceless, sun-dancing wilderness.

With dusk drawing slowly across the sky, the pair

watched while the sun sank, enflaming the sea in carmine colours before night claimed her realm. Then – in the dusk ahead of them – a flash.

Gunnar looked again. A twinkle. But it was no star. Elaine saw it and cried out too, her throat rusty with dryness. "That's a lantern. Oh Martyrs, let it be land."

"It can't be land. We would see the shadow of the headland. A boat, it has to be a boat."

His flintbox had been the first thing the soldier had left out in the sun to dry off, and now he ripped a strip of parched cloth from his expensive silk shirt. It burnt with a sizzling that put him in mind of a rasher of bacon.

Whatever the light was, it was growing larger, phantom silhouettes flickering across the darkening sea as it neared. Closer still.

Lantern light played across the shape of a nodding ship, the lamp swinging from a small fishing mast.

Thrusting itself over the side, a heavily bearded face looked them over. "Kalknorr has seen far better ways to travel, if you do not mind him saying."

"I have been in some of them too," Gunnar said. "May we come aboard?"

"I think you will not be lasting so long if you are staying."

The man called Kalknorr threw some nets over the side and Gunnar scrambled up them, Elaine leading the way above his head, where necessary using his shoulder as bracing.

Once aboard, Gunnar's racking cough returned and he waited for breath to come back. "We can't be the only ones who are lost; this, it is a cold water sea ship isn't it?"

"Eyes are good," said the tall, bear-broad man. "Skella mountains saw me born, but I am preferring the sun and heat. Unfortunate, don't you think? All that ice and snow, when my heart likes it more in a land like Lériddas."

"Lériddas – Martyr's teeth, yes that was the name of the

place our wines came from. Are we near there?"

Kalknorr scratched his straggly blonde mane. "You were floating out into the Enclosed Sea. Not a nice place anymore, if it ever was being so. Pirates from Gliarin; pirates from Taranto; *Wa'a Kaulua* raiders from the Princes of the Sand – better places are there to be than there."

Elaine seemed willing not to dispute the point. "You do not seem over-worried at that prospect."

Their saviour roared with laughter, his big chest expanding as if it was being filled by a smith's bellows. Kalknorr lifted up a slimy silver fish, still convulsing after being grounded. "Pretty lady, my treasure is not being so very attractive, you see. Besides this, the warm sun is not the only reason I am preferring this land."

He pointed to a strangely curved axe fixed to the wall of his hut-like wheel room. "From better days, before the *Althing* decided they did not like my company so very much and pressed their point harder than an honest man was expecting. Come, the winds are turning now. Help will be good, this boat is meant for two, but my partner was coming to an unfortunate end."

"How so? Gunnar asked.

"He was cunning with me. Selling our fish for more than he was telling me. But I mourn his memory sometimes, so that the all-father will see he does not go as hungry as he sure deserves in the Great Hall."

Excitedly, Elaine drew Gunnar aside before he could voice his commiserations over the ex-partners sharp trading practices. "Lériddas, listen sir, if we are going there, one of my aunts married an envoy from that land – Sanco Tal Hasteel."

"An uncle," Gunnar was surprised. "I trust the fact that they married at all is an indication that he owns a good portion of the estates there."

Elaine nodded. "It's simply perfect. He's rich enough to pay for us to get home. He also dislikes the rest of my family enough to not care about spiting them. They have always looked down their noses at his foreign titles, and with the exception of my aunt, he thinks everyone on the islands are rain-drenched barbarians. It is a delicious irony."

With a fresh spring in her step she approached the weather-worn fisherman. "Would you be passing though the city of Cuenns on your voyages, kindly Kalknorr?"

He laughed. "Kindly Kalknorr. I think you are trying to influence me, eh? But I go to Cuenns anyway, prices are high in the capital so I live in village port mostly – but to sell the catch, prices high also, you see."

Even in the darkness of late evening Gunnar could see that Kalknorr was not berthing at the coast. They followed a river from a wide bay, surrounded on both sides by a marshy form of the tumble, towering above them but occasionally slashed back from stockaded villages. These houses rose on stilts, the porridge-like marsh encroaching underneath; at times it was difficult to see where the marshland began and the river ended.

Listening to the jarringly unfamiliar chorus of marsh creatures, Gunnar gazed at their navigator. Kalknorr guessed what was on his mind. "Your cities surrounded by weirdwoods, yes? I have travelled to southlands and there they live with sand wastes that would be stripping meat off your bones in less than an hour. But this sure is the way to the capital, right enough. And here it is like this, but all the same, yes? Wild. Death for those that do not know clever ways. It is the all-father's punishment for the evil of the old ones. They even are having a special word for it here – *hubris*. This is why Kalknorr know my people prefer the sea. She is more honest with us, it is more easy to understand her hardness."

Waiting while the huge north-man worked their single billowing sail, Gunnar saw they were steadily drifting into an open stretch of waters, clearer and less muddied by the surrounding marsh-tumble.

Ahead of them, a string of lanterns climbed out of the waters, gently curving along the top of a massive stone wall. It was capped by defensive crenellations, and Gunnar could just make out the iron mouths of culverin pointing through the stone teeth, sentry shadows pacing the ramparts.

Now he saw why the capital was located here. Between the marsh-like tumble and the surrounding waters, there would have been few successful sieges in the history of Cuenns. Even if he had been sailing in here on the Gogmagog – and he in her crow's nest – the Realmsman would not have been able to see over the elevation of the towering white wall. But what lay sealed off on the other side of the imposing bulwark?

Docks jutted from the fortification, small cogs and shallow-water galleys moored on the wooden piers. Showing a thoughtfulness which Gunnar suspected was uncharacteristic, Elaine insisted that they help Kalknorr unload his wicker baskets teeming with landed fish. They piled them onto the cracked docks, an official Kalknorr recognised arriving to wave a lantern over the load. He wore a cockade hat with a green uniform, and having counted the baskets the man grunted, strolled back towards a moon-washed building built into the quay.

"Skella, Lériddas, headman wants taxes the same wherever you travel, yes? Kalknorr first out, last back. I tell you, these people are not knowing how to fish. Sun good for old bones like me, but for the growing of your children, it just makes them lazy and cunning."

Bare-breasted carriers in cotton trousers came across to carry Kalknorr's fish away, and the northman led his other strange catch of the evening towards the gate at the end of the wall. It was guarded by a soldier in a white uniform with red facings – bored in the extreme – the mustached guard flicking a collection of pebbles towards the night waters. He looked barely better shaven than Gunnar after two days on the open sea. The Realmsman surmised there was little danger of them being challenged.

"There is no curfew on the gates here?" Elaine asked.

Kalknorr shrugged. "Here? Why? There are troubles in the south, but that is where they seem to be staying. My God better than your God – who cares? Drink and be great, my Carl-priest used to be saying. Good advice, eh?"

The stairwell beyond the gate led them higher through the interior of the wall, emerging on top of the ramparts, a cool night breeze playing across their faces. The drop on the other side was considerably greater than Gunnar had been expecting, falling straight down to the floor of a valley – Cuenns's wall built on the crest of the surrounding headland. It was like a fortified dike, holding back the wild marsh and her waters.

Below, white-roofed buildings slouched across the basin, the yellow flicker of oil-lamps frosted behind the windows. Their rampart was wide, but the couple could peer over and straight down the rocky precipice. Vines grew up the rough rockface, though Gunnar would not care to risk their fate on a climb down them.

"Is good, yes? Sure no marshes down there."

What looked to be a wooden barn loomed over the side of the wall, and it was to this the northman led them. Inside, another soldier in an identical white uniform lounged across a wheel. A team of donkeys harnessed to the wooden cogwheel glanced resentfully in their direction. Kalknorr threw him a cloth-wrapped parcel and the soldier replied with the ancient thumbs-up sign, waving them onto the hoist platform.

"He be keeping his pretty lady happy with a little extra food on their table. You learn this about this city, you not be paying too many coins, when the favours you do for the right people!"

Leaving the creaking of the barn-wheel behind, they descended towards the valley, the weighty platform holding steady in the calm night, each corner held by a length of rope the width of the northman's bull-like chest. Finally it jerked to a stop in an empty square, the plaza surrounded by empty sow pens and strawdust for unloading livestock.

Waving aside Elaine's offer to see her aunt and uncle repay him, the unassuming Kalknorr pointed them in the direction of the most affluent area of the city then roved off into the night, telling them the inn he was staying at and they could see him there, and perhaps get the good Sanco to pay off his bar account.

Elaine's uncle might have been startled at their unannounced appearance, but Gunnar was equally surprised by the foreign nobleman. He had been expecting to be greeted by a tanned, senatorial politician with steely-silver hair, not the languid, almost effeminate man his servants eventually brought to the door. Tal Hasteel looked at the dishevelled sea-soaked pair in front of them and laughed.

"My life has been dedicated to the avoidance of trouble," said Tal Hasteel. "So it is cursed funny how much I run into."

Ushering them into an immense drinking room, his family arms set in stone above the fireplace, Elaine's uncle slumped into a leather couch, his thin wasted face watching them with an alert curiosity.

"Such a pity that your aunt is visiting her friends out in the plantations. She misses your frosty wet islands terribly, maybe we will send for her before you leave."

With elegant gestures and amusing digressions, the foreign nobleman drew their story out from them, Gunnar omitting only the real reason for their voyage. Apart from himself, only Taliesin, Connaire Mor and Bron had known the object of their mission – with their bloated corpses feeding the sea-devils by now. The dandy doubted Annan Pendrag would prove very forgiving should her secret be leaked to this strange foreign court.

Hasteel smiled, his piercing eyes glittering as if he knew that the young Realmsman was leaving out the important part of the story. When the unkempt couple came to their description of the terrible ship on wheels, Tal Hasteel could barely conceal his interest – although it was clear he did not want to make his attention too evident to his unexpected guests.

As Elaine had predicted, the Sanco applauded her acts of mischief, blown into the proportions of a romantic epic by her storytelling. "Ah yes indeed, you should live with passion when you are young, my dove. It is gone soon enough when the obligations of rank pass onto your shoulders."

Pausing while retainers brought them in warm wine which smelt pleasantly of oak casks, Tal Hasteel pointed towards a painting on the wall. It was the elegantly wasted nobleman in the full flush of youth, wearing one of the white uniforms which seemed the general pattern in his nation. "Such passions I lived. Before my father died I had seen a dozen lands in the Queen's service, burned a Wa'a Kaulua warfleet off the infidels' coast, driven those silver-grabbing bastards in Zamarere all the way back across their mountains. Now look at this old shell, the most exciting decision I made last year was where to invest the rents from the farms, my most dangerous adventure when I forgot to attend the Royal Promenade and the Queen thought I was insulting her new lover."

Elaine beamed at Tal Hasteel. "I am sure it is not so terrible to grow as wise as you are, uncle."

He smiled courteously. "But I am a terrible host. After all you have been through, my poor dove. I shall have my people run you a full bath and you must pick some of your aunt's clothes before we go out to buy you some new ones tomorrow. And you, young man, even before your impromptu immersion, your uniform would have been quite ordinary. How your Princes ever saw fit to drape their officers in such plain cloth I could never understand. Here, even our Sergeants look as if they were Marshals, men of courage have to be proud to fight!"

Gunnar's suspicions that the lure of a bath was a ploy to remove Elaine from the conversation proved correct. Leaning his thin frame forward after Elaine had shut the door, his rascal-eyes shimmered in the candle light.

"You would wish for an exit undistracted by the preoccupations of my niece."

"You are indeed a man of discretion, Sanco Tal Hasteel."

"Of course," Tal Hasteel lifted his crystal glass to the light. "Such a beauty as my niece's would not be greatly improved by sabre scars or a battlefield amputation. I am not properly apprised of what you are about, but as it is, I am sure my brother-in-law will call you out when you return home. You have not exactly, how shall I phrase it, observed the proprieties in relation to her."

Gunnar shrugged.

"Yes, her father is a most tiresome man. The problems I had marrying my wife. Ha, if he was in this land I could buy him, his estates and his esteemed noble lineage thrice over. Do they still duel with pistols over there? It makes both sides so equal. An insufficiency of skill and artistry. But how very, very, sporting."

Gunnar finished his measure of wine.

"Still, I am sure it won't come to that. Unless your patron is well placed, I doubt if they would wish for the publicity of – what do you call it – grass before breakfast? A couple of peasants with garrotes would be more that family's style."

"As you say, I'm sure it will not come to that." Gunnar laughed. "I would be very appreciative it if you would accept a letter of credit to aid me on my way."

"Such absurdity, I have enough Realm angels in my coffers to bribe your Arch-Truron to convert to ancestor worship. And I shall also lend you one of my ships, it will be humble, something discreet and hardly worth the attentions of a corsair. There are many pirates on the Enclosed Sea, profiting I am sad to admit from my good business sense. I would say to lose one ship beneath your feet would be careless – where as to lose two would be an act of consequential ineptness."

"You are a generous man, sir."

Tal Hasteel humbly motioned away the young Realmsman's acknowledgement. "I shall have one of my people bring back an appropriate description of my dear brother-in-law's reaction when I return his missing daughter to him. That will be repayment enough."

The clear light of Cuenns appeared almost crystalline in comparison to the yellow-green daybreaks of the islands; shadows so intense they were barbed, the air transparent and febrile under an unwavering sun. The shadows falling off the valley cliffs and dike-like ramparts were not the gray of the Realm, they were cast as black as a pit of Old Shadow.

They rose with the sun to find the streets outside already full of peons in chalky shirts and flowing dresses. Gunnar was now dressed in a similar manner, though not in the baroque white uniform that his host had tried to press on him, he wanted to blend in with the scenery, not have every foreign officer in the kingdom saluting him. His dirty brown jacket was packed away. Somehow he could not bring himself to leave it behind; a uniform which had survived so many battles. Lucky cloth.

Gunnar was planning to leave through the gardens to the rear of Tal Hasteel's large manse, and the noble waited for him on his porch, fingering his pony-tail while another of the badly shaven manservants lingered by his side – Gunnar's guide to the Sanco's private pier.

"Tell Elaine I said sorry."

Tal Hasteel nodded. "I would tell you something too,

before you go. Sometimes in life you have to see in which direction the wind is blowing and make a choice. That is if you want everything you have built in your life to survive you. One day, when you are older and have greater weights on your shoulders you may understand this."

Gunnar was not sure what the wasted nobleman meant by his remark, but he nodded amiably and looked towards the manservant.

While being led through the streets, the Realmsman kept a weather eye open for their saviour of the night before. But then Gunnar realised that the northman-in-exile would probably be out fishing again by now. He deserved to have been repaid in a more proper fashion. True to the Sanco's word, a small leather sack full of Realm angels sat in Gunnar's pocket, and if the locals did not recognise the head of Annan Pendrag, then they would at least appreciate the high-based silver it was stamped on.

It might have been the pure clear sunshine pouring down, but for the first time for many years Gunnar felt free again. All the killers and toppers that were hunting him in the Realm were an ocean away; his wealthy family and their chains of duty; the army he had disappeared into; the offended husbands and the scorned women. All dissipated in the haze of this pleasant land.

Gunnar hummed a tune and pondered his circumstances. There was no harm in sailing to Sombor. From what scurrilous gossip had trickled down to him in the streets and bawdy houses he frequented, the Queen's younger sister was the sort to fall in and out of love on the sweep of a courtier's cap. The only out of character part of the tale Taliesin had brought back was that the young lady had stayed besotted with her foreign lover long enough to have fled with him in the first place.

Perhaps he might try to enlist with Sombor's palace guard and do a little sweeping off his feet himself. And if Princess Ariane's new husband was still in the first flushes of the dangerously protective stage of their marriage? Well, there had been hundreds of principalities and kingdoms on his tutor's dusty globe – experiences enough for an enterprising young buck who had suddenly regained his anonymity. Fresh faces aplenty, with no idea of his reputation at the gaming table or his good standing with Milady Chance.

Gunnar's mental revelries were interrupted by his ill-shaven colleague. Looking around, the dandy found they were in a square under the shadow of the valley walls. Not the one they had been lowered into on the previous night. Now they were surrounded by warehouses, white-washed brick in the simple style of architecture favoured by the Lériddians.

Carts stacked with barrels of pickled fruit and vegetables rolled past, Gunnar gazing astonished at what he first took to be horses. The creatures pulling the carts resembled bulls, but far more muscled than any seen back in the Realm, thorny plates stretching down their black hind-quarters. Oblivious to the grotesque beasts of burden, his guide mumbled and pointed to the hoist.

Lifted up with bales of flax and hemp, they were raised to the parapet encircling the valley. On the other side lay the shorter drop to the swampy waters and beyond that, the dense interior of the bogs.

Tal Hasteel's private pier rose up on thick wooden columns, a number of small vessels moored to its side, licking against the water in the wall's shadow. Gunnar strolled down the planking, looking over the boats. Where was his cursed guide? He turned around. "Well then, sir. Will you tell me which one is to be ours?"

The man shook his head. "No."

A heavy docking-pin slammed down across the Realmsman's head and Gunnar pitched into the porridge-thick waters, the shock of the scum failing to revive him.

# Chapter 10

Roanne's hospitality consisted of a seven man cell, a musty atmosphere further polluted by the unpleasant reek of sour vinegar. If it had not been for traces of blood on the straw, Taliesin would have sworn the city's prison had recently been given over to storage of Finbar's wicked grape.

Warmed only by shadows, the damp survivors of the sinking had been infected with a funeral mood. "It smells like the last bugger emptied his guts over here."

A dragon-brown turned on the complaining sailor. "How many more times are you going to say that, scroat?"

"Until I'm out of here, landy. You too busy to listen to me now?"

Taliesin rammed a boot into the soldier's calf as he jumped up to threaten the mariner. "Martyr's sake, can't you wait for the noose? You have to have a bloody go at each other in here as well?"

"You're no doing any good, man," Connaire Mor said to the soldier. "If we are for getting out of here, you just save it for Pock-face and his friends."

Pacing, Taliesin went to gaze out of the small barred grill, the only window they had on the outside world. Across the dingy corridor he could see the door where the tinker and the remaining prisoners were being held. Connaire Mor had matched his considerable bulk against their bars earlier, the metal so rusted Taliesin had been amazed at the door's resilience. Perspiration had soaked the highlander, tendons and veins bunching out of his muscles like purple cables, but the wasted door had moved not a jot

– it was as if metal sediment had ossified in the portal.

From out of the gloom they heard approaching footsteps, then the copper glow of a lantern bobbing and swinging in the half-light.

A voice carried ahead. Not one that Taliesin recognised, certainly not the last one he had heard down the corridors – the donkey-like braying of the Moon Queen's fop, Six dam Saldair.

"Oh dear me, down here is it?"

Flanked by a pair of thuggish jailors, a stooped figure walked towards their cell, orange light glinting off the little man's octagonal eye-glasses. Taliesin had seen a similar pair on a tallyman who had lived above him in Llud-din's slum lofts.

He peered in through the grill, most of Taliesin's cell mates on their feet at the sudden break in the monotony. "This is it. Yes it is."

Taking a stubby set of keys tied to his belt, the taller of the jailors reached out to jam a key into the dragon-browns' lock. They did not seem pleased, and the officer wondered what it was that could possibly have upset the pair of sour and surly bruisers.

"Come, come," beckoned the stooped man, their door rasping open and sending a thin shower of red dust onto the floor. "Out you go."

Finbar was the first to waddle out of the cell. "Show us a little of the Martyr's mercy, we're not ready to have our necks stretched like mortal chickens yet."

On the opposite side of the corridor, the tinker and the others emerged, blinking in the sudden torchlight.

"Oh dear, this isn't an execution you know. No, no. Not at all. You are quite free to go, every one of you."

"What is this?" Taliesin commanded. "Some Martyr-buggered game of Six dam Saldair's to wear our nerves down?"

The stooped man shook his head. "Six dam Saldair is a rash man, quite injudicious, you have our apologies. You will be the guests of the Moon Queen. She has commanded it be so."

Connaire Mor moved forward. "So she's been saying this to – "

"Of course she did, I am her majesty's chamberlain. You must know that your own Queen is a relative of our most glorious majesty; you will be received as if you were members of her majesty's own loyal household, there's no reason why you should not."

Taliesin bit back explaining they had already had a taste of her family's welcome earlier on in the day. "We are free to leave the capital?"

"Yes, oh dear, well the Moon Queen has dispatched a courier to the Realm with news of your vessel running aground. I expect word and instructions will arrive back from your mistress in a little over four days. Until then, provisions have been made for you to stay in the town – though you really should remain inside the departments where peace is kept by the Moon Queen. Beyond that part of the city it can be, well, quite difficult to predict how our people will react to your presence."

Taliesin looked at the Moon Queen's chamberlain with undisguised suspicion. "Weapons."

"Pardon me?"

"Our sabres and the puffers taken from us. Every officer who has sworn a parole is allowed to keep his sword, and from what I saw of this city, we will need them."

Flustered by Taliesin's words, the chamberlain looked indecisive. "Well it is, that is to say her majesty said nothing of the matter. But if they are yours, then I dare say they will be returned to you. It is quite safe though, quite safe, as long as you stay within the boundaries of the Moon Queen's territory. Only outside will you be in danger."

Sitting in a palatial throne hall which perfectly matched the affluent robes of its owner, the Ecclesiarch of Roubaix pondered the message which the Martyr had seen fit to deliver into his hands. It was a terse communication, but then one did not expect carrier pigeons to carry manuscripts. It failed to bother Thibaudeau. Unlike some of the other Princes of the Church, he valued brevity. Sermons were for the masses, that and the duty to provide his coffers with the tithes which kept him in power.

Thibaudeau beckoned one of his clerics to approach the throne.

"Your holiness."

"These are definitely the men our brothers in the Realm sent word of?"

Fighting the urge to shrug, the priest bowed his head slightly. "Indeed your holiness."

"It may suit our Realm brother's purposes to have these men fail Annan Pendrag, but will it serve our ends? That is the question ..."

The cleric bowed humbly. "With only the distance of their meagre territories to care for, the islands have long been united under the true faith. As the late King's demise should remind us, it is in our land where the good struggle is being waged, not over there. The Arch-Truron cares not what his Queen's men are about, he only knows if they do not succeed, their Queen will be a distance farther from uniting the Realm under her own hand."

"What we need," Thibaudeau decided, "is to know what that devious bitch Pendrag's real business is. We owe our brothers little, the Realm's church has grown fat and idle in spirit; let the island Queen rise high to challenge their unity; let Annan shock the Arch-Truron from his complacency. It will provide our brothers with a reminder of the tests we face weekly."

"Just so, your eminence."

Thibaudeau waved forward one of his Hospitaliers. The clean-shaven warrior came to the throne and dropped to his left knee, his body washed in a chromatic scale by the illumination of the Ecclesiarch's stained-glass ceiling. On Thibaudeau's command, the knight of the Martyr rose again, the red fish revealed on his surcoat. A wickedly familiar sight if Finbar had been there to see it.

"Take your Order, Misamal, be my eyes, find out what the bitch Queen has planned for her captives. And see if Buonapar's knives know of their presence yet. We must discover our position in this web, only then we shall know how the Martyr's will is to be interpreted."

Misamal's almost transparent green eyes dipped to the floor, a gesture the Ecclesiarch recognised as a sign the humble warrior had a further question.

"Speak."

"To do this we will need to enter the lanes controlled by the Moon Queen's guard."

Typically, the unassuming warrior had made it sound as much a statement as a question.

"Misamal, we are not a Count's household, to be limited to the boundaries of territories and tollways. Our peoples' need for salvation is not so limited, and neither must be the Martyr's hand."

"Father, may these hands and eyes prove worthy of your trust."

Thibaudeau nodded and turned back to his court of clerics. He found the intricacies of the great game far more interesting than the tedious dogma he had to feed his fanatics.

Finbar's views on the party's new accommodation was an accurate summary of all the Gogmagog's survivors. "A better class of blessed floor altogether. Any wicked smell of vomit here will sure and be our own."

Their rooms were in the August Kin, an inn on an island of three streets; at the heart of the department of Roanne the Moon Queen's armsmen claimed responsibility for.

Soon after their unexpected release, Taliesin gathered the survivors together and put to them Annan Pendrag's offer. Then the choice: make their own way back to the Realm, or travel on by their own means.

Unsurprisingly, the hardest inquisitor was the foul-mouthed hunchback, Laetha.

"So we're stealing something back for the slut on the throne then, eh. What do we get out of it? A pissing pension and the joy of going back to the army?"

"Money," Taliesin said simply. "Enough gold angels to buy yourself out of the Crown's press and onto your own farm, or to idle your final years away in a bawdy house."

"And what if we decide to keep what the Queen wants us to steal? Sell it for ourselves?"

"Then either way, you can spend your rotten little dotage wenching and drinking coaching-inns dry back in the Realm."

Laetha laughed. "You are a canny bastard, Taliesin. You might have tricked those royal idiots into paying you a Captain's coin, but you still think like a rookery cut-purse all the same. But you tell me this, if the Queen wants us to go across half the sodding globe to rip some treasure from a local Ruri, then it's going to be bastard thick with bastard foreigners wanting to cut our throats at the other end."

If the suspicious hunchback came over, then Taliesin would have the rest of the company immediately.

"There is danger all right, but you have been fighting the qualities' wars for them for years. And for what? Two meals and scarce a copper angel a week. You want to run away now, Laetha, you return to your village poor, see if they'll welcome you and not give you straight back to the bugger whose warden you sliced. That might suit you fine, but if I go back to the Realm, it won't be to kiss and salute some rich toadshit with a sixty-angel Crown commission and a silk shirt. I'll be going back to buy an estate, hire one of the priests that used to whip me as my local friar, and have *that* bastard make free with all the sirs and madams."

"All right then, one-eye, you've led us a merry chase so far. We've done for the bastards in Emrys, Cornwall, Tryban and Astolat, so I don't suppose life on the sodding mainland is going to be any harder."

They voted, each of Taliesin's surviving dragon-browns choosing to remain for the trip eastward. All but one of the sailors too, Bron's privateers deciding the lure of a fortune was stronger than the lure of a life on the sea.

Taliesin turned to Finbar. "You in for the money, priest?"

"It's not for me to be worshipping at any altar of gold and silver. But precious fortune has thrown me out of my own Princedom, and there's a streak of the devil running through you boys that needs the care of the Martyr."

"That leaves you old man."

The tinker shrugged. "It's been a while since I have had a call to see the east."

Taliesin looked at the ceiling in exasperation. "That's no damn answer, sir. But I have the suspicion it hardly matters either way – if we slipped out tonight, why do I know we would only find you waiting in the next tavern down the road?"

"Travellers do as traveller does."

Connaire Mor came in from the street, closing the tavern door behind him. "A fair chill out there now."

Taliesin looked around. "Any obvious watchers?"

"I tell you man, this area is crawling with the Moon

Queen's guard. But I no think it is for us, there's a smell of murder about the place. Given the chance, most of them would be getting like that one."

Taliesin followed the mountain-man's gaze, seeing one of the Moon Queen's soldiers slumped over a table, red wine spilled across his uniform as if it were a duelling wound.

"Martyr's teeth, there must be close to a hundred bloody islands surrounding us, how hard is it going to be to get a boat and slip out with the night?"

The tinker's rascal eyes glinted. "You are not waiting to hear what word Annan has to say?"

Taliesin snorted. "I don't believe the Moon Queen sent that courier to the Realm, and neither do you, old man. I don't know what game the dollymop here is playing, but I have trouble enough with one woman's ambitions. A night to recover – buy what we lost on the Gogmagog tomorrow – then away, and Pock-face's quality can stew in her own poxed juices."

The tinker pulled his garish cloak in tight, more customers coming into the inn, the evening wind cool off the lake. "And of course, if Annan has been contacted, you might not like the answer she sends back."

"That's right tinker. I've got too much to live for to risk the caprice of Queens, ours, or the one here. If Annan finds out about Bron's loss, well, we'll bring her back something to turn her to forgiveness and more besides."

# Chapter 11

Staring at him, the seabird nipped his shirt, exploding into the sky as his chest stirred. Gunnar's head flopped to the side. He was at sea again, on the planking of a small vessel; his cheeks and neck burned red by the sun and the stinging salt air; both arms tied behind his back with what felt like rope.

Across from him lay Elaine, hands and legs similarly bound, with the addition of a purple bruise swelling up on her face. "Scum-pig," she said. "The bastard is selling us out to my family – my sweet scum-bastard uncle! Two of his bully boys grabbed me from out of bed this morning."

Tal Hasteel's last enigmatic comment returned to Gunnar with a fury.

Gunnar tested his lips with a rough dry tongue. Chapped and sun-burnt, he tried to talk. "He might truss me up like a fowl for stuffing, but in your case, wouldn't your father regard that as rather an insult to the family? Your uncle could have put you on a packet with some guards and have you back in the Realm a sight speedier than in this old bathtub."

Gunnar's mind spun, light-headed and fevered. Dumping their bodies at sea? But why? No it could not be that, the marsh was closer and the bizarre things that lurked there would have disposed of their bodies far more cleanly. Then it came to him.

"He's part of Annan's network of spies, Martyrs! He lived in the Realm long enough. All that money the old fraud's got salted away, half of it probably came from Annan in the first place. Bloody damn, she'll take my head if they drag us back there."

Cutting short his speculations, a whiskered face came

into sight. Given their predicament he seemed to be grinning with an obscene good cheer.

Standing under the boat's central sail he rubbed his face and grinned at the pair. "So my little chickens, you are awake. This is good."

"If you need extra shiphands, you've grabbed a deuced bad pair. Isn't it normally fishermen that are pressed?"

Finding this much to his humour the sailor rocked with laughter. "But you are my catch today. The lady I think I shall keep, but you, perhaps I should throw you back. No, but you are obviously a funny man, so then I shall keep you for company for a while. The Donna, she has not been so talkative and what she has been saying, beloved Martyrs, it is not very nice."

Another sailor peered from behind the mast, rolled up the sleeves on his rough grey-cotton shirt then whistled at the first.

Twirling his whiskers the man bowed mockingly to Elaine and disappeared out of sight once more.

Gunnar was assured by the sight of Elaine's elegantly cut dress; surely Tal Hasteel would not have wasted expensive, fresh clothes on someone who was only going to see the executioner's block? Rolling onto his side he could feel his empty pocket – the money bag had gone, probably into the hands of their leering jailer.

Then he heard it, the distant pulse of the demon-black boat. The eery throb in the stygian-cold darkness, it would haunt his dreams until death finally clawed up to him. An occasion that might not be too far removed. Yes, it was there, a dot on the frothing blue horizon and powering inexorably towards them.

"Martyrs!" Gunnar screamed into the wind. "How many of those Martyr-damned things are there on this devil-cursed ocean? Hey, smiler. Sail us out of here, oh for the love of the Martyr, you are tacking towards her. Dolts!"

Elaine added her curses to the hue and cry, and their grinning jailer returned to his charges. "So my chickens are clucking. What is it? Do you smell the wolf at the fence. Do not be afraid, I am here to protect you."

"Listen to that noise, damn your eyes, it will be the last thing you hear, unless you can outrun what's out there."

Unconcerned, the sailor reached down to touch Elaine's hair, his hand moving across to brush her breast. She spat at him and he seized her face, squeezing it. "Such beauty comes into my hands and I have to let it go once more, is that not the way of life?"

So. They were going to meet the devil-boat. Gunnar gazed out in puzzlement at the approaching craft. Had it been a Realm ship which had sunk one of her own privateers? Sending a company of the scrapings of her hated army to the bottom of the straits?

What game was that spider Annan Pendrag playing?

It was iron; lying there in defiance of every natural nautical law that Gunnar had been force-fed at his family's merchanteer knees.

The devil-boat was made of dark cimmerian-coloured iron. While it was true that the dandy had spent most his formative years avoiding ports and the responsibilities that lay there – he had to admit – never in all his years had he expected to see such an unnatural vessel.

Four on each side, eight iron wheels pierced a platform-like hull, the main structure laying fifty feet above the water – the wheels actually rolling her across the chopping waves. The main body of the sail-free ship was suspended above water, which caused problems for the fisherman's small craft. They were in danger of being swept underneath her belly and out again, before they even landed at the stairs the thing was lowering down.

Gunnar gazed up, looking for signs of life. All along the iron platform, oblong ports on her side were sealed shut, but if the hatch's size spoke of the culverin she could run out for battle, then there would be scarce a ship in the world fit to engage this monster. Could this craft really belong to

Annan Pendrag and the Crown fleet? Surely even the smoke-wreathed workshops of Llud-din would not be able to produce such a nightmare?

Their smiling captor pushed them up the stairs as the terrible craft slipped alongside, his mate fighting at the rudder to keep them steady. The devil-boat's pulse-like rhythm had ceased now, but the silence left by the black hulk was no more reassuring.

Once they were on the stairs the grinning thug leapt back down to his wooden deck, looking up at them while he glided under the sweep of the iron-boat, out of sight.

"Is there no one on this thing?" Elaine spoke in annoyance.

Gunnar looked down at the dark shadowed depths churning beneath them. Nothing to cling to – too far to swim even if they knew which direction to try for.

"Let's try the steps then." He moved in front of Elaine.

It was not the officer at the top which halted the pair in their steps. It was his two protectors.

Gunnar had fought their kind often enough in the Realm's deep forests. Demisapi, beastmen, these ones raised from something wolverine, sly-fox eyes craftily appraising them while tongues lolled over razor-sharp teeth. Bare footed, they wore matching blue tunics, cutlasses strapped around their dark furred waists. Gunnar had heard a coaching-inn tale of a Cornwall widow who raised a demisapi from a cub, teaching it to till her fields. He reminded himself to give such tales more credence from now on.

The human officer spoke. "Please to come with me."

Without waiting to see if he was being obeyed, he turned on his heels. Walking with the two beastmen guarding the couple's rear, Gunnar looked the officer over. Little different from the naval men who trod the decks in the Realm, he had a collarless calf-length coat the same sapphire-blue as his wolf creatures' shirts, and a pinched-in wig peppered with white flour.

He led them along the metal platform, between a fortress-like superstructure raised in the centre of the deck and the starboard side's rollers, each stationery wheel jutting out of an opening cut into the platform. Entering the superstructure, Elaine held close to Gunnar as they dived deeper into its depths. From outside, the thumping stroke of the vessel started again, the couple feeling the ship sway slightly as it pulled into the sea.

Introducing them to a surprisingly ordinary-looking oak-panelled cabin, the officer left while his demisapi remained. On the other side of his desk a short, balding man examined them through a monocle. From the silver braid and facings on his blue uniform Gunnar marked this fellow as the commander of the vessel.

"Welcome on board. My name is Bazin, a name for which I apologise."

Seeing the pair looking at him in bewilderment. the officer continued. "It is not quite a proper name for one of my rank, but these are changing times. Your age of Tals, and Dams, and Vons, your age is passing into dust."

"Why are we here?" Elaine demanded.

"Direct and to the point. Admirable traits. I shall return your courtesy. You are here because of the company you have been keeping."

Gunnar glared at the undersized officer as he straightened his tie-wig, fastidiously fiddling with the black ribbon bow at the nape. "My company?"

Bazin barked a succinct laugh. "Not your military company of course, young man. I am talking of your recent exertion on the Gogmagog. Privateers have been polluting the limits of the Empire's waters for too long. As you can see around you – " Bazin gestured at his vessel – "I now have the advantage to limit their activities. I find it most intriguing that an officer and noblewoman of a foreign state, albeit a somewhat barbarous and distant one, should have been receiving passage from a criminal of Bron's stature."

Gunnar snarled. "So you, it was this bastard iron bucket

that near drowned us."

"Alas. That was one of my sister ships. Believe me, I would not have forgone that opportunity lightly. Bron tweaked the Imperial nose many times in the past when our circumstances were not so ... unequal."

Elaine sounded surprised. "Empire? Since when has Roubaix been domesticating demisapi? How in the name of the Martyr can you be expecting to tame such foul creatures?"

Bazin shook his head mournfully. "Roubaix indeed. What an uneducated little barbarian girl you are. And what sort of heathen god can you find solace in that he lets himself be nailed to a tree?

"Ach, well let me drive a small degree of enlightenment into your insipid minds. This vessel has the honour of being the flagship of the Imperial fleet of Thuringia. The carving of the World-Tree on outside of my door means I am the High-Admiral of that fleet. The two demisapi behind you, the ones you believe can not be tamed, they mean that you will tell me what duties you were undertaking for the uncouth warlords of your equally uncivilised, squalid little chain of islands."

Elaine felt her face flush under the composed gaze of the officer. "There were no duties! We were running away from my family. We just wanted to be together."

"I know at least one member of your family who believes to the contrary. Yes, I find you quite charming my dear, but I am afraid I do not for a moment believe you."

At the reference to her uncle, Elaine's short temper slipped, Gunnar stepping across in advance of the beastmen to thwart her attempt on the Admiral's eyes. "You black-hearted little shit, I'll see you and that slime-sucking toadshit rot in chains for seizing us like this."

"Tal Hasteel has found the friendship of my people *most* useful. I guarantee you would find such a friendship so much more agreeable than the alternatives. You see, there is a death penalty in the homeland for known corsairs, and it is to my chagrin that Bron grew very infamous on the Empire's coasts. How a land as poor and as far away as yours could cause us so much trouble ..."

"She is telling the truth," Gunnar said.

Bazin stood up. "Can you read Latin better than you speak your bastardised form of it? Ach, can you read at all?"

Moving to the book shelf in his cabin, the Admiral pulled out a leather-bound volume and blew dust from the spine. "Did you know that most members of my House work in the Impstad's libraries? A happier calling than mine has proved to be, with scum like your friend Bron polluting our coasts. Now this book, for instance, it was written by an ancient called Heraclitus. So little survived the Sunken Empire – they were terrible brutes really. But listen to this for a moment.

"So if man should see another man, yet see a higher good come between them, then what savageries will he not work on his brother?

"Imagine that, this Heraclitus lived three hundred years before the Caesars seized your pathetic God and hammered nails through his hands, yet here was someone who already had this lucid vision of our inner nature. But I apologise. I am tiring your limited ability to appreciate the gifts of the mind. Are you quite sure you will not change your unamusing little story?"

Gunnar watched the Admiral lower his monocle. "There is nothing to tell."

"As you will. I am by nature a patient man. But these are impatient times."

With the same dismissive hand motion Gunnar's tutor used to use, Bazin signalled his wolfmen to shove the two voyagers out into the corridor.

# Chapter 12

The tinker looked across the table at Taliesin. "Hey-ho, these lodgings might be paid for by the coin of our *host,* but how are you going to get the other things you need?"

Bending over, Connaire Mor slid off his boot, easing out a strip of Realm angels from the hollow heel. Annan Pendrag's regal features were stamped haughtily across the silver.

"Most the coin was going down with the ship, but a man has to cover his bets."

"Ha," the tinker was clearly amused. "You have the life of a traveller in front of you yet."

At the wooden bar, Taliesin took back his empty draughts and returned them to the proprietor. Taliesin was wary of testing the plump owner for information – if the Moon Queen had arranged their rooms, then he was sure she would have chosen a host who was well ensconced on the royal payroll. But the officer had been in enough two-coin sawdust holes to know owners' weakness for gossip and tall stories. Drinkers treated staff as if they were part of the fixtures, happily spilling confidences with the wine, unaware that there were bored ears in front of them only too eager to play silent roles in the conversation.

"Are all your clients such good customers?" Taliesin pointed to the Queen's drunken armsman, brooding over his bottle of blackstrap.

"Reason enough to punish the bottle, these days. But that one, my little love, well, he's a man who has got more reason than most. Bless him."

"A soldier's lot is not a happy one."

She nodded her tubby chin. "Same problem we all got.

Your betters come and go, the church you're told you have to visit changes every week. It wasn't like this in the old days. People need a bit of quiet to live proper, not all this fuss and bother."

Taliesin knew he was on the right tack. A blatant loyalist for the bitch he suspected was still their jailer, even if the bars had been made more luxurious. "To better days."

"You're foreigners, aren't you, my little love, you and your friends? Yes, you wouldn't have known our old King, bless his poor bones. He was a lovely man. Never too much trouble when it came to his people, couldn't do enough for us."

"There's still the Moon Queen."

She looked into space entranced. "Bless her, yes. Every bit his daughter, the same blood you see. Born to it. Have to be to make a proper job of it."

Taliesin nodded sympathetically. "I am only a visitor to your land of course, so it's not for me to say. But we did have some trouble when we first came here, before the Queen in all her mercy rescued us. On one of the bridges, just riding in we were. Then a bunch of bludgers tried to waylay us. They were dressed in crimson, as red as devils."

"Ah," she nodded. "Devils enough, then. Those were the army. The King's new army. The bloody lobsters."

Taliesin jerked his thumb towards the drunken soldier. "Careful what you say."

"Oh no, bless you, he's for the Queen, part of her guard, and the King's before that, the real King I mean."

"Grandmother, I tell you, those dogs who chased us were real enough all right."

She nodded sadly. "Buonapar's an upstart, my love, his red-coated devils are all the claim to the throne he'll ever have. Oh, when I think of the darling girl having to marry that beast, him pawing her innocent little body."

"A sin indeed. But if she was your old ruler's daughter, why in the Martyr's name did she marry this bastard? Was she blinded by passion?"

"Passion," the tavern mistress croaked. "Passion indeed, she deserved royal blood but she got that of a swine. Oh there were troubles in the land you see, fighting and fuss and speeches and no food on the table. And where there's mischief to be had, there are rats waiting for scraps off the table. Buonapar was the fattest rat of them all, my love, led the army against his betters after my beautiful man fled into the north. Took the Princess for his Queen to make it all legal-like, practically raped her on her father's own throne."

There was one more thing. "Maybe the real King will come back one day, reclaim his seat and do for this devil Buonapar?"

"Oh no, my love. Poor, poor man. The King died of a broken heart during the troubles, to see his land pillaged and his people so troubled. I just thank the stars he never had to live to see what happened to his darling little girl.

"But there's those that still remember. We won't forget the Queen or let her down. Buonapar's red-coats won't be showing their faces in this quarter, not if they know what's good for them."

Taliesin nodded, starting to thread his way back to the dragon-browns' table when the door opened. Instead of the reassuring mass of Connaire Mor, the doorframe was filled by four men. They did not look like the Moon Queen's armsmen, but the uniformity of their white surcoats had the stamp of a military company.

From across the ale-room, Finbar jumped to his feet. "Mortal me, there's trouble blowing in on the night now."

Their landlady appeared no less bothered to see her latest customer's arrival. Taliesin turned to her. "Are they Buonapar's?"

"Hospitaliers," she hissed. "Soldiers of the Martyr. Oh, they're trouble here. Trouble anywhere for that matter. Those crows don't respect anything. Not our Queen, not that monster Buonapar, not the city watch. Fear them for it, my love. They are the chosen. They worship the path to the next life more than they care for their passage through this one."

Fortune favoured the priest, and Finbar's reaction was lost in the tension of the crowd. A space immediately cleared around the men. Grabbing their bottles, most of the drinkers were heading for the August Kin's kitchen and the back door.

Turning around, scanning the room, Taliesin saw the red fish sown over their surcoats. The four men certainly had the look of the worst of the priests who had administered Taliesin's poorhouse. Intense eyes which seemed to stare beyond the limits of their sight, rigid stances mirroring their inflexible code.

With a smile, the gaze of one of the soldiers of the Martyr rested on the Moon Queen's sad drunken armsman. He pointed the guardsmen out to his blades.

"Coignet," one of them laughed. "At last, you seem to have found your place in life."

The target of their attention glanced up and dismissed them with a contemptuous glance, far more interested in the contents of his bottle.

"You and your friends gave us trouble enough in the old days, eh? But where are they now?"

The armsman called Coignet looked at his bottle, then without comment lifted it neck first and poured the dregs on the sawdust in front of the Hospitaliers' feet.

"Of course, they're dead aren't they? Where you should be old man. You and your friends are living history now, you should all be put out to grass."

"I'm glad," Coignet began loudly, "that the church has done so well out of the new regime. It would be a terrible thing to see your source of converts dry up."

His sardonic comment angered the Hospitaliers. Taliesin heard the trace of sarcasm from the other side of the room. As antagonism built up between the two sides, the August Kin's big-room crowd thinned rapidly down, customers scurrying off into the night on suddenly discovered business.

"As your mistress has lost *her* position. But at least the

174

Moon Queen had some positions with you first, eh, my friend?"

Almost casually Coignet took the bottle and swung it across the nearest Hospitalier's face. With a massive wrench the armsman overturned the table on the others and drew his sword. "Why, this is just like the old days, except I was fighting men in those days, not boys. Twenty years ago Thibaudeau wouldn't have had you blades for his choir, let alone the Order Militant."

Snarling, the three fighters rushed Coignet while their leader picked himself up from the floor, feeling his torn face.

Taliesin looked closer and saw he had been mistaken, it was not a sword the armsman had held by the side of his chair, it was a longbow. Laughing and stumbling half-drunk, he was using it as a stave to ward off the Martyr soldier's assault. It was obvious that the younger fighters would soon have him dead, hyenas bringing down a lion.

"Cubs! If the Martyr's got no better servants than you, he must be twisting on his tree right now."

Goaded by his blasphemy, all four of the Hospitaliers intensified their attack, trying to kick tables out of the way so they could surround him.

Taliesin caught Connaire Mor's attention and pointed to one of the sabres which had survived their sinking. Reaching over, the mountain-man tossed it through the air, the blade cartwheeling across to where Taliesin snatched it by the guard.

"Have a bloody care you crows."

They turned on Taliesin, and for a moment, the Realm officer saw the glimmer of recognition in their leader's eyes. So the church knew they were in Roanne. But to what purpose?

"Your accent tells me this isn't your fight."

"This sabre tells me it is."

"So be it, we'll gut you both then."

Leaping across a crude bench, the fanatic vaulted in front

of Taliesin and converted the movement into a lunge. Taliesin remembered the advice he had beaten into him in his first harsh year with the Cornwall headcount: point beats edge. Whatever school the Hospitalier had graduated from, it had taught him that much too.

Short in subtlety, Taliesin swung the sword around like a butcher, deflecting the fanatic's blade in a shower of sparks. It was clear the Hospitalier had not been expecting that – too accustomed to the clever, flamboyant flourishes of Roubaix's fencers. Taliesin drove his leg up and connected with the Hospitalier's thigh, ramming the holy fighter against a bench, unbalancing him. Seizing the second of imbalance, Taliesin jabbed his blade forward, ripping into the chest of the man's white surcoat and twisting up to finish him in a savage murder.

Turning about, Taliesin found only one of the Hospitaliers was left. Two of his men pinned the fanatic against the tavern's staircase, the brutal hunchback hammering his fist into the man's face, Laetha laughing and working the soldier over with practised strokes.

The sodden royal armsman helped the dragon-browns roll the bodies out of the August Kin, not caring whether they were dead or wounded.

He weaved his way back to talk to Taliesin. "Your debt, sir."

Taliesin shrugged. "I have a fondness for a fair scrap."

"You'll get precious little of that from those daemons," Coignet snorted. "They like to make their conversions in mobs, as I know to my people's cost."

Standing nearby, Finbar moved his bulbous nose in suspicion. "Your people?"

"The Way of the Leaf, though there are few that will tell you those tales now, even in the north. Your friends here have seen to that."

"A blessed heathen is it? Old shadow. I don't appreciate these cursed fellows much more than you, but you'll be wanting to mend your wicked pagan ways or you'll be called to account for it when your time comes."

Coignet snorted again, fury igniting. "Damn you and yours to your own infernal fires! Our priests were gentle. They moved with the Green Circle and the seasons of life, we never presumed to tell others what to think or believe. Little good it did us when your Militant armies came to our villages, burning and killing. Men like that scum impaled my entire family in the name of your precious saviour."

"It is true, we've fallen into wicked bad times," said Finbar. "And it was the same back home. The Arch-Truron getting a might too fond of his luxuries, forgetting the simplicity of the way, selling indulgences and tithing the poor. But don't judge us all by the Militant Order's velvet fist, there's many a grand fellow walking into the light back home. They'll be a mortal few here too. Look to our message, not the fallibility of the Martyr's poor servants."

Superstitious in the way of those who live close to death, Taliesin cursed his weakness, needing to reassure himself by consulting a horoscope. There had been many fate-readers eking an existence in the dark, smoked streets of Llud-din. The inhabitants rarely undertook major enterprises in their short and meaningless lives without looking for an augury in the movements of the heavens – or the flicker of a crystal sphere. Would the marriage be a happy one? What trade should their youngest child seek? The questions were many and the answers rarely definite enough to ever be proved wrong. Out of habit he went alone, ill fortune to hear another's fate.

Taliesin ducked into the darkness of the fate reader's room. "I have come seeking wisdom." The ancient greeting, as old as the profession itself.

An old crone chuckled in the darkness. "Wisdom is in short supply, but sit anyway. What troubles you, boy?"

Taliesin lowered himself to squat on the bare hay-scattered floor. "I fear failure."

"As do we all, and there is so very much of it around

these days. The weight of events lies heavy on Roubaix and many are those who are swept up in her current. What is the symbol of your birth?"

Taliesin shook his head, discomfited. "I do not know. My parents were lost when I was a child, in a grain riot."

"No matter," the old woman bent over her table and placed a burning brazier on the surface. Humming and swaying she pulled some seeds out and scattered them across the coals, a yellow mist rising to cover her leathery face. "You will be travelling."

"Don't waste my time," Taliesin spat. "I'm a soldier, that's too easy."

She chuckled. "Ha, even your superstitions are shorn of belief. Now hush, boy, I need to concentrate. Ah… there will be perils. Death is in your shadow and your hands, and where you go, others will follow."

"Who follows, old woman?"

"An angel, it is fallen and its heart is filled with destruction."

Taliesin rubbed his unshaven chin. "Is the angel ours, or my enemies'?"

"Both."

"That's not much help."

Shaking her head, the old woman spilled more seeds across the fire. "The smoke shows many paths, countless directions. How you walk them is for you to decide."

"Who will seek to stop me?"

"The man on the tree."

"Then what is his nature?" Taliesin asked.

"He has been crucified and reborn."

Darkness concealed the officer's sudden fear. "Do you speak of the Martyr?"

"Your enemy has left the tree and has his followers. He makes his own titles now."

"Will we succeed?"

Moving her head around the pungent mist the old woman

shook her head. "You will see failure in victory and pain in success."

Taliesin had expected nothing less veiled, but the old woman sensed his disappointment. "You wish me to tell you you'll find a nice plump wife to warm your camp fire and tend you into your seventieth year?

"Listen, some I tell the truth. Fools and Kings I tell tales of spry children and golden years."

Taliesin shrugged, placing a silver angel on the table and standing up to massage his numb legs.

"Wait," she called as he left. "One last thing will I make known to you. When you must make your decision, remember, let none touch the unholy tree."

"And what tree would that be, grandmother?" Taliesin asked.

She cackled loudly and, ignoring his questions, waved him out.

Having extended his drinking trip to include most the inns on the way back to the Moon Queen's court, Coignet was late enough to have missed the free stirabout served to the armsmen by the palace kitchens. Made of scraps and whatever was old enough to be no good for the courtiers, the stew was a dubious privilege. Many of the Moon Queen's guard preferred to eat in the capital's ordinaries, the hundreds of taverns serving cheap but wholesome suppers for a handful of coins.

Winding his way through the palace's halls, galleries, courtyards and living quarters, his bloody clothes drew little comment from the other armsmen, but courtiers raised fans to cover chattering mouths, affecting an indignation they did not feel for the sake of their good-standing.

Coignet had wrecked himself, seeking oblivion from a dead King who had promised him peace for the northern provinces, then watched while the mountains of lies became mountains of corpses. With what little loyalty he could muster, the old soldier still served in the royal guard, although his honour had cost him everything he had ever cared for.

Stumbling on a set of stairs he laughed at the irony. King's Guard, that was a rare old joke. Buonapar had made himself sovereign. What use had he for the blue-uniformed soldiers and their loyalty to the old regime? Buonapar's new army of devils were the future of the land now. The armsman was a useless, living antique.

Tripping on another tread near the top, Coignet nearly stumbled into a party coming down the stairs. Then he saw the tumble of raven-black hair trailing down the side of her perfect face, petulant doe-brown eyes locking onto his own. Three bottles of blackstrap brought her face into an abnormal clarity: the haughty angle of her wire-thin eyebrows, soft skin and the aching curve of those lips.

Coignet thought the Moon Queen might say something to him then, her mouth quivering slightly. But her bodyguard pushed him aside hard, and he had to lean on his longbow to stop himself from folding over.

Ignoring him, she glided down the stairs, a trail of chosen courtiers and confidantes hustling behind with a great deal less dignity.

Coignet coughed as vomit climbed in his throat. "Bitch."

She had not always ignored him. Once, early on in the years when the girl blossomed into the woman, then he had been her favourite, her protector, and later on even her lover. The world had belonged to Coignet and his band of armsmen in those days. No intrigue had been too small for the gallants of the lion-badge, no task too dangerous or impossible to attempt for the King.

At last managing to climb the stairs, Coignet turned around, then stopped, his reflection angled across a mirrored urn. A grizzled face gazed back at him, the ravages of time and disappointment having consumed the looks which women had fought over thirty years earlier.

Coignet touched his cheek, hardly believing the face was his. "What happened to us?" he whispered.

But he knew the answer. His lover had become a monster. His master had gone insane and led the nation to ruin. His own people had been betrayed, and those of his friends who had survived the long war of attrition in Sisteron had been worn away by the heavy years, the wars, the intrigues and riots and starvation.

Sick of himself, Coignet pitched into the freezing ebony night, out onto the stretch of battlement which led to the Royal Guards' Keep. Underneath the wall, skiffs and wherries slid across the cold surface of the lake, carrying late night revellers and drinkers under the bridges and across the City of Isles. He thought it odd that people could be living such a normal life. Buonapar and his new order had brought a strange sort of peace to Roubaix. On the surface the Empire was as calm as the capital's massive lake, but beneath, beneath the garbage-ridden surface, savage fish weaved and jostled and gobbled each other in the darkness.

The skiff-poler's cries floated up to him, touting loudly for the dwindling supply of citizens seeking a safe quick lake-ride back to their homes.

Moving towards the square of light cut into the keep's side, Coignet's giddiness vanished in a sudden burst of adrenaline. Moving out of the door were a party of Hospitaliers, their hulking white bodies pure silver in the moonlight.

"Coignet! No," one cried out, and the armsman realised he had drawn an arrow and notched it to his bow without even thinking.

He saw familiar faces. The Moon Queen's Immortals, armsmen towering above six foot, giants even among the Guards. The elite of the elite.

"What is this?" Coignet demanded.

"We're about the Queen's business, so hold your tongue and move out of the way."

"Have your wits fled you? Dressed like that, you won't be able to get across a single island before an armsman or redcoat fillets you."

"We're going down there, old man." One of the giants pointed to the small gate below, and Coignet saw a large wherry moored in the darkness. "And it is us which will be doing the filleting. Those foreign island dogs in the August Kin."

Now Coignet saw why the Moon Queen's elite were masquerading as soldiers of the Martyr in the middle of the night, and felt the bile raise in his throat. "On our honour, damn you, they are under the Guard's protection."

"Not any more they're not. Now they're going to be under our knives."

"Standards have fallen," Coignet spat, "if the Guard's taking on toadshit like you. Do you not understand? We have taken it on our honour to protect them. If that situation has changed, we damn well tell them that it has been withdrawn first."

Contemptuously, the lead soldier pushed Coignet out of the way, the Immortals filing past him with murder in their eyes. "We will tell them, old fool, right after we have slid three-foot of Imperial steel through their island bellies."

Coignet watched the party of giant armsmen clamber into the gently rocking wherry and saw the small boat push off. Looking up at the bare stars glinting above, Coignet tried to find some order in the heavens. A sudden resolve hardened in him, defiance consuming the last vestiges of his hangover.

This desecration of their code was not going to happen!

He would impose his own order on the heavens and damn the cost. He would show everyone who had been laughing at him over his years of wreckage what following a way of honour meant. Why he and his comrades had marched in columns across a dozen battlefields with balls cutting ragged swathes among their ranks, why they had duelled, and fought, and died. And lived.

Coignet raised his bow to punch the stars and a weight lifted off the old man, remembering the salute of his dead friends. The word he had forgotten for so long.

"Glory."

Coignet sprinted across the streets and bridges, deserted, silent. He was relying on the fact that most sane revellers out at this time of night would be travelling by the safe, slow, lake-bound wherries. Even the ruffler Thief-Kings thought twice about crossing wherry journeymen, a major commercial power in the City of Isles. Criminals stayed away from the waters, confining their vicious trade to the capital's numerous bridges and crossings.

It was across these bridges that Coignet sped now, his lungs burning like a furnace, inhaling a chill night air which tasted of red hot needles and blood. It felt as if somebody had filled his boots with lead, the armsman wheezing a filthy curse at his tired straining body.

Coignet prayed to his forest gods that the Moon Queen's Immortals would choose to skirt the King's departments. It was the only chance he had to beat them to the Realmsmen's lodgings

Each householder was meant to hang a lantern outside his property to light the streets at night, but even the few that still honoured that responsibility did not bother to waste much oil in the small iron frames. After all, why waste good money on wastrels, thieves and the feuding guardsmen of each department? Good citizens barred their doors against the rufflers: prancers who would break into stables and make off with honest people's stallions; moonmen who raided town yards for the plump chickens and poultry that subsidised the slum areas' otherwise meagre diet; even the mischievous young anglers who went about their night's business with long poles, purpose-built to fish rich clothes off washing lines.

Now Coignet exploited the citizens' lack of care, dodging from shadow to shadow, avoiding the few puddles of candlelight thrown from behind second-storey windows.

He cut through the city like a spring-heeled demon, cries

rising up behind him, Coignet responding by darting down side streets and vaulting yard walls. King's men – Queen's men – Martyr's warriors – merchanteer's private watch – it mattered not, he flung himself through street after street, past shops, across bridges weighed down with taverns and along roads that could barely pass a cart.

Turning a silk-seller's premises, Coignet recognised the small avenue and exposed isle which accommodated the party of dragon-browns. It was bathed in a still silence, broken only by the brittle far-off coughing from one of the nocturnal toads swimming the lake. He gazed down the street. No sign of the Moon Queen's Immortals. Not a sign of life or the massacre the traitorous bitch had ordered. Had he arrived too late? Had silent blades already dipped on this murderous night?

Stepping from the cover of the shop's alcove, Coignet heard a sudden rasp. A weight smashed into his side and a curved slice of steel flashed up into the starlight. Paralysed, Coignet knew he was pinned and the second he had to stop the knife was spent.

The wicked point jerked to a stop at his neck. "Martyrs," the voice cracked into the night. "You stupid daft bastard, are you after getting your throat slit?"

Lantern light fell across the foreign mountain-man as he tucked his sabre back into his belt. Still shocked Coignet rolled over and the giant helped him to his feet. "A picquet."

"Aye, come on inside now."

Warmth from the common room's heath slapped the armsman as soon as he crossed the threshold, massaging the aching muscles in his legs. Muffled murmurs drew Coignet's attention to the serving counter, and he looked around to see the August Kin's proprietor trussed up and gagged as if she were a pheasant ready for the feast, bound with the remainder of her staff.

"You've picked a buggering bad hour to go drinking," Taliesin said.

Across the room the foreign soldiers were waiting in silence, their faces blacked with coal from the fire, grinning like devils. They held brand new flintlocks and wore stuffed packs, strips of bedding from the tavern torn up to bind and silence their loads – a clever precaution for night fighting, when every snapped twig was magnified to sound like the blast of an explosion. Coignet snorted, his blue-coats had been using that trick when these sweepings from a foreign gutter were suckling in their cribs.

Taliesin picked up a line of rope. "You'll forgive me if I make the knot a little tight, but I suspect you could give us a lot more trouble than our good hosts here."

"Pah," Coignet swore. "Put that away, one-eye, I haven't risked my head and lost a good night's sleep to be roped by the likes of you. The Moon Queen has sent her pets to gut you tonight, and they'll be following close on my heels."

Taliesin looked suspiciously at the old armsman. "And we are meant to believe you are telling us this for the good of your heart?"

"No, curse you. Not for you. I'm doing this for the colours on this jacket. They were better than a midnight murder, once."

"You will find your Moon Queen still wears the same colours, sir."

Coignet shook his head. "No. All she has done is to sow a lion-badge on a pack of knifemen and toppers. The best of us died an age ago. I died an age ago."

Taliesin nodded and let the rope fall to the floor. "Not much point in tying up a dead man, is there?"

By the window, Finbar motioned for silence. "There are a rare old number of them out there, lad. Out on the mortal lake and as quiet as water serpents, aye, coming to sting us dead with their venom."

Approaching the rear of the small island, the wherry full of the Moon Queen's assassins cut through the water. It would have been a deadly assault, silent save the gentle slap of oars pushing the boat forward.

"About as much as we expected." Taliesin lifted one of the new flintlocks from the table, distrusting the weapon and its unknown craftsmanship. Connaire Mor had had the luck to run into a merchanteer selling puffers crafted from forges in the Realm, or so the man had claimed. More likely the rogue had recognised their foreign uniforms and spun them a tale.

Stamped on the barrel was the proof-mark of the smith, but it was no forge the Captain recognised. At least in the Princedoms, Taliesin knew which workshops were reliable, here they had paid their silver and now it looked as if they must also take their chances.

"By the wall, move."

Fanning out into the tavern's back-yard, Taliesin's men knelt by a low wall and pulled out the paper-wrapped balls which made the clumsy business of loading their weapons easier. Biting the end off of the packets they quickly tapped the powder down their barrels, then drew out mauls to shove the balls down, along with the torn paper which helped badly-moulded balls grip the barrel. Pulling back their puffer's locks, the Realmsmen reached down with practised fluidity to bring up powder-horns, sprinkling fine-grained priming powder into the pan. When they commenced firing they would increase their rate by reloading the pan with low quality powder from the paper cartridge – a flogging offense in the Butcher's army, officers believing such sloppiness led to misfires.

Coignet looked on in amazement. These foreign killers had loaded their flintlocks with an incredibly quick, deadly professionalism, putting to shame the conscript armies of his spring years. And any army that could fire twice as fast as its enemy might as well be twice as large.

Taliesin timed his strike to perfection. The wherry pulled up to the rear of the tavern, a small dock which the lakesmen used to unload the inn's kegs and barrels. Just as it stopped and the Hospitalier-dressed soldiers rose, unbalancing the boat, a flurry of flames licked out to catch the Immortals like an axe sweeping the water. Smoke bloomed in front of Taliesin's men, their night sight made a field of dancing spots by the flash. They blinked it away and reloaded. Coignet did not realise the Butcher, like all Realm Generals, made every soldier learn to load his puffer while blindfolded, literally. Smoke from their culverin cannons and flintlocks rose to cover battlefields, and a soldier who could not pour out fire in that choking fog was of no use to the feuding Princedoms. It served Taliesin well here.

"Fire," the order came again.

Confusion reigned on the wherry, Immortals crawling bloody on the deck, coughing blood, then the next volley whipped across them, lifting men back across their own dead or into the freezing waters.

Yet again. Fire!

Coignet reeled in the darkness. He had fought battles of honour, where rival commanders met for breakfast and agreed the next day's timetable of battle as if it were a costumed masque. But this, this was a bloody slaughter, and at last he saw why his countrymen considered the islanders to be uncultured savages. How could they load their puffers so fast? Where were the reluctant headcount he was used to, men that had to be flanked by their own hussars just to stop the ranks from fleeing when a battle started?

Coignet shivered and was glad his kingdom was separated from these ruthless black-faced devils by the walls of a sea.

Taliesin pulled out his sabre. "Muzzle swords."

He said it in an even, casual voice, as if he was speaking to a friend and pointing out a particularly pretty women on the other side of the street.

"They're finished," Coignet started. "You can't – "

"They bloody will be." Taliesin stood up and his men rose with him. He had no great desire to close with the giant Immortals, but he knew that faced with a broken enemy his men would expect pickings, and if Taliesin was to carry them back to the Realm he had to have their trust.

Sliding the wicked serrated blades under their flintlocks, the Realm soldiers rushed the wherry, the screams of a pack of banshees fouling the night. Floundering in water and on deck, the surviving Immortals were speared as they tried to clamber across their brothers' corpses and to safety. An Immortal shocked and bleeding from ball wounds raised his arms, only to fall back gouting blood as one of the sailors shoved a blade into his throat.

The Tinker moved to stand by Coignet as the Realm soldiers threaded their way through the bodies, cutting open pockets and taking any coins they found there.

"Rawn's teeth, but they're barbarians, barbarians."

"Oh, I don't know. I would say that is relative, would you not?" The tinker moved forward, dipping a gnarled old hand in one of the Immortal's pockets and fishing out a coin. He bit it and, apparently satisfied, dropped it into a little leather pouch.

At last the slaughter was over and a silence fell over the back yard, the only sound the gentle creaking of the wherry in the water.

"You are a butcher, sir."

Taliesin wiped his muzzle sword on the white surcoat of one of the bodies. "No, you'll find that is my General. I just clean away the quality's shit for them. Wherever it is. So. Are you still with us, old man?"

"What have I got left here? Yes, the Leaf damn you, I am still with you."

"Good," Taliesin stepped back from the corpse. "We need to get out of the city, quickly. Even if your Moon Queen has warned her army off this area, sooner or later someone is going to come over to find what all the noise was about. What is the best route out of the area?"

Coignet though a moment. "North, we can head north. My people are there and they have no love for anyone in the Court, we will receive shelter there."

"Sure and we're among the mortal heathen now," said Finbar.

"Look on it as an opportunity to spread the word," Taliesin said. "Get those bodies out of the boat. Connaire Mor, the rest of the supplies from the tavern."

Used to oars, the surviving complement from the Gogmagog took charge of the wherry, the soldiers dragging their packs and supplies out to the craft. It was a tight fit, all the more uncomfortable on seats made slippery by spilled blood.

"I need to go back to the palace first," said Coignet.

"Martyrs." Taliesin looked at the world-weary armsman. "Whatever you are about there, leave it. Every minute we waste it one which your ruler could be using to muster more of those bastard giants."

"We go to the palace first," said Coignet. "Or you can find your own damn way out of the capital."

"Listen to me, old man, by first light every faction in your cursed country is going to be howling for our blood. That place is going to be packed with soldiers. Just leave it."

"We go," Coignet insisted.

"Martyrs! What is it with you? Just what kind of bloody score have you got to settle?"

"More than you can know, one-eye."

# Chapter 13

Coignet directed the wherry to land at the far end of the royal estate, a steep slope which led up to well-tended lawns in front of the palace's curtain wall. It was easily the largest island Taliesin had seen on the lake, the only sign of life coming from sentry lights high on the wall above.

The captain stood with Coignet and Finbar, noting the hedges they were using for cover had been shaped into animal silhouettes.

"Ah, we are going to need blessed angel's wings to get in there," said the priest.

"I am too old for such heroics, Martyr-man. There was a time when I would have climbed up and down the ivy all night, and thought nothing of it. Especially if there was a beauty waiting for me at the other end. But there is an easier way."

He led them along the lawn, across an orchard planted in orderly lines, then through a line of statues, muscled athletes throwing disc and javelin, stone cracked and hairy with moss.

"See over there?" Coignet pointed to a wall of tall hedges. Memories jogged Taliesin, a sight he had seen before. Of course, the merchanteer's court in Llud-din. In the small park there, the maze. Filled with quiet little enclaves where the city's lovers could meet on their trysts, destitute street children chasing each other around on guild days.

So courtiers in the Moon Queen's household valued similar distractions.

"Blessed nice, but let us leave now, before the devils discover us creeping around their garden like mortal midnight slugs."

"After me." Coignet waved the others forward as he crept towards the maze's entrance. The lawn under their boots was washed by the ghostly-blue moonlight, dewy turf sucking away all sounds of passing.

Weaving his way through the maze, ducking left then right, Coignet squeezed through openings in the hedge, waxy leaves catching his jacket. Even with the moonlight, Taliesin was glad the old soldier knew his way. It was a route he had obviously followed many times in the past.

"Here we are." Coignet led them along a blind turn and into the centre of the maze. A folly stood there, a small dome supported by seven pillars, stone benches in the shadows beneath.

Getting to his knees, Coignet groped underneath one of the benches, then with a grunt of satisfaction he found what he was looking for. There was a small click and getting to his feet, Coignet lifted the stone bench. It twisted over and Taliesin and Finbar saw the iron hinges fixed in its side.

Gazing into the space vacated by the bench, Taliesin found only inky blackness. Coignet climbed down into the darkness, fumbled about, then ignited an oil lamp. Greasy flames lit his face like a devil as he stared up at them.

"Nobody knows what's happened yet, so I should still be safe in the Court. If I am not back by the half-hour, leave without me. If anyone else climbs out of here, you can gut the rascal, because I'll be dead."

"You can be buggering sure of that," said Taliesin.

There was a chill in the tunnel and Coignet hoped he still remembered the way. The maze underneath the palace was far deadlier than the lover's game they had passed through aboveground, dead-ends and trapdoors scattered liberally throughout the labyrinth. Only the armsmen personally trusted with the King's safety knew of these tunnels.

Not that it had done his old master any good. He had escaped only to die in exile, or, as Coignet suspected, far more likely hunted down by one of Buonapar's executioners. Power was the real trap, it had destroyed his master with no escape-passage possible from it.

Cobwebs fell across his face. Coignet brushed them away and found the ladder he was looking for. He tied the lamp to his belt, iron flaked red with age dusting down as he gripped the rungs. Three stories climb and a fair way to fall at any age, let alone his.

At the end of the climb was the wooden passage, warmer now, the heat of the palace trapped and circulating in the small partition.

There were spy holes in places. Less for security than because the old King had been a terrible voyeur. Before madness took him, he had loved to watch his courtiers rutting, making a pastime of catching the household in unfaithful embraces. How he had loved to hint of his courtiers' clandestine passions – spreading a false reputation of the divine and omnipotent King.

Dust layered the floor, showing the King's secret had died with him. No-one else used these passages. But Coignet had a use for them of which he thought the old King would have approved. When alive, the ruler's fondness for practical jokes had bordered on the deranged, pointing to the long dark madness which was to follow.

Coignet stopped, running his fingers along the wall. He found the wooden circle and slid it aside. On the opposite side of the wall there was a room, lit only by the dancing embers of a log fire. The heath was stacked high with fresh logs, dribbling glue-like sap into the flames; the servants had just been in to stoke it.

The latch clicked and Coignet pushed the panel back. It was stiff with age, but made little sound as he forced it, a tribute to one of the King's ancient ancestors. The Moon Queen hated people coming in her bedroom, an honour afforded only to her favourite lovers, the men and a po-faced maid who was ancient even when Coignet had arrived at Roanne.

Moving silently all the same, Coignet went over to the Moon Queen's dresser, remembering the last time he had been in here. It seemed an age ago. Waking up from a drunken stupor, and in the candlelight seeing Céroline clutching a faded document marked with the royal red seal. Sobbing quietly to herself. Watching pretending to be asleep while she exhausted her tears then placed the manuscript back in the compartment. It had not taken long for the armsman's curiosity to get the better of him, reading it one night with the Moon Queen away from the capital.

Where was the release? It had been so many years and age was dimming his memory. In one of the wooden carvings, but which one? He tried each of the lion's eyes to no effect. The tail perhaps. Then he saw it. The lion's crown, where better to hide it. One of the crown's jewelled carvings pushed back into the dresser, a tiny drawer popping out.

There was the document. Laying on a fold of velvet and worth a throne, or maybe even two. Coignet smiled grimly. There was a time when he would have killed to keep that document from the hands of the King's enemies. Now it was just a guarantee, and Coignet would sell it away himself if the worst came to the worst. He tucked it into his jacket.

Coignet gripped the lion sown onto his arm and with a sudden jerk, ripped it off, laying it down on the green velvet and closing the drawer.

So be it. His fate was joined to a company of rufflers and Realm-scum now.

Frosty air squalled across Coignet's face as he emerged back outside, climbing into the cover of the crumbling old folly.

Taliesin lowered his sabre. "Are your affairs in order now? Or perhaps you'd like to take a few hours to write a couple of farewell letters."

"Go to hell, one-eye. And move your ugly bulk, now we go."

Staying low to the ground the three men moved back to

the wherry. Taliesin's men were already gambling away the coins they had scavenged from the Moon Queen's Immortals.

"They'll be plenty of time for that." Taliesin stepped across into the wherry while the sentries cast off. "Which way out?"

Coignet pointed across the rippling silver surface, towards the far side of the lake's bank. "There. We will need mounts if we are to outpace the ones they send after us."

On the other side of the boat, Connaire Mor shook his head. "I've already been out looking into that yesterday. The only horses to be had in this entire swining town were fit for the tanners."

"Ha, that's because you've been looking in the wrong place, boy. The armies buy all the fit ones here, or to put it more truthfully, they confiscate them."

"You'll not be thinking of adding the crime of prancing to your long heathen list of sins would you?" Finbar asked. "Back home, villages might stoop to an occasional cattle raid, but stealing a man's horse is a precious serious matter."

"Unless you've got a better idea, priest."

Resigned, Finbar made the sign of the tree. "It's a wicked pack of thieves I have fallen in with."

There were few other boats out on the lake, and if it was not for smoke curling from the occasional chimney, Taliesin could have believed the city to be an illusion of phantoms. They cut through the water with the sailors pulling long, experienced strokes. From one of the passing islands a watchman's voice rose to cry out the time, then fell away to be consumed by the cricketing of the lake's insects.

A mist was rising from the corner of the vast lake, the party finding themselves damp in the vapourous shroud. Moisture glistened on the sides of the wherry as the sailors' oars dipped and fell. In the front of the boat the tinker was murmuring a nonsense song about mist drops and ale hops, and Taliesin hushed him.

"These are army stables we are heading for?" Taliesin asked.

Coignet nodded. "Indeed. Not the main one, though. That will be too well guarded. It's the old armoury where they keep the previous King's siege culverin. Those weapons are antiques, hardly worth the space to store them. The barrels would explode if you loaded them with a full charge of powder. It's a good bet there won't be too many lobsters there, but there'll be enough horses for us."

"Lobsters?"

"Redcoats, the King's new army. Besides, I know the gate-man. A sergeant who lost a leg in the retreat from Sisteron. I carried him out of the last stretch of the tumble, so he might be persuaded to let us have the mounts without too much fuss."

"Let's hope so."

Coignet put his hand on Taliesin's sabre guard. "We do this my way, one-eye. These are still my countrymen."

Taliesin nodded reluctantly. "That won't stretch too far if they discover us."

Placed on a rocky promontory, the old armoury loomed large out of the mist. Dark ramparts stared down at them, light glowing from behind the loopholes betraying the presence of inhabitants. The rocks on the lake's shore were black and slippery. Landing the boat, the force slunk through the mist drifting off the lake, careful with their footholds. If there had been any watchers, the dragon-browns' appearance would have seemed supernatural, ghosts rising from the drowned Roman city lying on the lake bed.

There was only one approach to the old armoury, a dirt track leading up to a gate flanked by two towers. It might have been an ancient construction, but the architects had known what they were doing. No blind spots from the wall. Taliesin knew if they had been attacking a well-armed and pre-warned foe, they would have been cut to pieces by fire, killed before they had got within two yards of the fortification.

Taliesin and Coignet walked up to the gate while the rest of the party sheltered in the shadows of a small copse.

In reply to Coignet's banging, a small grill opened in the gate, a grizzled, bearded face pressing against the bars. "You still alive then."

"For the moment, you old devil."

A small door cut into the main gate swung open and Coignet and Taliesin ducked underneath. The grizzled old man on the other side waved away a younger soldier with a pike, the weapon's head flowering into a veritable hedge of blades.

Coignet walked into a small room on the tower's side. "So you're working for the new King now?"

"Pah, I find Buonapar's coin a little more plentiful than the Moon Queen's. You're wasting your time in the Guard, she's becoming as daft as her father was towards the end." The wooden-legged sergeant offered a bottle of blackstrap to Coignet and Taliesin.

"You're too old for change."

"Buonapar may be a ruthless bastard, but he's a canny one all right. He's running rings around the Moon Queen *and* the church. There's greatness in that man, you mark my words, and some of it'll rub off on the Empire before he's done."

Coignet started laughing. "Age seems to be softening you, old friend. You never wanted anything more than a day's rations and enough silver for a month of debauchery when the campaign finished."

"I'm tired Coignet. Tired of watching high-blood idiots running the land into the ground, never producing anything except an enormous litter of squalling brats who'll grow up to be just as pig-stupid as their parents were. Before I die, I'd just like to see someone lead us to a little glory. But that's just spit and wind, you and your ugly friend here didn't come out to listen to an old soldier's hopes."

"No," Coignet said. "You might say myself and the Moon Queen have had a falling out."

"The kind you might lose your head over?"

Coignet lifted his knife. "Yes indeed. She is going to want to make me a present of this in my back. If we don't get out of the capital fast, the only way we'll be leaving is floating face down on the lake."

"Good for you," the old soldier smiled. "She always was a buggering dollymop, Coignet, but you were too blind to see it. She just grew into the role a little better as she put the years away. Well, it doesn't take too much of a brain to figure out why you've come to me. But you are out of luck. There is an entire complement of lobsters posted here now, two hundred men, as sharp and eager as we were in our day."

Coignet looked at his old companion disbelievingly. "For what? A handful of chamber-culverin full of rust?"

Coignet's friend tapped his nose. "They're stockpiling here now. I told you Buonapar has dreams of greatness dancing around his head. And nobody thinks of coming out here."

Coignet cursed and Taliesin stood up. "It doesn't matter, there are no other choices left, we'll take our chances."

The old soldier shook his head sadly. "Well a life for a life, but I have no desire to see you kill yourself with your foolishness. Make it look convincing."

Coignet tore off a length of cord and bound his friend's arms and legs, then gagged him with a strip of cloth from his own uniform. Drawing his knife, the armsman drew a nick across his friend's brow, a slight cut but one which would make it appear he had been half-murdered when the old soldier was eventually discovered.

"I'll see you beyond the Leaf, old friend."

Taliesin opened the small gate's door and motioned the others to advance. From the other tower, the young soldier poked his head out and saw what the two visitors were doing. His mouth opened to cry out, then violently expelled air as Taliesin's boot connected with his crotch. Taliesin reached over and slammed the boy's head against the wall, pushing him down into the shadows of the keep. "Your friend would be better off if we finish this one. He saw us come in."

"Leave it," Coignet said.

Taliesin nodded. The officer had no stomach for a cold-blooded murder when the lad's only crime was being in the wrong place at the wrong time. If the King's army was anything like Taliesin's own, he would be loyal and fond enough of his old sergeant to keep his mouth shut. Especially when they found him trussed up and bloody.

Dark shapes filled the yard, and even in the moonlight Taliesin could see they were not the rusty antiques he had been expecting; heavy culverin mounted on block, carriages which would need a team of six horses to tow. Huge roundshot lay piled next to them, just large enough to be rammed down the weapon's wide bores. The new King was clearly planning to tighten his hold on the Empire, and with the equipment strewn across the yard, he would be able to present a very persuasive argument to his opponents.

Coignet and Connaire Mor led the men in a silent chain, scurrying past the shadows of the bombards and culverin. From one of the towers on the other side of the open ground, singing could be heard drifting across the night.

Taliesin did not give much for the armoury commander's chances of hanging onto his commission after this night. The Realm horse-thieves could just as easily have been a raiding party from the Moon Queen or one of the Princes of the Church, out to spike the newly cast culverin. They had crept across battlefields with raiding parties before, and hammering a sharp steel spike into the culverin's muzzle would make it impossible to fire without blowing out the breech. Smiths would have to file the spike away if they were to ever repair them, a tedious, laborious task.

"If they haven't been moved, the stables are behind the

central donjon," Coignet said, pointing past the main stronghold.

Keeping low, the line of soldiers moved into the darkness in the lee of the building. On the other side, a dark shape in the centre of the open yard blocked their path. A fire burned by the ground, lighting two sentries, a square of light cut high in the structure – another shadow moving there.

"Damn, a siege tower," Taliesin whispered.

"No tower," the tinker's tinny voice came back. "It's made of iron."

"Iron?"

"As in kettle-black."

Taliesin looked again. What he taken to be smoke from a tower fire were the fumes drifting out of a squat funnel. Two stories high, there was a plough-shaped blade at the kettle-black's front, massive wheels just visible on the other side of a metal skirt, wicked spikes jutting from the side to hold off would-be scalers. Fortifications ran along the top, covered by a thick iron canopy.

"Bloody Martyrs, what sort of war is this man expecting?"

From above them a scream sounded, a lady's high-pitched voice. Taliesin looked up to see a young face ducking back into the stronghold.

"Of all the times to take the air," Coignet cursed. Sentries ran out onto the battlements. Seeing the formless shapes below, they emptied their flintlocks down into the shadows. From the opposite end of the yard more soldiers tore out from the stables, pulling on red jackets.

"That thing," shouted Taliesin, the Realmsmen already darting into cover.

Both the lobsters at the foot of the massive automaton had fired their puffers, ramming new balls in when the dragon-browns charged, close to fourteen soldiers screaming down on them with muzzle-swords glinting in the pale white-blue moonlight.

As Taliesin expected, the guards took to their heels

immediately, sprinting back to their own troops trying to find their nightsight at the far end of the courtyard. In all Taliesin's soldiering years with the Butcher, he had heard of few engagements where armies met each other short-blade to short-blade. Normally, one side broke at the sight of men made maniacs by fear and closing with their evil thrusting plungers.

Well-disciplined, the redcoats formed a line two men deep, an officer swearing loudly at them. They would sweep the fortress clean of Taliesin's small force when mustered. Taliesin clawed at the rungs in the metal beast's side, the others scrambling up close enough to feel his boots brushing their hair.

At the summit, Taliesin discovered the shadow he had seen earlier, a corpulent barrel of a man trying to hide in the corner of the cabin. Furnace light flickered across his terrified face, flames he would need to keep constantly stoked – unless the land's new ruler had a couple of spare days to bring the kettle-black's aeolipiles to functional heat.

Taliesin turned to Coignet. "You know what you need to get him to do."

Squeezing past the timber box, the others emerged on the rear deck. Wooden planking creaked to the sounds of men reloading their puffers, and the officer prayed the iron sheeting outside was thick enough to hold off Buonapar's roused troops.

"This is wicked heavy." Finbar lifted a cast iron ball towards a small culverin run back from a firing port, his bulbous nose glowing with the effort.

Connaire Mor carefully measured the powder charge with a scoop-shaped shovel. "Same as our clan's culverin this one, my beauty Meg Mons. We saw off those Logriese devils with her, at least we did before Emrys lent their swining army to the lowland devils. Then it was a different song we had to sing. Aye, it's a lucky name still, that is what we should be calling this bastard fort on wheels, Meg Mons."

Taliesin snorted, but he was fond enough of the young mountain-man not to point out his family's huge cannon had hardly proved sufficient to turn back the regiments sent by Annan Pendrag.

Balls pelted their enclosure, a spent one fleeting off the side to roll past Taliesin's unslung pack. Answering with return volleys, the dragon-browns laid down a constant barrage of fire, the sound of plank-after-plank of wood splintering.

Someone had possessed the wit to move more redcoats onto the battlements, a clearer field of fire down into the automaton. A Realmsmen collapsed back as a shot cracked into his shoulder blade, hurling crude insults at the redcoats while the tinker tore away the man's shirt, trying to staunch the bleeding.

Taliesin sighted on an officer, an obvious target in his tricorn cap. His puffer kicked back, a choking cloud of fumes erupting out and snatched by the night breeze. He saw the officer on his knees, another redcoat trying to drag him back off the battlements.

From the cabin a keening cry sounded, Taliesin seeing a brown uniform rolling down the armour to be impaled on one of the kettle-black's spikes. A cluster of redcoats were storming their vulnerable side, seeking access to the ladder of rungs while Coignet held them off.

Reloading his puffer, Taliesin saw Coignet put three flights into the mob below, quarrels blurring down faster than anyone could hope to clean and charge a flintlock. A fresh group ran from behind the main stronghold, and balls cracked about Coignet, the old armsman ducking back from the hail of shot.

They had a minute before they would be overwhelmed, and it was not going to be enough. Pulling the butt hard against his shoulder, Taliesin's puffer coughed out another plume of sulphurous smoke, one of the climbers spinning back down to earth, crumpling into the small crowd below.

Finbar pushed past Taliesin. "Mortal happy is the man

who stands firm when trials come." In his hand he had one of the culverin roundshots, hollow, packed with powder and scraps of metal. A tarred slice or rope was twisted into the sphere.

Lighting it from the furnace, he pushed it out of the door, the ball rolling down the side. It caught the edge of the automaton's skirt and lifted back up into the air for a second, then there was a shattering explosion, a shower of metal ricocheting between the walls of the stronghold and those of the kettle-black.

Where once there had been men, now there was a hill of bodies, cries and groans rising up from among the corpses. One soldier crawled away on his hands, howling like a timber-wolf.

"Dear life. This is a terrible, bloody thing," said Finbar. "I could have joined the Order Militant and seen less blood and bones than this."

Taliesin said nothing. He had long ago learnt the professional's trick of pulling a veil across his feelings before a battle started. They had a task to carry out and staying alive became the only thing a soldier could afford to focus on.

There was a double quake, the kettle-black's culverin blasting out a load as the automaton shuddered forward under her own motion. Dark smoke billowed out of both her funnels, and the plough protruding from the front overturned every bombard in their path. Her passage was accompanied by a deep rhythmic hissing, like a dragon fighting for breath, shots raining across the automaton as the redcoats desperately tried to prevent them making off with their master's dangerous toy.

"On to the main gate," Taliesin ordered their fat captive. "Even this jiggered carriage isn't going to pile through the battlements."

Forming a human chain, half the soldiers set themselves up between the furnace and the timber-box, passing torso-sized chunks of fuel down the line. Their new transport had an insatiable appetite for wood and water, her flames licking out ever higher as they fed her.

An anguished cry sounded from the tower falling away behind them. Taliesin noticed a half-dressed officer shaking his fist at them. Leaning out, Taliesin laughed and replied with an ironic salute. He cupped his hands and raised his voice to a cry. "The Moon Queen's best greetings to you, sir."

"I hope you never intend to come back to the capital," Coignet muttered.

"By the Martyr, the bitch was planning to murder us wasn't she? Let her explain that away."

Ahead of the lumbering automaton, the armoury's twin towers stood high against the night sky. Clouds fingered by the first touch of dawn while soldiers manning the gate scattered to remove themselves from the path of the heaving, puffing monster.

With a worried glance, their fat prisoner turned around and looked at Taliesin.

"Ram the bugger! Straight through."

Slammed against the cabin's sides with the force of the impact, Taliesin was covered by a shower of furnace sparks. A half-burnt log rolled out and smacked into Finbar, the monk cursing his stars and the wicked fools that had convinced him to ever begin this journey. There was a scream like a cat discovering its tail through, and Taliesin realised it was the gate giving way. Shards of wood scattered across the cabin and the kettle-black was lurching forward again, a trail of thick smoke rising behind them.

"Keep to this lane," Coignet commanded, picking himself off the floor. "We'll head north at the cross-roads." He turned to Taliesin. "If we go far enough north we'll find the Cold Sea fishing villages. Ships from your islands trade with my people there, you should be able to buy a passage home for yourself and your men without difficulty."

"We are not going back yet," Taliesin told him. "Our business is only going to be finished one way."

"That jolt must have wobbled your cursed young brain, Captain. Not only are you going to have the Moon Queen seeking to ship your carcass back to her preserved in sour blackstrap, but the entire King's army will be looking for us too. It will be the first time Buonapar's been on the same side as the Moon Queen since he forced her into marriage!"

Taliesin picked up the armsman's bow and handed it to him. "We go to Sombor."

"What! Are you insane? That's on the other side of the world, next to the very Frost itself. The overland pass is a nightmare, and the Enclosed Sea's full of privateers preying on every ship attempting to sail across it; a good few of them your Realm's, as a point of fact."

"Maybe they will take pity on their fellow countrymen?"

Coignet turned away. "Pah, you are all crazy, crazy. Murdering savages who want to kill themselves. Have you heard your precious land is full of treasure? There's nothing out there but daemons and darkness. Roubaix is larger than all our neighbours – and her reach is longer than you can comfortably run. Your best chance is to head back to your islands before someone turns you in."

Taliesin shrugged. The only way they were returning alive to Annan Pendrag was with her soft-headed sister, so he would risk every kingdom and cross every topper from Roubaix to Sombor if that was what it took. And the Martyr help anyone who tried to get in their way.

# Chapter 14

Met at the door to the Moon Queen's chambers by her Lord Chamberlain, Uriel eyed the stooped old courtier with distaste. The Chamberlain eyed the silver timber-wolf which slunk along beside Uriel with an equal measure of loathing. But Uriel was an assassin, and as the best in the world they could indulge his eccentricities.

"Oh dear," the chamberlain fussed. "I'm afraid they won't let you through with your weapons."

Uriel sneered. "The Moon Queen has obviously not inherited her father's belief in his own immortality."

Two of the giant royal armsmen lifted his sword away from him and took the long-arm flintlock strapped to his back, then pulled back his cloak, discovering the killer's hand-sized bow and an array of knives. To be cautious the armsmen also took his rammer, powder horn, and the leather satchel filled with paper cartridges.

The thin, dead-faced man stood quietly by while they searched him. One of the giants found a long wooden flute, grunting a laugh that this notorious assassin possessed such a gentle object, then handed it back to him.

"Are you finished?"

"Quite, quite," the Chamberlain opened the door. "Well, through you go. We don't want to keep them waiting."

Inside, the Moon Queen was less than pleased to see the hulking beast following Uriel into the room, her smoky voice tight with fury. "You dare! You dare bring your pet in with you to my presence!"

"No pet. He found me, or did I find him first? It was some time ago and we have discovered good hunting in each other's company."

Her face reddening, she flicked her mane like an annoyed

colt. "You used to work for my father and his opinion of you was high."

Uriel acknowledged the remark in silence, replying with a slight nod.

"Unfortunately, my father – " her voice lifted in almost holy reverence when she spoke his name " – my father was often overtaken by fancies in his last years. Show me you weren't just another of them. Let me see your skills, paid killer."

He laughed, a dead sound like the rustling winds of autumn. With a mocking little bow Uriel slid out his wooden flute, then, pressing it to his mouth, began to draw out a lilting lament, a tune so melancholy it made the scattering of courtiers in the chamber feel they were having their hearts ripped out by the ache of it.

Céroline sat in shock that this thin man would dare mock her in front of her advisors. "Kill him," she screamed. "Take his head, I want to see his blood."

The three giant armsmen flanking her throne drew their sabres and rushed Uriel, the quickness of their charge telling the killer that this was the test the Moon Queen had planned all along.

Rolling to one side, his feet scythed across the space he had vacated, slashing the feet from under two of the ruler's armsmen. Flicking forward with the long flute, Uriel slapped it at the neck of the only guard still standing, cracking it back and forth in a blur.

Stunned, the huge soldier stumbled back and with a leisured casualness Uriel moved forward, took the guard's sword arm, and spun around, a horrific crack shattering across the room. One of the other guardsman was on his feet and Uriel lunged forward with the flute, stabbing the man deep in the gut then pulling him forward and tossing him across the wooden panelling. The giant fell, lying still with his neck at an impossible angle. Broken by the angle of the throw.

Still moving, the assassin spun around like a dancer, the

flat of his foot stopping the remaining giant's blade from slicing open his side. Using the flute Uriel slapped the man's blade arm twice, the sabre dropping as the giant's hand went numb. Uriel pivoted around with a short sweeping kick, the soldier's jaw snapping back and his neck cracking. Tumbling, the dead armsman fell across the other corpses. Uriel's timber-wolf yawned and stood up to sniff the bodies.

Céroline was leaning forward, her eyes glittering with blood lust. She touched her upper lip with her tongue. "We *are* suitably impressed. You may possibly be worth your fee after all."

"I do not kill people for free. That demonstration has cost you another three-hundred."

Céroline moved her fingers slowly down the long curve of her legs, "I can offer you much more than money."

"Yes, yes I'm sure you can," Uriel's lip curled in contempt.

"You've been out of work for some time in these parts," Céroline reminded him. "You really should be more selective about who you choose to murder in my land."

The memory of the fat man returned to Uriel. One of the rufflers – the Thief-Kings of the kingdom's capital. His sausage-like fingers sweaty and clammy around the purse he had offered.

It had only been later Uriel discovered the nature of the coin he had accepted. The girl, young and beautiful enough to have reminded the killer of another – in his own time. What had she done? Resisted the ruffler's advances? Spurned him or one of his friends, wanting to hold on to her all-too-brief childhood?

Uriel had returned the ruffler's money, shortly before strangling him with the lord's own silk belt, the ruffler thrashing and squealing like the swine he resembled as the cord bit deep into his rubbery neck. Then he had killed the thirty-odd mug-hunters who came after him for his feud price, and kept on killing them until he had made the gold a poisoned chalice no-one else in the trade would even accept.

Uriel looked the Moon Queen straight in her sea-green eyes. "Some jobs I take for free."

"Succeed for me in my matter," Céroline commanded, "and in addition to the money, I will make my patronage known."

"You overestimate the charms of working in Roubaix. Still, it would make it easier to operate here without having to kill every mug-hunter who crosses my path."

"There are other people for you to kill now, assassin," Céroline purred. "Foreign devils who have violated my peace and made off with my property. Led by a one-eyed bastard. And a traitor, one of my own cursed armsmen who helped them. He has a priceless manuscript with him, you kill them all, you hear me, every last one of them, but bring the document back to me. You do this for me, killing man, and I shall give you land, jewels, your own weight in gold; anything you want."

Uriel said nothing. Foreigners and turncoats would die just as easily as the three giant guards lying sprawled around him. They were just flesh and bone, like all the rest.


Six dam Saldair bent his pock-marked face in supplication, staring at the rich crimson rug which surrounded the Ecclesiarch of Roubaix like a red sea.

"She did not say what the manuscript contained, your holiness."

Drumming his fingers on his throne, the Prince of the Church looked at his informer. Briefly he wondered if this man whom the Moon Queen considered one of her most loyal servants was playing a double game. Then he dismissed the thought. Six dam Saldair was too deep in the church's own grip to risk revealing the truth and throwing himself on the Moon Queen's mercy now – not that the bitch of Roubaix possessed much of that.

For the thousandth time in his career, Thibaudeau wished

he could reverse the course of time, to undo his past folly. He had done nothing when Buonapar had seized the throne from the Moon Queen's father. The indecisive old fool had not deserved to hold on to Roubaix – introducing dual worship and making concessions to the heretics in the north, and for what? Just to attract the heathen into his new army so he could finally smash the power of Sisteron.

The King's hatred for their dagda neighbours had become a most dangerous obsession, bleeding the land dry for the money to bolster his great campaign. While the scheming Prince of the Church wished the dagda any ill which might befall their twisted little race, he knew no army of Roubaix could have hoped for victory on dagda territory. Mankind could barely hack enough of the forest away from their own doorstep for a sheltered city or a royal parkland. How could the mortal children of the Martyr hope to beat an enemy which lived comfortably within the wild enchanted forests? Making their homes there as if they were familiars nesting on the back of a demon.

As Thibaudeau anticipated, the old King stumbled out of Sisteron with his army in tatters and nothing to show for it but a slaughter. Terrifying tales from the few survivors; of the tumble's nightmares breaking upon Roubaix's conscript army of young farmboys. Wave after wave, after brutal wave, howling out of the darkness of the huge trees. Always striking in the night. Thibaudeau had not even made the attempt to stop Buonapar's mutiny.

But now Thibaudeau knew the true nature of the radical who had taken the throne. He had no respect for the church of the Martyr, nor any of the great institutions of state which had proved themselves the foundation stones of the Empire's stability. As far as possible, Buonapar had cut the church out of all affairs of state, appointing his own people to every position of power and ruthlessly purging anyone he suspected of old loyalties from office. Now the charismatic fool would pay for his short-sightedness and dangerous policies.

Thibaudeau turned over the possibilities in his mind. He had some small inkling of the contents of the manuscript the Moon Queen was seeking with such desperation. So, the old rumours had turned out to be something more than that, and now the church would deal a blow to both Buonapar and the foolish girl who had inherited the ruined nation her father had left behind.

And after the blow had been dealt? After that? The Twelve Houses' numerous candidates for monarchy would turn to the only unscathed power in Roubaix, and the Martyr would be only too happy to support some stupid little royal brat of an appropriately impressionable age.

"So, she has hired Uriel to do her work for her?"

Six dam Saldair nodded.

Thibaudeau was troubled. He knew the assassin's reputation. What he did not know was the killer's past, and with the tentacles of his network stretching the breadth of the land, that such a man could conceal his origins was worrying indeed. All anyone knew was that he had appeared east out of Neuistria years ago, and understood too much of Roubaix to be anything but a native.

"No matter. He is but a single man, while the servants of the Martyr have hosts to command."

Six dam Saldair started as a phantom-like figure wearing the sign of the red fish appeared at his side.

"What have you found out, Misamal?"

"They are indeed soldiers of the Island Queen, your holiness. Even Céroline does not know what business they were here on, but the spite for her husband led her to assume that if the foreigners were removed, it would hurt Buonapar's alliance with the islands. It seems Céroline ordered her armsman to do the killing while wearing our own white."

Snorting, the Prince of the Church waved his warrior to continue. "Transparent. Buonapar would have seen straight through such a ploy. Continue."

"There was a genuine altercation yesterday. Three of my

brothers were killed by the gutter-scum while on the Moon Queen's territory."

Thibaudeau nodded gravely. "You wish to revenge them, Misamal?"

The humble warrior bowed.

"Pick your men, my child, take only the most worthy. And take him!" This, pointing at Six Dam Saldair.

Six dam Saldair bridled. "My absence will be noticed, I will be of no more use to you in the Moon Queen's court if I am chasing down these fellows."

"Bring me back the manuscript, courtier. Just bring it back to me and I will care no more."

Weary now, Thibaudeau signaled his entourage that he would depart for his evening feast, a regular and ample assortment of swan, eels, oysters, honey-cake and fresh lake salmon. The care of the land was, after all, a most tiring burden.


They had come as far as they were going. Taliesin looked down the crevice towards the jagged rocks below. Brackish water flowed along quickly through the small stream at the bottom, carrying away foliage from the nearby forests.

Then he looked up at the bridge spanning the gap. Not wide enough to pass their huge kettle-black, not wide enough by half. Connaire Mor crossed back across the bridge and spat into a clump of bushes. "A wee small bridge for such a well-built road."

A worried-looking toll-keeper stared across at the vast kettle-black, his eyes wide at the size of the automaton and following the trail of black smoke pluming towards the clouds.

Behind them, a warning shot sounded from the cabin. Coignet was leaning out and waving. "Rawn's teeth, look to the rear!"

There was dust cloud rising on the road behind them. Taliesin rubbed his remaining good eye. "Well at least we had two days."

"They must have ridden their mounts fit to burst all the same," said Connaire Mor.

They scrambled back into the highlander's Meg Mons, and Coignet handed Taliesin the eye-glass. Taliesin was taken back as he looked through the dust-filmed lens, finally catching sight of their pursuers.

"It's the crows. Martyrs, we kill half the bastard army of their bastard King and ambush the Moon Queen's favourite blades, and who in the Martyr's name do they send after us? A pack of religious fanatics! How many of them do you think there are?"

"One hundred and fifty," Coignet said.

"You've sodding good eyes through all that dust they're kicking up."

Finbar made the sign of the tree. "No. It's a mortal holy number for their wicked business."

Coignet pulled his bow off angrily. "Holy! There was the same number when they put my family to the sword. Everywhere they pillaged, their companies had that cursed number."

"Too many for us," Taliesin said. "Even in this monster. He pulled Connaire Mor's dumpling from the giant's belt and waved it at their fat prisoner, then motioned the pistol towards the wall holding back the enchanted forest from the road. "On you go."

"No," Coignet pushed Taliesin back. "Better we stay and fight here than go into that."

"If we stay here we are finished."

"Damn you one-eye, that is not just the tumble, it is the edge of Sisteron. I followed a King in there once, what makes you think I'll follow a crazy bastard like you now? We had forty-thousand men, and we marched out of there a month later with barely enough to fill a good size coaching-inn. That place is evil, inhuman, it eats people and does it so cursed silently you will not even notice your friends have gone."

Taliesin warned Coignet back with the flintlock, then –

keeping him covered – stuck his knife in the prisoner's back. "Do it my overweight friend, or so help me I'll slice you here and leave you for the crows."

Shaking, the prisoner set the kettle-black on a headlong course into the wall. Meg Mons smashed through far easier than Taliesin was expecting, walls fanning out on either side as if they were twin slices of bread. It was only when the collapsing wall hit the forest carpet that the thundering sound of destruction brought a reality to the tons of masonry they had just exploded through.

Trees and greenery spouted up into the air about the cabin, their titanic front-plough breaking through the dense web of the tumble. Animal cries echoed out in response as they pressed forward. Their journey was accompanied by a screeching along the armoured sides, branches flaying a protest across iron sheeting. Connaire Mor shook his head, looking back at the wake of devastation and the thick smoke coiling above them. "They'll no have to use a verderer to follow our trail."

Forest collapsed behind them as the automaton continued her escape through the tall trees. Minutes fleeted past. One of the Gogmagog's sailors squeezed past the timber box, waving frantically at Taliesin. "They're following, the crazy bastards are actually coming after us."

Taliesin moved back onto the firing platform to look over the iron ramparts. "Persistent buggers."

Leaping fallen greenery, weaving around the weirded trees, the Hospitaliers were thundering full tilt in their wake.

Taliesin picked up a puffer, pre-charged with ball and powder. "Twenty paces. Aim for the horses."

Five men could face out of the kettle-black's rear, and five more stood behind them, ready with rammers and powder to reload.

"Let them close, let them close. Now!"

Flints cracked down and a line of fire swept the first line of horses. They could not miss in the press, beasts and riders tumbling down, tripping the soldiers behind them. Every white-coat was ridden down immediately and still the charge continued. Coignet arched arrows back towards the crows, matching the Realmsmen in fury, happy to be settling his score with the devils who had massacred his people.

Fresh flintlocks were in the men's hands and they sighted them again. Black smoke jumped out, another wave of horses falling, then a third, then a fourth. The pursuers were now riding less densely, deliberately. Every time a rank folded, the pursuing horses had time to jump their fallen comrades.

Taliesin shook his head. "They are as bad as Realm dragoons. Charging full pelt at anything that bloody moves."

Connaire Mor shoved two of the soldiers aside and pushed up the small culverin. "It's double-shotted, both with grape."

Taliesin grunted his approval. A double charge meant double powder and two shots in the chamber, but they were not going to be using the culverin again if it blew its barrel.

With a violent kick, the stubby bombard spewed two cases of metal out, the thin copper walls splitting apart, showering the horseman with blisters of canister and hundreds of lead balls.

Dozens of the Hospitaliers went down in a cloud of flesh and white cloth, enough to trip up four lines of mounts trying to bypass the mound of heaving bodies and horses, the rear milling about, thumping the air in frustration.

Bouncing across a rut, the Meg Mons was momentarily airborne, then she came down with every pound of her armoured bulk. A scream of metal protested at such treatment, a large wave of water flooding out from under the skirt, washing away into the hazy greenness of the world around them. Their prisoner folded in the corner, shaking his head.

Meg Mons' dragon-hissing died away, the forest

replacing the silence with a chorus of calls and animal song. Taliesin shouldered his leather pack. "Out, if we are caught up here, we're dead."

Leaping the last few rungs from the armoured side Taliesin landed on his hands and knees, the rumble of hooves close behind him.

Around them the true scale of the forest became apparent, silver-fir large enough to offer leaves as wide as a mailcoach's wheels out towards the sun. A distant mocking hoot signalled its derision of all the minor products of mankind.

Taliesin pressed into the shadowy forest. "Into the trees, force them to dismount."

Fleeing across powdery lichen the soldiers retreated into the brooding darkness. Clouds of green dust were raised by their boots, staining clothes and itching Taliesin's eye.

Laetha swore at his Captain's back, the hunchback furious. "Idiot. Idiot, this toadshit could have been the sort that can grow inside your lungs. You wouldn't even have realised until gorse started growing out of you curse-stupid bloody arse."

"Let him lead the way," called the highlander.

"After you, then."

Laetha tramped past cursing. "My back might be a little bent, but it's your sodding mind that's gone. Leads us into this, then charges out here like a drunk brothel-keeper who has never laid eyes on the forest in his life. We might as well put one of those holy white-coat bastards in charge."

Leading the party, Laetha made surprisingly good time, skirting trees which squirted poisonous sap and flowers that could impale a horse. The soldier led them past a steam filled with darting water vipers, *three-steps*, the number of steps a victim took before dying of their poison.

Clearings were few and far between, the forest possessing a cool emerald luminescence all of its own. In one of the openings in the canopy, they found a small pool, fed from a trickle off a house-high cliff. Laetha hobbled around the water and pronounced it safe to refill their canteens. Coming out, the soldiers luxuriated in real sunlight and the golden warmth, glad to have temporary respite from the endless eery-green tunnels.

Watching them from the cliff face was an all-white bird, eyeing the soldiers with a careless curiosity. Taliesin looked at it and the bird stared right back. He called Laetha over.

"What is it?"

Laetha grinned, an ugly gap-toothed smile. "That's a caladrius, one-eye. It's said to be prophetic. In fact its dung cures blindness, so give it a scare and maybe they'll be enough to give you two good eyes again."

One of the soldiers raised his puffer but Taliesin knocked it aside. "I've lived long enough with this patch. Leave it be."

To their west there was a crackle of puffers, a brief silence, then another wave of fire. Taliesin and the others listened to the sounds without a word. It continued for over a minute then fell away.

"The ones who live here, do they have puffers?" Taliesin asked.

Coignet shook his head. "Of course not. They are not people, they are dagda. They are as much a part of all this as those ferns over there. They have made a pact with this daemon-cursed place."

Coignet turned to Finbar. "Your Martyr wasn't much protection for his holy company, was he?"

Marching back into the carpet of leaves, a quiet fear gripped the soldiers. Taliesin watched the darkness between the trees intently. He could hardly see beyond the range of a dumpling. His first colonel in Cornwall had told him a man needed to hold a holster-flintlock flush with a soldier's chest if he wanted to bring a man down that way. Better to use a muzzle-sword. An early lesson in the army.

"Over there," one of the soldiers cried out panicking. At the edge of their vision a freakish creature watched them. It looked to be a cross between a hyena and a lion, leering at them, a disfigured mouth parted all the way back to twitching ears. Lifting its freakish head, the creature let loose a loud chattering noise. The sound reminded the Captain of a room packed full with talkers, all the more jarring emanating from this inhuman beast.

"A leucrota," Laetha said, forgetting to curse for once. "But the ones back on the islands shy away from people. Away with you, toadshit, come back when you're handsome, and take your laugh along with you!"

As if heeding his words, the leucrota slunk back into the darkness, the sound of its chattering receding into the depth of the forest.

Taliesin was suddenly possessed by the need to build a fire, the most basic of their race's urges. He swore at himself, the triple-cursed knot in his gut, and the sheet of frost sliding down his back.

"Rawn preserve us," said Coignet.

From out of the forest, phantoms appeared to rise from the floor, moving closer as the soldiers stared. Wrapped in robes and cloaks of green, the figures were all around them, hemlock spectres clutching black crossbow-like shapes. Hundreds of shadows.

Without conscious thought or orders, the Realmsman soldiers drew back into a square. On the battlefield they used squares to stand off cavalry charges, and no fully formed Realm square had ever been broken by horsemen alone. When the dragon-browns marched into one of their infamous squares, the enemy brought up culverin to hurl roundshot across their ranks until they no could no longer stand. That was the only way they ever broke the men who fought for Annan Pendrag. It was a record commanders like the Butcher took some small pride in. But here, all the badly-shaven Captain could see was wave after wave of menacing figures closing in, the silence of their noiseless approach more unnerving than any battle scream.

Suddenly Taliesin felt the familiar old fear curl into his gut, the soldier's companion, what Connaire Mor's people called the black dog. "Wait for twenty paces. Front rank, fix your muzzle swords."

Taliesin's voice broke the spell. They were part of the most professional scum that had ever marched across the Princedoms, killers who died for a coin a week and a daily ration of grog. They followed their very own devil and the figures in front of them were just figures once more.

Stepping in front of the square, the tinker's tinny voice sounded out, a surprising degree of command. "Hold fire."

"Out of the way damn you," Taliesin ordered.

"As you value your life, put a hold to your nonsense. All you can achieve by this is to die. Place your puffers on the grass."

Taliesin looked at the shadows surrounding them, then tipped his flintlock down with a malice, hating himself for clutching desperately to the hope offered by the garishly dressed old pedlar.

Coignet cursed the Realmsmen. "You listen to this old fool? I want an end that my family can sing about at the finish of the Circle, not tortured skinless by these daemons."

Connaire Mor wrestled Coignet's longbow away from him. "The tink does no look as if he's ready to die yet."

Surrounding them, the shadows stood silent-still under the bush and vines. Green hoods covered their heads and of faces there was no sign. One stepped forward and pointed his crossbow-like device at Taliesin.

Standing firm the Captain did not flinch. Seconds passed while Taliesin's heart hammered beneath his frayed pioneer's jacket, but it was the irritable hunchback who broke the tension first. "Have you got all day? Kill us all then, you cloaked piece of filth, but spare us your toadshit games."

His speechless accuser moved the crossbow towards the trees and his meaning was clear. They left their puffers and packs and moved off down the overgrown tunnels of heartwood, flanked at a distance by the shadows.

"Tink, man. What do they mean to do with us?"

The tinker pulled his patchwork cloak tight around him as if he was cold. "They'll do as they like, I expect."

Taliesin looked out at their guards drifting in and out of the oaks. "That is not buggering reassuring."

"More reassuring than being dead, and that's surely what you would have been if you had put up any fight."

Coignet refused to look at the others. "You have killed us with your cowardice. Roubaix lost an entire generation in this hell and most my friends with them. By the Leaf, I suppose it's the justice of the wheel that I should come back here to join them after all this time."

The tinker shook his head. "These ones are closer to your Circle than you think."

As they walked into the afternoon, the emerald shade growing longer, the Realmsman fell across the gruesome sight of the Hospitaliers. Their pursuit had ended in a knot of larch, bodies strewn across lemon-green leaves growing together in tufts. Hardly any blood had been spilled, but sticking out of the corpses' white surcoats were oak-like thorns, each the size of a thumbnail.

The tinker saw Taliesin's face and bent over to rest on his cane for a second. "From a bush which explodes seeds to scatter them into the ground."

"I don't see any bushes around here."

The tinker nodded. "That is what the dagda drop into those wooden crosses of theirs. Faster to load than powder and ball and a sight easier to clean."

Leaving the larch trees behind, Taliesin glanced back. The bodies were laid out like so many sacks of grain in the wild grass. They had been religious fanatics, willing to murder anyone to preserve their rightness of mind, unbending soldiers of their unbending God. But they had been people too. Now men who had once felt rain on their cheeks, seen storms and sun-filled days, had met their Martyr sooner than they expected. They were ending their lives as an unexpected prize for leucrotas, wolves and the forest's worms.

With the retreat of the sun, the green light which bathed every part of the forest evaporated like a mist. In its place a fuzzy greyness seeped over the bark and the soldiers. There was no rest, their guides keeping up a merciless pace which had the men stumbling along in numbing monotony, putting all their concentration into shuffling one foot in front of the next. The dagda seemed to need no rest or nourishment, and Taliesin found his canteen emptied by the day's difficult progress.

Along with the approach of night, the competition of forest song became muted, chatter falling away to be replaced by the creaking of insects and wind-rustled leaves.

"Have these daemons got no mortal weakness?" Finbar mopped his sweating tonsured head, struggling up an incline. "They're walking us into our blessed deaths. We need food and a drop of the barely bloody drinkable if we are to keep this up. Sure and a rest too, just a short little chance to ease our aching limbs."

The forest shadows halted at the brow of a heavily forested hill. Below lay a valley, partially cleared of the tumble, and on the facing slope three shapes pulled out of the forest, brushing the darkling sky.

Staring down, the party realised they were looking at three huge trees. At the foot of these mighty living titans the canopy of the wood grew around their base, climbing like stools of fungi beside an oak. The three trees grew so close it was impossible to tell where one started and the others finished. Lime-tinged lights glittered from the beard of the foliage, strung out like faerie lanterns.

Laetha looked down, awe touching his twisted face. "Babel-trees. There were rumours … but never this, look at those bastard monsters."

"Blessed life, you would need a pact with Old Shadow to prosper in there."

It was true. On land where no kingdom dared raise a home, their hooded foemen were living in a green Mountain of the Gods, untroubled by the myriad forms of life which moved through the shadows of the enchanted forest.

Picking a way down the side of the valley, their silent captors herded the soldiers towards the towering mass. Taliesin craned his neck. High above, buildings were carved into the bark, roped walkways strung between herculean branches. Where man would have cobbled together crude log cabins, everything done here was in harmony with its surroundings. Even the buildings above appeared to be a part of the mahogany-coloured column, moss-soft curves merging with the tree at strange angles, maidenhair vines curling upwards in sculptured braids.

Taliesin coughed. The air was damp with dew from a water source somewhere out of sight. Beneath the closest tree, another line of treeguards stood, halberds by their sides. They guarded a gate cut into the tree root, a gnarled serpent-like twist of wood which corded out of this monarch of the tumble, burrowing deep below ground. By rights, the roots would have to reach all the way down into an underground sea to satisfy the trees' thirst.

The dragon-browns were passed through the gate, into a passage lit by lime-coloured lanterns. Following a stairwell carved out of the tree's heart, the exhausted soldiers were shepherded into an amphitheatre circled by hooded figures.

More dagda waited on a dais above, the first ones the men had seen unhooded. Their faces appeared curiously soft, as varied as the soldiers' own, possessing large child-like eyes and shocks of long silver hair. The most striking feature was the skin; changing pattern chameleon-like, tiger-striped green and sap-brown, a constant dance playing across their bodies. Even their eyes changed colour as the islanders looked on with a mixture of revulsion and curiosity.

At last, a female dagda called down to them. "Why did you not fight?"

Taliesin stepped forward. "Perhaps we did not feel like dying today."

"Your feelings are of little relevance here. Sisteron is death, for your kind."

The raffish old tinker swept his cloak down in a flourish and bowed. "Wiser counsel, Mother-Queen."

Bending closer to look, the silver-haired dagda started, then lent back and resumed her stance of regal scrutiny. "Myridyn. The builder. Do you build still?"

"I travel, your highness. Here and there, and there and here."

She nodded. "Of course. I have small desire to trouble you, but these other ones are another matter."

"Hale travelling companions are a difficult commodity to invest in. You would have my gratitude, if you forgave their sin."

"Builder," a voice boomed down. "What gratitude would be worth the price we have paid at the hands of these killers?"

Emerging by the dais was a tall dagda, a glass tube clutched in his hand.

The tinker smiled. "Fandolwyn. Ever the compassionate."

"Do not waste your words on me, builder. Do the plagues of man still make their homes in dead lands with dead hearts, tearing down anything that lives and grows?"

Nodding, the tinker scratched his nose. "Yes, they do that."

"And do they enslave every creature they find, and massacre the ones with hearts too large to slink after them as pets?"

"Yes, I am afraid so."

"Would the kingdoms that besiege us fall down upon our people again, with their smoke and poison and iron? Would they think twice about treating Sisteron with the same barbarity they show when slaughtering their own brothers and sisters?"

The tinker looked thoughtfully at the ceiling. "Well now, I would have to say I think they *have* learnt their lesson on that point."

"As will these," the dagda said angrily "We survive here, but only because such ones as these know they risk becoming as dead as their empty hearts if they trespass."

"Have a little mercy, now," Finbar said. "You don't want to be bothering yourself with a poor bunch like us. We weren't meaning any harm, sure we weren't. Just give us a bite to eat and maybe a little drop of your grape and we will toddle out of here and say no more, all friends together."

Fandolwyn growled. "Are you so stupid, or is this mockery? Your people are the worst of all, you would burn everyone here at the tree for the difference of our hair. We took a party of your kind once. At the end we showed them their own compassion, nailing them to a tree so they could be closer to your saviour."

Coignet cleared his throat and lifted his voice to sound around the chamber. "Do you know me also?"

"We know the colour of your uniform," the Mother-Queen answered down. "And I believe you are of an age to remember what happened to your Empire when they last brought a crusade in here."

"You will forgive me if I don't recognise you. But the things you sent came mostly at night, when you raised the forest to reject us."

"The hatred life feels for your kind was already there, killing-man, we just directed it."

"That is as may be," Coignet said. "But you are right, sooner or later a royal son is going to be born to one of your neighbours, and his young head will be filled with tales of enchantment and the darkness hanging over this place. He will grow up flattered to fancy himself a hero by rich fools, and then another army is going to come tilting down on you. But I can stop that."

Waving aside her advisor Fandolwyn, the Queen of the dark people laughed, a sound like the tinkling of wind chimes. "You seem to lack the trappings of a weirdsman, and to achieve that you would need to work a very great sorcery indeed. Will you replace every noble child with a forest changeling? I understand that is the excuse your kind use to murder crippled cubs born to them."

Coignet pulled out the manuscript from under his shirt, the red seal of Roubaix soft in the warmth of the amphitheatre. "Sometimes a human weakness is all you need. For your eyes, milady."

One of the hooded soldiers passed up the scroll to her and she read through the decorative lines of text. Lifting her head back she filled the chamber with the echo of her golden laugh, then handed it across to a treeguard. "Lock this away. Armsman, you and your friends have your lives. Free escort back to the Empire."

Startled by her mercurial change of heart, Taliesin called up. "That would be no favour, silver-hair, the armies of Roubaix were not best pleased with us yesterday."

"Yes," she laughed again. "I am certain they were quite annoyed with you. Passage to a less hostile land, then."

Their audience ended and the tension drained away from Taliesin. "What was on that bloody scrap of paper, old man? That is what you risked my neck for when you went back into the capital, isn't it?"

Coignet threw his hands up. "It was a letter of confession by the old King. A most dolorous piece of literature, full of self-pity and recriminations; hardly worth reading saving the part where he admitted his wife had been dallying with an officer and had become pregnant. He knew the child could not be his. He had inherited his uncle's sterility, another well kept secret."

The tinker interrupted. "I do recall she only gave birth the once."

"Ha," Coignet grinned. "Pathetic isn't it? How fiercely the Moon Queen worships her father, and all that time he wasn't. She has no claim on the throne and that young fool Buonapar actually married her for it! The dolt. Céroline found out, and then she became even more infatuated with his memory, garroting people for criticism of the old madman. You try and find the sense there."

Finding this news much to his humour, the tinker kicked a little jig. "Oh, that's worth a fortune that is. How the Gods must be laughing. Two rulers both hating each other and a single secret which could destroy them both."

Connaire Mor was less impressed by the foreign quality's debauched manners. "And what about you, tink? Unless I'm going daft, those green-faced devils were going to let you go and do for the rest of us. Why were they calling you the builder?"

"I think when I was here before, I did tell them I was builder," the tinker explained. "It must have been a good little tale to stop them nailing me up to a tree."

"Aye, there's a tale there somewhere, but I don't think it's that one. You, you're as slippery as a cobblestone in a storm."

"That scroll would have been worth a fair weight of angels," Taliesin looked at Coignet. "Everyone in your land would have wanted the power of that."

He shrugged. "I'll die a poor man."

Finbar looked at the treeguards flanking their journey deeper into the living titan, less numerous now the Mother-Queen of Sisteron had given them their freedom. "It is like being back in the blessed monastery, don't these devils have anything to say to each other?"

"But they talk too," said the old tinker, cracking his cane up every step as if he were a blind man. "You just haven't been taught to listen quite as well as they do."

# Chapter 15

Elaine and Gunnar had not heard any other voices since they had been sealed in their small, featureless brig. The passage of time appeared to have absented itself, without a porthole to gaze out. The dandy guessed it would now be close to evening.

Elaine pressed her back to their bare iron wall, letting the damp rivets knead her spine through the Lérridian dress. She had not asked what the Realmsman had really been doing on the Gogmagog, and Gunnar wondered if it would be a kindness to tell her.

Would the Empire of the Tree torture him for what they suspected he knew? Would he tell them if they did? If they tortured Elaine, would they kill the noblewoman before they found out she really knew nothing at all?

No, he would give the Thuringians what they wanted long before it came to that. Better an uncertain fate if he betrayed Annan's secret, than a certain death for both of them on this black rusting hulk.

Sliding back the cover in their door, a human pair of eyes looked them over. Food at last? Gunnar realised how hungry he was. There was a clacking from the door as a heavy metal key turned the lock, then a hand holding an oil lamp swung the light in front of them. Blinking in the sudden illumination, Gunnar found himself seized by tense, shaggy hands. Beastmen pulled him into the corridor; Elaine behind him. It was a mixed crew of the tall Thuringians and beastmen, sailors and demisapi in blue tunics. An officer in a tricorn hat pointed his octagonal barrel in their direction.

Forced up a length of ladder-like steps, the couple were

manhandled onto the deck. They were drifting in shallow waters and Gunnar could see no land under the spartan light of the stars. Having come on deck amidships, the sailors silently dragged them towards the back of the vessel, where the helm and rudder would have been were this any natural ship with sails to catch an honest wind.

Walking forward, one hand on his cutlass to stop it from tripping his breeches, the officer pointed to the block of a wooden tackle suspended above. "I would hope you are enough of a gentleman to want to spare the lady this. We are not barbarians."

Gunnar looked at the pulley, then at the face of the tie-wigged officer. He knew what it was for. About the only thing Realm sailors feared more than the ample floggings their Captains handed out. Keelhauling!

"So. We let you have a drink of the sea first. Ensign, the hoist if you please."

The ropes were wound around Gunnar's waist in a sheet-bend knot and looped over his shoulders. Their captor pulled the rope in tight and Gunnar winced. "Better this does not come undone, yes?"

Three of the wolfmen took hold of the rope and Gunnar find himself being raised into the air, the harness of rope taut on his chest, cutting into his armpits.

"I very much regret the necessity of you having to watch this, milady."

Elaine grappled with the demisapi creatures restraining her, one of the beasts angrily cuffing her across the face as she struggled. "What are you doing to him? What are you doing?"

"There is not a man at sea with the fleet who has not lost a relative to the deprivations of your friends. Do you think our merchanteer Barons smile benignly on your activities? Do you think a letter of marque makes any differences to the burghers whose sons never return to harbour?"

Gunnar was dipping down past the raised platform-deck,

then he was underneath, watching the lower radius of the iron wheels churning the dark water. Frost-cold sea grabbed at his feet and the current of their passage dragged him back, the rope running to its limit until it was taut. Slapping him, a black wave rode him down and Gunnar was underwater, bubbles escaping from his mouth as his feet flailed in panic. Then he was on the surface again, gasping and battling for air as surf sprayed across his hair.

He tried to kick to keep himself above water, but the rope twisted around like a corkscrew and he found himself flipped under the surface again, briny water flowing into his mouth and choking him. With a jolt he resurfaced in a trough and the cold night, a wall of water curling high above him. It whipped across his body while his lungs burst for air. Teasing him, the sea seemed pleasured by this opportunity to play her cat-and-mouse game over and over again. A brief heave of air; then the painful malevolent strain on his lungs, desperately trying to withhold life from this cruellest of mistresses.

It was never-ending. Measureless. And in the fever of exhaustion Gunnar found the rhythm to match the turmoil of his embrace. He gave himself to the pain and in return all he asked for was that brief flash of life and air; the long agonies of pain, then the lightning burst of joy. He submerged his personality to the sea, gave her his all while he endured her slaps and rolls, the dark mysteries which lay under her surface.

He had been here for a day. A week. A year.

Surely this was the finest of loves? Every iota of life he had to give being sucked out of him, his body convulsing with the numbing icy pleasure, shaking with fever, no feelings to worry him, protected from the sensations of pain which was all the gift life had ever seen fit to proffer.

Suddenly his love was taken from him. Trembling, he was being raised away from her warmth. Kicking and crying, his feet did not move and no voice issued from his mouth. It had been his purest experience, she needed to be told what she had meant to him. His head lolled back, and the velvet spread of the sky spun across his eyes, her distant diamonds sparkling on the edge of his consciousness. Were they jealous of him? There was a throbbing rhythm, and Gunnar knew it was the universe singing out for him, a sonnet for his failed passion.

His ascent towards the heavens slowed and halted.

So, even the stars had rejected him.


On the iron platform, Elaine had been tied to the rails, the beastmen tired of her incessant squirming and curses as the day turned to darkness.

"He is a brave young man," said the officer, recalled a few moments ago by one of his human sailors. "Six hours. I have seen men dead in far less time. Our galley served the Admiral the most exquisite pork stew in the Cuddy tonight. Your friend would be far better served by being fed some of it. I assure you, his diet of sea-water will get very monotonous. Just say the word, we will be happy to winch him back down to the deck."

Elaine aimed a kick at the officer's breeches. "Bastard. I don't know anything! I was a stowaway, and do you think he really looks like one of the Realm's most trusted advisors?"

"I doubt if your friend will survive another keelhauling, you know."

Fuming at his stubbornness, Elaine gave up trying to break her ropes and stared pure hatred at the foreign officer.

"Such energy you have, but so badly served. As a gesture of mercy, I shall leave him hanging up there for the duration of another watch. When he comes to his senses I shall pray to the World-Tree that he cares for you more than you evidently do for him. Now he knows the nature of the sea, well, I doubt he will wish to see you exchange places with him."

Striding off, the officer's collarless calf-length coat flapped in the night breeze. It was badly lit to the rear of the ship, Elaine's only illumination the spill from the lancet portholes on the superstructure. Occasional silhouettes moved there, along with shadows walking the parapets of the fortress-like structure. Near the top of the winch, Gunnar's limp body twisted in the wind. She could not see his features in the twilight.

"Gunnar?"

No answer. Martyrs, she prayed, don't let him be dead.

They had slowed down, perhaps stopped altogether, the rhythm generated by the evil black ship sufficiently muted for her to hear waves breaking against their monstrous iron wheels. Night gulls dived across the platform, shrieking, one with a fish or a crab in its beak. Didn't that mean land was close?

Someone was shouting, and a church-like bell peeled from the battlements, the thumping noises dying altogether. She breathed a sigh of relief. They must be anchoring for the night, which meant they would not be dragging Gunnar – or her – across the sea until the next morning. Night wore heavy on the noblewoman's eyelids, but try as she might, she could not fall asleep while she was trussed up to the railings.

Then she saw it. A tentacle rising on the opposite side of the iron platform, she shivered to scream but a hand closed around her mouth.

Mumbling curses under the tight grasp of the palm, she saw what she had first taken for a tentacle was the shadow of a strangely helmeted figure. Others were pulling themselves up. There was something like a claw sticking to the deck railing next to her, wrapped in cloth to eliminate the noise of impact. One of the shadows came across to her, fingers flickering in some form of sign language. Her captor must have answered with his spare hand, because the one in front of her stole silently away.

"No sound," came the whisper. "You speak, I blade you."

Elaine nodded and the hand was removed, her bonds falling away with two quick slicing motions. Small kegs were being rolled across to one of the vessel's wheel mountings, the raiders stacking them in its black shadow.

She tugged on the raider's sleeve and pointed to Gunnar's flaccid form dangling above the deck. There was a growling sound from the man's throat, but after a moment's hesitation he went over to the pulley, and with another of the shadows, they slowly let Gunnar sink back down to the platform. Throwing him over a shoulder they carried him off. Elaine glanced over the side. There were two longboats underneath, more raiders manning the oars. Her liberator patted his back and indicated the noblewoman, but Elaine shook her head. There had been plenty of trees tamed back from the enchanted forests on her family's estate – she could climb well enough. Swinging her legs over the side, she grasped the rope and slithered down, making sure she had a firm grip on each knot in the rope before she moved to the next.

The longboat tipped to one side as she swung into it, the other rowers adjusting their position to accommodate her. Down the grappling-line the rest of the raiders scrabbled, all in near total silence, kicking out into the small boats.

Even by the dimness of the night's crescent moon she could see they were a mixed bunch of rogues, and they slid their oars out into the sable-dark sea, pulling back in practised movements which noiselessly cut the water.

Without conversation the men and their boats retreated, Elaine looking around to see they were heading for the jagged outline of a volcanic island. Following this course, the raiding party slipped past the beach, tracing a passage around its limited coastline. It was small, though obviously large enough to have figured on both parties' navigation charts. An ideal place for crewmen to stretch their legs and go hunting for bird's nests and rain water – too small to support the creatures which might be tempted to add sailors to their own menu. There, by the lee of the island – the raider's own ship, secure in the cloak of the volcanic mountain. Her sails were being unfurled, drifting down lethargically from the rigging. She looked eminently ready to flee the scene. Footholds driven into the hull allowed the raiders to scale their vessel, the men laughing and blaspheming at last in the rush of success.

There was an eruption behind them and for a brief moment Elaine thought the volcano had snatched into life. But the fume of flame in the darkness spun up from behind the mountain.

"Do you want to wait around here and find out how fast she is with one wheel less? Or are you going to stand to your stations, you dogs?"

That voice startled her. It was another woman.

Across the deck the figure swaggered, flared silk-like breeches wavering in the night breeze. "I didn't realise we were taking prisoners tonight."

A sailor moved forward. "They weren't our prisoners, Graine, they was theirs. This one here looks as if Bazin's been giving him a good old Imperial dunking."

She noticed the unconscious form of Gunnar for the first time, bending over him. "Well at least thisun seems to be a fair young buck. But now why did you go and be bringing back his bawdy?"

Elaine was about to retort when a shadow loomed up on the upper deck. "If their loss means anything to Bazin, then you have all earnt an extra ration of grog this night."

Elaine stepped back. Had she fallen from one devil-ship only to step onto another? Twin horns curled from the shadow's head, baneful red eyes fixed on her from within the darkness. It came down the stairs and stepped under the light of a mast-lantern.

It was a beastman. Bunched, muscled features twisted

around the maw of a bull. Snorting like the minotaur of some ancient civilisation, the creature advanced on Elaine. When the splinters brushed her neck she discovered she was backed up against the mast.

"A curious prize for this night's work. Unexpected. Tell me, young lady, why was Bazin holding you on his new iron toy?"

Elaine looked into the savage face of the demisapi. "We … we picked the wrong ship to sail in. Bazin sunk us for it."

"And what ship would that be?"

"The Gogmagog."

At this the crew raised a cry, clustering around their prisoners and jostling closer to hear what the girl had to say.

"You see," the beastman turned to the sailors. "You see now how it is. The sand-hairs will scuttle us all, one by one. They mean to sweep us clean from the ocean and burn us out of our homes."

"Burn you out?" Elaine looked at the crew. "But who are you?"

"My name is Ibn-Dali, and let me show you my ship." Laughing – the sound of a rumble of barrels rolling across stone – the beastman climbed over to the bow, lifting a lantern to light the flag fluttering there in the clasp of the wind. It was a curved *yataghan* cutlass reversed out of black.

And above it was a skull.


Elaine knew about corsairs. She had been at Court when the Queen's Office of Revels commissioned a troupe of travelling players to stage a winter production of *The Tales of Dragut Rais*. So entranced had Elaine been by the romance, the grand sweep of that play, she had kept the copy of the stage sheet in her dresser. She could even recite the text of it from memory.

*The Tale of Dragut Rais, who were hang'd at execution*

*dock. Giving a more full and true account than any yet published, of all their murders, piracles, maroonings, places of refuge and ways of living.*

Dragut's adventures and his valourous crew seemed a long way removed from the coarse, vile collection of killers which swarmed over the *Khair-ed-Din.*

Three days at sea now with these rogues.

Elaine suspected that whatever command the beastman master had over his crew, it had much to do with the fact that Ibn-Dali could rip any seaman apart with his monstrous fists. She doubted Ibn-Dali would have settled for Dragut's method, the ballot of the corsairs.

Elaine sat by the windlass of the Khair-ed-Din, a heavy needle in her hand as she sowed into a fold of sail. She had not disabused the minotaur-headed Ibn-Dali of his assumption their position on the Gogmagog had been that of crew rather than cargo. As fellow corsairs they seemed eligible for protection, but as passengers, their true worth would only be measured in the amount of angels her family might be willing to pay for her return.

It had come as quite a shock when the noblewoman discovered that their lives onboard were governed by regulations every bit as strict as the Realm's navy. Where was the brutal carousing of brave Dragut? But considering the diversity of the crew and their violent life, it made sense for the problems fated to explode in the closed world of a corsair vessel to be judged by common rules.

Elaine's stars had smiled on her. Not only had the Khair-ed-Din's sail-maker lost his journeyman understudy in a recent engagement, but he was elderly and bordering on the infirm, hardly alert enough to notice that the only needlework Elaine knew had been learnt at the draconian knee of a Countess of Cornwall.

"Hey girl, I was on the maindeck earlier. Your friend was looking as if he might break his fever soon." It was the old man who claimed to have once been the worthiest of Play

Directors in Lotharingia. Unless he had staged Dragut Rais, it seemed no qualification for a life of piracy.

"You get that if you swallow a little too much of the bad stuff. I've seen men die from it, but that one, he may be young but he looks as if he's seen worse and lived."

Elaine smiled. He was one of the few men on the vessel who did not look at her with lechery hungering in his eyes. Not for this first time, she wondered what Ibn-Dali's views were on her position of sufferance. Or the code she could not ask questions about without arousing their suspicions.

The dark-haired wild woman, Graine – Ibn-Dali's lieutenant – was the only other female on board. And she had casually broken one of the mates' nose after the sailor had gone too heavy on the grog and made advances to her. He had not even touched Graine, but he had been lying on the floor close to death while she waved a dirk around, daring anyone else who felt like it to try for another of her 'kisses'.

Graine barely contained her contempt for Elaine. Perhaps she had relished her lost status as the only woman among dozens of rogues, devils and cut-throats? Flaunting her admittedly supple body: then extinguishing the ardour of the more foolish among them with sudden bursts of savagery.

Elaine's ex-Play Director saw where her frown was directed. Graine swaggering along the upper deck, occasionally making adjustments at the helm.

"Better not be making an enemy of that one, girl. She's Martyr-tight with the Rais, and she's got a fire in her hotter than a torturer's coals."

*The Rais.* That was what they called the Captain.

"They're not, well, you understand …?"

"Ibn-Dali," he laughed. "He's taken a vow hasn't he. No drink, and none of the ladies. They're funny like that down in the southlands. But Graine's awful fond of him anyway. I don't know the all of it, but they met when the Rais was still a slave on Bazin's boat. Those was in the day's when Bazin and his rascals were fighting us fair in real sodding ships. Imperials didn't use to have their beastmen in those days either, but they did not have anything against a little slaving. They took the Rais with a bunch of *Wa'a Kaulua* sailors after a battle."

"But he is a demisapi?"

"Aye. Where the Rais comes from, they live by the word of a heretic, and this Prophet wrote a place for all the creatures in his book. Even the buggering ugly ones, but don't be telling the Rais I told you that. They're not like the feral ones that might have chased you though the forest, if you ever took your young head out herb hunting."

Elaine sniffed. "Oh, how very barbaric."

"If we ever get taken in the west, the Militant Order would have us on their racks quicker than spit for cavorting with the heathen. But then, they'd probably stretch us all for piracy anyway, so what do we have to lose?"

There had been members of Elaine's family who had lost their heads in the games of the Court – her grandmother sprung immediately to mind, foolishly crossing Annan's father. But it would be an ignoble end indeed to become the first in a long and lustrous line to have her corpse wrecked by the black crows of the Martyr. Not quite the future her darling father had in mind for her.

"It's good to have you on board girl, but one thing is certain, the Rais stealing you away is not going to make our lives any easier. The Admiral and the Rais, they've got a hate going the like of which I never saw in any of my productions in Lotharingia. Not in *The Tragedy of Gartfriedel*, not even in *The History of Hrungnir,* and that was my best piece. It's an epic, girl, that's for certain. And the only way it is going to end is when one of that pair is feeding barnacles down in mother deep."

So, she had landed in the middle of a private war. Sea-thieves versus the distant Empire's mariners. Elaine looked around the deck. Men scrambled over the rigging, heaving the sounding-lead in the shallow waters, hauling ropes and swabbing planking.

Ibn-Dali's crew were rounded up from the scrapings of a dozen lands, deserters from every navy in the Enclosed Sea. There were quality fallen from grace in the delicate machinations of foreign Courts, merchanteers who found taking goods more pleasurable and profitable than selling them, dozens of fishermen glad to abandon their families. Otherwise, they were just those who possessed a plain taste for blood and plunder.

It was one that Elaine suspected lay firmly in the last category that came up behind her, snaring the noblewoman's canvas sheeting.

Graine.

"Enjoying the sun on deck are you?"

Elaine bit her tongue. "Very pleasant."

"Very pleasant," she mocked her accent. "Yes, I'm sure it is. I know what you were on Bron's ship, and it wasn't one of his sail-makers, was it?"

Staring at the raven-haired corsair, Elaine prayed to calm her speeding heart. This vicious hoyden must be able to hear the beating. What would happen now, ransom or a quick thrust of one of the knives belted around her crimson sash?

"Look at your pretty little eyes, your pampered hands. That annoyingly winsome way of talking which you seem to think is so *very* impressive and regal. You haven't seen a day of real work in your life, have you?"

Elaine stared, mesmerised by the fury locked behind Graine's tempestuous eyes. "Shall I tell them what you really are? Oh I think the crew would love to know."

So this was the end of them. Would they kill Gunnar too? Would they drag him out still in his fever, and toss them both into the sea?

"Whore. Pretty little dollymop. Did their crew enjoy you

every night, did you please them?"

Gasping, Elaine let go of the canvas. She thought she had been kept for ... that. Graine smiled, mistaking the noblewoman's shock for an admission of guilt.

"No, I won't tell them. It would be bad for discipline – the filth on this ship. When we make port you can crawl back to it. There are lots of of taverns where we're going, they'll pay plenty for you to slip between perfumed sheets again. But you stay away from me on the Khair-ed-Din, just keep downwind so that you don't trouble me."

Graine walked away and Elaine had to keep from screaming. How dare she! Back in the islands such rubbish as her would not have been fit company for the family coachmen, yet the pirate bitch, she had marked Elaine down as nothing higher than a bawdy-cabin whore. Her! A noblewoman of one of the most powerful, wealthy, distinguished Houses in the Realm. Why last year, she'd had the young Princes of Dal Albaeon and three more Princedoms following her around like love-sick puppies until their families stepped in to cool their ardour. And this vixen had the temerity to cast her as a ship's dollymop, a poorly-paid role which was notoriously unpleasant even in the tiers of *whoredom*.

Gunnar felt as if someone had hollowed out his bones, filling his veins with air to replace the blood. So light he might float out his hammock and clutch onto the brass candle-holder swaying from the ceiling.

Delirious, he lifted his eyelids.

They were rocking in a gentle swell and it was dark beyond the bow windows, a thin sliver of moon in a cloudless firmament. He had dreamed of stars, great fields of them, singing in such unearthly harmony; but the meaning of their heavenly opera had eluded him. Teetering his head around, Gunnar saw he was in what looked to be a round-house cabin. Had he been transferred onto a ship equipped with a surgeon? He doubted if a room like this existed outside the insane Admiral's own cabin, and Bazin would be unlikely to vacate it for his suffering prisoners.

Opening the door, a tall raven-haired women entered the cabin. Apart from brightly-coloured diaphanous clothes she could have been any of the dusky Lériddian women wandering through Cuenns. That made sense. If Bazin was going to bundle them off the devil-ship alive, he would as likely hand them back to Elaine's treacherous uncle.

"There was a girl with me."

This obviously was not what she had wanted to hear. Savagely, she forced the weakened Realmsman to lay back in the hammock, a firm grip on his blond hair. "But there is almost nothing to her. How can you lie with something that? You would scrape yourself to death on her scrawny bones."

So Elaine *was* here. But had he landed on a ship of lunatics, one of his father's phantom vessels, manned by the shades of those who had perished at sea?

"Look at me, sand-hair, am I not as fine a sight as you have seen?"

She was that. Buxom, with a body as lithe as a mountain cat, a face that would set bucks in most the coaching-inns of the Realm duelling for her hand.

Almond-green eyes flashed as she flicked her long dark mane across his face, drawing close and pressing her full lips against his. Gently biting his tongue she raked her fingers down his chest, and Gunnar had to admit, if anyone was capable of raising the dead, it would be this human firestorm. In Tryban he had once seen the dance of a gypsy maiden, one of the extended families which lived a dangerous nomadic existence travelling the Crown highways, paths torn back from the dark forests.

This one was the same as that dance; feral, unbroken, radiating raw defiance, so full of the energy of life that she could devastate a man and leave him an empty broken shell

– just by the fact of her existence.

Laughing, she dropped herself off the hammock, every self-aware movement the step of a dance. "Now tell me that you don't want me."

Gunnar lay there as if he had taken the concussion from a roundshot.

"The same men who wanted to drown you. They tried to make me a whore too, once. But they lost interest after I'd bladed my fourth sailor."

Gunnar felt his sweating forehead. His mop of hair was soaked too, the white hammock wet where he had been resting it. "Where am I?"

"My cabin. I made you soup when you couldn't even remember your own name, I held you when you cried all night like a dying dog. Then I covered you in blankets when you shivered in the heat of half-day. That makes you mine, sand-hair. You owe me a life. Yours!"

Elaine stirred more of the dark dry nuts into the open canister. It still seemed strange to her that pitching seed-like things into boiling water would made such an addictive drink. No one had yet got drunk from Ibn-Dali's *carfeel,* but many of the crew would sooner take wooden pitchers of carfeel in lieu of the brown-coloured grog which left them thirstier afterwards than before they had quaffed it.

Elaine had taken some down to Gunnar after she heard he had recovered, and the officer had seemed strangely hushed, though doubtless that was only to be expected after an attack of fever. While no-one else was in earshot, she updated the young soldier of their precarious situation, and the fabrications they had better adhere to if they were to survive it. Gunnar thought he could remember enough of ships to bluff a history of sea-borne iniquity. To keep their morale up, Elaine had expressed the hope that the dandy's familiarity with flintlocks and sabres would gloss over such occasional failings.

Scooping out a mug of the drink, the sailor who claimed a once-vigorous theatrical genius warmed his hands on the steam curling from the canister. It was chilly, the night sky cloudless.

"We'll be at port soon, right enough."

"Will we be flying our flag when we go in?" She pointed to the evil grinning skull.

"Girl, this is one place where they'd blow us out the water for *not* having it up."

"How so?"

He tapped his nose and smiled. "You'll see, lass. It's a fine old place we're going to. No airs or graces or getting sniffy about having us in town. And that's a rare thing these days. Why, last year we sailed into Gliarin and the locals grabbed some of our boys. You know what they did? The bastards blew them from the mouths of the port culverin, scattered them across the briny-blue as they chased the Khair-ed-Din out. Gliarin, for love of the Martyr! People like us built that island, made them rich. It's those Imperial bastards behind it, spreading their gold and their merchanteers across every neighbour who'll let them in."

Elaine smiled at the old man.

"You want to know what a real pirate looks like, lass? He gets some greedy Emperor – who's stolen all his land from the peasants in the first place – to sign a charter which says he is now a Free Company and can do as he and his avarice bloody pleases. And any port he wants opened to him, gets a visit from their bloody big fleet that blows the legs off all the locals until they see sense. Corsairs, we're bloody amateurs compared to the Empire of the Tree, girl."

"That's a good drink, what is it?"

Elaine looked behind her. Gunnar, his face ashen but still strong enough to test his legs on deck.

"You shouldn't be out here," she fussed. "It's getting cold."

The old sailor passed his mug over to Gunnar. "Don't be

all ado, girl. A tang of salt air has had plague victims up and dancing before. Be getting a gulp or two of this down your throat, mate."

From the mast above, a shout rung down from the crows nest. "Land ho. Land ho."

Elaine rushed to the forecastle deck. There was no land in sight, but there was a fog. It lofted above them, a huge bastion of rolling white smoke.

As the sea detonated, Elaine screamed. In front of them, a streaming column of magma funnelled into the air, hot tears of molten rock spraying across the sea to starboard. Black dust followed the rain of rock, drifting in the night breeze and blowing across their deck.

To port another column of fire howled towards the stars, lacerating the night with red afterimages. All around the corsair vessel, the waters were seething as glowing rock landed over the waves; the wind so hot the very air rippled and twisted as if were being tortured by devils. They would be boiled alive as if they were lobsters in the shell of the Khair-ed-Din.

Gunnar grabbed Elaine.

Martyrs, so this was it. Of all the sea stories his father had terrified his young son with, of all the horrors, this tale was by far the worst. Cannibals, mutiny, seaslugs, they paled in comparison to the absolute nightmare. One island which had been twisted and warped beyond human understanding, a punishment for the evil necromancy with which the demon-possessed ancients had perverted the course of the world. Taranto.

All that remained of the Sunken Empire.

# Chapter 16

There was little room for wandering around the chamber given to Taliesin for the night. The dagda's concept of architecture appeared completely alien to the dragon-browns. If it was not for the curious elegance of each curve, the rooms and tunnels of the tree-city could have been caves hollowed out in wood – womb-like in effect.

Carved close to the bark, a sheet of semi-transparent sap had been fitted to look out onto the constellation of lights, lanterns sparkling across the world of leaves. On a disc-shaped balcony, Finbar found the company's officer looking out into the chasm between the trunks.

Taliesin's noticed he had company. "It smells nothing like a city does it? No soot or smoke, no hawkers screaming their wares. No muleteers swearing at each other caught up in a cattle drive. No women throwing their slops out over you."

Finbar smiled. "No blessed little children running after the foreigners to pelt them with rotten turnips."

"There it is again." Taliesin motioned towards the buildings clustered barnacle-like higher up the tree.

Music showered gently across the two Realmsmen, fragile notes, the same unearthly tinkling which could be caught in dagda speech.

"No mortal place for the likes of us," Finbar wheezed. "Us poor fools shouldn't be here, we should be back home, you leading your brave fellows and me drinking a toast to your army. Ah, but perhaps the Martyr made the forest as fearful as it is so these ones could have a home here."

"These are daemon lands, there are no reasons here. You are either as strong as the land or it destroys you. Those silver-haired devils would have turned us into worm food, if Coignet hadn't given them a weapon to hold against their neighbours."

"It's a rare hard place that's true."

"There is not much I fear. My stars have taken me through battlefields in every bastard Princedom in the Realm. I've stood and seen horseman ride regiments into the earth, watched the Foot trying to hold their intestines in with nothing but a strip of leather. My eye was splintered in a hail of grape outside Fanrig, and I had to look on using the other while they closed the wound with boiling pitch. In all that time, I knew I was never going to be one of the poor sods who ended up on the butcher's bill. But when they caught us out there in that green hell, I thought we were for dying then."

Finbar knew the one-eyed killer would not have told this to anyone else in his band. They followed him as much for his legend of invincibility as a Crown commission; the Captain who would march into the underworld to beard Old Shadow in his den if there was an advantage to be had.

Perhaps Taliesin would have talked to the tinker, but the strange old man had disappeared once again. Their dagda hosts remaining even more uniformly silent over his absence than usual. In his gut, Finbar did not trust the raffish mysterious tinker, and that fact worried him more than it should have done.

Turning his attention to Taliesin, the renegade monk pulled on his bulbous nose. "So you worry about mortal dying. Did you also worry about not being here before you were born?"

Taliesin grunted and looked down into the gloom. It was not death he feared, but failure. That someone would one day look on his grave and know there lay a man who had been born into nothing and died with only the same.

Disliking the claustrophobia of their burnished sleeping

chamber, Coignet wandered the serpentine tunnels of the tree with Connaire Mor and a solitary guard, the hooded dagda there to warn away any over-curious onlookers. The highlander was looking forward to retrieving their provisions. As much as he hated Annan Pendrag, he felt naked without her heavy Realm sabre by his side.

The tube-like burrows they passed through were empty of citizenry. Not that Connaire Mor suspected they would have heard the silent creatures, even if there had been a coaching-house's worth on the other side of the wall.

Winding its way out of the trunk, a walkway jutted out across the chill night, swaying slightly in the wind. Following the treeguard onto it, they looked down onto bulb-shaped minarets, buildings and towers blossoming like rose buds from the lower branches. Circling underneath, a cloud of night ravens soared in the warm air patterns surrounding the trees.

Crossing the chasm, the highlander and armsman walked into the burrows of the neighbouring trunk, climbing higher and higher up the colossal growth. Under the lime-green lantern light they entered a cove of hollowed timber, realising this was the end of their journey.

Here was scattered the debris of man's intrusions into the strange land of the dagda: banks of piled swords, helmets, pikes and engraved gorget plates glimmering in the pale lantern light. Looking it over, Coignet saw their puffers and packs had been clumsily thrown near the front of the precipice of equipment.

It spoke much of mankind and her ruling class's universal hubris. Black armour from the small nations bordering to the north, a brace of holstered dumplings, flintlocks which would have belonged to a wealthy horseman, polished chest plate decorated with ribbons and feather plumes.

Connaire Mor lifted up a flintlock. It was not one of the cheap numbers produced in the smoke-filled workshops of the Realm or the mainland. The mountain-man ran a hand across its wooden furniture – oak carved with the head and jaws of a forest cat – then scooped up a matching flask filled with priming powder. Pulling back the flint from the puffer's pan, the highlander found it was cracked and blunt. Whoever had last owned it had been too desperate towards their end to exchange the flint for a fresh one. He looked down the barrel and felt its weight.

"You can keep your flimsy puffers from the forge, man. This must have belonged to some real quality."

Coignet said nothing. He had seen the island savages fire off thirty balls to a pound of powder, with their puffers from the shoddy workshops of Llud-din and Gwynedd. Pouring out fire faster than any Roubaix regiment ever had. Gold-etched axes and velvet gloves had not saved his King, nor turned back the beasts wailing out of the darkness. Coignet doubted any elaborately engraved tools of death from this army of ghosts would help improve the Realmsmen's rate of fire, or their fortune.

Spilling over with a crash, a hill of powder horns slid across the floor, a sooty cloud of fine-corned priming powder spraying out. Lying on his back, their hooded dagda companion was inching across the flasks, a cheap militiaman's bill thrust into his chest while purple-red blood coursed across the opulent armour.

Uriel stared at them across the mounds of dispossessed weapons, no sign of the assassin's wolf to be seen.

Coignet picked up a sword. "You're in a damn foul place not to have silver hair."

"That is an interesting accent," Uriel said. "You must be the Moon Queen's bed warmer. She wanted to try me, but then, I do have my standards."

Pulling a hand out of his jacket, Connaire Mor pitched a throwing knife at the thin assassin. It flashed over the fallen weapons, cracking into the wood as Uriel took an indifferent step to the side.

Connaire Mor was already charging the killer with another two knives, one in each hand. Seemingly unarmed, Uriel slid his boot under a grounded stave and kicked it up into the air, catching it and stepping forward.

Trained in short-blades by generations of bloody clansman, Connaire Mor came up for a deadly low ripping belly-thrust, but Uriel cleaved the stave across to block the right blade, turning it around like a windmill to smash into the mountain-man's arm. Stumbling with pain the giant twisted out and threw his surviving blade arm towards the assassin. Uriel pushed the longer reach of the stave down and rammed it onto Connaire Mor's knee; as he folded to one side Uriel stepped in and kicked out, smashing the giant soldier down to the floor.

"Plenty of strength but no technique," Uriel said, raising his dead eyes to stare at Coignet. "That is not a mistake an old man like you would make, is it? You can't afford to."

"Whose damn creature are you?"

"You've taken something that doesn't belong to you, old man. It would be a very good thing for you and the island savages if you gave it back."

Coignet laughed and advanced on the assassin. "Then we will be all friends together, isn't that so?"

"Have it your own way."

Coignet stepped in fast with his rapier's point, Uriel's feet dancing a pattern to the left, shifting his centre out of the sword's path. Swaying forward, Uriel snatched Coignet's sabre arm and appeared to rock it up and down, two snapping sounds popping across the chamber while the armsman screamed.

Uriel flipped Coignet over and stamped on the soldier's right leg, dislocating it with a mean splintering. Coignet tried to grasp onto the pain. Anything to remain conscious.

Searching expertly, Uriel ran his hands through Coignet's jacket, trying his silk shirt, then took a knife to the uniform, slicing into the lining. Uriel grunted and pulled the boots off, then prised open the heels. There was a hidden pocket in the soft leather of the left boot, but no manuscript.

Uriel flipped Coignet over again. "Old man, where is it? Tell me which one of your friends has it, or you will discover there are nerves in your body that you never knew existed."

Coignet said nothing, he was trembling and his breathing was slow and shallow. Uriel cursed and felt the armsman's chest.

A stroke.

Spreading one hand flat on Coignet's white overcoat, Uriel made a fist with the other and hammered it down. Coignet's body arched slightly but his breathing was fading quickly away.

Soundlessly Uriel repeated the hammering action but the armsman still did not respond. "Fight, old man. Just long enough for a minute for me."

Uriel pulled out a wooden rod from under his cloak, beating the armsman with it in a measured rhythm, touching precise areas around the man's chest and side. A racking cough sounded like a snore from the old man.

Behind the assassin there was the vibration of a shifting board, and spinning around, Uriel curved two jagged steel snowflakes into a forehead apiece. Even as the two treeguards doubled over, a brace of the dagda's crossbow-like weapons discharged in a shower of red dust. Walnut-like seeds blew their shells apart and thorns flicked into Uriel. Numbed, the dangerous man slid across a piling of halberds, his face setting into a corpse-like rictus. Crowding around, the silver-haired creatures moved in, carrying the dead assassin's body away.

Lifted to his feet by the dagda, Connaire Mor staggered over to Coignet. "Do something man, he's as cold as ice."

Tracing his hands over the armsman's chest, the courtier Fandolwyn shook his head. "His heart has burst, there is no healing in the world which can save him from this."

"You're soft," Connaire Mor yelled. "There's plenty of life left in him still. Bring a bastard leach in here, he'll save him."

"The wheel has turned," Coignet's voice hacked, his eyes struggling to quiver open. "My time is over."

"Don't be daft, man. We would all be red meat for the ravens if it wasn't for you. They'll save you, you will see."

"Hush boy, I can – see – them. You live, well, for me. Do you hear? They're all there, Helig the Sword, dam Delidor, every lion-coat who died in this stinking hell. Can't – you – see?"

"Open your swining eyes, Coignet, tell me who else you can see. Who else!"

Fandolwyn pulled Connaire Mor away. "He has gone, leave his shade to walk in peace."

Above Coignet's corpse, clouds of the ravens nesting in the huge living tree circled the funeral platform, a squadron of winged spirits to escort his soul into whatever warrior hall the old man had followed during his long life. Watching in silence, the Realmsmen saw a torch dip and touch the body, then suddenly it was consumed by a wave of flames. He had been bathed in wheat-oil and the body rippled in an intense white fire.

Finbar nodded, and followed the white clouds up into the heavens, clear blue with the frost of the morning. "He was a blessed wicked offender against you, there is no doubt, but if you are as grand as I think you are, you'll be sure to look kindly on him anyway."

On the other side of the tree trunk, the soldiers filed out from the shadow of the giants and departed into the tumble, two dagda guides at their head. Finbar waited a minute then walked after them, the lament of ravens attending the body behind him.

It was dark in the small chamber and Fandolwyn lit one of

the lime-green lanterns. Across the room, Uriel was separated from the dagda by a wall of bamboo-like bars, his hands and feet secured by heavy black manacles.

He looked at the silver-haired courtier without a trace of emotion. "You have an antidote for your seed spine."

"Obviously."

Uriel pulled at his heavy chains. "You flatter me. Am I so dangerous?"

"And you interest me. How did you get to Llfhome without the unity detecting you? No-one of your kind has ever done that before. Even your cursed human weirdsmen have few deceptions to make themselves invisible from tree and leaf. And you are not one of them."

Uriel sneered and sniffed the air. "What is that stench I can smell?"

Astonishment broke Fandolwyn's mask, then he regained a measure of control over himself. "So, you have mastered your glands' essence. What a very subtle creature you are, there are few who can use their essence to regulate the lesser beasts in that way. You may be unique among your kind, but then I think perhaps not. Who taught you our ways?"

Uriel laughed. "Father oak and sister yew."

"You will tell me," Fandolwyn said. "Why show me you know our ways but deny me the rest?"

"Your Mother-Queen was the one who instructed me, silver-hair. And in return I taught her everything she needed to know about rutting out her bawling little ugly brood."

Fandolwyn battered the bars. "Animal. Filthy man-thing. I shall rip your secret out from you and leave you a dead and empty husk."

Turning his head away in derision Uriel stared at the graceful curve of his cell's ceiling.

Setting a stool outside the bars, Fandolwyn sat opposite Uriel's shackled body. Changing colour with the movement of Fandolwyn's emotions, his dagda pupils stirred from the passions of crimson, reforming as an ebony-specked grey.

Thrusting out, the dagda's mind shattered against Uriel's own, trying to force a passage into the assassin's memory. He whipped against Uriel's defences like a snake writhing against granite, but there was not an inch of surrender to be found in his captive's consciousness.

Uriel's head arched back, his eyes burning in pain while Fandolwyn tried to push into his mind as an axe cleaving into the heart of an oak. No child born of a woman should have stood the intensity of that strike, but Uriel struggled still, his body whipping from side to side.

Who! Who! Who! The inquisition lashed across Uriel until the dagda's green face grew crimson with the exertion of squeezing the assassin. Moisture trickled off silver hair and flowed down the his exotic face, Fandolwyn leaning forward, squeezing the cell's bars until his knuckles went white with strain.

Uriel screamed and fell limp, the chains clinking down until they finally caught the slack.

Wary of the deadly assassin, Fandolwyn struggled up pale-faced, issuing a silent command for his treeguard to come down to the cell. Carrying their seed-thorn bows levelled, four green-hooded soldiers waited by the shoots of the bars while their master traced his hand across the assassin.

"He is dead. Burn him, and scatter the ashes far away from Llfhome, *fifewydar* will grow where his filthy body rests."

Fandolwyn stalked away, disquiet eating away into his confidence. How had one of the cursed man-things managed not only to use their own ways to walk through the forest undetected, but possessed the strength of will to turn away an attempt to peel his mind, to the very point of death itself?

With the twin dagda guiding the Realmsmen's passage,

their journey through the deep valleys and forests of Sisteron was uneventful. Sensing the presence of the dagda, the twisted beasts of the tumble shied reluctantly away from the small column of soldiers, and the dragon-browns skirted the worst areas of the tumble, green abysses waiting patiently for warm-blooded life to spill and soak across its roots.

They made good time, given confidence by the dagda's quiet knowledge of the perverted and flourishing paths of their home. After four days journey through the dense tunnels of underbush, their guide's finally halted. "There," one pointed. "Your kingdoms."

There was little difference in the forest ahead of them, but between the trees there was a carpet of downy white pasture reaching as high as a soldier's boots. It seemed to flow in the breeze – then Taliesin realised it was not grass, but fine haze. Hanging there like a wall, the mist yielded silkily to his legs and Taliesin turned back towards their guides. "What land is this?"

The dagda were already reduced to spectres in the trees. "It is the Many Lands. Your names pass so quickly…"

Connaire Mor unwrapped the vellum map he had bought in the City of Isles, cheap and damp from the mist. Its accuracy could barely be trusted, but precise maps were expensive, not to mention jealously guarded by Kings, coachmen, and the merchanteer caravans. "I say we would be here. Finbar, you have Latin, what is this swining word?"

Finbar took the map in his sausage-like fingers. "Ah, it is the Thuring states. I know of this place. It was the mortal home of a Holy-Emperor King, but that was a good few ages ago. It is split into hundreds of lands now, it could be any of these."

Finbar squinted at the small faded script again. "The Theme of Räuber, Sennfontein, Triesbaden, Weider-Felter. Yes, one land but now it's blessed many, true enough.

Sweet life, but this is a poor turn! It is a wicked place, full of war and killing. The tales I have heard of these lands; they'll stick a blade in us as soon as give us a feed. We should be going home, not into this evil place."

Taliesin pushed out across the lake of mist. There had been few tales in his youth – and only one book, the same one the poorhouse forced on all its wards. The urchins had only the hopeful fantasies produced by other children. Hoards of gold which a daring and clever lad could thieve in the congested avenues of Llud-din. Or the girl who discovered her parents were not the miserable brutes beating her every day, but a Lady and Peer who had had their daughter snatched by Llud-din's rooftop thieves – the worshipful company of skymen. Stories for children. Struck by melancholy, Taliesin looked out into the tumble.

Locating one of the lofty trees which Lactha spat was safe enough, Bors, a surviving sailor from the Gogmagog, shinned up it with the same ease he had clung onto his sails. Looking out across the measureless canopy he found no sign of man's mark, only the towering crests of the wood.

They marched on.

Everywhere the pallid mist flowed across the dirt and meadows. Taliesin had known fogs following in the aftermath of great battles, the cloying smog of culverin and puffers drifting out to shroud the killing fields of man until the weather could stand no more and covered over the fetid reek of death. But this, this continuous sea of vapour sucking at their boots, it was unnatural.

Again the sailor Bors climbed a tree, finding only the clear stretch of the tumble's canopy. Not a sign of inhabitation. They marched down a valley and into a copse of giant yew trees perverted by the strangeness of the forest, tree trunks bent and swollen into dozens of human faces; knots of grotesque mouths, knobby brows, pinched noses coated with coarse moss.

At one point a Bonnacon confronted them. But it

appeared some distance away, and when the bull-like creature dipped its curled horns in challenge, the soldier scouting the lead lifted his puffer and fired, the thunder and smoke terrifying the beast as it leapt sideways and bolted back into the weald.

They had little choice but to spend the night in the wilderness. For a camp, the Realmsmen finally found a hillock rising out of the floor of mist. It was a distance from the nearest trees and there was enough deadwood lying around to kindle a good-sized blaze. Uneasy sleep fell across Taliesin while distant animals trilled out their calls from the tumble, the pacing of sentries the only friendly sound.

Morning crept out into the clearing, announced by the aria of bird song. Washing down a swallow of the honeyed liquid which the dagda had filled their canteens with, Taliesin abruptly pulled his flintlock up. Where there had been seventeen men camped around the knoll, now there were only sixteen.

Grabbing their sentry, Taliesin shook the man. "Damn you to hell, you were sleeping last night."

"Not me," protested the man. "Ask Brakriu, he saw guard duty. With me and Laetha!"

Taliesin looked around. It was the soldier Brakriu who was no longer in the encampment.

"Martyrs," Taliesin swore. "Curse this forest to damnation. What sort of bastard creature is it that could come in here and pluck a man out without a scream?"

Finbar made the sign of the tree. "This is a wicked bad start to the day. Out of one hell and into another, and not even a drop of man's mortal food to sustain us in our perils, just these tree-devil's loaves to feed us."

"Move out," Taliesin ordered. "We'll march to whatever passes for civilisation in this shadow-world if it kills every last one of us, and Old Shadow can take his buggering forest."

Dragging their hemp-leaf sack to the summit of the pyre, the dagda treeguards rolled the bag along the platform. More corpse sacks waited below, but when one of the workers tried to lift one, the treeguards stopped her and pushed her back.

"They will not join with the one up there, that one is *fifewydar*. He will burn alone."

Stepping back, the pyre attendants looked aghast. Earth-cursed, one of the hollow hearts, dead-life which could only pollute and ravage the greenheart. But it was from a race which had passed the levels of regret and rapture, so must still be burnt according to the law.

Astonished, one of the treeguards noticed a timber-wolf sitting opposite the pyre, its pelt as metallic-silver as the hue of their own hair. He produced the odour of tolerated-inconvenience and sent it at the wolf, but the beast still lay there, looking sadly up at the pyre.

"Oh, it does no harm," sent the attendant. "Let it stay."

Irritated, the treeguard lifted his clay vessel of wheat-oil and climbed up the pyre. It was not part of the order of things that a simple wolf should be so interested in their ceremony of rejoining. Still, it should have a healthy fear of fire, and no doubt it would spring back into the forest when he ignited the *fifewydar*.

Glancing back to the sack he saw it was empty, torn and bare. He reached for his belt but his thornthrower was no longer looped there. Uriel twisted the dagda around as the treeguards below broadsided the platform with tiny barbs, thorns piercing their comrade's chest. Wheat-oil spilled over the pyre and ran into the guard's torch, blazing up into a sudden inferno. One of the treeguards in the meadow twisted back as the wolf slammed into him and another dagda collapsed over his sacks as Uriel's weapon spat back, a spine bursting out to bury itself in the creature's neck, flames licking across the assassin's boots.

The cross too slow to reload, Uriel leapt into space and flailed down into their ranks, feet and hands a blur as they cracked limbs and found dwell-points among the strange web of dagda nerves. He broke one's neck and converted the pattern into a swaying kick, driving a nose-bone back through a brain.

In the giant shadow of the tree, a dark spectre lifted itself out from the collection of corpses, purple-red blood running down its hands.

Starting to chase after one of the fleeing pyre-women, Uriel called back the wolf before it brought the panicked dagda down. "Leave her, wolf."

His heart was beating like a battering ram with the physical strain of restarting it. Slowing it down so low and for so long was a seriously dangerous trick, and now he would suffer fatigue for the next few days. From the pain Uriel guessed he had been asleep for two days, nearly three. He gazed up the length of the three massive trees, stretching into the firmament like the columns of Olympus. Arrogant imbecile. It had almost been a child's game to goad the forest lord into torturing him into his coma. Show contempt for no foe, underestimate no enemy, the words replied from Uriel's memory.

Stripping the bodies of every weapon, assassin and wolf turned back into the silence of the forest together, a pyre crackling behind them.

# Chapter 17

S pirals of chimney smoke bore witness that the
Realmsmen had reached one of humanity's landscapes,
fumes rising to snatch languidly at clouds gliding along the
face of the perpetual forest. Where the tumble had been
slashed by estate workers, the bizarre foot-high mist halted,
as if aware this was the boundary of its realm.

Across the hinterland of lush open pastures, a city
shimmered in the heat, a run of buildings bordered by a
wide circle of ramparts, toy-like in the distance. Closer, the
character of the houses became clear. There were no stony
walls, or thatched roofs, no lead tiles, not a stretch of
cobbled road or any of the crumbling brick-blocked
rookeries which had comprised the twisting ghettos of
Taliesin's youth. It was an entire city of timber – wooden
lodges and pliant log buildings – few over three stories tall.
The dragon-browns crossed a stream, wading though the
spuming-green ford to get to the opposite bank. Joining a
road on the other side, they found themselves among
hundreds of travellers making their way in and out of the
wooden city. Families, players and merchanteers. The
farmers in high wide-wheeled wagons, loaded to the
tailboard with milled barley, cures of smoked bacon, casks
of honeyed wine and chests of silk, people queueing to get
through the city's gate. Flanked on either side by watch
towers, a rampart of logs led across the ditch protecting the
palisade, the Realmsmen finding themselves moving
through unchallenged with the press of people.

Between timber houses and across streets layered with
planks, the town was a lively place, bustling with geese and

swine being led to market while farmhands cursed the children chasing and scaring their animals. Taliesin had seen enough recruiters to recognise the sort of man who approached them out of the throng.

"Four angels a head if you take Riebknecht's coin, but you will have to leave by tomorrow."

Taliesin wasn't sure if Riebknecht was a general or one of the thimble-sized kingdoms their map showed scattered across Thuring. "Maybe tomorrow."

"You won't get a better offer from anyone else," the man persisted, trailing after them. "Buy some tankards of huffcap and think it over. There is no war in Eichswehr anymore, not unless you want to be on the losing side, you ask the caravans. Don't sign up with them."

Taliesin waved the hook-nosed man away. "We'll think it over."

"Look, man," Connaire Mor said. "We could be home."

It was true. Now Taliesin scanned the crowd carefully, he could see dozens of parties of soldiers, few with matching uniforms, all grimy from wear and battle. There were coats made up of small iron plates sewn onto leather, cuirassiers with heavy plate, foot regiments with clumsy-looking puffers and impossibly long barrels, not to mention squadrons of hussars and their trademark braided dolman jackets. Where mercenaries gathered – the carrion of war – trouble would be fast on their heels. It appeared as if the pygmy lands were as antagonistic towards each other as the feuding Princedoms of the Realm.

Taking shelter in one of the lodge-like inns, the Realmsmen found themselves accosted by recruiting parties representing dozens of interests – Sovereigns, Ruris and Peers. All with grievances, and a need for killers and the sharp steel they brought with them. In the islands, rogues had made a career by cheating the Queen's recruiters, taking coin for joining one recruiting regiment then deserting to enlist with another. Few of Taliesin's cutthroats did not know how to play that game, toying with the men and accepting every drink proffered in the hope they could be loosened into enrolling.

Taliesin used the men for information, quickly discovering the land they had entered was Goricht and they had chanced across its only city of note – also Goricht. Goricht possessed few of the troubles of her neighbouring nations. Across the forests, kingdoms warred and fought each other with a regular, bloody monotony. It had started as a war worthy of the name three hundred years ago, with one league of nobles attacking another. But now it had degraded into an anarchic mess of tribal, religious and ethnic slaughter. Mercenaries looted and burnt as they willed, villages fortifying themselves against their own armies, ploughmen fleeing into the tumble while crops burnt unharvested across the few good fields remaining. Goricht nestled in the corner of the patchwork map, the kingdom of Engarn – her large neighbour to the south – guaranteeing Goricht's safety, sensibly desiring a buffer to carnage which was excessive even in the dragon-browns' savage age.

If, the recruiters explained, there was any black cloud on the horizon, it was that Goricht's King Ganderman was barking mad, ruling with a bloody and erratic hand. He was currently labouring under the impression he had swallowed a glass piano and could play melodies by gargling with huffcap.

Huffcap was what their lodge served too, a glutinous hoppy drink which slid down swiftly, bringing a pleasing warmth to all the tired soldiers. Finbar took great delight in tipping vessel after vessel of the potent mixture down his hang-dog face, banging the table until the owner crammed his disk-shaped table with swan pies and cuts of goat meat.

Unlike the benches in the Realm's coaching inns, this establishment placed short four-legged stools across the planking and sawdust. Taliesin perched on his and watched another recruiter approach them. The Captain doubted if he was a professional, he had more of the look of a merchanteer about him, calculating eyes and a thick velvet cloak which had not seen too much harsh service.

"Love of the Martyr," Taliesin called to him. "We are not interested, I don't care if you're working for the Sunken Empire and want us to fight the Lord of the Fish."

"You haven't seen my coin yet," said the man quietly, tossing a gold disc at Taliesin. "Happen it's not the drowned land you'll be fighting for."

Picking up the angel, Taliesin saw the proud rearing dragon of Emrys struck into its side. "That is an interesting coin. Take a chair."

Seating himself opposite Taliesin, the man glanced over his shoulder. Finbar was gorging himself with food while Connaire Mor hurled his throwing knifes towards a wooden circle on the far wall. Mercenaries stomped the floor approvingly and shouted rude cheers, exchanging money with a swarm of wager-bursars. Satisfied they were unheard, he turned back to the Captain. From beneath his jacket he slid out the iron seal of Camlan. "The Realm's merchanteer factors are looking for you up and down the coast, so what are you doing here, you cracked idiot?"

"You'll tell me who you buggering are first."

"Martyrs, what does it matter? Marius, I follow the trading road from Ciendsvin, and as an extra profession I take the coin of a mutual acquaintance, Domnal Mac Aedo."

"And why looking for us?"

"Why? Happen a boat from the Princedoms fished out a

half-drowned sailor from the Tolisi, and our good friends back in Camlan wanted to make sure there were no other survivors spreading embarrassing prattle about what you were about. Take some advice and get rid of either your patch or that uniform, the combination makes you too easy to spot."

"Bad news spreads fast."

Marius shook his head. "Just as fast as a dove flies with a message band."

Taliesin stared to speak but Marius threw up his hands. "I don't want to know what you're about either. It's a sight unhealthy to find out too much about Domnal Mac Aedo's doings. I'm just going to give you a purse and you can take a ship back to Camlan."

Taliesin pointed his finger at Marius. "We are not going back yet."

"I have been told you are. Orders. Every survivor back to Camlan or fixed so they can't talk any other way."

"Threaten me – " Taliesin gripped Marius's richly embroidered shirt – "and you'll find it's not just Annan Pendrag's pets that you'll need to watch out for."

Frightened, the merchanteer pulled out of Taliesin's grasp. "Don't be a fool. What does it matter to you? You think they will be relying on you to do their business for them now? The Crown does not work like that. They have probably sent two lots of killers to their deaths before they sent you, and I'll wager there's another two on their way by now."

"You send word back that we're still doing what we have to, you tell them that a lady in Camlan once told me to acknowledge no higher authority. I don't intend to."

Marius shook his head ruefully. "Happen that Domnal Mac Aedo is paranoid, can't you tell? He's spread his factors over every land within a hundred leagues of the

Realm, and most of them couldn't even tell you where the Princedoms are if you asked them. If the Ruri of Skella caught the pox, Domnal Mac Aedo would know about it before the boy's leach. See, he's a butcher. You cross Mac Aedo and he'll hunt you down. Martyrs, look at you, the message I received said more than twenty-score went down in the Tolisi. You've got less than two-hand left now. You going to take on an army somewhere with that? I think not. You must be fair cracked."

"I fought my way this far," Taliesin said. "And if I have to take on Annan Pendrag's paid knife-boy to see this through, I shall."

Standing up Marius pushed his stool away. "I'm looking at a dead man and he doesn't even know it."

Connaire Mor came over as the merchanteer wormed his way out of the crowd. "Aye, and another one making us an offer."

"It wasn't a very good one."

Unrolling the vellum map, the mountain giant pointed out a line charcoaled across it by the inn's owner. "This is the road which travels down to the gulf. We can try our luck for a ship out of there."

Taliesin nodded approval.

Unnoticed by the two soldiers, one of the other drinkers was staring at their table intensely. As if making a decision, the bald-headed watcher pushed his tankard back, striding away and leaving the room and its smell of stale hops. Dordias – the black-hearted weirdsman – slipped out into the night and was gone.

# Chapter 18

The Rais Ibn-Dali roared his barrel-rolling laugh when he saw Gunnar's face. "We do not have the skirts of the Island Queen and her Princes to scuttle behind, little man. No rainy harbours or Annan's royal papers of plunder for us. Did you think we would nestle up into some Thuringian port and ask them to show us their hospitality?"

In the sea all around them, volcanoes grumbled and thundered, breaking the surface like an infection on the face of the world. Great white clouds steamed up from the oceans as volcanoes hidden underwater boiled the waves and rocked the Khair-ed-Din.

Gunnar looked pale. "It's cursed, daemon-cursed."

"How did you infidels ever come by your kingdoms?" Ibn-Dali growled. "It would be death if we did not know which passages to take through these waters. And make no mistake, outside our town there are wastes so grotesque I would sooner fight thirty sand-devils than spend a night in them. But there are no daemons on the island, or shades of the Sunken Empire. At least, they have never attacked us if they do make their nests there."

Ibn-Dali looked at home on the deck of his vessel; boiling steam blowing over the ship, reducing their visibility to a handful of feet, the fire and molten explosions throwing hellish vulcan light across the Captain's minotaur features.

Slowly, the heat was intensifying as they picked their deliberate way through the volcanoes, following their charts and employing sounding leads to be sure they were not drifting over underwater mountains ready to spear rock and brimstone through the hull.

Those crewmen that owned them started discarding their shirts, working the ship in striped breeches and the silky billowing trousers styled in the southlands. Others wrapped water-soaked scarves around their parched mouths, wiping black dust from glistening foreheads. Gunnar felt as if he was reliving his fever in this dark shadow-world, quivering red shadows from the fire-mountains writhing on their sails, dancing erotically.

How inconsequential their ship appeared, floating among these chimney stacks connected to some lost layer of hell. But their three-master was small anyway when compared with a decent-sized merchantman. The Realmsman supposed she had to be, her livelihood consisting of hit-and-run, the shallow draught enabling Ibn-Dali and his devils to hide in narrow creeks along the coastline.

From the crows-nest came another cry, and buckets of water were launched up on ropes, extinguishing a scorch in the sail. Someone thrust a shovel into Gunnar's hands and he joined the others scooping hot coals from the deck and casting them over the side. It smelt awful, like rotten eggs and burning salt.

Then it was over.

With the bubbling ocean growing more quiescent, the swirling fogs gradually washed away behind the Khair-ed-Din; the haemorrhage of magma becoming a distant but constant growl.

Before them a black coast reared out of the sea. Even at this distance it was clear the thorny tumble was so rank, so virile in its daemon-altered growth, that it stripped the rising dragon-horns of the mountain range behind. In the distance, more volcanoes burned to the rear of the peaks, the sky above glowing orange from reflected hell-fire.

So ill was this vista that it took a minute before Elaine realised that there was a harbour huddling on the coast.

Coming towards them was a crescent-shaped port protected by the walls of a palisade.

Lights shone from the occasional window, though this was a waste of good candle tallow, under the fiery glare of the distant volcanoes it might as well have been the middle of the day. However base the inhabitants of this pirate port, the locals still placed a high value on their counterfeit light, preferable to the crimson-stained landscape which otherwise haunted their waking and sleeping hours.

Ibn-Dali was not the only visitor to the town. A variety of ships nuzzled the harbour's stone moorings, some larger and others smaller than the Khair-ed-Din. They all flew the black flag of the corsairs. There were motifs sporting hour glasses, bleeding hearts, bloody tear drops, devils and daggers, but almost all contained the skull and skeleton bones of their own vessel.

Ibn-Dali turned his severe gaze on the town. "Port Hesperus."

Gunnar nodded. Hesperus, demon of ice and snow.

Which corsair first fleeing here had baptised the blackened hell-scape with such a perverse name?

# Chapter 19

Night brought little serenity to the streets of Goricht. Outside the wooden lodge, a player composed poetry which could have earnt him excommunication, drunken gangs chanting along as they sprawled over each other. A riot of jackal-like laughter drifted in from the back of the tavern, setting Taliesin's hair on edge. This was followed by a round of women applauding and hooting. It was as if the visitors were attempting to redress every tragedy of violence and slaughter in the neighbouring states, revelling in the simple joy of being alive. But there was a desperate, manic edge to their pleasures. The last days of empire.

Inside the road-house, their host was rousing his staff to eject the remaining drinkers, a task achieved with as much diplomacy as possible while the patrons battered swords and flintlock butts on their tables.

Soldiers washed out into the street and stumbled off in search of somewhere which kept longer hours. Taliesin looked around the room. Half the dragon-browns were already asleep across log tables, those that could stand were hauling their fellows up steps into the cheap sleeping loft.

Carpentry skills were commonplace in this tiny, distant land, and climbing the stairs Taliesin marvelled that the lodge had been built without a single nail, peg or screw; clever joins being all the artisans had needed. In addition to a talent for raising buildings hacked from the tumble, they had shown an elaborate touch with carvings, delicate patterns chiselled into the rafters and wall-panels.

Taliesin was halfway up the stairs. Glass shattered below him. The officer looked out of a window. Revellers were being rudely dispersed by a mob of mercenaries in the street, and a small riot had erupted. Behind the fighting, a figure moved into the light of a flailing torch, then disappeared. Taliesin kicked over a stool in frustration.

Marius.

He had counted on the calculating little rodent sending back to Camlan for instructions from his mistress. Now Marius's coin had convinced a mob of hired sabres that a night of slaughter would be a profitable diversion from the centuries-old anarchy.

Slamming a beam across the door, a lodge-man screamed as blades plunged through the gap between the logs, slashing his chest. Still befuddled by drink, the Realmsmen streamed down the steps, lugging their puffers and packs with them.

Climbing through the smashed window, a mercenary was flung back in a hail of metal and stone splinters. "Bastards."

Behind Taliesin, the inn's owner held a puffer with enormous flared-iron lips. Dipping his hand into a pouch of nails and stone fragments he grabbed a powder horn to reload.

"Are these your friends or mine?" bellowed the owner.

Taliesin emptied one of the dumplings into an intruder's face, the man pitching back with his head a ruin. "Ours."

"No matter," he rammed the nails down with a thin maul. "They should have more sense than to try and settle something in Cordoba's place."

Cursing his stars, the Captain risked a glimpse outside. There were just too many of them and his men were in no fit state for a fight. Rebels retreating from Astolat had once left kegs of blackstrap in their wake, knowing if the dragon-browns stumbled across it before Camlan's officers, they would drink their pursuit away into insensibility.

It was a useful trick and the rodent Marius had timed his strike perfectly. To join the army, men had to be desperate, the headcount of the Realm drawn from the appalling squalor of the rookeries and the poverty of village acerages. Drunk for an angel – dead drunk for two angels was the saying, and Marius had known Taliesin's men would be no different.

Breaking down the back door, a bearded soldier with an iron mace burst in. Connaire Mor shoulder-slammed the mercenary then scooped him up, lifting him into the air like a sack of barley. With an explosion of wood the giant crashed him down onto a table.

Picking up the ownerless mace, Finbar swung it wildly around his head, blundering forward and glancing it off a man's chest armour, denting the plate and leaving the bludger clutching his stomach as he writhed about over the sawdust.

Connaire Mor up-ended a table to barricade the rear door, and the owner came up to detonate his antiquated but deadly weapon, a salvo of metal shreds scattering out into the darkness.

From the front, a gang of mercenaries with torches rolled a cask towards the lodge, and Taliesin knew what would be inside it. Oil. If they torched the building the Realmsmen would not stand a chance. Flames would tear across the inn and ignite half the wooden town with it.

Taking careful aim, he snapped the lock down and his puffer bucked, a ball spinning into the band. One mercenary crumpled to the side and still the others heaved the barrel forward.

"Have you got water?" Taliesin cried back.

Moving forward the lodge's owner blinked into the dark street. "Crazy. They'll do for the town, they will."

He called back and sent his people into the kitchens, dragging out wooden stock-pots of water which they knew would not be enough to save them.

One of the torches flashed in the night then went dark. Suddenly the night was filled with a swelling carpet of giant black shadows, huge wraiths shambling through the mercenary's ranks. Clawed hands rose and fell as solid-muscled limbs lashed about the street in a frenzy. Soldiers ran only to be ripped from their feet and rendered in two, blood splattering out across Goricht's timber foundations.

"What are they?" Taliesin asked in shock.

"King's Guard," said the owner. "Tribes of Urr."

"Demisapi," Connaire Mor said. "Aye and they've only tamed themselves a pack of beastmen."

Cordoba shook his head. "Hardly tame. But they do follow the King."

Finbar looked out of the shattered window. Showing no mercy, ursine forms hunted down the survivors of the massacre, mercenaries clawing up buildings only to be pulled down and gashed into pieces by the beasts. In the Realm, demisapi came in many forms, wolfmen, bearmen, pardmen, boar-like killers. During the age of Empire, the Islands had been a distant outpost and few demisapi had outlasted the Sunken Empire. Those that had survived, lived deep in the enchanted forests, tracked down ruthlessly when they hunted near the estates of man.

Finbar pressed his sausage-like fingers together. What madman would try and wield the Godless creatures into a legion again? When even the might and witchcraft of the Daemon Prince Vulcanus had not been enough to master the wild creatures at the end.

Smashing down the front door with contemptuous ease, one of the bearmen looked into the lodge. Barrel-sized silver armour enclosed the monster's chest – a royal acorn enamelled across the metal – and it ducked through the doorway, a made-to-size battle axe strapped across its brown furred back. Gazing at the Realmsmen, it growled back into the darkness.

Answering the call, a human soldier walked into the room. "Those men outside, whose were they?"

"Gutter scum. Whose gutter scum is another matter," Taliesin lied.

The soldier grunted. "It's always good to make an example, can't have enough of them you might say. Too many jackals around who have learnt their courtesies in the states on the other side of the border."

"We'll be heading across them ourselves."

"Not yet you won't," the soldier held up a fist. "It wasn't the city runners that brought us here. Do you think the Guard hasn't got better things to do than sully ourselves in street brawls? No, you've got an invite to come and dine at the palace tonight, my lucky jacks."

Connaire Mor looked out at the ranks of bear-things surrounding the lodge. "What if we were telling you after this we are no in the mood for feasting tonight?"

"My father always said big men don't have large brains. Our Kings come from a sensitive line, and they don't like to have their feelings bruised. I would hardly be doing my job properly if I let you upset a man who pays me so generously, would I? Leave your sharps behind, eh?"

Taliesin placed his rifle on the table. Another mercenary, then. One who would gut the company without blinking if they interfered with his livelihood.

Crowds of revellers vanished as the regiment of demisapi moved out into the logged avenues of Goricht, the Realmsmen emaciated in comparison to their massive bearman escort. Only Connaire Mor come close in height to any among the alien regiment. Taliesin was disappointed to see none of the corpses in the street was that of Marius, the filthy little merchanteer had obviously left before the fighting started.

"I thought your paymaster was crazy, barking mad I was told," Taliesin needled the beastmen's Captain.

"Ja, he is touched alright, but you'll be more touched if you go talking that up to his face. See, your quality doesn't have much sense when it comes to money. And a crazy King, well ... you can see the possibilities."

"Yes, I see."

"I don't think you do, eh," said the mercenary. "I was born in Nathgratz and don't you believe what they say, it was a shit-hole before they burnt it to the ground. Probably worse now of course. You might say that was one of the formative lessons in life for me. There I was, scarce a man's hair on me, and all the flames bursting and sizzling across the place. It was like ... like a Goddess had breathed life into that dirty stink-hole for the first time. It was better than having a woman or downing huffcap on a hot day. Never seen anything like it since. Did quite a few kingdoms and burnt a good few places since then too, but it was never like that again. Anyhow, me and my lads ended up here and it has been finest pheasant on the table ever since."

"You and your overpaid menagerie?"

"These ones?" He said slapping one of the bearmen on the back. "No, they're traditional. Aren't you, Rawyr?"

A growl-like confirmation came back from the demisapi marching in the lead, twin patches of red thatch surrounding its eyes.

"Part of the family you might say. First jacks who set up in Goricht had them all the way back then. Right useful they have been for the quality too. Dare say they're one of the reasons why the troubles haven't spilled across this way. Course, they need someone who appreciates them, to give the jacks a bit of a lead in things, someone to tell them when to get into mischief and when to stay out of it. But they're proud of their record, eh, Rawyr?"

"Nobody beat us," it snarled back.

"I tell you, I've been with plenty of jacks who've sold their own quality out when the other side made them a better offer. But not these ones. Loyal as a hunting dog to the King. If I had the knowing of where their wild cousins were hiding out in the forest, I'd be of quite a mind to trap me some cubs and sire an army of them. You could take any kingdom in the Thuring states."

Finbar snorted and the mercenary looked back angrily at the priest. "If I was you, I might conduct myself with a little more appreciation of my predicament, fat man. I'd make a good King and there are plenty who've done it over the borders. Quality hiring the wrong men to get them out of their little difficulties."

"Your King's lucky to have you then," Taliesin said.

"Ja. Damn right," he said, missing the irony in the officer's voice.

Two palisades barred their way into King Ganderman's palace of logs. The first girdling the entire wide rolling hill, the second fortification circling the headland, protecting an entire citadel raised by the axeman's skill. Dominating the corner of the city-kingdom, the citadel looked down on the timber structures below, the town nestling right up to the baskets of earth fortifying Ganderman's palisade.

Manning the posts was Goricht's regiment of bearmen. Most demisapi had the huge battle axes, but close to the wall they held flintlocks – also sized for their ungainly paws. The weapons bore little resemblance to the soldiers' own. Closer to the Realm's small mobile *galloper* culverin.

Moving into the palace, Taliesin could see the timber had not been hewn from any tamed orchard. The scale of the corridors was such that it only have been felled in the weirded forests of the tumble.

Hastened through a cathedral-like hall of oak arches, the group found themselves facing Ganderman the Magnificent, the chubby, balding little monarch roosted in a wooden throne. As good as his word, Ganderman was seated behind a table covered with peppered geese, partridge, flagons of huffcap, wines, pies and baskets of fruit. His eyes were crystal-pebbles, flashing with frantic energy.

"Oh my sweets," Ganderman leapt out of his seat. "It is true, blessed day. Come in, come in. Come share my table with me."

Empty of other guests, the table was attended by stewards in brown surcoats, the heraldic crest of Goricht's silver acorn vivid on their drab uniforms. Filing out to line the room, the escort stood motionless while the Realmsmen warily seated themselves opposite the sovereign. The mercenary officer sat himself down next to Taliesin.

"Eat, my sweets. Fill yourselves," he looked at Finbar. "A follower of the Martyr. Has the Martyr brought you here to me today? Surely he has."

Finbar picked at a plate of ham. "Ah, sir, he has kept us in all places where we have gone."

"Of course, of course. I let your church into Goricht, you know. But some of the villages didn't like it. It was Rawn this, Rawn that. But I said to them, there are already seventy Gods in Goricht, I think we need some more. Don't you think that's sensible? The more Gods that smile on me, the better off we will be, that is what I told all my sweets. Does your Martyr get on with Rawn? They should, after all, the ancients nailed him on a tree didn't they, and Rawn likes trees too?"

Finbar looked into Ganderman's intense eyes. The cult of Rawn the Hunter was rumoured still to survive in parts of Logriese, though no doubt very quietly given the Arch-Truron's attitude towards the pagan. "I'm sure the Martyr gets on mortal fine with all the world."

"Yes. Yes. Your arrival is a sign, I see that now. I'll let them build their cathedral here now. Aren't you pleased?"

"Right enough the Martyr will be blessed pleased."

Ganderman looked towards the red-haired mercenary. "But what about my people, Silver? Will they be happy with a new cathedral here?"

"Don't think they'll be too many of them complaining, my liege."

With a laugh like the sound of goat giving birth, the King thrashed around his chair. "Of course not. No. I had the druids impaled, didn't I? I would have given them to Rawyr and my brave fighters, you'd have liked that wouldn't you Rawyr?"

"Meat too stringy," said the bearman.

Leaning close to one of the Gogmagog's sailors, Ganderman pointed furtively at the line of demisapi. "My mother said we should never feed them real people. They might get the taste for it you see, then where would we be? Here priest, celebrate your new cathedral, cut my pie for me."

Finbar took the knife from the King and sawed into the crust of a shield-sized pie. As its edges folded back, there was a sudden movement and tiny sparrows erupted from inside the pastry, flying towards the high ceiling beams. A startled Finbar tripped back and nearly fell over a drowsing hound, the dog skittling sideways and throwing a distressed look at the monk.

Ganderman was in hysterics. "Oh my sweets, that was good! This is the best day I have had all year! I was a bird too, once, when I was younger. A gosling, but my mother made me change back because I was frightening all the visitors from the other lands. Can you imagine that? All those Princes and Arch-Dukes being frightened of a little bird. It is no wonder they hate each other so much when a little bird could scare them."

Taliesin pushed away one of the stewards attempting to fill his wooden mug. "What are we celebrating here?"

"You don't know? Oh my sweets, but you simply must. You have brought my son back to me."

"Your blessed son now?" Finbar wondering what the balding lunatic was taking about.

"This is splendid, splendid. You're toying with me, ever since my mother died, nobody brings any frolics around here anymore. It is all doing this and doing that. You, you there, bring in the painting."

Rushing out of the chamber, stewards hurried to obey their ruler's command.

They returned stumbling under the weight of a tall painting. On the canvas, a beautiful woman stood in a wide-bottomed dress, pictured next to a martial figure holding a sabre. Under the weight of the man's heavy muff-cap, Connaire Mor's face was sketched.

Taliesin gasped. Apart from the distended ears, the figure in the portrait was a near perfect double of the giant mountain-man. "It can't be?"

Leaning across, the mercenary Silver grinned and spoke softly. "Of course not. He had his son flayed to death four years ago. Our young jack wanted to leave the palace grounds, but the King had commanded he couldn't until the boy took the throne. They found him trying to join a free company down in the town."

Jumping to his feet, the quick tempered highlander was pointing at Ganderman. "You're as daft as a brush, man. I've no put my eyes on you once before and that's the truth of it."

"Martyrs," Taliesin called, trying to get Connaire Mor to placate the lunatic ruler. "Have a care."

Ganderman rounded on Finbar. "Yes! Yes! Martyrs. It is you priests again. Interfering crows, and smug, self-important druids. You and your church mercenaries have turned my son against me with your words and your holy books. Have you turned my son against me?"

Stewards fled the hall fearing their master's rage, backing out through the armoured demisapi.

"How many priests do I have to kill?" Ganderman screamed. "How many before you learn to stay away from my sweets? Get away, get away from me!"

"Sir?" Silver said, unsure of what the King wanted and

knowing only too well the dangers of misinterpreting his mercurial desires.

"Do I have to tell you everything, am I the only King in all of Goricht? Lock my son away. Put him away where he can't hurt himself again."

"And the others, your highness?"

"You," Ganderman pointed a shaking finger at Finbar's bulbous nose. "You really want to be martyred don't you? Just like all your friends I had dragged to the tree. How many saints does your filthy God want me to make? No cathedral for you now, no cathedral for your God now. I won't be listening to any more of your mewling sermons while my sweets nail you on to the branches. You will cut them down instead, that's what I'll have you do. Join the timber parties."

Two of the massive beastmen dragged a struggling Connaire Mor to the floor. "You cracked dunderhead, you are as good as killing them all."

Ganderman stroked his cheek. "Oh my sweet, they've bewitched you with their sorcery, haven't they? But you'll be safe here. No one will ever take you away from me again."

Taliesin stared at the lunatic ruler from behind the wall of beastmen. "Next time I see you, I'm going to slit your bastard throat for you and put you out of your misery, you madman."

They were dragged away.

"Into the tumble with them," screeched Ganderman. "Work until they fall and all the forests drop with them."

With the dragon-browns gone and Connaire Mor marched away, a gangling figure emerged from a small doorway. The man whose face was indelibly scarred in the soldier's minds. A weirdsman they would never forget.

"As I told you, your majesty," said Dordias. "They are evil sorts – they mean you only harm."

Ganderman shivered with the thought of them. "Oh yes. What a wily merchanteer you are. My mother always said, if you want to know what your hands do when you are asleep, ask a trading man. I think I shall sign your treaty, I think I shall."

"Free commerce is all we desire," said Dordias, bowing carefully.

Night in the devilish forests was a featureless darkness, flooding the hollows and nettles. Wolf lay uneasily, watching his hunt partner as he thrashed and cried in his sleep. Uriel should have known better in the dangerous heartwood, but too often the assassin was like this. Timber-wolf sniffed the air and was satisfied. There was a stag two leagues away, but nothing more dangerous than the owl spying on them, foolishly thinking itself unseen on a high branch.

"Why?" Uriel whimpered, lashing out from under his blanket. "Take me, not her. Make me strong, strong. Make me strong."

Wolf hunkered down under the darkness of a bush. Clearly his brother was insane. But wolf still remembered the travels in the land of the long-dark. There had been a terrible winter and the sisters and brothers were forced to hunt across the territories they normally avoided. For good reason. His pack had died in the terror of the long dark, one after another the brothers and sisters were claimed by horrors which themselves preyed on the hunters. Leaping and twisting things which even their life in the dangerous heartwoods had not prepared them for. Timber-wolf, the last to survive, had been surrounded by the shadow things. Snarling and leaping, he had waited for the evil calm of their touch, but then Uriel had appeared, rising out from the long-dark like a wraith of death; in the fire of his cold fury the shadow things broke, fleeing back into the mountains.

No, timber-wolf would not desert his hunt partner, not even if he was insane enough to howl pack song into the malignant darkness of the forest.

It was a simple task to recognise the men and women who had been incarcerated for over a month in Goricht's tree-felling companies. Their clothes hung off the prisoners in long dirty shreds, gaunt feet shuffling along in homemade clogs carved from stocks of stolen wood.

None of them shared the faces of the hard and careful men who stole livings from the dark forests back in the Realm. These were farmers and townsmen, each condemned by their ruler's arbitrary madness. It had been only a few days imprisonment, but already their time was blurring into a haze. No interval to mark its passage. Some days, the lake of mist which climbed up to their knees would return, and the labour gangs would toil in the eery moistness. Other days it drifted away as if it was being inhaled back into the mouths of the primeval forest Gods.

Beside Taliesin, a boy raised an axe and chopped down into the towering oak. Withdrawing his axe, the boy coughed while Taliesin hacked into the trunk, splinters flying across the tough mat of wild grass. Wearily the boy pulled his own axe up, slapping it into the oak again.

His uncle had hidden a goose from one of the King's tax party officials and this was the uncle's punishment. To lose his only nephew to the forest. It was a punishment that went beyond a cruel emotional chastisement. Goricht was not the overcrowded lanes of Llud-din, where life was cheap across the dilapidated, airless slums. Where Taliesin's own uncle had accepted his dead parent's pitiful legacy then sold him to a church poorhouse for a handful of angels. Here it meant poverty for a childless uncle, no kinsmen to till a strip of land and provide for his imminent old age.

Hacking up yellow saliva, the sweating boy swung at the

oak, the axe barely glancing into it. Taliesin did not need to be a doctor to recognise the boy's sickness. It was the same one dozens of the prisoners had. Climbing-rot. Dust from the deadly slimy fungae which grew all over the base of the weirded trees. The other prisoners claimed mixing water with ash burnt from ivy-stems helped calm the inflamed chest, but the remedy had done little for this one.

Taliesin swept his blade into the oak and waited for the boy to follow through with the next one. It never came. He had folded over and was lying on the grass, his face ruddy crimson.

Pulling on his cumbersome leg chains Taliesin dragged himself to the boy's side. The lad's breathing was coming out like a murmur, cold purple lips trembling with the fever.

A shadow fell across them, one of the Goricht mercenaries. He kicked Taliesin aside and knelt by the boy. Touching the boy's heart with his ears then feeling his burning forehead, the guard called across to a demisapi. "Bring the keys. This one's for the pond."

Taliesin climbed to his feet. "He can still make it, you bastard murderer."

Lashing out, the guard hit Taliesin in the mouth, cracking his lips. "The pond."

Goaded beyond sense Taliesin smashed a foot into the man's exposed paunch. As he doubled up, the Captain twisted a length of chain around the mercenary's throat. Pulling him to the ground, the man gagged with his face crushed into the mud, lungs bursting trying to breath, then a cudgel slammed into Taliesin's neck and the officer fell slack.

On the chain, the sailor Bors tried to stop them unchaining the boy but two mercenaries clubbed him down, pulling his limp body away.

Passing the body across to one of the huge bearmen, the boy was lifted away. The pond was deeper in the forest.

Bodies laid there would be dragged away by the forest beasts when they came out to water, saving the logging parties the extra labour of burying the corpses.

Wiping mud from his face the guard scowled at Taliesin. He grabbed the Captain by his hair and pulled him back. "Filth wants to make trouble does it?" He cracked his fist into Taliesin's kidney and the Captain convulsed. "Looks as if we'll have to learn you a little better. Tie him against the planks. His friend too."

Pulling Taliesin and Bors into the open clearing the work parties had made, they shoved the two Realmsmen up against the mound of felled trunks. Viciously their arms were twisted around, hemp-like cord binding their hands, then their wrists were lashed across the branches.

"I'd do this myself," said the mercenary. "But I don't want to be spraining my arm."

One of the demisapi crossed the clearing with a rope flail, long bands of knotted-wet chord dangling from the handle. The mercenary tested it, flicking it against the air, then satisfied handed it back to the huge beastman. "You do it, lad. Bad people, yes, want to hurt King."

"Bad," growled the half-man. It trotted forward slowly and stood behind the two Realmsmen.

"Bite into your jacket or you'll lose your tongue," warned Bors. "Martyrs, but this was one of the reasons I jumped ship from the navy back in Emrys."

Taliesin nodded and moved his head down, biting into the collar of his dirty Cornwall Pioneer's uniform.

Hissing out like a stinging medusa, the ropes curled around Taliesin's spine, circles of pain flaring across his eyelids as he closed them. Then the ropes struck out at Bors, his teeth piercing the soft neck of his shirt as he held back a scream. It whipped out at them in a fierce rhythm, once to the left, once to the right, then back again.

Switching them with all its strength, the demisapi

continued the beating for long minutes which extended into a searing eternity for the two soldiers. There was the swish of air as the ropes curved back in the air again, but a laughing voice cut the swing short. "What is this then, eh?"

Silver sauntered across the clearing with his retinue of bearmen, the mercenary officer tapping his leg with a knife the length of a short-sword.

"A good little lesson for these two, sir."

Placing his arm around the guard, Silver smiled and pointed at the two prisoners hanging flaccid from the lumber. "Have a little professional courtesy, eh? That one runs with another free company."

Silver drove his knife between the guard's shoulder blade and the man howled as he fell sideways. Kneeling over him Silver drew the blade across the guard's throat, blood spraying across the grass.

He cut Taliesin's straps and the Captain fell down across earth burnt by the timber parties. Silver motioned one of the beastmen for a flask of huffcap and dribbled the thick liquid across Taliesin's chapped lips.

"You see, Captain, I like you, ja. You remind me of my first general. He took me and one of my cousins in, gave us a good start to life. He was a foreigner too, Lotharingia I think. We hanged him outside Riebhias when he tried to stop us looting the town, said we had been paid to defend it and would risk never getting work again if we took the place. You see where having just a few virtues can get you? It's more dangerous than having none at all ... or being a saint."

Taliesin tried to roll over and coughed. "Nice thing about being dead, I wouldn't have to listen to any more of your shitty stories."

Silver laughed even louder. "Professionals, that's you and me. I'm glad I took the detour to come here. There's some news for you, your oversized friend back in the palace ..."

"Connaire Mor."

"Whatever. Ganderman's valets tried to cut his hair into a tail at the back. He drowned one of them in the oak tub and broke the other's neck. I thought you'd like to hear that. Can't be that much larking going on out here."

Silver got up and tossed the canteen at Taliesin's body. "Keep it. I'll come back in the summer, see if you're still alive, Ja. Not that I want you to build your hopes too tall, most seem to last no longer than a season out here. "

After Silver stalked away, the bear-things towed Bors and Taliesin back to the chain and clasped their manacles on. Finbar looked down the line and swung his axe into a trunk, then lapsed heavily onto his knees as the prisoners were given a rest-break.

"Take this for your back." The monk threw across a bundle of moss. "Oh this is a wicked old fix we are in now. I've been dumped into a freezing sea, locked up, pursued by most of the Order Militant and dragged across the tumble by a bunch of mortal tree spirits, and now we are to be starved and worked into our graves by a gang of terrible great talking beasts."

Taliesin tugged at the iron leg-chain. It was rusted green by the damp forest but appeared as strong as when it had been newly cast. Tapping the chains in frustration, he tossed the mercenary officer's flask across to Finbar.

"Bless you, lad," the priest said, guzzling at the rounded brass head. "That's fine old hops and all the better for being out in this cursed wilderness."

Looking around, he saw the hungry eyes of the villagers gazing enviously at him. "Ah well, it is hardly as good as the ones I tended back in the monasteries." Finbar passed it down the chain.

"Up, up," cried a demisapi, cracking a rope flail across the idling prisoners. "Rest gone, now!"

Rising, they picked up their axes and hacked away at the

forest again, the position to the left of Taliesin empty. It would not remain so. They had been trapped here for three days and already new prisoners had arrived. Apathetic peasants with faces deadened by their harsh lives. Too numb to resist, they accepted their fate and shambled listlessly about the trees, embracing the endless monotony of blade-thud against wood. It was hard not to hate them, even though there had been hundreds of faces like theirs to be found in the filthy rookeries when Taliesin was growing up.

From near the head of the chain there was a screaming. Flopping out of the forest's crown, a leathery blanket slid out of one of the massive trees. It landed on a villager and a long whip-like tail flashed back and forth, piercing the man's body. He rolled across the carpet of leaves, yelling and tearing at the thing.

Pulling away, the horrified peasants pushed back into the brush, but the Realmsmen rushed forward, dragging over the villagers on the chain. At their lead, the foul hunchback Laetha battered the flapping creature – others pinning it back with axe handles while Laetha swung his axe down, its innards spattering against his uniform. Still buffeting the dragon-browns with its edges, Laetha cut open the creature with a venom.

At last it flapped no more and the demisapi moved in, prodding the thing with their weapons. On the ground the villager was already dead from the beast's poisoned sting, a look of indignant surprise frozen on his paralysed face.

"Pond," growled the bearman.

Pond. They would all end their cursed lives as corpses waiting for a wolf or a leucrota to drag them away into the forest.

# Chapter 20

Port Hesperus was no town to wake up to. Certainly not after the meagre few hours of sleep the dandy had snatched. Gunnar walked down the streets of the port, eddies of black dust rising with every step; both his and Elaine's white peon's shifts filthy with the volcanic debris. Her uncle's last gift was proving nearly as useful as the traitorous noble's hospitality had been.

There was little work for carpenters in the hidden harbour – a wise precaution with regular falls of hot ashes – the only wood in Port Hesperus was found in the palisade and corsair's ships. Every stone buildings they passed seemed built from Taranto's blackened stone. That and the grey magma rock. He remembered how amazed he and Elaine had been the night before, that it could weigh so little. The weakest sailor on the Khair-ed-Din was able to lift up boulders of the plague-pocked stone

Ibn-Dali turned around to make sure the island couple were still with him. He indicated a long low building with a flick of his curling horns. "The council will be held in there. Wait with the others inside. I need to talk with the other Rais before it starts."

As they were called to bear witness to the sinking of Bron's vessel, Gunnar and Elaine were allowed entry to the corsair's Great Hall in the spectator's section. There was hardly anything to the hall, a barren stone-and-timber room with blocks for listeners to sit on, facing the curved wooden table with twenty chairs for the Rais-Captains.

Many of the Rais were already seated, only six of the chairs left absent, Ibn-Dali's among them. Mobbing the room, ship crews shoved each other, imbibing alcohol, eating and swearing loudly at rivals. It looked more like a coaching-inn crowd than a debating chamber.

One of the Khair-ed-Din's crew displayed his knowledge of the Captains at the table, eager to impress Elaine. The devil in the tie-wig was a Thuringian who had mutinied and sold his Captain to slavers, sawing one of the officer's arms off first so he might keep something to remember him by.

Then there was Captain 'Red' Janz, infamous in Roubaix after he seized one of the Empire's merchantmen. Janz had released all their crew, all except the cook, who being a fat and greasy swine – a man Janz had taken an instant dislike to – fried well after they lashed him to the mast and burnt his ship.

A swarthy, handsome corsair, with a moustache so thin it might have been drawn on was pointed out as the Rais Calico. Also known as Sharp Calico, on account of the time the scoundrel had tricked a ship into surrendering by forcing the prisoners on a third ship he had boarded to hoist a dirty towel as their black corsair flag. It had fooled the newcomer into thinking Calico was fielding two ships, the heavily armed merchantman striking its colours without even a fight. On the table in front of him capered a tiny monkey. The monkey, hardly larger than a kitten, was dressed in a miniature naval coat and it tried to attract attention with its antics, rolling over and dancing across the table-top. It was ignored by most the serious-faced Rais, but the jaunty Calico indulgently teased it with a handful of nuts.

Elaine looked on fascinated. This was the grandest collection of scum, adventurers and murderers she was ever likely to see on a single day. Or for the rest of her life, if it ever turned back to the luxurious, stately pace her station in the Realm afforded her. Even the tales of Dragut Rais paled in comparison to this.

There was the heavily bearded devil, Sanco Tal Rack, a man who braided smoking fuses into his beard when he swung across to seize fat merchantmen, a personal touch guaranteed to sweep a ship with fear, sailors throwing themselves into the sea rather than face his cruel reputation.

On the end of the table Genevieve the Swan sat in a blaze of colourful cotton. Elaine had heard of the fey-beautiful woman even before the sailor pointed her out. The woman's husband had been one of Annan's privateers before they fell out, he having his head departed from his neck in the course of the disagreement. Genevieve the Swan – then known only as a shy buttery worker – had stepped into his shoes and sailed into infamy at the Court in Camlan.

She had faced Annan's Naval Board at Execution Dock, announcing that far from holding a grudge against the Queen, if her husband had fought like a man, he might not now be hanging like a dog! A brace of swan-handled puffers jutted out from behind her belt, silver plated, delicate etchings adorning each barrel; both flared at the muzzle to make it easier to hammer ball down on the rocking confines of a ship-deck.

Ibn-Dali entered the hall with another Rais, a dusky corsair with a devil-goat beard, his hair hidden by a wrap of blue silk.

A man stood up at the head of the table. "Let the council of this port recognise we are in sitting. All brethren of the sea will have their say."

With this brief formality completed, the cook-burning murderer Red Janz jumped to his feet and pointed his finger at Ibn-Dali. "I'll tell you what I have to say! Your blood feud with the Empire of the Tree is costing us all dear. I have sailed up from the southlands; the Deys have only one topic of conversation on their lips; they are talking about barring us – each of us – from their harbours. Where am I to sell my slaves if they line their galleys up against us? Where am I to buy gold cloth and spices to trade if their arcades are shut to me? Where am I to sell the prizes my crew win?"

His grim minotaur features clenched in anger, Ibn-Dali ignored the cheering of the rival crews in the hall. By the wall, the corsairs acting as stewards exchanged nervous glances, shifting their flintlocks and cudgels.

"Do you think, Rais Janz, that without me the Imperial navy would suddenly welcome you into their ports? Would their merchanteers sail past you and offload their cargoes with a cheery smile on their fat faces? It is Thuringian gold which is closing ports to us, not the blood which lies between myself and Admiral son-of-the-devil Bazin."

"I hear the Empire of the Tree are at war with the Princes of Nathstadt, Hissan and Lieksa. That means they will be issuing letters of marque to disrupt their enemies' trade. We can take those letters. Steal a pardon from them."

"They are always at war with each other," Ibn-Dali shouted. "Always. State against state. Prince against Prince. Ruri against Ruri. Baron against Baron. Do you want to be the kept plaything of those fools? Corsairs take what they want, we don't bend our knee to infidels."

Red Janz shook his head. "I'll take any religion that makes me rich. I'll bow to their World-Tree, I'll bow to the man the ancients nailed to one, I'll bow to the Prophet and the Seven Gods of the Sea if it brings me a buggering pile of silver."

Taking to his feet, the handsome Rais-Captain Calico addressed the muttering crowd. "I don't know about you, but I know why I became a seaman. I did not care for Ruris and Dukes and priests and their Gods telling me where to go, what to think, and how to do it. If the cost of getting life back to normal is having to kiss their asses and smile while they piss all over me, then you can go to hell."

"Your rhetoric is all very well," said Genevieve the Swan, her voice smoky from a life of strong grog and sea air. "But it will not put gold on the table! Who cares what papers we carry? Our ships sail the same if they sail in Nathstadt waters. Their merchanteers burn just the same as if they were ad-dinat traders or Aragon cogs. Their gold, and I have tasted it, is no less sweet for having permission to steal it from some Impstad governor."

Ibn-Dali looked at the lady Captain. "Was that what your husband told you, before his meeting with Annan Pendrag's axeman? Have you learnt nothing! What the blessed ones give with one hand they will surely take away with the other. I say we fight back. Burn their ports. Burn their ships and drive them off the sea."

"Your feelings about Bazin are well known, Rais Ibn-Dali. They are getting in the way of your ability to think clearly. We have very few choices left open to us."

Ibn-Dali leapt to his feet, pointing at Gunnar and Elaine. "Beard of the Prophet, I shall show you the choices Bazin will give you."

Pressing through the crowd of corsairs, the couple stood before the sweeping table, a brief silence falling over the room as they became the unexpected focus of attention.

Red Janz's hostile gray eyes bored into Gunnar. "Who are these two? They look like pissing Lériddian farmers."

"They were enjoying the *hospitality* of Bazin and his devil-boat when we pulled them off. Before this they served with the Gogmagog – that vessel consumed by the ambitions of the same man who you, Rais Janz, in your eagerness, would now fawn over."

Bellows of fury broke out in the crowd at the news of Bron's death, sailors jumping to their feet and shaking their fists, others trying to be heard above the clamour.

"Tell them your story, islanders. Tell them of the 'peace' that Bazin made with Bron."

Gunnar held them bewitched with his tale, using every trick of embellishment the soldier had picked up during a lifetime of carousing through the Realm's coach-houses.

Bron's hopelessly inferior last stand became an epic of mythic proportions. No hero of antiquity could have held a candle up to the stalwart defence mounted by the Captain, wading over the corpses of his brave crew as he raged defiance at the devil-boat, the barrels of their culverin cracking under the heat of the barrage of ball poured onto the Imperials.

Cross-examined by the panel of privateers, Elaine took over the story in the spirit Gunnar had set forth. Yes. To the last Bron had refused to surrender, standing on the bow and pissing into the water as the Gogmagog burnt into the waves, laughing at the Empire of the Tree and calling their Admiral a stunted manikin.

When the brave privateer at last ran out of roundshot, Bron had emerged on deck with a chest of gold, and they had blown clouds of the precious shrapnel at the Empire's unnatural craft, peppering them until the greedy sailors on the devil-boat abandoned their own culverin to exhume gold splinters out of dead beastmen.

With the tale closing on the sea's sad embrace of the proud, sinking wreck of the Gogmagog, Ibn-Dali's rogues were on their feet, waving daggers and cutlass. The animated applause and cheers was led by the ex-Play Director, who knew a good performance when he saw one.

After the deliberations of the council, Rais Janz looked with ire at the two Realmsman. The passions the couple had roused was dooming them all to a course of suicide.

"This is your decision?" Janz barked. "To have the Empire hunt each of us down like they did Bron. To lose everything we have ever taken from them?"

Ibn-Dali looked at his rival. "It is the decision of the majority, Rais Janz. Will you abide by it?"

Sweeping to his feet the corsair waved his crew out of the hall. "I take no orders from you, beastman. I would sooner become a monk than be led to my death in your pissing feud. Blood take you all!"

Two other Captains felt the same, storming away from the table with their crews.

"Cretin infidels," Ibn-Dali cried after them, smashing the table with his monstrous fist. "Your lack of guts will not save you. There can be no pax with the Imperial devils. Away from this port they will take you wherever you sail, they will burn every one of you at the stake."

Elaine's ageing sailor pushed his way through the

jostling masses to congratulate the Realm couple. "That was sharply done, by the Martyr it was. Why, if I had you back in one of my cities, what a pair you would make. All the classic roles could be yours, every merchanteer in the land would be vying for tickets. And you lass, with your beauty the nobles would be lining up to hand over their crowns to you."

Elaine smiled, that was a dubious eulogy. Back in the Realm, women who took to the stage were looked upon by those of quality as little better than whores. Though it was true, the more successful and beautiful among them certainly had their choice of wealthy, titled lovers.

Now it was over, crowds flocked out onto the ash-strewn streets of the port, milling around, swapping hearsay and opinion, trying to talk away the dangerous events they had witnessed. Gunnar looked down the hill. Rais Janz and his supporters were striding towards their ships, making ready to distance themselves from their brother seamen.

Laughing, Gunnar pulled Elaine in close to him, brushing her hair away from the scattering of freckles on her face. "You were magnificent."

"And you were extraordinary."

Mirroring the frenzy of the satanic volcano light, Graine glared jealously at the couple, the pirate woman hidden by a tavern's shadow.

So this was how it was to be!

She pulled a dagger from out from behind her sash, testing its edge on the rock of the blackened building. Sharp enough for both of them.


A single tinder box was given to Goricht's prisoners to allow them to make the fires preventing them from freezing, as well as holding off the more timid forest creatures. Fixed to a single stake in the ground, the prisoners could not move off without sounding bells attached to their chain. Not that the dragon-browns would have got far with a line of sick peasants and starved townsmen, even if the natives could have been threatened or cajoled into fleeing.

Prisoners huddled in the moist sea of mist, tendrils of vapour curling around the trees, albino fingers shifting in the night air.

By the fire-light, Taliesin saw Laetha reaching back into a thicket. His hands slowly withdrew with a handful of solid-looking black stones. The hunchback looked across at Taliesin. "You know why there are not many beasts out here that'll steal an oak-pincer's eggs? No, of course you don't, you one-eyed idiot."

Taliesin glared at the soldier. "The thing that was in the tree this afternoon?"

He laughed. "Clever man. Now make sure none of those poxed overgrown dancing bears are looking over here."

Gathered around a fire in the safety of the clearing, the demisapi were feasting on a haunch of beef which had arrived with the evening's logging wagons, blood rolling down their furry cheeks as they mauled the meat.

Lifting a block of wood, Laetha cracked it down onto one of the black things. Splitting open, an ebony liquid flowed out across the chain links, a caustic reek assaulting their nostrils. Steam fizzed off the chain while the leaves underneath curled and bubbled as the liquid splattered across the earth.

Taliesin turned away and nearly vomited with the stench of it. He had walked across battlefields where men had poured their blood and guts into the ground, but this was far worse.

Laetha laughed softly, hardly bothered by it at all. On the ground the chain had been eroded away into a contorted necklace of smoking iron.

"There's not enough eggs for everyone," Laetha said.

"It doesn't matter, we'll get the keys."

Laetha cursed at Taliesin. "Fool. You think you can take on those sodding monster dancing bears? Take them on by yourself. I'm off and out of here."

"You will stay here. And give me one of those."

Laetha tossed it at Taliesin, and still swearing, Laetha broke open another egg across the remains of his twisted chain.

Burning off his chains with the pungent black fluid, Taliesin crawled towards the axes. He scooped up an armful of blades and kicked his way back to the trees. Laetha was still there.

"I though you were for getting out."

"Just sod off," said Laetha, angrily picking up one of the axes. The weapons were passed down the line of chained soldiers, the soldiers threatening the cowering villagers into silence. Taliesin gazed out at the camp in the clearing. It was the beastman with a horned helmet who held onto the thick bundle of keys. Like the others it was looking into the fire and grumbling as it chewed at a meaty bone.

"Silently, until they see us," Taliesin ordered.

Clutching an axe in both hands, Taliesin and Laetha raced across the clearing. By the campfire a demisapi looked up and roared while Taliesin replied with an insane scream. Outpaced by the Captain, Laetha hobbled close to his heels, twirling his axes like twin windmills and crying like a banshee. Under the bright half-moon Taliesin loosed an axe towards the demisapi, burying it in the back of one of the giant bearmen.

With the other axe he danced forward and hacked at the horn-helmeted demisapi's waist, slicing the beasts thigh and lopping away the keys. It keeled over clutching its bleeding leg and screaming. Behind him, Laetha grabbed a loop of ammunition bags hanging from the wagons and pitched them towards the camp fire. "Down one-eye!"

Taliesin ducked under a floundering demisapi as it powered a fist towards him. Flowering out with a ear-splitting retort, the sheet of flames licked over the circle of creatures, knocking them back. Seizing the keys Taliesin slashed out at the stumbling beasts and fought his way past the howling animals. Retreating, Laetha's twin blades flashed in the clearing and he cackled like a witch at the slaughter he had wrought.

Throwing himself into the line of tumble Taliesin flung the keys at Finbar. "All of them out!"

Behind him, the line of giant beastmen roared towards the prisoners. With only murder on their minds, they were enraged into a killing frenzy by the flames and blood. Now the feeble prisoners would pay for their foolish attack with a massacre. Like a statue, Taliesin stood his ground with Laetha, prisoners freeing themselves back in the tree line. Villagers scattered out into the darkness, their fear of the enchanted woods totally overcome by the attacking beasts. Soldiers grabbed axes and moved out to stand by their Captain. It was no line the dragon-browns were accustomed to, where they marched up flintlocks to fling ball and flame into the enemy's advance, stiletto-thin muzzle swords to plunge into any army foolhardy enough to charge the most professional killers in the world. This would be bloody slaughter. Steel, tooth and claw.

Taliesin shouted. "When the last one of us is free, we pull back."

Suddenly the furry giants were among them and the battle fell apart into a dozen desperate brawls, a heaving mass of soldiers and bearmen lashing out, thrusting with steel and iron. Used only to facing mercenaries who had learnt their skills of war while raping children and beating elderly ploughmen, the demisapi were shocked to find here was a foe that fought back.

Taliesin blocked an axe-thrust with the head of his own and slammed the crest of it forward into the demisapi's snout, crushing bone and sinew. They were strong, but the creatures were too used to living in a land where children were scared to sleep with the beastmen's reputation.

Another burst out of the scrum of jostling bodies and Taliesin thrust his axe forward low, scraping it past the animal's leg, nearly slicing it off below the knee. It bowled over howling then lurched onto a soldier slowly bleeding his stomach out over the clearing.

To his side, Laetha laid about him with a vengeance, twin axes flailing in the shadow of the giant demisapi. He looked like a deformed god as he grinned and swore, a crippled trickster from legend come to bring death to this tribe of monsters.

At last the size of the beasts began to show through and the soldiers were forced back towards the tumble, slashing and cursing. Hoping all the company were freed by now, Taliesin opened his mouth to shout for the retreat, his words cut off as the underbush came alive behind them.

From the treeline, leaping reivers hurdled out into the clearing, passing the Realmsmen's line at a run and throwing themselves into the ranks of the demisapi. Wearing wolf-skins, the ferocious warriors hacked about them with short sword and battle-axe.

The savage bearmen could take no more and facing a new foe, they turned and ran, the reivers cutting them down as they broke. While the two forces fled across the clearing, Taliesin and his dragon-browns checked their butcher's bill. One of the soldiers had fallen as well a comrade of Bors. There would be no healing. They had been hacked to pieces in the press, and if their souls were anywhere, it would be in the mercy of Finbar's Martyr.

Taliesin stood back, sick to his stomach with the slaughter. He understood the forest savages might have mangled the Realmsmen's line in passing – just as easily as they had the demisapi's. Would the reivers be allies of convenience?

Emerging from the wolf-shirts was a woman, her conical helmet a sinister mask. She cleaned the sword on her jerkin and looked over the Realmsmen from behind her iron eyepiece. Tugging the helmet off, she tossed her long hair back, a dark mane which had been constrained by the helm. She pointed at the soldiers. "I'm surprised they sent you here to die if you fight like that. Good killers are always in short supply in Goricht."

"We fight our own sodding wars," said Taliesin. "No one else's."

She laughed. "And proud. Of course. I have a need for fighters. Unless you care to wait here for the guard to return in better number."

Taliesin looked at her. She was a beauty, no doubt, but where had he seen her before? There was something familiar about her quizzical brown eyes. "I'll hear your offer out."

"You do me a great honour," she mocked, walking back into the trees.

Finbar hustled after her, followed by the Realmsmen and her own reivers, the warriors strutting out laden down with the demisapi's weapons and some of the corpse's own pelts, fresh and bloody from being skinned. "Bless the source, lass, but what's your mortal name now?"

She put her fingers to her lips. "No lord of the light here, Martyr-man, it is the lord of the forest you should mind in this place. But you can have my name … Freyjessi."

It meant nothing to Taliesin. "Where have you come from, Freyjessi?"

"Why, here. Where else?"

"You're blessed young to be a forest doe, and precious pretty too, if you don't mind me saying it, lass."

"I do not. There are many in the forest now, and not just those that were born here." She indicated the savage reivers picking their way carefully though the dark forest. "Those fled from Goricht, as well as refugees from the turmoil across the borders. People can only take so much butchery before even the wilderness is made to look like a haven."

Taliesin looked at the ferocious reivers. "And these ones mind you sharing their forest?"

"Some do. Not these."

"And why would that be?"

Freyjessi laughed again. A liquid sound. "You might say it is in the spirit of charity."

Moving across the mist-wrapped landscape, the reivers

led the dragon-browns deeper into the tumble. Night made the forest a realm of cool gloom, moonlight penetrating the canopy and open groves. Torches bobbed in the darkness, wands of wood wrapped with slow-burning vine. As they travelled, the reivers made hardly any sound, the Realm soldiers tracing the savages' passage. It was not difficult. How many times had the company crawled silently past enemy sentries on cloudy nights? And living off the land often meant being able to steal into a farm plot and snatch a hen or a swine without stirring a chase of dogs. Even if looting was a hanging offence in Annan Pendrag's armies.

In a deep valley their escort showed signs of slowing the punishing pace. Pushing their way through a forested incline of yews, the soldiers and the reivers slithered down onto the valley floor. Waiting for them, clouds of fireflys flittered through thickets of evergreens, flights of tiny faerie-lights showering trunk and turf with an orange illumination. Hanging back, the mist seemed undecided as to whether it should invade the hollow, tendrils whisking out in the night wind like long phantom fingers.

"This way." Freyjessi led them deeper into the valley. Seeing a figure through the darkness, Taliesin started. Then he saw the silhouette was a statue in a grove overgrown with nettles. Twisting in a swirling toga-like dress, the sculpture was of a woman. She had been captured in the measure of a dance, endowed with a timeless grace even climbing vines and moss could not conceal. Dozens of fireflys turned around her sad face.

"Polykleitos," said Finbar, seeing the statue.

Freyjessi looked at the priest. "Your monastery must have a store of many manuscripts."

"Oh, a grand old number. More than my poor, thirsty head can remember after all our wicked troubles."

As they emerged into a sparse area of trees, Taliesin saw a legion of lean-tos, campfires burning between the towering weirded yews. In the corner of the copse was the ruin of an ancient building which had survived from one of the distant ages. Broken marble columns stretched out, cool under the lunar radiance. From behind the campfires a wide variety of faces stared at the newcomers. There were villagers, fishmongers, blacksmiths, players, young mercenary deserters, children and many scatterings of the fierce reiver warriors. A look of expectancy was on all their faces.

"What are they doing here?" Taliesin asked softly.

Freyjessi pointed to the old ruin. "Can't you see? They are waiting."

"And what would they be waiting for at this blessed time of night?" Finbar asked.

"Rawn. The Huntsman. The Raven King."

"You'll find gods are wicked slow at showing themselves to us poor sinners. Their ways are mortal subtle."

Freyjessi tucked her helm under her arm. "Hush now."

Beneath the ruins a silhouette had entered the copse. Shadowy garments drifted out with the wind, spindles of mist floating alongside the figure. It gazed left and right, two horns curling out from the murky shadow of a hood. A black raven sat on its shoulder, tight eyes blinking into the blazing torches and fires.

"The paths of life are moving closer," a strangely dilute voice drifted across the assemblage. "Those who walk with the path of the forest have drawn nearer to those who live as outsiders. This is as it should be.

"A circle of darkness spins itself large in the realms of shadow and will soon, so soon, seek to write a long dark night across every life's heart. Destruction lies in its trail. Look around you. See the person who sits by you. Find your strength in them, find the strength in your own heart, for the time will come when there is no other light but this."

Laetha hobbled forward and spat on the ground. "Miserable bugger, isn't he?"

"When that time comes you will stare into the abyss, and only then will you know yourselves. I seek... silence."

So saying, the figure withdrew slowly into the cover of

the mist, the raven on its shoulder glancing about at the forest people.

Taliesin looked around. The reivers were getting off their knees and Freyjessi with them. "I think it will take more than speeches and a druid in a mask to sway our hearts."

"You would deny the evidence of your eyes?"

Taliesin grunted. "No, but I'll keep the use of my brain."

Crossing the copse, Taliesin approached the ruins. Pale and broken, the crumbling walls and overgrown floors had been painted with once-vivid frescoes and mosaics. Now the faded procession of figures blew their curling pipes and carried their funeral biers while cracks and decay wore away their beauty.

Taliesin vaulted a pile of masonry. Freyjessi ran after him. The atrium was a mound of tiles across what had been a rain water pool – small trees and shrubs flowering there with the libation of the collapsed underground well. Threading through the rubble Taliesin found himself in a collonaded garden, its roof eroded by centuries of rain. But the collonade still stood. Wilderness had long since replaced hyacinths and violets with wild roses and thick thorny bushes, growing over the fountain and stone terrace seats.

"Where is he?"

Freyjessi laughed. "In the trees and the wind."

"Martyrs. You must think I'm damn soft."

"Have you never seen a forest spirit before, foreign man?" She moved back outside.

"I've seen weirdsmen. And I've seen players with a clever slight of hand."

Freyjessi shrugged. "It is of no matter. Does the wind care if you believe in it? But it is a fool who does not see the leaves carried along by it."

"And what do you need fighters for, you still haven't told me?"

Drawing herself up, Freyjessi looked at the scornful face of the one-eyed captain. "To take these ones back to

Goricht. To make a land where our people don't have to fear being thrown out of their homes – or starved – or beaten on the whims of a madman. To make a place where the people in the other states would know they could flee the carnage and packs of killers."

Taliesin laughed and looked around the pitiful encampment. "What, with these? Shoe-repairers and farm girls?"

"The reivers also," she flung an angry hand at the savage forest people.

"Oh yes, they fight like madmen in the forest. There's not an army in the world that would want to march in here and try to break them. Any regiment would be cut to pieces by ambushes and bled away by raids, those that didn't die of green-rot fever first. But there's not an army in existence stupid enough to be dragged into this hell, not even a mercenary band led by that loon Ganderman."

"We can take Goricht," Freyjessi cried.

"You march these people against a line of mercenaries, with puffers in the open, and as bad as the hired sabres are, you'll be cut down before you get close enough to piss on them."

"Bad? Why bad?"

Taliesin sat on the stub of one of the shattered marble columns. "Because they fight for money."

"And I suppose you weren't paid when you fought? You battled for free?"

"Men don't fight for angels. Oh, you pay them, and slop out the occasional plate of prog so they don't desert, but they don't fight for that. They fight for their friends, their colours, they fight to show the bastards that lead them they're not going to give them the pleasure of their dying. You give a soldier a few coins and tell him they are fighting for gold, you haven't got an army there, you have got a mob of killers one murder away from turning back on their commanders."

Freyjessi touched Taliesin's shoulder. "So what do you fight for?"

He looked across the encampment, close-mouthed. He fought because there was someone to fight. He fought because it was the only thing he had left in his life.

Taliesin did not know why he stayed. Day after passing day drilling the refugees, while he told himself it was all so they could rescue Connaire Mor. But wincing at the clumsy peasants falling over their flintlocks, the Captain knew they would be better off raiding the palace on their own and quickly escaping Ganderman's wrath, rather than daring to topple the maniac ruler.

Having cajoled the reiver's smith into making a pair of crude trumpets, Taliesin called time while the Realmsmen tried to move the would-be companies along in formation. "Ordinary step."

They marched forward slowly, the trumpeter blowing orders out over the meadow clearing.

"Open order."

Falling two steps behind each other, the three lines moved apart.

"Enfilade."

The left wing of the line swung around while the front rank kneeled, the rear two ranks standing with their scant row of flintlocks raised. Without muzzle-swords, the front rank bristled with pitchforks and bale spears. Taliesin winced as the marching flank shuddered apart, the villagers lurching over a bank. They would halt a lot quicker with an enemy line pouring ball across them.

Standing in front of them Taliesin put his hands on his hips. "Were you born in a sheep-herd, lad?"

"No sir," spluttered a plough boy.

"The damn you sir, don't wander around as if you are trying to round the entire line up! Close order means you lock your bodies together, tight, tight to stop the bastard enemy breaking through."

"Toadshit," one of the men in the back line muttered.

Taliesin laughed, a roar like the sound of a culverin ball exploding across the men. "I like a soldier to have spirit. No, I do. Every man from there to that tree, lift one of those rocks over your head and run to the end of the valley and back again. Bors, if you see anyone slacking they can do it twice, every last stinking one of them."

From behind the yews one of the grinning young mercenary deserters laughed. Taliesin swivelled to see where the sound had come from and stalked over. He kicked a space of ground clear and threw six small rocks onto the dirt. "Each rock is your battalion squares marching through this valley. The creepers are a line of charging cavalry. Disposition?"

Discomforted by the savage Captain's one-eyed glare, the mercenary placed the rocks in a crescent formation.

"Congratulations," Taliesin said. The mercenary smiled. "Congratulations because you have just unnecessarily added a third of your men to the butcher's bill. You are being charged down the valley floor, not the Martyr damned sides. Move them like this." He repositioned the rocks in an alternate chequerboard fashion. "Like this, each company has the support of another. If your squares hold firm the horses will have no choice but to ride around the length of the companies and they will, sir, be cut to bloody ribbons."

Chagrin descended across his face.

"Join the others!"

Although the motley party possessed few flintlocks, one of the villagers had worked in a powderman's workshop. In a wickerwork hut she sang lewd songs to herself, mixing saltpeter, sulphur and charcoal, filtering the black grains out into rows of sheepskin sacks. It was a course mixture, but it served its purpose, dirty black smoke leaping from flintlock pans, flame pluming out of barrels. Lacking lead, the smiths improvised by smelting small iron balls of the same calibre.

So they practiced with live shot. To the best of Taliesin's knowledge, no army outside of the Realm practised the laborious drill of loading and firing with full loads. If they filled them at all, they rammed half-loads down, saving coin on powder and saving troops the pain as puffers slammed back into their shoulders. When Taliesin had told them they were to practise with full powder, a mercenary had even argued they would all go deaf. There was nothing so dangerous as an amateur killer.

Supervising the training men, Laetha hobbled up and down the line. To make firing practice even harder there was little consistency between the muskets, soldiers clutched dumpling-like holster arms, longarms with engraved locks, puffers with multiple pepperbox barrels, butts ridged with brass spines, all-metal cavalry weapons, and even a hideous looking monster which a smith had combined with a hunting sword.

None of the fierce reivers used flintlocks, they wielded crossbows and were expert enough with them that Taliesin saw no point in trying to retrain them in powder weapons. More powerful than normal longbows, the devices were cocked by sliding back a lever built into the bow. It seemed a faster way of loading fresh bolts, at least compared with the Realm's hunting crossbows which were made ready by twin handles at the tail, winching back the murderous string.

Laetha cackled at his line. "I thought I had been born ugly. But it is not half as sodding ugly as you base-born swine reload your puffers. Not half as ugly."

"It's these village weavers," cried one of the mercenary men. "They think a puffer's something to scare the crows off a field."

Taliesin walked over. "Who spoke?"

"I did," a soldier with a red uniform walked out. "And it's true, these barley-reapers aren't going to be worth spit in a fight.

"And you are different?"

"Straight I am."

"Show me," Taliesin ordered, unshouldering his

flintlock. "Load your puffer faster than me. Two rounds."

Breaking up the line, the other deserters crowded in. Freyjessi had no right to put this foreign one-eyed monster and his ugly devils over them. Who was he to lounge about and force them to pound weapons away until their shoulders went numb, working them until they stumbled from duty to duty? Now they would humiliate him and force Freyjessi to reconsider.

Both men stood ready and Laetha called the start. Having none of the paper-wrapped cartridges which held ball and powder together, Taliesin was now on an equal footing with the mercenary. He swung up the powder horn and tipped a measure down the barrel, pushing a ball in and reaching for his ramrod. Slapping the charge down with the maul he crashed the puffer back up and tipped another measure of powder into the side-mounted pan. He squeezed the trigger, the flint came down and the pan erupted with smoke. It blew back across Taliesin's face and he heard his rival's weapon fire.

Sparing no time to glance at the mercenary, Taliesin grabbed his powder horn and piled another weight of black grains down. Seizing the maul Taliesin knocked the second ball down on top of the powder then primed the pan. Banging out, Taliesin's other ball ricocheted across one of the trees and there was silence from the deserters. Realising he had been beaten, the other soldier had stopped cocking his flint. In spite of himself Taliesin was impressed by the young mercenary. There were not many men in the Realm's army who could have done it as fast as that, and he suspected there were even fewer among these foreign incompetents.

It was not the time to show admiration. Tossing his puffer at the deserters, Taliesin pushed the townsmen and farmers back into line. "Too damn slow. These men will be guarding your backs when you march. If you haven't taught the villagers to load at least at your speed by the end of the week, I'll have every second man on half-rations, starting with you."

"And if we manage to teach them?" said the incensed soldier.

"Then boy, I'll teach you how to load and shoot like a real soldier."

Freyjessi came over towards Taliesin. "What good will these people be if you grind them into the ground?"

"More good than they'll be if they're disembowelled on the sharp end of one of the beastman's axes."

"They're ready to drop," she shouted.

Taliesin pulled her to one side. "You wanted fighters, I'll give you fighters. But you don't turn dough into bread without some kneading. I'm not going to be able to pull my lieutenant out of that madman's coop with an army of cobblers and merchanteers."

"Friend! Why can't you say the word? You would not stay around here to save one man unless he was your friend. I sometimes think you're as inhuman as Ganderman, but at least he has got the excuse he's crazy."

Ganderman! Suddenly Taliesin knew why Freyjessi had seemed so familiar when he first saw her in the logging camp. Why the villagers followed her around like hound pups after scraps. She was the woman from the portrait that Goricht's lunatic king had hauled into the throne room.

"Martyrs, you're Ganderman's daughter aren't you?"

Freyjessi looked away.

"No wonder you want the bastard toppled."

She turned, running away from the captain.

"Ah, but those were mighty unkind words," wheezed Finbar. "For the poor girl had a terrible secret."

He swore and stared after the princess, then gave chase. Catching Freyjessi by the decayed villa, Taliesin turned her around to face him in the clearing's spectral light.

"You just don't know what it was like. To grow up in that madhouse of a fortress with Ganderman as your father, his insane whims, no courtier with the guts to stand up to him after my grandmother died; the ones that did question his edicts exiled into the forest. I saw so much … so much."

Tears flowed down the edge of her nose, tumbling towards the dead pastels on the weather-scoured mosaic.

Taliesin remembered the churchman standing over him with a lash, the petty cruelties of the poorhouse, his parents pitching to the street in a crush of bodies and hooves, the severe existence of a ruffler on the streets of Llud-din, joining the army as a young drummer before the boy had shaved a man's hair.

He touched her hand and gently lifted her chin to look at him. "The Martyr knows, I have few enough answers for my own life. But I do know one thing. Sometimes, all you have is each other."

Softening against his chest, Freyjessi lay her hair on the captain's brown uniform, burrowing against his solid body like a doe seeking warmth. She closed against him, seeking something substantial to hold onto, testing his arms, his face, the set of his leg muscles, as if she believed if she didn't hold onto him the officer would fade into the mists which submerged Goricht's enchanted forest.

Freyjessi drew him to the floor and Taliesin kissed her on the neck, her midnight-dark plaits tossed over the mosaic as her head arched back. He kissed her gently, but she dragged his face down and pushed against him with a deliberate passion. Slipping a hand across his jacket, she tugged at his silver buttons, the metal of the Realm's crown and dragon cold aside her arm.

Taliesin stroked Freyjessi behind her ear and she lost a breath, somewhere between a sigh and a moan. "I came here to steal a princess."

"Then you have found one. Steal me now."

Ibn-Dali owned a sprawling two-story warehouse building in the secret port, three expansive halls on the ground floor, the sailors hanging their hammocks there as if they were still at sea.

It was clear that with the Empire of the Tree strangling the corsair's trade, they were having difficulty selling-on their booty, one of the halls being taken up with barrels of spices, swathes of cloth, and boxes of seasoned oak containing stacks of flintlocks buried in wood shavings. Gunnar looked these over with a professional's eye. Sea air had done the weapons no favours. The flintlock mechanism scraped noisily back to half-cock, and the frizzen plate which covered the powder pan was hardly in a better state. He slid it back in the box in disgust. Ibn-Dali would be hard pressed to find nobles desperate enough to want to equip their men with puffers of such low calibre.

One of the sailors saw his reaction to the rusty weapons and laughed. "There's always some quality on the mainland who'll take 'em, eh? They're not fussy when it comes to burning down each other's estates and raiding villages. It's the poor sods that works for them that does the bleeding."

Gunnar agreed. The Khair-ed-Din's crew had been much friendlier towards him since their performance at the corsair council. It had been his initiation. In one leap he had gone from being the jack from a rival's crew to one of their own, and anyone who had survived a devil-boat scuttling had to have been favoured by Milady Chance in the eyes of the superstitious seamen.

Passing him a flagon, the corsairs urged him to drink. Gunnar gargled on a swill of the yellowy liquid and tried not to retch. It was the drink Realm farmers called Arch-Truron's brew – some monk on the mainland had spent a good year or two on this potent ale, raising coins for his diocese. He took another swig. Years well invested.

Pointing to a table covered with cards and circled by boisterous cursing seamen, the sailor clasped Gunnar's arm and grinned. "There man, have you played Primero before?"

If Gunnar had a personal angel, she was laughing.

"No, I don't think so. Is it very difficult?"

Not wishing to venture out in the oppressive port and its hellish illumination, Elaine walked bored through Ibn-

Dali's store of treasures. With few windows in the hall, the dark room was lit by candles. Items of real worth such as gems and jewellery were kept in one of the guarded rooms upstairs, but there was a store of more eccentric items down below.

Somehow, Elaine had difficulty imagining the fierce killers swinging back to their ship clutching some of these prizes. Stuffed animals sat next to burnished breastplates and helmets, strange creatures with sharp teeth and incredibly colourful feathers. Books in a language Elaine could not read, a spider-crawl script illustrated with lustrous metallic illuminations. Flicking through the pages, the noblewoman noticed all the figures in the illustrations were wearing the billowy silk-like clothes favoured by Ibn-Dali and many of his crew. They were gorgeous books, quite comparable to the works turned out by monks in the Realm's abbeys. Quite unlike the cheap volumes set by the great city's wooden presses, although to give them their due, it was the rude printers that turned out the romances she had commanded her maids to conceal about the family's estate in Emrys.

"Can you read then, girl?"

It was Graine, the raven-haired corsair standing on a pile of rolled carpets, malevolence shredded right through her savage eyes.

"The Rais told me a story once. About a whore who was condemned to death by a Sand-King. So that she didn't die, she spun him out a different tale every night."

Elaine curled her lip in contempt. "How very interesting."

"You superior little slut." Graine removed a bell-guarded dagger from her sash. "Have you any stories for me, harlot girl? Something to amuse me before I slice your chattering little tongue out. It will be interesting to see how much men'll pay for you with some of my embroidery across your cheeks."

Elaine looked into those deadly viper's eyes. The woman was serious.

Advancing on her, Graine flourished the dagger, taking pleasure in the Realmswoman's fear. Glancing desperately around her, Elaine's attention hooked on a pile of armour behind the stuffed animals.

Bolting back towards the weapons, Elaine scrabbled through the rattling pile, lifting a small round shield and a mace-like rod, both pocked and pitted where jewels, gold, and rich ornaments had been stripped off by the corsairs.

Graine was not perturbed. "Let me slice your face, harlot girl. You try to put a scratch on me, and I'll hold you down and open your throat. Have you seen that done to a man? That is an embrace where your blood'll paint the ceiling red."

"Here's my throat," Elaine said. "Let's see you cut it, you filthy-common little maenad."

Graine screamed in anger and lunged for the noblewoman. Elaine stepped forward, ducked the knife and slammed her shield into Graine's belly. That had been a lesson she had heard the House's vicious aging sabremaster shout at her cousin. A man attacks you, he expects you to step back. Step forward. Unbalance him, you little shit.

With her adversary doubling up, Elaine slid her mace sideways, cracking into Graine's ribs and watching as the corsair woman slipped back through an open door.

Elaine looked through. Graine was tumbling down a wooden stairwell leading into the corsair's cellar. Far from being horrified by what she had done, blood-lust swelled higher in Elaine. Every humiliation the pirate had heaped on her was going to be avenged this day, every last indignity forced on her by this lowborn barbarian. She imagined bringing down the mace again and again onto Graine's contorted body, smashing her until the corsair screamed and cried for mercy.

Throwing herself down the steps, Elaine closed on Graine, the corsair coming out of her stunned daze in the realisation that it was not a meek bawdy-cabin whore she was facing, but someone every bit as willing to spill blood as herself.

At the bottom of the steps the women launched themselves at each other, weapons spinning and stabbing, without regard for their own defence, moving only to inflict pain in their shared fury.

Cries erupted with the flare of a lantern coming about the cellar's corner. And it was not from the top of the stairs. There were other people down here with them!

Elaine yelped in surprise and Graine looked around startled, stories flooding back of corpses buried in cellars.

Whoever was down here was obviously as surprised as they at being disturbed, the scouring sound of cutlasses being drawn as shadows darted towards the two women. One blow glanced off Elaine's shield as she raised it, the attacker returning a man's cry when Graine stuck the figure with her dagger. Graine had a blade in both hands now, grunting in the midst of the shadowed combat, piercing death cycloning across the cellar.

A single shadow circled around the stair's steps, and Elaine slipped past the furore Graine was causing, lashing out with her heavy mace. Elaine's muscles ached as if they had been torn with the weight of the thing, but the head of her bludger's weapon impacted where the shadow's face should have been. With the figure stumbling back to the wall, Elaine swung the shield like a scimitar, arching around into the attacker's groin.

Behind the noblewoman, the remaining shadows were shouting and retreating in confusion, the life of two of their number ebbing away in a lake of pooling blood. Graine howled like a banshee, scooping up the fallen lantern and flinging it around the cellar corner. It impacted across a wooden rack, bursting into flame.

Exposed by the light of the unexpected pyre, the cursing figure of Genevieve the Swan stood in front of them, a pyramid of kegs laid before the mouth of her tunnel. Bricks lay strewn where the rival crew had broken into the cellar, her people struggling back down the tunnel.

"You!"

Genevieve the Swan pulled out one of her brace of enamelled silver puffers, the pommel-shaped handle shaking with anger in her hands.

Its flared lips detonated towards Graine just as the Realmswoman's mace slammed into the Swan's shoulder. Floundering back, Genevieve's ball grazed off the stairs and skimmed into a mirror leant against the wall, shards of glass shattering across the dust.

Clutching her elbow in pain, the corsair commander scuttled back into the darkness of the tunnel, cursing the name of her attackers.

Graine tracked after her, but stopped at the mouth of the tunnel excavation. There was a hissing by her knee-high boots and she stamped on the ground. With a splutter the fuse-cord died and Graine kicked at the piled kegs sending them spilling over.

"Stay here in case they come back." Graine tossed her dagger at Elaine.

She gaped at the corsair.

"If they attack here, they can attack above! Stay."

Graine's fulminations were enough to work necromancy on a legion of corpses, and the roused crew of the Khair-ed-Din spilled out into the streets, brandishing their shortswords and emptying flintlocks at the sky.

"Treachery!" Cried Ibn-Dali, circling his scimitar in the air. "I will tear your wings from you, Genevieve the Swan. I will leave you a bleeding skeleton in the gibbet before this day is done."

Sailors flooded out across the streets from the barracks and tavern opposite. At their head was the athletic figure of Rais Calico and his gang of buccaneers, his aristocratic mustache twitching in annoyance.

"By Gods! Ibn-Dali you're shouting fit to wake the Sunken Empire. What? Has some cheeky wench sawn off your horns while you slept?"

Graine rounded on the light-hearted Rais. "That bitch whose legs you enjoy so much – Genevieve the Swan – she has just tried to fire twenty kegs of powder up our arse. There was enough barrels beneath us to blow most this street out into the sea."

"What is this?" With a casual leap Calico swung up on to his tavern's awning, peering out across the harbour from his height. "The Silver Swan is unfurling her sails. She is running."

Ibn-Dali faced his men. "Red Janz! As the sun sets red, it is the hand of Rais Janz standing behind this filthy indignity. His lick-spittles are after seizing control of the Port. To your ships you dogs, call the other crews."

Gunnar looked around. From the warehouse Elaine was emerging out into the orange light.

"She's got too much of a lead on us," a sailor said.

"I'll sail the Khair-ed-Din over the fire mountains to catch that treacherous bitch. Move!"

Calico tipped a knowing wink at Elaine. "Hey there, that is reassuring."

Sprinting down the hill, the seamen charged towards the docks, hooting and discharging flintlocks. Families of the corsairs shrunk back into their houses as they caught sight of the undisciplined rush.

Out in the harbour, Genevieve the Swan's vessel pulled about, trying to find the wind. She was not ready to stay and fight every corsair in the harbour, but then she was not about to miss targets of opportunity while she exited.

Patters of smoke mushroomed along her wooden hull and Gunnar flung himself and Elaine down onto the volcanic street. Overhead there was the canvas-ripping whir of flying balls followed by explosions in the town. A building burst apart back up the passage, raining the sailors with Taranto's buoyant rock.

Shouting them to their feet, Ibn-Dali resumed the madcap flight to the stone jetty. Far behind them came screams, and

Gunnar glanced back. One of the explosions had blown apart a section of the towering palisade which surrounded the secret town. Through the gap, a black horde of leaping chattering things poured into the back-streets of Port Hesperus; at first glance they could have been larger cousins of Calico's tame monkey, but their eyes opened as large as saucers, long talons curving off deformed paws. Baring fangs they screamed and mobbed the people still in the street, scrabbling up the houses and smashing the windows, pulling at doors in their wild fury.

"Come on," Ibn-Dali shouted. "There is nothing we can do for them except avenge them. To the ships."

Their gangplank groaned as the remaining crewmen pounded aboard the Khair-ed-Din, throwing themselves up the rigging and running out the culverin below-decks. Seeing the escape of the Silver Swan and her bombardment of the port, Ibn-Dali's watchcrew had already raised the anchor, and with the last corsair hurdling the gap, they cast off.

"Make ready on the culverin. Chain shot. Fire as we take them – put a long one across her rigging."

The Play Director brushed past Elaine. "He'll be Martyr-damned lucky at this range."

Inhaling wind, the Khair-ed-Din's canvas billowed into life and they wrenched out into the sizzling waters. Gunner scrambled into a cross-tree, midway up the ship's aft-mast. There was already a corsair on the platform, emptying a charge of powder into the pan of his puffer. Inspecting his own weapon, the Realmsman lent around to his borrowed satchel, picking out one of the rolls of paper. He bit the end off and emptied a little into the pan, saving most of the powder for the barrel. Ramming the wad of paper and the ball down with his iron maul, he brought the puffer up.

With the rolling of the ship and the strong sea winds it would be even harder than firing the weapon on land. It was why soldiers fought in columns and lines. Without a mass volley there was often little chance of hitting the enemy.

Gunnar had talked to enough of his family's naval friends to know that the Realm discouraged putting snipers in the rigging – the risk of powder flashes sparking off fires in the canvas. But then, when they reached the boiling hell of the sunken volcanoes, the risk would hardly matter.

Noticing he was not alone, his fellow marksman nodded at the dandy. "We'll get them, mate. No worries. The bull, he is the best I have ever sailed with, him and his evil Sand-Prince sorcery."

"Pity for us they are not wearing uniform."

"Aye, but that it is. That's why I prefer taking on your regular line-ship. Some arrogant sodding quality wandering around on deck with ribbons and a big hat. Still, you do what I do, aim for the poop. Any buck strutting their boots up there is going to be someone worth putting a hole in."

Genevieve the Swan was at the edge of the harbour now, the wall of boiling volcano mist only minutes from swallowing her and her ship.

Leaning over the rail of the top deck, Ibn-Dali cried over the bustle of the vessel. "We're turning to starboard. Place them across her stern. Make ready."

Her enmity put aside, Graine looked at Elaine. "Now girl, if the waves favour us, I'll show you why the Khair-ed-Din is the choicest ship of this and every other ocean you are likely to sail on."

They nosed down into a trough, and as the boat was pitching up again, Graine shouted the order. Fire!

Culverin all along the deck banged back, dirty gray smoke squalling over the crews. First, it appeared to Elaine the balls were curving out short, slapping the sea and sending up a spray of the blistering water. But then she saw they had skimmed up again, glancing off the sea and into the ornamented stern-transom of the Silver Swan. One explosion shattered the Captain's round-house cabin and another piled into the sails, driving a square of canvas into the ocean.

Loud cheers echoed around the deck.

"That's how you toss them farther than the Swan cares for," Graine yelled, exultant. "Bitch! You will be sleeping on a bed of splinters tonight."

Already the crew surrounding each culverin were mopping the barrels of their iron beasts, clearing them of burning powder which could ignite premature explosions on the next load.

Elaine looked to their stern. Six corsair ships were following in their wake. Behind them smoke clung to the hillside of the port. Enough sailors were staying behind to drive the hideous black leaping horde back into the tumble.

Ahead of the Khair-ed-Din, scorching waves of fog were coiling around the traitor's vessel, the hungry thunder of mist-masked volcanoes rising to greet them as they approached the passage of fire.

Graine slapped her thigh in anger. "Damn, we'll lose them in that. We'll have to catch them on the open sea."

She started to swear again, then halted. The White Swan was reversing back out of the wall of fog. "The fools, we have them!"

Elaine looked on, a nausea rising from the pit of her stomach. It was no ship of wood. An iron devil-ship stirred its way out of the steaming white barrier. And another. And another. And another.

# Chapter 21

Blue light arched across the gentle curve of Freyjessi's spine, moonbeams filtering through the villa's broken roof. A rustle of feathers made Taliesin turn, a figure appearing to step from out of the frescoes.

Silver raven eyes blinked in the darkness as Rawn the Hunter loomed in front of the soldier.

"Do you expect me to fall on my knees?"

"I expect nothing," whispered the figure.

Taliesin moved away from his sleeping lover. "Then you make a poor god, sir."

"A station you claim for me, not I."

"Those people out there would say the same."

Rawn the Hunter flitted past Taliesin like a shadow, his cloak darkness. "Everything in life has an elemental force, even a forest. I am a reflection of life, nothing more. There is little I can change. In many ways, even Freyjessi, laying there so still, is more powerful than I, for within her she possesses the power to create new being."

"Perhaps." Taliesin looked into the curious eyes of the raven staring at him from Rawn's shoulder. Then he gazed down at Freyjessi's serene form. As if reading the officer's mind, the Raven King broke the silence. "She will not wake while I remain here. Her House is bound to mine in ways you could not understand."

"Come now druid, be truthful with me," Taliesin said. "You have a purpose with me this night? You lead these people."

"Lead? Lead, no. If they follow, they follow their hearts. But their designs coincide with mine."

"Which are?"

"I see you, island man. I see you, Taliesin. You have become the eye of a storm and our future rests on your shoulders."

Taliesin laughed while Rawn circled him like a twist of flintlock fumes. "What burden rests with me? My people are fighting for a handful of coins and the chance to buy ourselves out of our toadshit army and into a better life. Nothing more."

"There is a force, island man, which would order my world. Which would violate the beauty of this place and replace it with neat lines of wheat and rye, a forest of regular, barren certainty, chained by the insanity of a single changeless mind."

"You are talking of mankind's realm," said Taliesin. "A poor argument if you are seeking to convince me. The forest has always tried to kill me, and by the Martyr, I intend to kill it back."

"Your realm too. As thin as your souls are, you have the need to grow within yourselves, to become more than you are. All life shares the urge to climb. What I sense is a clawed fist which will squeeze the kingdoms of man as eagerly as it would strangle mine."

Taliesin shook his head. "Whose hand, druid? I have seen rulers and families killing each other for a share of their privileges, the games of Kings and Ruris. I have travelled through the savagery of the wild – where owl eats mouse and wolf eats owl. And with one eye shot out, am I so blind that I have failed to see the army of daemons waiting to enslave us?"

Rawn's goat-head mask dipped as if he were an angry bull. "Daemons! There are daemons in this world wearing shapes you could not even comprehend. Daemons in men and daemons in the forests. They would consume you, annihilate your purpose, and after they have done with you they would sweep the names of change and evolution into history."

"My purpose, druid," Taliesin said. "I'll tell you what my bastard purpose is. I'm going to the cut the head off the lunatic who sent me to rot out here, then I'm going to bring back the sister of the royal bitch whose head graces the coin of the Realm, and in return she's going to pile enough of those same coins in front of me to buy half the merchanteers of Llud-din. I can think of no better purpose, and your mystic seeings be damned."

"You walk a different path, even if you see it not."

"You've been sucking on too many roots, druid." Taliesin lent his shoulder against a broken column. "You see spirits where there is nothing but the savagery of people and the loneliness of the forest."

"I do see that you believe in the horoscope, Taliesin. Would you have me cast one for you now? I am the equal of most the fate-readers you will have met in your rookeries."

"I may follow my stars, druid, but I am not stupid. So let me tell you of *my* future. I'm going to steal myself a Princess, and if man, beast, demisapi, or the very legions of Old Shadow should wander into my path, then you and I will both discover whether steel and ball and Realmsman blood are wanting. And as the sun rises in the east, I guarantee you that one party will earnestly regret the encounter."

Catching the glacial moonlight, Rawn the Hunter's horns glinted as he left the shadow of the rubbled villa. "That we will, Taliesin of the Islands, that we most certainly will.

"I seek… silence."

Taliesin moved out to look for the druid, but he was gone, leaving no tracks in the dew-headed grass. The officer snorted.

"Conjurer."

Taliesin looked with irritation at the sketch of Ganderman's wooden citadel. "Your ancestors knew what they were doing when they had this place built. Still, your rag-tag army is as ready as they are ever going to get out here, unblooded in this cursed wilderness. But I do not see what they can achieve with your father's defences this strong."

"There is no way then?" Freyjessi asked.

"If there is, I don't see it," Taliesin scowled. "Look, there are two curtain walls, each one positioned higher up this hill. By the time you attacked the first – even with surprise on your side – the other one would be manned fit to withstand any siege, and you don't have the equipment or numbers to sustain more than a quick, decisive blow.

"The builders have even protected the hill's precipice, here at the rear. See how this river streams past the back wall and continues down the slope, feeding the wells and helping to keep the moat full in summer? How much grain is stored under the fortress along with that water? I'll wager it's enough to last the best part of a year."

"Grain. That's food for poultry, not solid fellows with heroes' hearts," said Finbar, fingering the map with his oversized hands. "Can we not be getting in through one of these wicked river drains at the back of the palace?"

Freyjessi shook her head. "No priest, there are iron grills down there thicker than your legs. Besides, it's too small. When I was a girl one of my friends drowned down there in the wells. She couldn't squeeze out and she was only seven at the time, what chance would the reivers and the free companies have?"

Taliesin spat. "None at all. Damn this place to hell. Humbugged by a wooden fortress, wood by the Martyr! If I had a battery of Annan's culverin I could tar the balls and have that palace burning down around Ganderman's ears inside a day."

"I heard the woodsmen soaked the fortress's planking in a mortal clever solution," said Finbar. "It helps stop the place blazing up in summer, so there'd be none of that even if Annan was of a mind to send some fine fellows to help us along – not to drag us back to the islands in chains."

"Oh that's good," said Taliesin, lifting up his flintlock. "Our buggering stars. Barrels of second-rate powder, not even enough of these antiques to go around, and now there is a wooden fortress which won't burn! I might as well march us up to the walls and call Ganderman out. At least he is probably crazy enough to consider a duel."

Finbar leapt to his feet dancing a jig. "It won't burn, ah but mercy, you have hit the nail on the head, lad. It won't burn will it? No, of course it won't."

"Your Martyr-man is touched." Freyjessi pushed aside the reivers who had run over, attracted by the monk's lunatic dance of joy. "Has his head been split?"

"Oh no lass, it is a precious miracle sent down by the Martyr, that is what it is." Finbar waved at the crowd of gathering onlookers as he cavorted across the clearing. "And it is for all you unbelievers too, each and every last one of you heathen devils."

Taliesin looked out at the lanterns on the citadel wall. The officer was surrounded by the last vestiges of the enchanted forest and accompanied by Freyjessi's makeshift company of soldiers. A reiver nodded at Taliesin, his face a whirl of spiral paint and tattoos, then vanished silently back into the forest. He would rejoin his brothers and sisters in the tumble near the town proper. With luck their raid and the fires they caused would be enough of a diversion for what Taliesin had planned for the night.

Ganderman's wooden palace might have been cured with an ancient treatment to fire-proof it, but if enough of the house builders down in the town were of the same avaricious breed that had erected the twisting warrens of Llud-din, then there would be a tempest of blazes in the town tonight.

Darkness hid his face while he recalled the time the east bank of Llud-din had caught alight. All the children from the church poorhouse had ran out laughing into the streets to watch the sight. Great billowing clouds rising above the buildings and floating back across the river, cinders landing across the cobbles in the road while the fierce owner of the wooden printing press across the street, Seri Crabfast, loaded his oak machine into a cart, swearing at the children as they pelted him with dry horse droppings. Liberated for the day by the scent of insanity and anarchy in the air.

Taliesin remembered what Silver, Ganderman's hired bully boy, had said to him while they were being escorted up to the palace for the first time.

*– It was as if a goddess had breathed life into that dirty stink hole for the first time –*

He shivered that the course of his life could have run so close to that of the amoral mercenary.

"Will there be much of a noise?" One of the recruits spoke, hoping to cover his nervousness with the hushed banter.

"Too far away," said Taliesin. "But you watch for a small flash behind that hill. That's how you'll know when it has been done."

Nodding, the farm boy pretended he had known that all along.

Freyjessi was surprised how differently Taliesin treated the men now he and his soldiers had dispensed with their murderous training regime. Where before nothing and no one had been good enough, now he listened with patience to the soldiers, told them tales of how the troops of his own people had faced wild demisapi and raiders and rival armies, fighting with a brutal lack of care for their own lives and a studied scorn for the enemy.

She had grown up with beastmen bodyguards who unthinkingly would have laid down their lives to protect her; but that ferocious blindness – born from a mixture of pack instincts and bestial loyalty – was nothing like the stoical, black-humoured strength these strange islanders fought with.

Finbar gazed up into the night. Clouds draped the moon like a shawl over a dancer, her veil slowly being teased down the canopy of the sky.

"What is man, that thou art mindful of him?" Finbar wheezed. "But then, lad, you don't look like one for precious classics. Perhaps this would be more to your taste. Mother lunar's wiles, while the fox in its lair smiles."

Grunting, the sweating mercenaries rolled the last of the barrels to the top of the cliff face. Below, the rush of water could be heard in the dark ravine, tempting them with its cool passage.

Finbar suspected Freyjessi had lumbered him with these soldiers so the young hot-heads would be limited in their choice of atrocities when it came to taking the town. She did not want to alienate her countrymen any more than necessary while they attempted to unseat her insane father.

"That's it now, when you are good and recovered, we will pop them down the blessed holes we went and dug earlier."

One of the deserters winced in annoyance at the priest's interpretation of 'we'. As far as he could recall, the tonsured bruiser had done nothing but lounge around in the shade of one of the wilderness's monstrous trees, giving orders as if they were an informal sermon but expecting them to be obeyed nevertheless.

They started spading a layer of earth onto the half-buried barrels. "Why in the ground?"

"Why, my fine lads? Because it is in the ground we must sow if we are to reap." Finbar uncoiled a length of hemp, the hairy cord still damp from being soaked in the reiver's nettle wine. "And it is the good ground we want to receive the bounty of this wicked offering, not poor honest men like ourselves who might be standing a little too close to it."

He beckoned over their reiver guide, a wild-woman with eyes the colour of broken flints. "Now then lass, pass me your torch so we can light this, then you had better lead us about our way through these haunted heartwoods of yours – and be a might sharpish in the leading too!"

Dipping the tar-soaked brush to touch the length of cord, Finbar stepped back and waved the party away from the edge of the ravine.

"You parted a sea for him – all this poor fool is asking for this night is for a blessed little closing of a river."

From the border of the tumble, Taliesin heard the first shouts of panic rise up from the buildings. There, in the centre of the town, lanterns were lighting up behind the windows as the townspeople woke with the reiver's acts of arson.

It was muffled, but the distant cries were rising in a crescendo, the fire watch adding to the noise with the peel of tower bells. Next to him Freyjessi bit her lip, and Taliesin guessed what it must mean to her to have to do this to her own city.

One of the village rebels leant forward. "Sometimes, milady, you have to burn the fields of stubble if you want to raise a fresh crop."

She smiled at the kind words but said nothing.

Taliesin touched her hand as she breathed in the night air. Soot and smouldering wood.

From deeper in the forest, behind the rising hills, there was a brief flash and the faintest suggestion of a report, as if the air had stirred.

"Nicely met, priest."

Laetha hobbled forward. "Silly bugger used too much powder. We shouldn't have been able to hear the poxed thing go off from here."

"As long as they didn't notice inside there." Taliesin pointed to Ganderman's fortress.

"Bugger me. A palace. At last, a sodding palace."

Taliesin knew what the hunchback was thinking. "The

Butcher's provosts might not be with us, but how far do you think you'll get through the tumble with a bundle of loot and these ones after you?"

Laetha looked at the evil iron masks of the reivers and scowled. "What's the sodding point of getting into a palace if we can't get out again with some of the quality's trinkets?"

"You know what we're about. We don't leave behind our own. Besides, think of the look on Ganderman's face when you slide your hatchet across his belly."

Laetha's face split with a cruel grin. "What do you think was keeping me warm at nights when that bastard chained us out in the tumble?"

From behind his fierce mask, the leader of their attachment of reivers waved a snub crossbow at the fortress. "We attack now?"

Taliesin could hardly understand the wildman's accented voice. "Do you have a god for your rivers?"

"Rawn – spirit of the heartwood – all that which flows though it also."

"Well sir, I can tell you four of the tributaries fed by your friend with the raven have just been closed off, and the fifth runs straight though the corner of Ganderman's fortress. Have you ever seen a mudslide? In truth I can't say I have. But I have a description from someone who saw the effect of an avalanche blocking a river beneath his monastery."

Nodding in understanding, the tattooed reiver stared at the river feeding his enemy's wells. It was already starting to bubble at the walls, frothing up as if boiling in a druid's cauldron. Water was flooding out across the river banks, gushing down the channel as debris was sucked along in the flow, spinning in the muddy surge.

Breathless, a soldier assigned to watch the front of the fortress brushed past the trees to speak to Freyjessi. Columns of Ganderman's tame demisapi had marched out to restore order in the town. Rawn's tribes had done their work well, using the rebel townsmen's knowledge they had set their first fires by the lodgings of the largest free companies boarded in Goricht, and now each regiment suspected its rivals of trying to burn them out. Even with the fear they generated, it would be hours before the beastmen cleared the streets of brawling soldiers.

Now the corner of the fortress was flooding, water battering the palisade and drowning the hill in a morass of mud.

Looking at Freyjessi's hair, as dark as the pitch of a burning torch, Taliesin felt the cold metal of his sabre guard. "My parents died when I was young. One of the only things I remember about my mother was a tale she used to tell me. It was about three brothers who made houses and what happened to them. The one who made a house of wood lost it when the tide came in. He had built it on a beach, you see."

Freyjessi smiled. "I don't think that was a very sensible place to locate it. How did they die?"

"There was a famine after a long winter." Taliesin checked the lock on his puffer. "We lived in a city, one of the largest in the islands. There were riots for food. My family and I were caught in one when the merchanteer guilds that ran the town called in the dragoons to break it up. I remember thinking how proud they looked in their shining breastplates, then of course they rode us down with lance and sabre. Horses have to be well trained to do that, I found that out later when I joined the army. You would be surprised by how little training well-fed men need to do it."

Collapsing like a pole-axed stag, high sections of the wooden palisade fell outwards, the rush of mud and water driving past to spill across the gardens revealed inside. Along with the palisade logs, more mud slid down the hill to pitch into the moat. The rear of the fortress had been transformed into a landscape from hell.

Taliesin lit his torch. "Skirmish line forward."

Mud sucked at Taliesin's leather boots, a thick glutinous bog filled with dirty-brown flood waters. Fighting the pull of the man-made marsh, the lines of rebels charged up the slope, unaccompanied by fife and drum and holding back their cries until their enemy showed itself.

So sudden had been the flash flood, there was still no warning cry from Ganderman's depleted garrison. Inside the garden, a disoriented demisapi stumbled, its head cut open by the falling palisade. A reiver laid into it with his axe and the unfortunate beast sank into a bed of thorny flowers

Taliesin grabbed Freyjessi. "The quickest way to Ganderman?"

She pointed at a three-storey building adjoining the citadel's second curtain wall. "This way."

The Realmsmen survivors followed Taliesin, the rest of the revolution streaming past on either side in their disorganised mobs, breaking through gates and attacking demisapi scurrying off the wall and out of garrison buildings. A torch whirled through a open window and hit something flammable inside, the reivers shouting excitedly as mercenaries and demisapi weaved out into the darkness in flames.

"Martyr preserve us if we're relying on these amateurs to win the battle. We need your father as hostage, or those bear-monsters down in the town are going to rip us to pieces."

Testing the door to the building and finding it locked, two of the soldiers slapped their woodsmen's axes across the frame, cutting it down with a savage rhythm.

Freyjessi led them inside the deserted room, dust rising from the floor. Gardening tools lay piled on the floor, including an old iron roller with a harness meant for a pony. She started to heave on the roller and the others added their weight behind the rusted hand grip. Rolling it back, Freyjessi lifted away a herringbone rug, revealing a faded square of wood.

"It is the old loading hatch to the beer cellars, You can only open it from inside."

"You can get into the main apartments from there?"

Freyjessi nodded.

Taliesin passed his flintlock to the soldiers and took an axe, Laetha limping over with his double-headed blade, looking for all the world like some travelling player's parody of an executioner.

It was wood brittle with age, splitting open before the two island soldiers had a chance to work up a sweat. Laetha kicked down, caving the hatch in.

Iron rungs led down into the darkness, the jumping flames of their torches throwing pools of light across the barrels and bottle racks.

Hoisting a bottle off a frame, Laetha smashed its neck off against the wall and greedily poured the contents down his throat.

"Never tasted anything like that before, sodding good grog though."

"I'll fire on the next man who tries that," Taliesin threatened. The scrapings of the islands, most his men were quite capable of drinking themselves senseless before, during, or after a battle. "If any of you devils are still alive after this, then you can come back down here and tap barrels until you're pissing blackstrap – but not before."

There were murmurs of discontent and Laetha tossed the bottle into the darkness. "You had better mean that, one-eye, or you will be leading yourself the rest of the way on this campaign."

Freyjessi shook her head in bewilderment. "Your rulers actually pay these scoundrels to fight in your regiments?"

"If we had something better to live for, we wouldn't be taking the Queen's silver."

Passing though dozens of the arched storage chambers they finally halted by a cranky staircase leading up to the exit, steps broken and a thin wedge of light piercing the darkness to the side to the door.

"This is the closest to my father's chambers. We're near the centre of the palace. There's the kitchens outside the door, through there into the main banqueting room – then his apartments can be reached by a stairway to the floor above."

"Is he likely to be in his apartments, with all the trouble outside?" Taliesin asked.

Freyjessi nodded. "Oh, believe me, the last place you'll find him is leading the defence by the Urr. He's too squeamish to bloody his own hands, that's what he pays people like Silver for."

Deserted, the kitchens smelt of fresh bread and onion soup. Some of the staff had been baking the next day's loaves, fleeing back to their quarters when the attack started. Taliesin dipped his finger in a cauldron of the chestnut-coloured soup.

Still warm.

Freyjessi motioned silently to a door in the cooking chamber's corner and the soldiers scuttled towards the wall. Levering it open, the Realm Captain peered through the crack. There were two demisapi guarding the stairway across the dining room, giant statues in black pelts. Both wore axes dangling from belts, but even more worryingly, the beastman on the right had one of the oversized puffers designed for their clumsy hands.

A soldier patted his flintlock, and Taliesin shook his head, put his finger to his mouth then pointed to his sabre.

Drawing his sword, Taliesin reversed the blade across his forearm – a style he had noticed Goricht's officers affect while in marching order.

Carefully opening the door, Taliesin marched into the banqueting hall, feigning surprise as he looked at the two demisapi. "Damn you eyes, what in buggery are you two doing here? Answer me now!"

"Orders. Protecting the Lord," one growled out.

"Orders is it?" Taliesin closed the distance. "Cowardice is what it is – your brothers are dying outside while you warm your ugly snouts in here. Who gave you these orders?"

"Silver commands us."

Taliesin lashed out with his sword, running the puffer-armed creature through the heart. Its comrade might have been a laggard at telling human officers apart, but it recognised actions well enough. While his sword was still jammed in the falling beastman, the other whipped out a club-like paw and sent Taliesin reeling into the stairway.

That single blow was powerful enough to knock the Realmsmen into a stupor and he weakly kicked out with his boot. Brushing it aside with contemptuous ease, the beast slashed bare claws across the length of Taliesin's jacket, opening up his chest through the cloth.

Contorted with pain, Taliesin felt the beast collapse onto his back – surely it was going to rip his throat out! Then the creature was rolling off him while the Realmsmen soldiers reached down to steady him back to his feet.

An axe was buried in the back of the thing's skull.

"You want to put on a little weight before you start wrestling demisapi," Freyjessi said, feeling his chest with a worried expression that belied her words. "The old ones used to pit entire gladiator teams against a single fighter from the Urr."

"What is a gladiator?"

"Someone who was paid to fight better than you do. Can you walk?"

"The wound isn't deep, I was just stunned. That thing has a fist like a falling tree."

Laetha pushed his way past Taliesin. "I was there when you lost your eye; you'll survive. Come on, idiot, I'm for doing for the old bastard that tried to kill us."

On the stairway they could hear the sounds of battle

filtering past the palace walls. Along with the breaking-wood crack of flintlocks firing there were the smothered screams of men and the howls of demisapi. Whether of anger, fear, or victory cries, it was impossible to say.

Fully lit chandeliers hung down the passageway like floating ice palaces from a child's tale, warming the opulently furnished chambers and halls. Clucking their tongues in appreciation of the wealth – anticipating the money it might bring if they walked out with some of it – the dragon-browns let Freyjessi lead their way.

A group of retainers stumbled into the corridor, the silver acorn bright on their brown livery. They saw Freyjessi and the hard faces of the island killers and fell on their knees. "Rawn preserve us. Save us, your highness."

Freyjessi appeared annoyed Goricht's own people had grown so craven in the service of her insane father. "Face me on your feet damn you, where's Ganderman?"

"In the library your highness, he ordered the Urr to slaughter all the staff for letting the forest savages in. But we did not let them in, I promise you that we – "

"Leave through the dining room! If you can get down into the town, tell all the people that will listen that Ganderman is dead and I rule here now."

Nervously glancing behind them, the retainers fled past the soldiers, blessing the name of their Princess. From the savaged corpses of the attendants they passed, the retainers possessed good cause for their terror. Freyjessi stopped by one and tears welled in her eyes.

"This was my nurse, Canerine. Even when my mother was alive, Canerine was always the one who cared for me, who used to play with myself and my brother. Ganderman, he has passed beyond the pale this time. How could anyone order this slaughter? How?

Taliesin did not have any answers to the question, and the group followed her towards the library.

There was no door to the chamber, just an opening into a

narrow room, two storeys high and circled by a walkway. There were mercenaries on the walkway but when they saw Taliesin's soldiers they shouted, fleeing out a side entrance. Two beastmen charged across the ground floor to be slammed off their feet in a quick, angry fuselage of balls, the Realmsmen raising their puffers level, blowing smoke and death.

As the pan smoke drifted out of their eyes they saw Ganderman at the opposite end of the room, Silver standing by his side. Ganderman was scrambling to fill a velvet sack with books. What could possibly be so valuable that the vicious monarch would spend his last hour plundering the palace library?

"When I heard the racket out there, ja I just knew it was going to be you." Silver pushed his sabre back into his scabbard. "I knew you were another professional. A banquet for these tired eyes to see you again too, Freyjessi. Forest air has proved good for you."

"What are you waiting for?" Ganderman screamed. "I'm your King, kill them. They want my sweets but they can't have them."

Silver smiled. "I believe I have just resigned, your highness. The pay was handsome, but the odds don't look good, and quite frankly, the conversation around you and the Urr always was lacking."

Ganderman dropped his bag, pebble-like eyes flitting between Taliesin, his daughter and the island soldiers. "I'm the King, you hear me, I *am* the King."

"What you are," Taliesin said as he walked forward. "Is a miserable little madman who would be far better off heading the bloody butcher's bill you and your beasts have run up across this land. I made you a promise last time we met, why don't you tell me what it was?"

Ganderman obviously remembered the conversation. "Half my little pretties, Silver, everything that's in the treasury room. Jewels, gold, coins from a dozen states. Just make that one dead for me, make him dead!"

Silver looked at Ganderman, then looked at Taliesin and drew his sabre.

"Don't be a fool, Silver. You'll be spending that coin at the Martyr's side."

"Ah well, thing is, I've never had very much money before. A sum like that, well I wouldn't need to work for people like him, I'd be one of them. That money would pay for an army to make me an Emperor all on my own. I could reunify every kingdom in Thuring with a fair-sized army. Imagine that, me Emperor, and all the people telling fireplace tales to their children about how I took over and brought them peace back."

Taliesin blocked Silver's first thrust.

"Don't be a sodding fool."

"All that power."

Taliesin turned the blade and kicked a chair over to protect his side.

"Women fawning all over me – quality begging me to marry their daughters."

Dropping into a fighter's crouch, Taliesin flicked out his sabre's sharpened tip, but the mercenary had seen his arm tense and deflected it.

"Statues of me in every village square."

Taliesin side-stepped the hired killer's blade and there was a detonation, Silver collapsing back onto a table, then tumbling off onto the oak-red carpet.

"You took long enough to get out of the way," Laetha complained.

Taliesin stared in anger at the hunchback.

"Sod off, one-eye. If you want to impress the lady-quality with your sabre games, sodding do it when we are all alive and out of here."

"That was hardly... even-handed," Silver choked from the floor. "I don't think it was meant to end this way."

"I could have had you," Taliesin said.

Silver hacked out a laugh. "Pigshit you could, you're nothing but a damned clumsy beginner. Now – you – see where having just – a few virtues can get you …?"

His head gently slumped back and Taliesin looked over to where Ganderman was cowering.

"No, don't hurt me, I was just being the King, that's all I was doing. Please, the throne, my daughter, the treasury, all my sweets. Take them, you can be King too, I'll just become a little bird again."

Taliesin picked up his sabre and stood over the pitiful figure. Ganderman the Magnificent and every other self-made title. His atrocities and insane whims.

"I tell you who I should see hanged, every stupid bastard at Court who saw you grow up and still placed that crown on your head." Taliesin let his sabre arm drop.

Freyjessi pushed past him and the officer saw the glint from the barrel of her small jewelled puffer. Its pan exploded and the main powder ignited, the ball jerking Ganderman back, pitching across Silver's corpse, a single weeping entrance tunnelled into his forehead.

"You don't have the right to forgive him."

Taliesin saw the fire of loathing in her eyes, and at that moment he knew that in a long life of stealing and soldiering he had never really hated anyone before. Not a real hate.

Freyjessi handed her axe to one of the Realmsmen. "Cut off his head."

"What?"

"We'll need to show it to the Urr companies when they return to the palace. With my father dead the leadership of the family falls to me. They know this, there will be no trouble when they see his head. They will understand. It will be over."

Taliesin moved over to Freyjessi but she pushed him away. "Take his body from here, please. Find your mountain-man friend, I would like to be alone for a few minutes."

Dragging the dead ruler's corpse across the oak-red carpet, Taliesin looked back at Freyjessi.

"I won't cry for him."

Taliesin nodded and walked away

Outside, Laetha was cursing: cursing the King's palace; his slut of a mother for bringing him into the world; the misfortune of his hunched back and every officer who had ever served in the Realm's glory-soaked sodding army.

He threw away Ganderman's velvet sack in disgust.

Taliesin sheathed his sabre. "Throwing away your chance to retire rich?"

"Rich," Laetha spat. "Here's your filthy riches."

He kicked open the sack, a book sliding out of the bag. Laetha tore off an illuminated page, a scene of a woman floating above water, mists gilded in gold leaf. "Once time there was a good man called Filer of the deepwood, Filer was a woodsman and his sweetest heart was the Princess of the Lake by the Sea."

Taliesin felt the claw rips in his jacket and the drying blood underneath. "What's a happy childhood worth to you, Laetha?"

"How would I buggering know, one-eye? They burnt me out of every village I lived in before I'd grown a man's hair. I'm going back down to the cellar to drink a bastard toast, with the head of good-King Ganderman and sodding woodsman Filer both!"

Connaire Mor stretched out on the cobbled docks, feeling the bright sun bathe his cheeks with warmth. His face was looking distinctly rounder now, and strength had returned gradually to his giant frame. When Finbar had first found him during their search of the palace, Connaire Mor had been suffering sorely for his refusal to let Ganderman spoonfeed his 'son'.

Taliesin was tracing his fingers across the scars of his

own encounter with the demisapi. After days of starvation, the gaunt highlander had still possessed the strength to break the back of the beastman Ganderman sent to strangle him.

Finbar saw Taliesin gazing into the north, towards the two-day distant capital of Goricht. "Mortal life, lad, but things are best left the way they've worked out. That lass has the dream of bringing peace to those kingdoms, and if she is to do that, she'll best be left outside the Martyr's blessed union. She will be making unions of her own, alliances of state for which she'll need to be fancy-free."

Laetha was of a different opinion, stealing his way into the conversation. "I still say you're touched. You could have been her General, and what's it matter if some poxed druid waves a tree branch over her and some foreign Ruri? She'd still be warming your sodding stupid feet most nights, wouldn't she? That bunch back there; we could have walked all over those village-sized kingdoms. I could have been one of your sodding Colonels!"

Taliesin said nothing. He looked across the docks. A group of children were following their Urr bodyguard around, much to the beastmen's annoyance, the demisapi a rare sight in this distant coastal town.

"Martyrs, the only time I get a women like that is when I pay out a month's wages, and you're too proud just to be her moonlight exercise? Sod it, but then maybe you are right. My family didn't give me much to remember apart from this hump, but I do remember what my grandfather used to say every time he saw me. Pigshit people come from pigshit families. Maybe you are lucky to have got away."

Taliesin grunted. If that was meant to be consolation it was meagre fare.

How could she have done what she did and not be changed by it? Closed up like the petals of a wild wounded flower. And yet even that fragility, that vulnerability, had been so desperately appealing, so tempting, making him want to hold her until all the pain had bled away.

"You can marry a woman," said Finbar. "But there's not many that can be marrying a precious country."

Grunting, Taliesin stared out to sea. What would it have meant to be born a Ruri-Prince? An existence of hunting and banquets and progresses around the great estates of the islands. Would he have been here if he had lived a different life? Would the situation have been any different?

A longboat pulled out from the ship they had arranged passage with. A small three-masted carrack which traded down the coast, The Princs Hooge had spent her life cruising past the patchwork Thuring states and their savage hundred-years war, past Nathstadt, even sailing as far as the nations whose seas covered the Sunken Empire.

Looking the vessel over, he had found it in a state that made the Gogmagog's sailors wonder if her previous owners had tried to scuttle her in a moment of madness. There were better ships in harbour, but none that had a charter to go direct to Sombor to pick up a merchanteers' entire stock. Taliesin was eager to finally meet the Queen's petulant sister; and he did not feel like calling in on every two-lobster-pot port on the way. If Princess Ariane was as vapid and fickle as most the quality he had seen at Annan's court, then with any luck she would already be regretting her marriage and making her husband's life miserable with infantile demands – Sombor's King might not even put up too much a chase when they snatched her.

They had to finish it soon. The longer their mission's end was delayed, the less their chances of a warm welcome by Annan Pendrag, even if they returned with her stubborn sibling in chains.

How long could she put off interested suitors without losing face to the other Princedoms? How much easier to announce a death from the fever. How much more embarrassing if they returned with a miraculously 'resurrected' Princess of the Realm!

No. It might not be the Queen waiting for them in one of the island's harbours, showering them with gold and royal estates. It could be Domnal Mac Aedo and his assassins waiting for a ship full of marked men. Their encounter with that little rodent Marius had shown their true colours.

A clamour interrupted the Captain's musings. The Urr bodyguard was stopping someone trying to get to the pier where they waited for the Princs Hooge to finish her loading.

Now Connaire Mor was adding his powerful lungs to the tumult and Taliesin pushed himself off the coil of rope to see what had provoked the tame bearmen.

"Och away, I'm telling you he is with us, you swining great talking monster."

Taliesin looked past the demisapi's brown shoulders.

It was the tinker!

"There is nothing in my left hand," the tinker told the hostile beast. "And there is nothing in my right."

He waved his hands in the air, then reached behind the startled creature's ear to produce a silver coin. Watching the commotion, the port's children cheered and started dancing. Turning towards them the tinker bowed and jangled his arms at his sides as if he were a puppet.

"Put your puffer away," Taliesin told the demisapi. "He may be a madman, but he is travelling with us."

The beastman nodded. This was the one-eye who led the thin brothers he had to protect. If he wanted the disturbed old-one, he was most welcome to him.

"Where have you been man?" Connaire Mor demanded. "You come and go as if you were a polka. Why, we've been dancing with murder while you've been off sampling every bawdy house and coaching-inn in this swining country."

"Where do you think I've been?" asked the old tinker, his mischievous eyes looking out to the Princs Hooge swaying in the harbour's swell. "A bit of travelling. A bit of visiting.

336

Old acquaintances."

Taliesin stared with suspicion at the spry old man. "One of those old acquaintances wouldn't happened to have been walking around that green shit-hole with an ugly black bird on his shoulder?"

Smiling, the tinker shielded his eyes with a hand and looked into the sun. "I don't think much of our ship, do you?"

As the Realmsmen's vessel left the harbour, a figure in a frayed uniform pulled himself out of the crowd, the port people recoiling back at the sight of his wild intense eyes.

It *was* them. On deck. And he had missed them.

Mistrael sheathed his sword back under the robes of the Militant Order. He had known he would find them, just as the Martyr had protected him through the unholy green cathedrals of the forest. Yes, everyone else had died, their soldiers' hearts impure and tainted by their lack of faith. Even Six dam Saldair, the nobleman blessed by the same hand as he.

But Mistrael was blessed upon the work of the lord, untouchable in the light. As the Realmsmen would find out to their cost, when he discovered which port their ship was bound for.

# Chapter 22

From his mast's cross-tree, Gunnar saw the flotilla of metal vessels emerge, the thumping of the devil-boat's hearts muted by the louder growl of the volcanoes. In the febrile wind, pennants waved from their fortress-like superstructure, the red tree sitting on a black background.

"Two hundred years," Gunnar's companion said. "For two hundred years corsairs have used this port, without a pilot betraying the secret of the passage of fire."

"Someone's told them now," Gunnar said, stating the obvious.

Below, Ibn-Dali railed at the heavens; turning towards his crew they stepped back, fearing his twisted beastman head might truly breath flames over them. "Bazin – Bazin – this is the end between us!"

As if in answer the culverin on the wheeled ships boomed out, columns of water exploding to the side of the Khair-ed-Din, hot sulphurous sea splashing across the corsairs. Each devil-ship opened up, their cannons like the thunder of the Vulcan mountain gods which swam Taranto's black coast.

The Imperial culverin were huge metal obelisks, bruisers which jutted out of raised platforms, spitting balls the height of the standing stones found in the Realm's valleys. Cutting through the air, shots slammed into the harbour, crushing houses and splintering ship hulls. Most the corsairs were still at dock, and as the monstrous enemy vessels bore down on them, vomiting smoke and flame, it was clear they were unlikely ever to weigh anchor again.

One devil-boat engaged the six corsairs behind them, the ships scattering like a family of weasels before a lion, annoying it with their insignificant teeth.

Her wheels churning up the ocean, the last devil-boat swung slowly towards the Khair-ed-Din. Ibn-Dali saw the gold trident pennant of the Admiral fluttering with the others, and howled at the sky, the battle cry of a wounded animal. The cry died in his throat, becoming a murmur.

"North by nor-east."

His helmsman looked at Ibn-Dali. "But there are no passages there. Just fire-mountains."

Ibn-Dali grabbed the man and hissed in his face. "How do you think the Khoja traders originally opened up this port? Did they fly over the flames? Into the steam, *ja hapur!*"

Tacking out, the Khair-ed-Din lent into the wind and fled towards the white wall, crewmen shouting when they realised where they were heading. Graine cursed them down.

"It's the only way. Do you want to burn here or burn when Bazin lashes you to the stake? Back to the loft, you scum-faced sea rats."

In his wheel-tower, Admiral Bazin wiped his monocle clear of steam. Bugger these cursed hot waters and that beastman devil.

At his side, Bazin's tie-wigged Captain passed the Admiral his cylinder-like viewing glass, staring over the parapet in disbelief.

"They are not sailing through the passage."

Bazin wiped the sweat off his balding head. "Then there is another passage into the island!"

"There is no other passage through the flames," said the officer. "We are sure of it."

"Follow them."

"Admiral," the Captain sounded if he had been abused by his superior. "You can not in seriousness mean that order?

If Ibn-Dali sails his dogs in there, then they are a ghost ship already. We would be cooked alive too."

"Will you obey my order?"

Bazin's Captain clicked his heels. "I will not, sir. I must request you relieve yourself of your office and confine yourself to quarters. The Impstad will not stand to see this vessel destroyed without a valid reason."

Bazin waved to two of his demisapi in blue tunics. "Take the Captain and toss his titled head into the first fire-mountain we pass over."

The beastmen seized his arms, the other officer on the tower-deck jumping to his feet just as Bazin shot him. The ball shattered the sailor's eye, his corpse falling back to wedge itself between an embrasure.

"You think because I am not from one of your Great Houses you can mutiny like I was a common fisherman!" screamed Bazin. He pressed the octagonal barrel of a second puffer into his wheel-man's neck. "I may not be an Impstad Baron, but you will make a heading after Ibn-Dali's ship as if I was Emperor himself. I shall not be vanquished by my own slave, I shall not be beaten by a raised beast. Do you hear me!"

He searched for the wake of the Khair-ed-Din, then looked down at the sailors gazing up at him from the iron platform-deck. "I am a man of intellect, a scholar. *Sinn und bedeutung.* No heretic slave creature shall be my equal."

Geysers of burning sea seethed into the air around them, the Khair-ed-Din rocking close to the point of capsizing in the choppy waters. How Ibn-Dali navigated through the volcanoes was a riddle only the beastman could answer, his red eyes intent on the swirl of the current and the eruptions of half-submerged islands. Crew muttered under their breath about his weirdsman ways, but they were still glad of his heathen techniques.

High above the listing deck, Gunnar choked, clouds of salty steam surging past his position in the mast. With their flintlocks abandoned, the dandy and his fellow sniper clung to the platform and tried to spy what hazards they could in the drifting clouds, shouting down directions to the top-deck.

Fiery magma exploded to the port of the ship, rocks decapitating one of the sailors higher up the rigging, his headless body tumbling down into the sea before vanishing with an angry sizzle. There were screams from the highest cross-platform, the top-sail on fire.

Seamen swung over and tried to beat it out, but their own silk shirts burst into flames. Two of them collapsed, billowing and twisting deckward.

"We'll have to cut it down," said the other marksman. "If it spreads there won't be enough canvas left to catch a sneeze, let alone outrun the Imperials."

He tossed a dagger to Gunnar. "Come on, mate, let's be having you."

Mounting the ratlines they pulled themselves higher up the mast, black ashes sweeping across Gunnar's vision while they dragged themselves ever higher, handhold by painful handhold. Even the strands of ropes were covered in hot volcanic dust, making his hands slippery with sweat as he climbed.

"Get to the shroud, lad, we'll sever the connections to the yard-arm and kick the thing back out into the briny blue."

Passing the flaming canvas, heat scorched the Realmsman's face, Gunnar clinging onto the ratlines for dear life, another rain of hot coals slapping his shoulder and blistering his neck again. He cried in rage, as if the sea might take notice.

"That's it mate, take my hand."

He kicked and hauled himself onto the high platform, the sailor's grip taut on his forearm.

"Blades out, let's slice the bugger off."

Gunnar hacked at the bunt-lines holding the yard-arm to its mast, fumes from the smoke bringing tears to his eyes. Three lines went, then another two. It was hanging slanted now and the sailor lifted one end of the large wooden stave. "Sharply done, matey. Now, you cut the last two off and I'll heave it away so it don't be landing on the poor old Rais."

Riving the last two rope-lines, Gunnar let the yard-arm drop, the sailor kicking out and pushing the tumbling wood and canvas towards the sea.

"Let's not punish our luck. I'm for the deck and sod this."

Gunnar agreed and slithered back down the rigging. For someone who had been as good as disinherited for refusing to go to sea, he was spending cursed inconvenient tracts of his life on, in, and under the watery blue.

The dandy was passing his original position on the mast when the underwater mountain awoke. Flame funnelled into the air, molten streams of earth's blood splattering the ship, waves dancing up and smashing the Khair-ed-Din to one side. Cannoning into the aft-mast, a boulder snapped through the hull as if it were match-wood, splitting their spar as neat as an axe. Falling to one side, the sailor shouted, "Leap for it!"

It was a standing jump from the cross-platform, but Gunnar hurled himself off the collapsing spar and towards the opposite sail. For a moment he was soaring in the air, a bat in the sooty darkness enveloping the ship. It was a crazy feeling – like the flight of a God – like he might never fall. Then he slapped into the swelling canvas, his dagger tearing into the sail. Gunnar slipped down the sheeting, but the grip of his dagger in the canvas checked his slithering, sliding descent, the soldier making a snatch at the rigging. Trembling but alive he was hanging high above the smouldering planking.

As his heart slowed, Gunnar looked around. The other marksman was spread-eagled across the wood below, unnoticed in the panic of running seamen.

Gunnar's hands were still quivering as he descended onto the quarterdeck. Sailors cut this way and that, flinging buckets of water onto the flames which burned along the length of the ship. Gunnar could not see the fire-mountain which had detonated, but he could hear it across the steaming sea. A deep basso lament of rendered rock, fire pumping skywards.

Frantic calls from below-decks told him they were taking water, begging for extra hands to man the pumps. Gunnar was about to answer when someone thrust a bucket at him. Resigned, he joined the chain of crewmen heaving water over the fires on deck. Numb with exhaustion they lifted bucket after bucket, spilling seawater over the blazes. How ironic that below-deck sailors would be bailing water back out, while on top they were desperate for more of it.

Then there was the sight which Gunnar though he would never see again.

Clear blue sky.

Wedged above an equally calm ocean. Not wreathed in steam and lit by hellish vulcan light, but natural ... golden ... serene. Never again would the Realmsman complain about the display of a stretch of honest ocean.

Gunnar's relief was shattered by the appearance of a worried sailor, the same old man who had befriended Elaine. He did not say a word, but led the soldier back towards the rear cabins. Across their deck a fallen spar had collapsed on top of Elaine, the noblewoman's body unmoving beneath.

Gunnar was still bending over Elaine when Bazin's devil-boat broke the steaming wall of fog. Her bowsprit had been melted by the exploding lava, and two of the massive iron wheels hung dead in their mounts, the others shaking the water unsteadily. Her pennants fluttered on fire above the fortress platform.

Whatever nautical instincts Bazin had followed when navigating, they had proved disastrously inferior to his beastman rival's.

A bombard on the fore of the devil-boat blew a plume of smoke towards them, signalling the duel was still on. It was a weapon made for dropping balls down on citadels and cities, and the projectile arched hopelessly high over their heads.

Gunnar looked at Elaine, her long strands of scarlet hair flat across the wet ash-strewn deck. He felt her breast and the flicker of a heartbeat.

"She's unconscious," he yelled. "She is only unconscious."

The ex-Play Director looked over Gunnar's shoulder. "Be-gods, lad, we need to get her out from under there."

She was trapped in the lee of one of the hatches leading to the decks below. If Elaine had been standing one pace either side, the falling mast would have cloven her in two. As it was, the mess of ropes, wood, and rigging had pinned her at a bad angle. Both legs trapped.

"I'll get the carpenter and his assistants, they'll be hiding in the boatswain's stores if I know 'em."

"Go, for the love of the Martyr go."

Across the ocean the two ships closed, the demon-boat, and the corsair commander who looked like a devil.

The hate of their two Captains was something palpable, tangible, alive. Its magnetism had drawn them to each other like moths to candle-flame. Across seas, islands, ports and numerous vessels they had crossed cutlass with each other and now they were to be consumed by the flames of their hatred.

Both ships were in range, and the defiant Khair-ed-Din

344

let her culverin be heard, opening up with a broadside, each booming recoil absorbed by their rope pulleys. No longer could the devil-boat use the advantage of her superior range. Shots flailed over the waves and struck the iron platform, rendering razor-sharp gashes in her superstructure and buckling the wheels.

Bazin's reply was forthcoming, his larger culverin spewed smoke, two balls ravaging the Khair-ed-Din, one piling into the main hull, the other nearly clipping off the bow of the corsair ship. On the devil-boat, her large-bore culverin had been charged with half powder loads, ensuring their roundshot travelled at its slowest velocity. The effects of this were evident below deck. Sailors screaming out from horrific splinter injuries, her own hull turned against the corsairs as a deadly weapon of oak-shards and wooden fragments.

Gunnar saw the ex-Play Director and the ship's carpenters emerge from the rear cabin. Their carpenter had indeed been getting drunk while his two young apprentices cowered in the boatswain's stores. They looked loath to risk the battle-scorched deck.

"Move," Gunnar screamed.

Urged on by the theatre man, the three carpenters scuttled to the fallen spar and looked the wreckage over. Down the deck another projectile collided into the ship's hull – somewhere near the waterline – seaspray and burning wood spouting over the side.

"What are you waiting for?"

"Well now that depends, young sir," said the elderly carpenter. "On whether the Rais is going to strike our colours or not. Because I can tell you how we sit here. This vessel will be underwater before we've sawn through half of this spar."

Gunnar seized one of the apprentice's axes. "Cut her out, damn your eyes. Cut her out, or I'll be finding out how much work you bastards are capable of with your hands removed."

"They're right," said Elaine's sailor. "Martyrs, but they are. We're shipping water below-deck like a bath. She'll be dead and drowned before we get half-way through the spar. But there is still a way to save her."

"What, man?" Gunnar looked imploringly at the sailor.

He pointed to the saw. "Her legs. We take them off and drag her out."

Gunnar gagged. Not Elaine, not her. On how many battlefields had he seen the surgeons sawing off blind-drunk soldier's legs and arms? Men who might have lain wounded on the field of battle for days before they were amputated. Elaine, who lived for the balls and masques of the Court, reduced to a crippled source of black humour for the other quality.

"It's the only way, mate. Alive and scarred – whole and dead – which is it to be?"

"Take them off," Gunnar whispered.

While he spoke, a dragon's breath of burning shot ricocheted across the Khair-ed-din, catching the hunched carpenters and spraying them over the wrecked deck. Fire exploded across every nerve of Gunnar's body as the ground seemed to suck him down.

With the collapse of the Khair-ed-Din's floor supports, the quarterdeck had caved in on the culverins and corsairs below. So quickly was the wreckage dumped down on them, the culverin decks below had been transformed into a ruin of corpses and moaning seamen, men crawling and floundering. Now free, Elaine lay stretched over a box of the wads sailors packed powder charges with. Elaine was still insensible, but by her side the last curtain had finally drawn on the life of the Play Director. Whatever genius he had possessed – in his mind or in reality – it had been extinguished for ever. He had slid down across a line of boarding pikes, a row of steel thrusting through his stomach.

Culverin silenced, the Khair-ed-Din was a ship in name only, the listing vessel still harassed by the rain of death from Bazin's devil-boat. Her sailors were survivors enough to realise when the game was up, those left alive throwing themselves into the sea, clinging onto wreckage from the shattered craft.

Ibn-Dali stood rooted to his top-deck, guiding the wheel of the Khair-ed-Din. He stared at the approaching enemy, oblivious to the destruction wrought on his own ship.

Then, climbing up from the wreckage of the lower deck, Graine pulled herself out of a hatch.

"Leave," boomed Ibn-Dali.

Whether this was directed at Gunnar, Graine, the surviving sailors, or all of them, the dandy was not sure.

Graine mounted the stairs, shaking her raven-dark hair. "I will not leave you."

Coughing, Gunnar slung the limp body of Elaine over his shoulder. The ship was a mass of flames and creaking timbers, smoke pouring out of hatches, the yells of people still trapped below.

Graine laughed and called down to Gunnar. "You might as well pleasure yourself on a farmer's rake, sand-hair, it would be less scrawny."

He looked up and blew her a kiss. Then Gunnar kicked himself off the deck and into the sea.

Graine's reckless laughter followed them down.

Elaine's back arched as they hit the water, the shock of the volcanic-warm sea reviving her. Remains of splintered hull bobbed all around the sailors and Gunnar paddled with Elaine to one of the floating messes of rigging, sail and timber.

With a single sail intact, the Khair-ed-Din and Bazin's damaged devil-boat bore down on each other, preparing to ram, neither Captain wishing to break first in front of their hated rival.

"They're both mad," murmured Gunnar.

Across the wake of the blazing corsair ship, sailors trod water, watching the final destruction of home and livelihood both.

There was a moment when the Rais and the Admiral's eyes locked. Bazin on his metal battlements and Ibn-Dali on his blazing wooden top-deck. Then the Khair-ed-Din was underneath the Devil-Boat's raised platform, her last sail sliced back as the metal monster ran her down.

Bazin cried out in rapture and pushed his helmsman aside so he could turn the massive churning wheels over the corsair, smashing the ship into firewood.

"Beast! Beast! Filthy animal." Bazin crowed, shouting down over the embrasure of his tower. "You are finished. You are dead. I have you."

Buried in the sinking ruin of Ibn-Dali's orlop-deck, the beastman's fuse finally spluttered its last, his entire magazine erupting. Eighty-seven barrels of powder packed into the stygian darkness.

Split in two, the devil-ship lifted up on a mighty holocaust of flame and smoke, its iron carcass rising and rising, then dipping seaward and impacting with the waves, sinking immediately. An iron wheel landed near Gunnar and Elaine, the waves knocking them free of their precarious hold.

Gunnar flailed his way to the surface, hearing the cries as Elaine surfaced. Across the sea the survivors of the corsair vessel were yelling and cheering.

Raising their lungs fit to attract a sea serpent.

# Chapter 23

His heart hammering as he dashed across the street, Marius's cloak quivered like a velvet pennant in the night. He was in Goricht's commercial quarter now, and if he could only reach the safety of his warehouse and the gang of bludgers that served as his staff, he might live through the night. The warehouse was quietly paid for by Queen Annan's factors, as were his coach guards, but there was a limit to what silver and gold could buy. Especially when the wrong sort of man was chasing you – the sort of man who couldn't be bought off.

Panting, Marius rushed past the walls of a storehouse that had burnt down in the recent troubles. Its wooden skeleton poked towards the stars, green glue-like sap having boiled and leaked across the planked street, the soles of Marius's soft leather boots slapping through the mess.

Behind him a whining drifted along the wind. It could have been a street dog working the bins outside one of Goricht's taverns, but Marius would not want to stake silver on such a poor bet.

Cutting down a small passage which rambled the length of one of his rival's breweries, Marius was choked by the the smell of yeast, the odour of fermenting huffcap. He risked a glance behind him. There was nothing, only the miniature red motes of rodent eyes, attracted by the scent of dough and staring out from the darkness of the shadows.

For the second time that night Marius cursed himself for having relied on his two bodyguards for protection, not even carrying a dagger with him. Though few would have believed it of the man as he stood today, in his youth the crafty merchanteer had been adept as a duellist, learning the craft from Roubaixian fencers before practising it in the service of the Realm's network of eyes and knives. O for such a bladearm now! Marius resisted the urge to panic, and forced his mind through the classic fighting positions as he fled. *Quinte, sixte, septime.*

But the two guards who had accompanied him had known all those and more. And they had still vanished in the bustle and crowds of Goricht's only theatre, disappeared as if they had never existed. There was nobody in Goricht who was good enough to have done that to them ... if there had been, Marius would have hired him long ago. No, all Goricht was home to was an army of second-rate woodsman mercenaries and the strong if dim-witted demisapi regiments.

Both of his bodyguards had even been trained in the southlands – Kal-addins of the Order of the Desert Rose – holy killers for one of the southerners' heathen prophets. The Martyr only knew where Domnal Mac Aedo had unearthed those two ethereal-quiet ghosts, but their poisons and quick slashing blades had deprived Marius of the company of his more active competitors, as well as serving the Crown's interests on the continent. Who in Goricht was capable of removing such men as if they were tossing the contents of a chamberpot from a bedroom?

Falling upon the entrance to his warehouse, Marius dodged inside and banged on the door to the guard's bunk room, splinters burning his fist as he pounded for help. "Out with you devils, up and out for your incredibly generous employer before my heart bursts."

Hearing no answer, Marius tried the door. It was unlocked. Inside, bodies lay strewn across the drinking tables and cheap straw mattresses, some with arms and legs snapped out at unnatural angles. Smelling the stench of sulphur, Marius stepped on a broken flintlock and backed into a spilled rack of weapons, sabres and puffers which had crashed across the floor.

"Your other two hirelings put up more of a fight."

Spinning around, Marius found a thin-faced man waiting with a timber-wolf. The man he didn't know, but the tale of the silver wolf and the one who accompanied it he did.

So this was Uriel – the only man who had ever turned down an offer of employment by Domnal Mac Aedo and lived to tell of it.

"Trained by one of the sects of Hasan-ben-Sabbah, if I were to hazard a guess. *Hashshashin* – their clothes always smell of that ridiculous battle drug of theirs."

"Happen I can offer you money…" Marius clinked his fat purse.

"Of course you can," Uriel smiled. "But unfortunately for you, I can only sell my reputation once. Now, stop talking what you know to be is nonsense. There will be no assistance, I was quite thorough in removing your people from this area."

As Marius tried to break for the door, Uriel let his wolf bring the Crown agent down, the beast knocking him to the floor with an easy leap. Placing his foot on Marius's calf, Uriel prodded the spy like he was testing the meat on a butchered chicken, then Uriel pivoted. Screaming as the bones in his right leg splintered, Marius scrabbled under the killer's weight, his fingers clawing at the floor.

"Now then, questions, questions. I hear you hired a free company to kill some friends of mine."

Flushed with sweat, Marius shook his head. "I can't tell you that – Domnal Mac Aedo would kill me."

Seizing Marius's arm, Uriel twisted it around, pushing it up and driving detonations of pain into the merchanteer's slight frame.

"You have more pressing problems, Marius you little rat, than Queen Annan's favourite blade. You may find it inconvenient to accompany your goods on their voyages if you have to do so with two broken legs – or as a corpse in a coffin. Where are they going? Your one-eyed officer,

Taliesin and his men. What are they planning to do?"

"I don't know," Marius protested. "Mac Aedo trusts none of us with more than we need to know. I was told to fix their trip home, that or their silence, nothing more."

Increasing his leverage on the merchanteer's arm, Uriel bent in close. "A half-truth, Marius, one suited to a liar as unctuous as yourself. You strike me as a man of some curiosity, one who would want to nose around such an undertaking in case there was a profit to be turned from it. What did you find out that didn't come with your orders?"

"Sombor," Marius shouted. "For love of the Martyr, they're going to Sombor and let go of my arm."

"Sombor?" Uriel sounded bemused. "There's nothing there but plains and the wagon people. What are they travelling to Sombor for?"

Giving up his struggle, Marius let himself go limp. "They've gone to bring back the Queen's sister, Ariane. She's run away from a marriage in the islands ... and you spread that story and the Crown'll see us both dead for it."

Uriel stood up, watching his wolf nose at the clothes of one of the corpses. "Yes, where would the world be without romantics?"

Shaking, Marius tried to crawl backwards. "Don't kill me, please ..."

A genuine look of surprise crossed Uriel's face. "You? Who'd pay for you?" He settled down on the edge of the table, rubbing his eyes as if he was suddenly tired. "I could tell you tales, little paid-knife. The places I travelled to when I was trying to die."

He had said too much. Listlessly, Uriel stood up and whistled for timber-wolf to follow him.

Outside, the assassin noticed one of Marius's servants approaching the repository. He was probably from the townhouse that belonged to the Realmsman; Uriel had considered capturing Marius there, but there was too much danger of Goricht's watch calling in their beastmen soldiers if they suspected trouble in the rich trading quarter.

Mistaking Uriel for one of Marius's toughs, the old retainer waved at the assassin, his breath misting in the damp air. "Sharp air tonight, eh? Where's his lordship then?"

Uriel nodded back towards the storehouse.

"He's been gone for so long, why cooky was worried her pie had spoiled," the retainer spat. "You know him and his filthy temper when his food spoils."

Shrugging, Uriel walked away. "Tell your household Marius'll be kicking the servants with his left leg for a while."

So it was Sombor that Taliesin was making for. He hadn't been there for a few years, but Uriel nodded to himself, it was a good land for killing, for catching up with Taliesin and the rest of the Realm gutterscum. The perfect place for murder.

Uriel disappeared into Goricht's mist, still tendrils enveloping the man before cloaking him with the forest. Behind him, timber-wolf glanced back towards Goricht, log lodges and lines of pine towers washed cold and silver under the moonlight.

Then it too vanished into the enchanted wilderness.

COMING SOON

Taliesin's adventures continue …

The Second and Concluding part of the
Triple Realm series

**THE FORTRESS IN THE FROST**

ISBN 0952288516

What follows is a short
preview chapter taken from halfway through
the second novel

Black dunes of sulphur crystals stretched in front of them, dark fields of rocks laying as if a millennia of skeletons had been heaped down before fossilising across each other.

Skirting a lake of thick boiling mud, Taliesin's company crouched as another stream of the scolding goo erupted into the air and spattered them. Uriel's timber-wolf yelped and turned angrily on the lake, the mud already solidifying on its sleek silver coat.

Steaming clouds obscured the volcanoes behind them, and Laetha held his nose as he passed another gurgling fumarole. "Holy Martyrs, get me out of this. I'll renounce drink, bawdy houses, anything. But just take me back home where it's sodding green and there's only a hundred varieties of beasts trying to do for you."

Magma dribbled down the volcanoes ahead, rivulets of burning rock hissing where it came into contact with the black rain. Ashes and charred lava blew across the dunes, choking the Realmsmen, even the tinker coughing and wiping the tears from his eyes.

It was a desolate, jagged land. Taliesin had not seen anything larger than a rock rabbit since they'd left the blue caverns of the eldritch forest. And now evening was closing in. Not halting for a rest since leaving the blue forest, they had been walking all day through the black dunes and knife-sharp rises.

Taliesin came across a piece of blackened metal, a dome-shaped fragment of steel jutting out of the ground. "Somebody has been through here before."

Uriel examined it, then looked at the Captain. "It is an armour-piece from an Ugrian knight, one of their Militant Orders. By the sea to the north, they are the only nation to live beyond the protection of the Wall. As you would expect, they are by necessity exceptional warriors. Their rites of passage do not normally carry them this far south, this one was a brave man. Or exceptionally stupid."

"I know which one our sodding General here is," Laetha said.

Manoeuvring past thumping mud pots, Taliesin came to the crest of a set of steaming springs. Beyond lay more black dunes, sulphur fog, and the dented cauldrons of erupting fire mountains in the distance.

Then he saw it. Between them and the dunes, a rainbow-like wall hung in the air, dancing light shifting across the cinder plain.

Taliesin pulled out his telescope, the leather-bound tube dented from his escape from Spartia. Extending it, Taliesin looked along the length of the strange soap bubble effect, as insubstantial as a mirage. "Well, I'm damned if I have never seen its like before."

"How very interesting. But fi and fo," the tinker gazed up over the dunes, "it's through that we must go."

They picked their way down the slope, stepping past the shores of pools filled by an ugly red carpet of algae. Bubbling in the hot water, a resilient living mat was dyeing the blistering liquid blood-red, magma gushing like veins through the rocky channels. It vented with the reek of putrefied eggs. Laetha sniffed again in disgust.

Taliesin halted in front of the shimmering curtain of energy, light dancing in front of the travellers as if a film of oil had been draped across the black crystal dunes. Uriel kicked a rock through the curtain and watched it roll across unharmed.

"There are mountains to our side, but they are believed to be impassable, even at this time of year. And there are winged lizards, simargl."

"Through we go then," Taliesin said, dismissing the assassin's detour. He stepped across the barrier, a flash of brightness, then he was through. The others followed behind him, Uriel's wolf clearing the barrier with a single bound.

"Oh my," the tinker said.

They had stepped from the dim light of late evening and volcano-fire into complete darkness, sky velvet and starless, mist curling around their feet.

Taliesin turned to look back through the curtain. Impossibly it was still daylight on the other side.

Hawking onto the ground, Laetha looked around the black dunes, the ground obscured by mist and night. "Bugger this, you can't tell me this is natural. Let's take your mountain route, mug-hunter, dragons and all."

"Are you afraid of the darkness, little man?"

"I don't need to be told what to fear by a sodding Roubaixian knifeman," Laetha retorted. "You lead, I'll follow."

Moving through the aberrant night, the party marched across a landscape of craters, arid bowls smoking and adding to the thickening fog. Lava sculptures had coalesced around the crater brims, presenting the appearance of fleeing demons coated in rock, tortured souls running and burning in the avalanche of magma. Their only companion was the silent, primordial darkness.

Even at a mile's distance, the officer could still feel the dry heat of the distant fire-mountains warming his skin. But Taliesin saw no sign of illumination from the volcanoes; in this unnerving night he would have welcomed the devilish glow of the mountains they had left behind.

One of the soldiers looked towards the cone-shaped peaks to the right of the craters, obscured by steam from the rocky cauldrons surrounding them. "What was that?"

Turning around, Laetha peered into the steam. "I heard nothing."

"Your ears play you false," Uriel said. "There was the sound of whistling. Look at wolf."

By his side his silver beast's ears had perked up

suspiciously, fur on its back as brittle and stiff as a pine cone. Taliesin checked his flintlock was charged. "A jet of lava?"

Out of the crater fog, a blue wisp of smoke emerged, luminescent in the darkness. It swirled on the hot breeze towards them.

One of the fisherman brothers laughed in relief. "It's just steam from the - "

He stopped as the wisp wrapped across him and solidified around his body. Tremors shook the soldier as blue lightening flared inside the cloud, sparks blistering across him, igniting his uniform like a torch. From behind the cloud other wisps slid out of the fog, spectral tendrils followed by an almost delicate whistling.

Taliesin's puffer erupted and he realised he had squeezed back its iron trigger, the ball slapping through the spectres only to be engulfed by the fog following them.

Dragging the other brother back, shouting and screaming in disbelief, the group abandoned their burning comrade's corpse and scrambled through the maze of lava sculptures. Like snakes the blue phantoms darted after them, curling over rocks and pushing against the breeze.

"You cannot fight them," Uriel shouted. "Run into the wind."

Racing feverously into the breeze they dodged demonic sculptures, the flute of the misty tendrils sounding behind them. As they ran, a bizarre thought struck Taliesin. This was a nightmarish reversal of a Realm Squire's recreation of hare coursing. And the dragon-browns had been turned into the sport!

Driving their way through the tangle of lava rock, they found themselves teetering on the slope of a canyon, the eerie fluting near and getting closer.

"I am too old for this foolishness," the tinker panted. Uriel's wolf had already started bounding down the boulder-strewn slope.

"Come on," Laetha spat.

"Hush now," the tinker said. He plunged his cane into the dark ground and started muttering quickly in latin.

"Only a travelling man," Taliesin said sarcastically.

"Go Captain, I will not be able to hold them here for long."

"Hang on just a minute," Laetha demanded.

Taliesin pushed Laetha and the surviving brother down the slope. "Move, damn your eyes, run or we are all dead men."

Tumbling down the slope Laetha hung onto his pack and flintlock. "He may be a crazy old sod, but we can't leave him up there."

"I suspect he's got more chances of getting back home than we have," Taliesin said, his chest burning from the exertion and molten-hot air. "And it was him that led us into this."

From the cliff above came the sound of thunder, a sudden wind whipping over their heads and scattering down crystallised sand. More lightening followed, the sea-spray sound of electricity crashing high above them. The party had reached the bottom of the gorge.

Surrounded by eroded canyon walls, Taliesin brushed his way through what had once been the rapids of a river. As blackened and sulphurous as the rest of the hell, diamond-sharp silt crunched under their feet as they sprinted through the corridors of the canyon floor.

"The old man is dead or they have slipped past him," Uriel said, pointing to the trail of blue luminance following them.

"Bugger them," Taliesin swore. "That crevice over there, we can squeeze through."

Uriel reached the gap. "These are true hunters, they will follow."

Cramping through the split in the wall, the party found themselves in another corridor along the chasm chain, a narrow ribbon of sky revealing only primordial darkness. The canyon floor was filled with rocks the size of farmers' cottages. A dead end!

True to the assassin's word, the blue ghosts were snaking their way through the crevice, tendrils searching out for the fire of human souls.

Turning to face the nebulous blue horrors, Taliesin heard a voice, one he first mistook for the tinker's. But it was no mortal resonance. "Begone!"

With a sound which carried the power of one of the volcanoes they had passed, the blue spectres sprayed out like candle-burn being ripped apart by a cyclone.

From the rocks an orange outline coalesced in front of them, a devil-bearded face, its features sketched in a net of shimmering fire. Again the thundering voice trembled the rocks.

"Who brings disorder to the realm of Vulcanus?"

Sobbing on his knees, the soldier who had been a fisherman cowered in the black silt.

The Daemon Prince which had drowned the Sunken Empire had returned, the evil which had corrupted Rome and the very earth about them. And with it came the power to sunder the universe.